The Brooklyn Rail
Fiction Anthology

The Brooklyn Rail Fiction Anthology

Edited by Donald Breckenridge

with editorial assistance from Jen Zoble

Hanging Loose Press
Brooklyn, New York

Published by Hanging Loose Press, 231 Wyckoff Street, Brooklyn, NY 11217-2208. All rights reserved without the publisher's written permission, except for brief quotations in reviews.

Printed in the United States of America
10 9 8 7 6 5 4 3 2 1

Hanging Loose thanks the Literature Program of New York State Council on the Arts for a grant in support of the publication of this book.

Cover design by Amelia Hennighausen

Layout: Marie Carter

Proofreading: Jen Zoble

Permissions may be found at the end of the book.

Library of Congress Cataloging-in-Publication Data available on request.

The Brooklyn Rail Fiction Anthology / edited by Donald Breckenridge

ISBN: 1-931236-69-0
        978-1-931236-69-0

1. Literature—21st Century. Prose, Experimental, Satire.

 Produced at The Print Center, Inc. 225 Varick St., New York, NY 10014, a non-profit facility for literary and arts-related publications. (212) 206-8465

Table of Contents

INTRODUCTION

The Brooklyn Rail originated in the fall of 1998 as a broadsheet circulated in Williamsburg and the East Village. It was designed as a series of short column-length pieces on arts and politics that would make for lively reading on the L train from Bedford Avenue to Union Square. Playwright Emily DeVoti, one of the paper's founders and later its theater editor, thus named it *The Brooklyn Rail*—with *Rail* referring both to the forceful opinions contained in the paper and to the L subway line. Its intent, as the *Rail's* original (and current) editor, political journalist Theodore Hamm, would write, has been to provide "slanted opinions, artfully delivered." Phong Bui, a visual artist, has been the publisher of the *Rail* since it became a full-fledged paper in the fall of 2000. In the last five-and-a-half years, *The Brooklyn Rail* has grown exponentially. It is now a monthly paper (10 issues per year), in tabloid format, averaging 70-80 pages per issue with very few of those pages given to ads. As its size and coverage has expanded, its goal remains intact: to combine radical politics with avant-garde aesthetics.

I discovered *The Brooklyn Rail* in February of 2001, when I almost tripped over a stack that had been left just inside the front door of Mercer Books. A few weeks later, I submitted some of my fiction, it was published that June, and, that December, Theodore Hamm asked if I would be interested in editing the fiction section. As a self-taught writer and ardent reader of formally experimental fiction, my goal as the *Rail* Fiction Editor has always been to highlight the talents of emerging writers, many of whom live in Brooklyn, as well as to showcase the current writing of established authors who have been marginalized by an increasingly risk-averse, profit-driven publishing industry.

Unfortunately, only one-third of the fiction that appeared in the pages of the *Rail* during my tenure as fiction editor is included here. This anthology was conceived not as a "best of" the *Rail* fiction section, but as an accurate overview of the various types of short fiction that have been published.

Jen Zoble, the Assistant Fiction Editor, has contributed her significant gifts as a reader and editor to this anthology; her work has been invaluable. The generous financial support of the New York City Department of Cultural Affairs made this book project possible, and Bob Hershon at Hanging Loose Press not only saw the potential of this book project, but helped to make it a reality. In addition, my thanks to Theodore Hamm, who has always given me the page space in the paper that I have asked for, and has become, over the last four-and-a-half years, a close friend. Amelia Hennighausen, the *Rail*'s former graphic designer, generously offered her time to design the cover of this anthology, and Williams Cole has been another important contributor to this project. Tam Tran was instrumental in putting together the grant proposal that made this book possible. Johannah Rodgers has been both extraordinarily supportive and generous with her time, creativity, and affection. And finally, none of this would have been possible without the hard work of Phong Bui.

Donald Breckenridge—Summer 2006

"The difficulty of fighting against your mania to understand is in proportion to your isolation. I am only now, thanks to a few friends, beginning to liberate myself to a certain extent."

Robert Pinget

Six Stories
by Diane Williams

DANGERESQUE

Mrs. White at the Red Shop showed me the beady-eyed garment, but I can't pay for it. I'm broke! I already own a gold ring and a gold-filled wristwatch and I am very uncomfortable with these. My eyes sweep the garment and its charms.

I am tempted to say this is how love works, burying everyone in the same style.

Through a fault of my own I set off as if I'm on a horse and just point and go to the next village.

This village is where flowers are painted on the sides of my house—big red dots, big yellow balls.

At home, stuck over a clock's pretty face, is a note from my husband to whom I do not show affection. With a swallow of tap water, I take a geltab.

By this time I had not yet apologized for my actions. Last night my husband told me to get up out of the bed and to go into another room.

My husband's a kind man, a clever man, a patient man, an honest man, a hard-working man.

Many people have the notion we live in an age where more people who behave just like he does lurk.

See, I may have a childlike attitude, but a woman I once read about attempted a brand new direction with a straight face.

11

HER LEG

"I would do anything for my son," she said. "But how little we know of what he really wants."

Meanwhile, her arm would release me. She told me what she serves for meals.

"It's all going to all work out," my husband said. "She will love you as much as she loves me."

His mother had a way of being strong, but not nasty. It was so sensuous. She and I both are short, short-haired women without eyeglasses. My husband has big eyes and he is large and muscular. I am very shy. His mother put her arm plus her leg around me—just live with it for a while. I, myself, how gladly I do.

Before long legend has it that when a partnership works, it is no accident. More accurately, more importantly, this illustrates this: I learn more about the arts and skills.

THE WIDOW AND THE HAMBURGER

I can't be expected to remember his privates—a pink head or yellow head. She wipes cream off of his face and I thought, I like his haircut now. She needs to take out whiskers. I don't see why any opportunity can't be taken to do something beautifully. I look for people to admire and she is one person.

I have on Billy's robe. The robe is filthy.
I saw his penis.

She wiped shaving cream off of his face. Those two never helped the poor because they were too poor.

Sometimes he sat near her, but tried to get away if she tried to smooth him.

People say the dog lay on its back, some blood near its tail.

Their house has plain bricks painted red and a shaded porch. They set their table with a cloth and the dishes and the cups keep dashing off through empty space.

If she had worried about money all the time, she'll have much more money.

For instance, your wishes are fulfilled and the dream comes true.

It is a great pleasure to be in a fascinating group.

JASSAMINE, EWING, ERASTUS, AND KEANE

I mention to Happy the honor of knowing Earl. I have loved Earl for months and for months and now get relief from not loving Earl.

I try to put a good face on it—I tell Marquis Abraham. It could have been the Marquis, but the Marquis's hair would not bunch up like that.

"Happy! Happy!" I say.

"Eat this," Happy says, "it will help you."

A loaf with a sauce.

They fired Happy, then Megdalia was fired and Sandra, not Marvin. Percy can't help me any more.

Perry once helped me. He made a hole and took my blood. He said, "I just want to cut through the fat!" He said, "Everybody who comes in here has the same color blood!"

"Take the food with you, your underpants, and the directions," one woman who created and arranged me said.

I don't find that very interesting.

JEWISH FOLKTALE

Around here, I see plenty of Haddock, an overall figure with his meaning growing, with a friendly frown, flanked on each side by a dog. I wonder how his bowel movements are.

I saw Mr. Haddock at the bay perhaps picking up his spirits. It's peaceful at the bay and Haddock says he does not have an ailment. He has no eye problems and perfect ears.

You know—fluid-filled space!—a bay, the bay!
Fancy cushion clouds at the bay are the same shapes and sizes as I saw when I had an exact understanding of conditions greater than my emotions.

Mr. Haddock's laugh—yeah, it is similar, but that's not what it sounds like. I remembered what it sounds like—then when you did that—I forgot.

There are a lot of young, forgetful people going around these days. At least, I am young and pretty and can make my claims.

Fifteen years ago there was a cloud I saw which moved around, traveled, came by, fled into the woods, exerted a strong influence, spent more than half an hour there, was free to roam, before returning to the village, where the cloud added up to a source of pride.

AFFECTION

She did so very slowly and needless to say she had to go get something in the dark room. She stepped into cold liquid. There was the crap in the dark and she hadn't reached any stream! She cried!

Like her father she had an ordinary way with walking, paying no attention to daylight or to artificial light. Sometimes she would pass on her philosophies to her son. Her husband also encouraged her. His job was mainly looking for nests and getting into mischief and he made quite a name for himself. Their house sits beside a dried up tree. All the gaiety and the color she finds in sex.

TRAUB IN THE CITY

by Brian Evenson

I.
Toward evening, well before Traub expected it, came a notable transformation in the face. The nose became more and more accentuated, like a blade, the cheeks grew hollow, the skin began to tighten. Traub continued trying to draw the profile, but the face was changing with such rapidity that he could only capture it, when he captured it at all, at several removes. He had the distinct impression that he was observing not one but several faces, coming one after another, quicker and quicker until finally, moments before death, the rush of faces was so rapid that it made Traub feel dizzy, and he forgot the paper, the pencil, and just watched, and in the vast shuffle of humanity nearly caught sight of himself.

II.
Days later, back in the city, having left the mountain inn, the body buried and left behind, Traub found himself shaken. He began to see heads in the emptiness, in all the space that surrounded them, isolated and remote. On the platform in the metro surrounded by hundreds of people he saw nothing but a series of heads, each suspended in a vast emptiness, each face in the crowd parcel of a single face that was changing with a rapidity he could no longer comprehend—as if a progression in time had been instead smeared out over space, all the faces of the city a record of one man's death. No matter where he was he had the distinct impression that there was only he, Traub, sitting beside a bed where a body was slowly giving way, through a desperate flurry of faces, to an implacable and faceless corpse.

III.

How many nights, Traub wondered about himself, night after
night, as in the darkness that one face broke into multitudes
and spread all about the ceiling separating out until each face
was surrounded by a terrifying silence. All around him in
the light of the street, the light of the moon, the room was
rendered harsh and was taking on at last its true character, its
true face: no object, he realized, touched any other— the
legs of the chair, weightless, no longer touching the floor; the
table too, shimmering and discrete; the curtains not touching
the window, but rather each panel riding remote and alone.
Everything was its own solitary world, he realized; if he tried
to touch something, he would touch nothing. He rode on his
bed above a void, was suspended above a solitary world that
was a bed in his own solitary world, all of it hanging in a void.
He lay there, feeling faces tick across his flesh like a clock,
slowly now, but a little faster every day. *And who shall draw my
profiles*, he wondered, no longer certain of who he was. *And
who shall render all my faces as I die?*

MEANWHILE

by Caila Rossi

Once, in a thoughtful moment, he told her why he had married her: "Because I knew you'd make a good mother." There was no mention of love, but it didn't matter anymore. After nine years, she wondered only how much more she could take.

He was Eurasian. A tall, thin Chinese boy, she'd thought when she first saw him, one of the new, green bankers brought around to meet the company librarian. "We'll be seeing a lot of each other," she assured them. At twenty-four, she was smarter and more experienced than they'd ever be.

The Chinese boy returned the next day with his first request. "I hate to reveal my ignorance," he said in a voice that belied his humility. It was a worldly, wry, all-knowing, English voice, a profound, not only intellectually, but deep, rumbling, Oxford-educated voice. His nose was aquiline, his eyes round. He had full, soft lips, a cupid's bow. She saw him more distinctly and she didn't see him at all. She saw a flood of joyous light, a blinding explosion, a clinch was what she saw, she was struck by lightning, dumbstruck. She fell off her high horse. When she got to her feet she could see again, but her vision had changed.

Some people know the person they're going to marry when they meet them, but that wasn't true in her case. She recognized only the tip of her desire, motivation enough. Recently, she'd been thinking of her bad luck with men, that she would never fall for the right one, but whether or not he was right never occurred to her, she only wanted to sleep with him.

"You're so talented," she said the first time.

He was resting on an elbow above her. "What do you mean?"

"You can make love to me and smoke a cigarette at the same time."

Never sure of anyone's irony but his own, he was flattered. So she kept her mouth shut about how romantic it was for him to have kept his underwear on. It was alcohol that made the sex bad, not his arrogance, which she liked. For weeks she'd followed him to bars after work with a group from the office, until he finally understood that she was coming for him, not the drinks. He'd had several more, then they went back to his place. He didn't stop drinking for years.

Just as well that her desire for him was not only physical, was so multi-faceted that there were, inevitably, enough successes to keep her going. He had a great delicacy; he trod gently on the earth, not like the marauders most men were. He had ways of wreaking devastation, but he always started with himself. Mostly, he was subtle, a gentleman like her father, who had died when she was fourteen of a brain hemorrhage. This gentleman she wanted to save, did save, would probably save again if she had to. Even now, hearing his footsteps crossing the bedroom, opening drawers, closets, his key when he entered the house, not just the smell, but the sounds of him were a rousing prelude. Even if what followed was often disappointing.

In the beginning she thought about him all the time, about what would please him. Maybe she couldn't be beautiful herself, and she was not, despite what her so-called lover said. Her dead so-called lover, who had hovered on the horizon as a portal to joy that she might never know now.

Though joy was not what she'd wanted. She'd wanted to own beauty: beautiful clothes, a beautiful vase, and this one, beautiful man.

Her husband hadn't married her because he thought she'd make a good mother, did he forget? He'd married her because he was transferred to London and the firm would pay for her to go with him only if she was his wife. They'd been living together for almost a year by then. Later, he would say, "I knew what I was doing." Maybe he did, but to her their marriage was an experiment. As easily as she had moved in with him, then quit her job to avoid the gossip and jealousy at work, and because a better one had come along, she could get divorced, return to the States, get another degree, in business, maybe. She might get married again, though not to her so-called lover; she never thought about marrying him. But there would be changes; she counted on them. Her husband would have to stop drinking, this time permanently. She couldn't stand what he was doing to himself or how, when he drank, he forgot everything. How she might as well not have been there.

Meanwhile she had London. Her children were born there, two years apart. She had a circle of friends who were also mothers and wives. They lived off Sloane Street. Down the King's Road to Fulham Road, to South Ken. To the museums, Harrods, up the gardens, to Hyde Park, to Oxford Street. She knew all the squares and mewses, museums, specialty shops, department stores, and parks in the area; she wheeled her children everywhere in Lewis of London, the Rolls Royce of prams. She never thought about other men, then; she was a one-man woman.

It was while they were in London that her husband decided he had to choose to be either English or Chinese. She wanted him to choose English; it was so much more convenient. Really, she didn't see why he had to choose at all. She told him

21

they should go back to the States, that an identity crisis like his would be much less severe there, but he leaned toward Hong Kong. He had a sudden great nostalgia for the place. He felt he'd betrayed a nation by leaving.

And what was this nation but a whopping big cash register, a suffocating people jam? Its charms were mostly topographical: the view of green islands in a turquoise sea from the air, the panorama from the Peak, the monolithic rocks off the southern coast. Their family stayed for a month with his mother in Pokfulam, a middle-class residential area with some breathing space near the university. His mother taught chemistry there. She was short and thin, smiled often and tried to be gracious, but couldn't help being blunt. "I don't like babies," she said the day they arrived.

This was what he missed? His mother's family had done well in Hong Kong. They were from northern China originally, from Fushon. He spoke angrily in dialect to her. It seemed she resented not seeing him for six years and he didn't want to keep her in the dark about why.

"At least your father waited until lunch," she said when he toasted her with brandy at breakfast.

"Don't pretend to remember who my father was," he said. By evening he was lurching around the apartment with a cigarette, making witty conversation that he never remembered.

She left the children with him and the amah one day, to wander the city by herself, to discover its narrow streets and alleys. There were many cheap, colorful trinkets to buy. Later, her mother-in-law would say she'd got taken. She took the Star Ferry, had tea in the Peninsula lobby, took the ferry back and, in a taxi on her way back to Pokfulam, she found herself taking stock. Look where desire had lead her, one blind step at a time: to a new job, to London, motherhood, to Hong Kong, to new friends and family, all in the space of a few years. To a charming, gentle drunk whom she adored and found endlessly interesting, and who found nothing surprising about her.

The sky is clearing to the south. She knows it's south, because her garden is on the south side of the house. Not a backyard, a garden, her garden. Shortly after she left him in London, taking the kids and moving back to New York to live here with her mother, her mother got sick, went into the hospital and never came out. She felt like Candide turning, after many adventures, to the small plot of land at the back of the house. She pulled up all the bushes her grandparents had found so easy to care for, but kept her mother's Japanese maple. Her life was bound to tragedy. Her parents were gone, her marriage over; she would have to accept that, but had no idea what to do with it. She plotted, dug, planted, dug up, replanted, and waited, but not being properly thought out, many of her plants failed in the shade of the tree and in the soil which may be alkaline or sandy, she didn't know. Some plants best for the shade didn't take, while others that needed sun did. She never had much patience for gardening, never took time to observe how the sun crossed the backyard. All her patience was spent elsewhere. Then, one morning years later, long after her husband had returned to them to begin his sobriety, years after she had stopped thinking all the time about her so-called lover, it suddenly required no effort to note how the sun fell on the upper branches of the tree, on the purple asters and the yellow roses climbing the wood fence. Later it alighted on the hostas, the ivy covering the fence on the east side of the garden, and on the pink physo-somethings with the long green and white leaves. In the early evening, right before dusk, when color is most intense, her

23

garden warmly applauds her. She returns the affection. All that money, time, and effort thrown so carelessly into the dirt paid off, nature collaborated.

He comes out to help her with the shopping. A tall, slouched, aging boy, he takes wide, unsure steps like a sailor on a pitching deck. An inner ear problem, but he was never good at walking. It's genetic, he says: His feet are too small for someone his height; he's never sure of his balance.

"Did you get stamps?" He sounds slightly less Shakespearean after all these years in the States.

"Oh!" She forgot, but she remembered everything else. "Your shirts, your rice."

"My rice?" His heavy rounded eyebrows rise like accent marks.

"The rice you asked for." She's his consort, that's what he used to call her, not his servant. "I got your medication, I went to the butcher."

As he wheels the cart through the living room, the dry cleaning slips to the floor. She picks it up.

"What'd he say about the skirt?" he says, as she hangs the clothes from the kitchen door.

"Who?"

He doesn't answer, but lowers himself into a seat at the oval table in front of the window.

"I ordered a case of spring water. You should drink at least a bottle a day."

"The dry cleaner."

"It wasn't a skirt, it was my blue dress. And that was two weeks ago."

He turns to look at the garden. "I should probably see a doctor."

Has she missed something? Glancing at him, she sees only the back of his graying head, with its vulnerable spot at the crown.

"This memory lapse can't be much fun for you, Jean."

Jean is not her name. He disarms her, he yanks her back from wherever she was; he's far less predictable than she. He thinks so, too.

"You've forgotten more important things," she says.

"Like what?" And when she doesn't reply, "Did you forget?"

His humor is inappropriate, but he doesn't realize that yet. He's spent his day reading the paper, following the stock market on his computer, eating breakfast, perhaps lunch, cleaning up, talking on the phone. He's never bored, perfectly happy to do nothing, for which he dresses neatly, casually, much the same as her so-called lover did. Each so fragile in his own way. She doesn't see herself as fragile. But then, she thought her so-called lover would outlast them all.

"Rob called," her husband says.

"Is everything okay?" Their son had been in Venezuela working for a non-profit. He learned from his father's uneven career to do what felt good.

"He wants me to go to China with them for two weeks."

"Go," she says dryly, knowing that though he said "me," he meant "us."

"It has been ten years." Not since his mother's funeral.

"So go."

He looks at her evenly. His face has coarsened over time, but any wrinkles and worry lines were diluted in years of drinking. They discuss his looks as if they were a mutual investment. Do his eyelids droop too much? She likes them that way. Should he comb his hair to cover the spot? Touch up his jaw line? What does she think? What do her friends think? Her friends and family think he is elegant, sophisticated, well educated: they are fascinated by him. If they see what she sees, they don't say so; that he is an anachronism, an Edwardian gentleman, rather hapless. He has a quick wit; takes nothing seriously but himself, though less so now, perhaps. He used to wonder what he had done to deserve her good opinion of him; he was clueless as only a narcissist can be. He was afraid of losing her veneration, but lost it anyway, incrementally. That is, he is no longer mythic to her. Destiny has shown itself to be a mix of genes, self-fulfilling prophecy, unfilled wishes, luck, good and bad, and circumstance, and diminished, even reversed expectations, not only of him, but also of everyone, of life. Not a bad thing, a good, a Zen-like thing.

"Is it something I said?"

"What?" She has made herself busy rearranging containers in the refrigerator.

"You've been in a mood since yesterday." He's noticed. She forgets, sometimes, that he's more aware now of sharing the arena. Having behaved badly at the beginning, he compensates, he pays attention.

It used to be so easy to hide things from him. "It has nothing to do with you," she says. Nothing has anything to do with anything else, the other used to say.

"Who does it have to do with then?" He smiles, trying to coax it out of her, and he will, she wants him to. The secret is out, anyway: she's not young anymore. He might as well know what a fool she's been, how she clung to the illusion. Was she deceived? Only by herself. She'd used her imagination mightily to keep some fantasy alive. Though she might mention that it had always required imagination to sustain desire, she never felt she had an equal partner.

Who will look at her now? Who will she think of when she buys clothes, when she gets her hair cut, her teeth polished? It was always her so-called lover. He was the silent one listening to her voice at the end of the line, his television always on, though he claimed to hardly watch it. She was sure he was observing her, too, from a distance. She felt him watching. It was the sort of scrutiny ascribed to angels and lovers, of which he was neither. Also to the newly dead. Though since this morning, she hasn't felt him. His gaze, real and imagined, is gone, the spotlight is off.

Her husband watches her. He thinks her crises are nothing—holes in her blue silk dress, spoiled meat—because she's always diminished her problems or not mentioned them. Maybe she did talk about herself in the beginning, when she still thought he might be interested, but looking for her reflection in his dark eyes, she never found it. Sometimes she'd have to check in a mirror just to make sure she was still there. His attention became the lesser part of her desire for him, and all she'd wanted from the other.

He's gone silent. She's going to have to say something, the least bit possible, just enough to keep him from thinking it has something to do with him. "Someone I know died."

"Who?"

She tells him, thinking the name will mean nothing, but he remembers. "I thought that was finished a long time ago."

She didn't expect him to remember. "It never got started."

"I don't believe that."

Too late now, she's jumped. Who knows where she'll land? "We were friends, that's all."

He turns away from her toward the window, draws the curtain aside, lets it go. Women had pursued him, too. They'd call the house and leave their names. She can't remember any of them.

"Don't expect me to attend the funeral." He's working himself up. It's an effort; he's constitutionally mild. He gets up, sits down. Is this shock? Neither of them seems to know what

28

to do. Distance feels most appropriate. They can't get too close, anyway, with this fault in the ground between them.

It had suited him to think her life was a neat package; then they could work on his. They couldn't fix everything, though. He is still easily wounded. Over the years, things she said and did, even unintentionally, have accumulated in his nursery of hurt. He never forgets. He's self-absorbed, absent-minded, helpless in many ways of the world, still a child, still needy, even more so. He's very much himself, and for that she loves him.

"He died weeks ago," she says, attempting a lack of affect. "I didn't even know." She tells him about the call from the former friend yesterday. "She thinks we had an affair."

"And you convinced her you hadn't."

"I don't care what she thinks."

"Who else knows?"

"Knows what? There's nothing to know." This is an argument for young people, people who still have a passion for each other, who can still feel betrayed.

"It wasn't an affair." How small her voice is, so high in her throat; her poor leg, trembling.

"Then what was it?"

"Nothing. I don't know. Friends." Steer a steady course to the truth, or the closest port to it. The truth is damning enough; the truth isn't even the truth.

"A friend you had to hide from me."

"We never made love, believe me."

"I don't believe anyone." She's anyone.

Look at her, so pitiful, a shaky bird on a thin limb. She feels young, or old. She remembers a poem about dying a young person's death: reckless, sexual, ridiculous.

Between them: an expanse of green tablecloth crossed by thin yellow lines that enclose large pink and white flowers. It is shot with small, fraying holes, but in a past life, the life she feels she has just left behind, she liked the way it looked against the window, with the garden beyond it. Now it looks like a souvenir. Everything has stopped, come to the end of its decorative life: the brass napkin holder his mother brought them when she visited from Hong Kong, such a cold, thoughtful gift; and the matte yellow teapot. She doesn't know what time it is. Early afternoon, late morning. A gray and white cat poises atop the wood fence, then jumps on the lid of the compost container and down to the wet grass, delicately shaking its paws. The houses attached to either side of them are quiet. They contain families whose cheerful faces belie what she hears through the walls, though maybe they are happy enough. Real crises occur in silence. Then the bodies are carried out.

COMING OF AGE

by Lynda Schor

I put my third cup of coffee in the microwave, hoping the fuse won't blow again. I'm not dressed, haven't taken a shower. Am trying to finish that article on how to talk sexy to your husband in bed. If I get it in to my editor by tomorrow, and it is accepted, and I made all the required changes in two weeks, I could count on being paid in a few months. I push a stray, graying lock of hair behind one ear, and sit down at the kitchen table, which is also my desk. The book I'm using for a reference says, "I want you to think about the word *penis*. Now close your eyes and try to visualize your husband's *penis*. As you are doing this, slowly mouth the word penis without trying to make any sound. Just feel the way your tongue and lips move. Say it again. And again." I recall, with a sudden panic, that I haven't seen my daughter for a few days. That's what that heavy feeling was, I realize, as I run, barefoot, across the rough floors of the living room, through one tiny bedroom towards the last, and largest, room of our railroad flat. Her door is closed. Studying its cracked and yellowed paint, and the also yellowed childhood drawing of a square red brick house with a smoking chimney, on a spacious bright green field, which had been hanging there for about ten years, I feel the panic I'd been feeling lately when approaching her now always closed door. My heart pulsing in my throat so deeply I feel I might black out, I wonder why I'm afraid of my kid. It was just that lately she didn't seem thrilled to see me. But was it only my fear of rejection? That's not mature. Finally I get up the courage to knock. There's no answer, but I can hear something. A floorboard? Her squeaky bed? I can tell she's in there. Still, I'm tempted to leave, finish my article. If she isn't answering, then she's fine, and if she doesn't want to see me, OK. At least she knows I want to see her. Then I realize I'll feel better if I actually see her and speak to her.

The last time I saw her we had a huge fight about her sociopathic friend Tami—who she had a cult like relationship with—and their visits to the Lower East Side gang, Sick Death. I'd found her diary on my desk while I was writing an article called "It's Great to Marry for Money," for which I had to do lots of research, since I'd never been smart enough to try it. Usually I don't invade my daughter's privacy—for instance, if I saw her diary in her room I'd never look in it—but somehow I wondered whether she wasn't crying out for me to read it by "losing" it right next to my word processor. Also, she looked like hell lately—scrawny, filthy—and was always grumpy. I realized with horror that it was like having her father—who I'd divorced years ago—around the apartment again—my tiptoeing around explosive and possibly violent outbursts with sullen silences in between. My high blood pressure creating fireworks that burst in my head leaving sparklers in my peripheral vision, I'd opened the lavender vinyl cover of her journal. If I'd once hoped she'd become a writer, here was, once and for all, the proof that that was out. In purple ink, and in a sloppy, rounded handwriting, with circles for dots, and a multitude of misspellings, I saw repetitions and variations of one idea—was Tami fooling around with Cool Breeze behind her, Lauren's, back, or wasn't she? I told her that her closeness with a friend she didn't trust scared me, and her going to the Lower East Side scared me, and her fooling around with members of a gang scared me. I was afraid to ask what she meant in her diary by "fooling around." I was afraid to ask about drugs. I was terrified that she had an eating problem. She screamed at me. I felt like a child being yelled at by her mother. I cowered, and covered my face with my notebook. "You're scared of everything," she shrieked, her light brown ponytail falling down over her slender shoulder. "I'll die before I turn out like you." She didn't accuse me of the one thing I was afraid of—invading her privacy. She was so angry, but yet she looked so frail, so vulnerable, that I began to cry, the first time I'd ever cried in front of her. Her hazel eyes widened with fear, and she put a thin arm around my shoulders. "Everything will be okay," she crooned as she rocked me.

I am about to knock once again when my daughter's bedroom door opens. She's lying on her bed, propped up on her pillows. Or *are* they her pillows? They're scarlet velvet, and I don't recognize them. Strangely, she looks years older than when I saw her a few days ago. Maybe that's because her hair is moussed back—no more bangs; her forehead is exposed. She's wearing a peach stretch t-shirt that has tiny sleeves, and is cut low, exposing what has become—quite suddenly, it seems to me—a large ripe bosom with a deep cleavage. I just stand there surprised. From behind me, a man's voice: "Lookin' good, ain't she?" My daughter squirms with pleasure. I notice, in the tanned, flat space between her low-cut tights and her short top, a gold ball in her navel. Where did she get the money for that? I wonder. The thin, light-haired youth sits down on my daughter's bed. Her now-womanly, well-rounded arm wraps around his narrow, hairless chest. Tattooed letters that I try to read emerge from the edges of his pale blue sleeveless T. I think I can make out the word "hate"—at least the "ate" part—and what looks like a swastika. "He's so supportive," my daughter purrs. Looking closer, I think I can see, through my daughter's blouse, a small ring next to each nipple. However I wasn't going to get hooked into screaming about the piercings or whatever other ornaments might be adorning her once-pristine body. Didn't I write an article about teens called, "Don't Sweat the Small Stuff?" I sit down on the other side of her bed, noticing with pleasure that she still has her pink *Mulan* quilt. "How did you get into her room?" I ask. "His name is Chico," my daughter says. He couldn't have gotten in without passing through my bedroom. The thought of him, with his dirty nails and fusty smell, sneaking through my apartment gives me the willies. I look at my daughter. She's running her delicate fingers through Chico's pale, oatmeal-colored, absolutely straight hair. The only windows in the apartment that aren't off an airshaft are behind my daughter. These windows face a small concrete backyard that has two large ailanthus trees in it, growing from a small crack. I could see the green above my daughter's hair, which has a reddish glow around her head, like a fiery halo.

"He came in through here, Mother," she says. How come she's calling me Mother, and not Mom or Ma as she used to? I look at where she is pointing. There is a doorway in her room where there used to be just a slightly dirty white wall, against which her bookshelves and toys used to be. "What's going on here?" I ask. My daughter gets up, and indicates that she'd like to show me around. She's grown so much in the last few days she towers over me. Her platform boots don't help. "We were able to rent the apartment across the hall, and they connected here, so we renovated, and now we have a gorgeous ten-room apartment." My daughter leads me through a maze of beautifully furnished rooms with oak floors and trim, with three fireplaces and a fantastic kitchen, with hundreds of cabinets. There is an island with a stove, like in *Frasier*, where ruddy gleaming copper pots of various sizes hang from a rack overhead. This is like one of my apartment dreams in which I'd suddenly notice a door somewhere in my apartment that I'd never noticed before. I'd open it, and find a few large rooms I never knew I had. Or an enormous terrace or garden that I could put chairs in, and a picnic table. "Where did you get the money for this?" I demand. "You're only fourteen." She had been baby-sitting since she was eleven or twelve, and had even bought her own Sony television. But an enormous renovated apartment? "I knew you'd be jealous, that's why I didn't tell you right away. What do you think I've been doing?" my daughter asks. "Give a guess. Don't try to pretend

34

you don't know. How else was I going to get the things I needed and wanted? From your magazine articles?" "What? What?" I sputter. "Quit pretending you know nothing," she squints at me. "You as much as gave me your blessing. That's your game, isn't it—ignoring what you don't like so you don't have to deal with it?" I look over at Chico, who's gathered his thin hair in a ponytail and changed into a grayish-brown Armani suit. "We're partners," my daughter says, linking her arm in Chico's. "Business partners," says Chico, winking. He has tiny, deep-set, pale-blue eyes with pupils like bullet holes. I must still look blank or shocked. "That's right, Mom. I'm a call girl, a high-priced hooker. *Very* high-priced—one of the best in the business." "Yeah, right," says Chico. "Your little girl here gives the best blowjob in the business. She's famous." He brings his beady eyes close to my face. "She can take twelve inches." My daughter giggles with pleasure. "I do everything but digest it," she says. Her laugh is the same delighted giggle she had when she was a baby.

My daughter places her bright vermilion lipsticked lips on Chico's pale thin ones. He pulls her closer by tugging gently on one of her nipple rings. I look away. It sounds as if they're panting, but I realize it's me, hyperventilating. I look around in vain for a paper bag in case this turns into a full-blown anxiety attack.

"You stupid child," I say, knowing that's exactly the wrong thing to say. I expect her to yell some insult at me, but instead she looks at me like a devastated one-year-old—like she did the first time some kid socked her in the playground, surprised and hurt. "You're being exploited," I continue, but in a softer tone. Maybe I'm reaching her. I don't have much time to reach her—maybe it's even too late. I was going to have a talk with her about sex, but I thought the time hadn't come yet, and now look. "You could get pregnant," I say, "you could get some disease. And what about college?" I expel some air, pull my ratty robe together across my chest, but not before I notice my own small, saggy breasts. The word "dugs" comes to mind. "Remember those feminist marches I used to take you on? Marches for Choice, marches for equal rights for women?"

"Yeah," my daughter says. "I remember those depressing marches, all those poor women in ugly t-shirts and shorts, and jeans with butterfly patches..." "I can't believe that's how you felt about all that...for me that was a most exciting time. You've inherited the benefits of our struggle." "What benefits?" my daughter asks, pursing her lips in disgust. "We worked hard so you wouldn't be totally exploited." I scream. My voice cracks, my robe opens. "And now it looks like you're *choosing* to be exploited." I look over at Chico, who's checking his tie in the mirror. "Exploited! How am I exploited? I'm the one who's earning a great living, who's getting rich, who has great clothes and a great apartment, who has a great mate. And I'm only fourteen. I guess you want me to make the same mess of life that you did—no money, exploited by those stupid dates you always had sex with, a dirty, rent-controlled apartment with no windows in two of the rooms, clothing from thrift stores. By the way, I am pregnant already, Mom."

I stand there with my mouth open. A writer, I'm usually very verbal, but with my daughter, either nothing comes to mind, or inanities burble out as if I'm bewitched—all the trite and horrible things mothers have said to their daughters through the ages. I recall myself, small and sullen in front of my own mother, brows knit, tears on my cheeks, vowing never to say those things she was saying, vowing I'd be much more understanding, open, totally different from that woman yelling at me.

"A baby. What are you going to do with a baby?" "We're going to let you take care of it, Mother. Since you freelance, you're home all day. Although I'm not that happy about how you'd bring it up." Chico nods.

"I may be home, but I'm working. How do you think those articles get written?" "You were never available to me," my daughter says. "While I languished for attention, you were always busy." She bites on a cuticle. She looks the same as she did when she was teething on a rubber circlet. Her two front upper teeth still have their "fringes"—the name we gave to their deckled edges.

I can't believe how she's interpreted my life—our life together, all my struggles to change things, partly for her benefit. "I always felt that I never had a moment of privacy, or even enough time to do a good job at my work. I was always available to you," I say. "And what is he?" I shrug a shoulder in Chico's direction. "Isn't he a pimp? Or does he have a day job? Isn't he exploiting you?" "No, mother." She fluffs those scarlet pillows, but looks as if she'd like to throw them. She gets her voice under control. She's sure she's right, which makes me madder. "We're in business together. We work together, and we make a great living." My face is hot, and it feels damp. "It's not his body that gets used in your business, is it?" I can't hide my disgust with Chico, though I'm trying. "I'm not the one with the gorgeous body, or the special talent," Chico says, squeezing a pimple on his chin. "I'm the one with the influential clientele." "You have the totally wrong idea, mother," my daughter says. "Chico's been to Harvard Business? A lot of his friends have helped us, and are now our clients. His real name is Arlen Trent Drumwoodie III." "The Republican senator's son?" I ask. "That explains it." My daughter stares me in the eye. "None of your usual sarcasm." She's protecting Chico. "That sarcasm is probably why Daddy had to leave," she says. "It's probably why you don't

37

have any man living with you now." Chico clasps his diamond Rolex around his thin, hairless wrist. It clicks definitively. I can't believe what she's saying. Our entire life together—everything I've done, everything we've done—is being interpreted by her in some twisted way. From the mirror I look back at myself, and can see that I need to calm down. My forehead is wrinkled with worry, and around my mouth are those lines that make me look like Charley McCarthy, the puppet. I stand straighter, pull my robe closed, and re-tie my belt. I modulate my voice. "You just don't understand how I lived, so don't make judgments. Daddy didn't leave because of my sarcasm. I made him leave because he was hideous." Her snide smile indicates that once again I've said the wrong thing. But is there any right thing?

"Not all girls can take twelve inches in their mouths. Those with this talent are surely entitled to public recognition. But our society denies the prostitute both appreciation of, and the opportunity to exercise sexual virtuosity," Chico explains, as my daughter helps him squeeze a cufflink through his well-starched French cuff. "What kind of talent is this?" I ask. Now I'm speaking to Chico. "She used to draw and paint. Even as a baby she had a wonderful sense of design, color. She was good at making pottery. She loved it."

My daughter puts her arm around Chico, which isn't difficult, as she's the taller one, as if they're posing for a family portrait. "Listen," she says. "I didn't want it to come to this, but look how we lived. And do you think your work writing those ridiculous articles isn't prostitution? Don't you complain that you have to write those idiotic, meaningless and pornographic, anti-feminist articles all the time and don't have time to write what you want? And the editors hound you with the stupidest changes, all based on their advertisers' ludicrous demands, they take months to pay, you still have no money, and you still have a shitty place to live? Is that a better, more moral life?"

I'm limp. There's too much going on here, and I have no more answers. "At least *we'll* be able to send our child to private school," my daughter adds. I cover my face with my hands, and sit on the edge of her bed for a moment. My daughter rushes over to my side, and sits next to me. Chico, who I see now looks just like my kid's father, gets on the bed too, and places a warm, reassuring hand on my back. We sit for a moment in silence. Then my daughter puts her face alongside mine. I can smell her sweet bubblegum breath, feel her cool, firm cheek. She places her hand on my arm, rubbing gently, soothingly. "Everything's going to be okay?" she says, the way most of the kids speak nowadays, ending their statements as if they are questions. Her slightly stubby fingers (like her Dad's), with their gnawed tips, and chipped, blue-polished nails, look like those of a tiny child.

ANOTHER EXAMPLE

by John Yau

I think it would be extremely pleasant and even comforting if I could find a new or at least different way to fuck up my life. If only I could delude myself for a few minutes more than usual, if only I could have a few minutes when I believe that what I am doing will turn out okay. It never does. It never has. The possibility that any brief segment of my life will be better than the previous segment, get ecstatically enhanced as the ad says with a nonstop wink, is about as likely as the Pope admitting he masturbates while listening to Black Sabbath. If there were a graph made of my life, and the prospects that have awaited it, the line cutting across the blue-lined paper would be flat and straight, the sign that the bearer is no longer breathing. A life of no trajectories, no dips or rises, not even a bump indicating someone in the bus farted and was relieved to do so.

Being a fuckup doesn't take work. That's a popular misconception. You don't have to work at it. Chances are if you are a fuckup like me, then you don't have to do anything. You don't take chances, they find you no matter what little burrow you have crawled into.

This is how the last one happened. The names we used are all that distinguish it from the time before. Why I say happened is a mystery because I no longer think things happen to someone, to me. I think they are just waiting there, like a room full of musty fabrics hanging like loose skin from their wobbly armatures and twisted skeletons. You enter the room this room of shallow breath and sallow light, it's really the color of urine, because there is no other room you can enter. Had you chosen to enter a different room, it would have been the same as the room you did enter.

I had been staying in a compartment in a converted domicile where the other chambers were occupied by those who never opened the door more than the thickness of an official envelope, their inclement cyclopean eye scrutinizing the depleted circumstances before they scuttled out into the dust clogged imminence, arthritic and crablike, though often they were not so old, but were in fact as young or younger than the one who lived inside my rented hive and who sometimes told others his real name.

I am lying when I say this. I never tell anyone, not even myself, my real name which I buried along with my parents glad to be rid of this last umbilical cord to the past that tries like the military to drag me back.

Otto, I say. My name is Otto. It has been my name intermittently and yet so often that I have started thinking of it as a pet that I carry around with me and sometimes show people. That was my mistake. Letting Velma pet Otto. I should have shooed her away, hissed and wagged my spiked tongue. I should have listened to my name and backed out as soon as I bumped into the well-molded facade she used to fribble with the scaly and the scamps.

Velma isn't her name, but it is the name I called her because the name she thrust at me, like a crust of stale bread, didn't seem to fit. It enhanced her and I didn't like her enhanced, as I could see that she was already more than I could handle.

It's not that I am small of stature and that Velma is stout. The opposite is closer to the measurements you are looking for.

I thought she said her name was Vermin but I was wrong and learned so when I repeated what I thought she said and she cuffed me with her furry saw-toothed arm. It wasn't enough to stop me. And it wouldn't have mattered if it did because behind every Velma is Vermin and behind every Vermin there is the bodily circumstance that has been waiting for you, patient as a mongoose.

I say circumstance but I might as well be saying circumcision or circus or cistern, in any case a place full of posterior odors and potent mukluks.

Velma and I shared ourselves with each other for six months. We left our germs and flakes of dead skin and I am sure much else that is teeming on each other's weathered parapets and rancorous downgrades. It was never fun. It wasn't even perfunctory. I would say dowdy but that adds a touch of voyeurism that is without merit, even to those who insulate themselves with maritime manure. But we had succumbed to our shrieking parliaments and the incriminating hunch that we would never be more than a periodical of perishable food so we soon couldn't escape periodically charging into each other like blind dogs who believe the meat is hanging right in front of them.

I used to scream out the wrong name at the right moment, that is where I have slipped each time my body is placed in something closer than proximity to another's promontory. She could have had the common courtesy to think that I was hallucinating, that I was seeing little scatterings multiplying in the grooves of my baggy skin. She could have thought I was a picaroon waxing picaresque syllables in an attempt to further heighten her motility units. Couldn't I have been whipping myself with erratum?

I could have screamed Vermin or Velma but no I screamed out another name the name of no one I know or knew a name that just sprang out of me one night in the neon interrupted dark.

42

I say no one I know or knew which isn't exactly true but is completely the truth. You see I screamed out my own name, my own two-headed little pet, my anonymity, my little room, as if I was calling to someone who was walking in the other direction, a plaintive cry, a mewling whimper maybe more like it, I can't recall, repeated over and over until finally I felt the fists landing on me and I returned to where I was and discovered what I was supposed to be doing.

You see it doesn't matter which name I tell you, whoever you are, is mine because one day in a moment of irrevocable irrigation that name will be the one that leaves me heaped up on the linoleum floor, a crumpled chapel to my dutiful childhood. That is when I start out again, knowing whatever road I am on is the same one I foolishly thought I left in a room I didn't plan on returning to.

DETROIT 1972

by Barbara Henning

1
Hunter's in the bath.

Linda's sweeping the floor around the edge of the door.

"Hunter, I wish you would put your own clothes away."

Hunter eases himself down under the bath, his ears fill with water, his long hair floats out at right angles—a halo of red hair.

He watches the bubbles now at eye level.

Down again and up for air.

"Hunter, can you watch the baby today while I go to work? I have to model from three till six."

Down again in the world of bubbles.

In the kitchen, he can hear her cleaning off the table.

Her footsteps in the hallway.

"Hunter, could you wash the baby while you're in there?" She opens the door and stands in the frame holding a chubby little girl with folds of fat around her knees and elbows and a big smile.

Hunter looks up from the soapy water and closes his eyes. "All right."

He sets the baby on his stomach, leaning her back on his knees. She splashes the water.

"Hunter, what kind of bubbles are you using? I hope it's not dish soap. That wouldn't be good for her skin." The woman combs her long hair until she is encircled by it and Hunter can't see her nose as he looks at her sideways.

"Hunter," says the voice inside the hair, "What kind of soap did you use?"

"Dish soap."

She turns, sets the hairbrush on the toilet tank with a clank and walks past him impatiently, whipping the baby off his lap and drying her with a towel. "I wish you wouldn't use that kind of soap."

Hunter pushes the door closed behind her. He steps slowly out of the tub, wrapping a long green and white striped towel around himself, looks into the mirror then and starts to untangle his hair.

2

Hunter comes home drunk in the middle of the afternoon and follows Linda around the house while she cleans and takes care of the baby.

"Remember the time, Linda, when the doctor in the hospital tried to get me to talk to those kids about drugs, how they were bad for them, how they killed and I told him the truth: Yeah, but doc, you can't deny one thing about heroin. It makes you feel good. Nothing else in the world makes you feel *that* good."

"Hunter, please…"

"No, this ain't nothing," he says. "I'm just talking. That's all."

Linda wipes off the mantle. "Hunter, drugs gave you that valve in your heart. The click, click sound that keeps us awake at night came from using that beautiful drug."

"That didn't come from the drug. It came from the needle, silly. The drug is beautiful."

He follows her in the bathroom, loses his balance, and grabs the shower curtain to steady himself. It comes down easily, the pole, too.

"Hunter. Why don't you just sit down. I wish to hell you would find a different job besides tending bar in that dump."

"Hey—What is it you want, Linda? Huh, what is it?"

"I don't want anything but some goddamn sanity in this house." She slams the ashtray down on the coffee table in front of the rose-colored sofa and lights a cigarette while the baby nurses.

"All *I* want, Linda, is a trailer, a trailer and a truck so I can travel around. I don't want this house, this furniture, none of it. I'll just pull my trailer up to the curb when I want to stay and pull away when I want to leave."

"You couldn't possibly leave the piles of shit you have accumulated here, Hunter."

"*That* would simplify things."

"Sure, I can see it now, beer bottles falling out in a heap every time you open the door. That would be very simple, wouldn't it?"

"I can tell you one thing for sure, Linda," he says as he stretches on the sofa, the toes of his brown shoes lined up on the floor. "I'm not going to keep working for the rest of my life just to make the bills."

They both shut up then and listen to his heart click.

3

Linda sits with her chin in the cup of her hand, her elbow resting on the bar. She smokes a Marlboro. Hunter wipes down the counter and tells a drunk who is sitting at the end of the bar that his time is up. "Joe, hit the road. You've made your limit." The drunk stands up, puts on his black trench coat, flicking his ponytail outside his collar. "Just remember Red, I always pay for my drinks," he says as he stumbles out the door.

Crack—the balls are spinning on the pool table. Linda stirs her rum and coke with the straw and pulls the brim of a 1930 style hat down around her face. A woman wearing a tight black skirt, high heels and dramatic makeup sits next to her. "You seen Lamont around?" she asks. "No, Vanessa, I haven't seen him all night," Linda says. Then she stares at the bottles in the mirror, using her hat to cut the woman out of her line of vision.

The night before she and Hunter had given a young girl a ride. Lying on the floor in the back of their car, she was crying and shaking—afraid Lamont would find her. They dropped her off at some house on Commonwealth Street.

Hunter moves up and down the bar. She can hear him

whisper to some pimps, Got some good grass. Then he shoots a game of pool with Chuck. Chuck takes five dollars from Hunter, and carefully puts it in the middle of his roll of bills.

"Watch out for that guy in the corner over there," Hunter tells Linda. "I think we're going to have trouble." She slides down closer to the end of the bar away from the action.

The guy in the corner—a tall skinny guy wearing red pants—puts a quarter on the table. Chuck turns around and faces him. "You motherfucker…You keep away from my girls!" Chuck smacks the guy on the head with his pool stick, cracking it in two. Suddenly the bar is full of people.

From behind the counter where Linda is hiding, she can hear the woman yelling: "Lamont! Put that gun away! We don't want that girl!"

"Shut up, bitch!"

Hunter flashes the lights on and off. His voice sounds over the fight. "Everyone out! The cops are on their way. Everyone out!"

The group pushes and shoves each other as they go out the door. Then Hunter locks the door, dims the lights, and the noise starts to move into the distance.

4

He glides from one end of the bar to the next, setting in front of each customer the correct drink, with a twist and a straw. Earlier in the day, in the Majestic Grill over orange juice, eggs and bacon, he and Linda had reaffirmed that they didn't want the false security of married life—a house with a manicured lawn. "We'll be together for the rest of our lives," she had said.

48

"A marriage certificate won't make any difference." They ate their breakfast. "We'll just keep on like we are—we won't let our lives change." Linda said this and Hunter agreed.

Tonight Linda drinks gin and tonic and she racks up the balls and then smack—the number five and the number three fall in corner pockets. Indian Joe, a regular, misses the ball—he's too drunk to do much more. With each shot Linda makes, she sinks two or three until she's won the game. A dollar in the back of her tight Levis and Hunter tells Joe it is time to go home and sober up.

The next quarter on the table is Lamont's—his ladies are across the street at Anderson's Garden tricking the johns and collecting twenties for his roll. He's going to pass a little time now, shooting a game of pool. "You sure are looking good, sweetie, since you had that baby—put on a little meat here and there."

A woman drops a quarter in the jukebox and Marvin Gaye sings: *I bet you wonder how I knew. About your plans to make me blue. With some other guy you knew before…"*

Linda chalks up her stick.

"I told you girl—anytime you want to give up that beatnik, I got a place for you. The baby, too. I'm definitely not jiving you."

He racks and she leans over, slides her stick over the felt. The cue ball hits breaking the rack sideways and three balls sink.

"Lucky shot, honey. I can tell you're a winner."

Hunter keeps drying glasses and washing down the counter, singing along with Marvin: *"I know a man ain't supposed to cry. But these tears I can't hold inside…"*

Linda walks from one side of the pool table to the other, sinking balls and occasionally hitting the lamp above the table, its angular light flashing back and forth between them.

Lamont steps back rubbing his hands on his iridescent red slacks. "Ain't nothing but luck for a woman to get those balls."

Hunter chews on a toothpick.

Linda purposely aims off center, grazing the number six.

"Like I told you, hippie girl, you were just lucky."

Lamont takes aim and knocks two balls into their respective pockets.

Linda banks the cue ball and puts the number two in the corner pocket. Then she takes all the rest.

Lamont peels off a five dollar bill and looks around the bar. Everyone is looking at him: Chuck's ladies at the bar, a group of hustlers by the window, and three or four others.

"Ain't no goddamn woman gonna beat me," he says under his breath. Then he removes a fifty dollar bill from the center of his roll and challenges her to another game. One of Chuck's girls crosses her legs and comments to her friend, "Come on Sally, let's watch this fool."

Linda puts three balls in on the break.

She stands taller and taller after each shot, brushing her long hair out of her eyes. Lamont chugs down a shot of vodka and then, leaning on his stick, he smiles at everyone in the bar. When he shoots, the cue ball drops in a corner pocket.

Seventy-five. Linda takes the second and the third game. One hundred dollars. "Ain't no woman gonna take my money," he says.

Vanessa comes strutting into the bar then and she walks over to him as Linda counts up her bills. "I'm out here, Lamont, breaking my ass for you and you're in here giving my money away to some white bitch?"

"Can't you see, Bitch, that I'm busy." He orders another drink.

• • •

Hunter lies on the sidewalk outside the apartment building and laughs hysterically.

"Hunter, get up. It's 4:00 in the morning. Hunter the police will arrest you. Hunter the babysitter needs to go home. Hunter I have to go to work tomorrow morning. Hunter…"

Hunter says "Oh Baby" between laughs and then he stops and lies still. He is very quiet.

She leans over him and shakes his head and tugs on his jacket. "Hunter…Come on. Are you all right, Hunter? You know you shouldn't drink, Hunter."

Suddenly, he laughs again, teasing her. She turns her back on him and starts walking home. One half block away though, and she looks back like a mother does to her young child who refuses to walk. The street is empty and the three story apartment buildings all have their shades drawn. The street lamps leave triangles of light on the pavement. Hunter stops laughing then, stands up, and they walk home together, arm in arm, just like usual.

CONTRIBUTOR'S NOTES

by Michael Martone

Looks Like

Michael Martone was born in Fort Wayne, Indiana, and grew up there. When Martone was in high school, it was often commented upon by family, friends, acquaintances, and even total strangers that he looked like Paul McCartney, one of The Beatles, a British rock-and-roll band that had recently visited America for the first time selling records, playing concerts, and appearing on television programs such as *The Ed Sullivan Show*. Soon after that, The Beatles' first movie, *Hard Day's Night* was released. By that time Martone had let his dark brown hair grow longer like most of the other boys in his school, and the longer hair increased the occasions when he received comments about his uncanny resemblance to the singer/songwriter. He imagined that he could see something around his eyes, the drape of his lids, he supposed, or there was an echo of the angle of McCartney's chin in Martone's own. But it was mostly the hair, he supposed, falling straight down his broad forehead to his overly bushy brow that he had only recently begun shaving on the bridge of his nose. Coincidentally, Martone was involved with a short-lived cover band inspired by the success of The Beatles' performance in the movie. The new band would lip synch the songs and imitate The Beatles' goofy antics, being pursued through the neighborhood by their screaming younger sisters. His bandmates, excited by Martone's evolving mimicry of one of their role models, urged Martone to take up the electric bass and begin memorizing the lyrics from *Meet the Beatles*. Oddly, and for reasons too complicated to explain here, Martone preferred to play the part of the band's manager, Brian Epstein, whose looks nobody then had any idea of, and stay backstage safely out of sight. Over time, Martone's and McCartney's shared facial characteristics began to diverge. For one thing Martone gained weight, his cheeks becoming even fuller and rounder than they had been, his neck merging with his chin and jaw line. McCartney's face, on the other hand, began to sag and the folds under his eyes grew deeper in shadow, the lids more hooded, setting the eyes themselves deeper in their sockets. There came a point when the casual mentions concerning the similarity of their shared appearance ceased all together. People would stare in startled confusion into Martone's face when he mentioned that once other people thought he looked like Paul McCartney. "I don't see it," they would say. There was a time, then, as he approached adulthood when Martone, as far as he could ascertain, looked like no one but his parents. His mother always said that if you broke Martone's face in two, the top half favored his father especially the nose and eyes but that the lips and chin were undoubtedly her contribution. Soon, Martone began to receive more and more comments that would draw a comparison between his appearance and that of an emerging character actor from Chicago named Joe Mantegna whose face, of course, was memorable but whose name unfortunately was not. Mr. Mantegna was, often for Martone's informants, the guy, you know, the actor in *Things Change* or *House of Games* or later the last *Godfather*. "Joe Mantegna?" Martone would answer once the pattern had become clear. And the resemblance was and is remarkable. Once, Martone, himself, had to look twice at a film still printed in his local newspaper. What, he thought at the time, am I doing in the newspaper? The similarity is most striking from a certain angle and stronger in profile. For some roles Mr. Mantegna will grow a beard, and Martone, whose hair now is best described as salt and pepper, believes that the actor probably colors his. Recently, another name, an actor again, is mentioned when people are moved to compare Martone's looks to others. Adam Arkin, the son of the actor Alan Arkin who he, Adam, resembles, comes up almost as frequently as Joe Mantegna as someone Martone looks like. Or when someone is searching for Joe Mantegna's name to tell Martone that he looks like him, he or she will say, you know, it is the actor that looks like the actor who is Alan Arkin's son. Martone suspects it is the eyes, the shape of the head, the hair where his face and the faces of these actors intersect. At a wedding reception recently, the mother of the bride commented in the receiving line that Martone had George Clooney's eyes, and, later that night, Martone pondered this new information. It just so happened that *One Fine Day* starring George Clooney was being shown on television. Martone stared at George Clooney's eyes as they appeared on the television screen before him, attempting to see the likeness but found, perhaps because he was a bit drunk from the wedding reception, that it was very difficult to look at someone's eyes or a picture of someone else's eyes then look at your own eyes in a mirror in order to determine if the two sets of eyes look in any way the same. The eyes on the screen and in the mirror kept moving. Secretly, Martone believes that he looks most like a cartoon character named Fred Flintstone. The particulars all seem to be a match. The thick neck, the shadow of the beard, the dark eyes and hair. Martone realizes that his self-image is probably a distortion, a projection of his own insecurities about his real appearance, but he can't help himself. And he isn't too surprised that when, in an unguarded moment, he asks someone he has just met if doesn't think that he, Martone, isn't the spitting image of Fred Flintstone, and the acquaintance squints and says, "Yes, I can see that."

Interns

Michael Martone was born in Fort Wayne, Indiana, in 1955. He taught at Harvard University where he was The Briggs-Copeland Lecturer on Fiction after teaching for seven years at Iowa State University in Ames. Martone noticed the difference between the two schools right away. On the first day of fiction writing class, he asked his new students to introduce themselves including in their introduction details as to their class standing, their academic interests, their preferences in what they read. He also wanted to ask them where they were from. He was curious having just come from Iowa to Cambridge. "Where are you from?" he asked the first student. The student answered that he was from Lowell House. Martone, expecting an answer like Illinois or Indianapolis, didn't know what to say in response so nodded his head and smiled in a manner he hoped conveyed he did in fact understand and even approved. He asked the same question of the second student who answered without hesitating that she was from Adams House. After several more students answered in the same way, volunteering that they were from this or that house, Martone figured out they were talking about their dormitories. It also occurred to him that he was meant to understand that knowing the particular house was to also know a great deal about the one who was from there, one's tastes and preferences. It was a code that took him most of the first semester to begin to decipher, but he finally figured out which house was preferred by athletes, for instance, or actors and musicians or those students who had a scientific bent. The rest of the first class was a disaster. Martone lectured to a restless and hostile room. He kept going while he tried to figure out what was so wrong. His students in Iowa had responded to his broad-ranging improvisations and his manner of peppering his talks with arcane trivia and personal anecdote. At Harvard, this appeared not to be working. The students sulked in their seats or stared blankly out the window. Suddenly, Martone realized that he was talking. That is to say that the fact he was lecturing was what was wrong with the lecture. He had grown used to the natural shyness and silence of his students in Iowa. At Harvard, his new students were not handicapped in the same way. They could not wait to speak, were more than prepared to do so, and once Martone realized this and allowed the students to speak, the initial discomfort disappeared at once. During the remaining five years of his tenure there, Martone barely uttered a few words each class session. In retrospect, he believes he was adored by his charges, winning teaching prizes each term and receiving excellent assessments in the student evaluations. He lived off Central Square, within walking distance to Harvard Square and 34 Kirkland, his office building at the university. Walking to work, he would pass several stores that specialized in selling used tuxedoes. Martone found it curious the number of such establishments. Formal wear for him had always been acquired from a rental store, the racks and racks of suits somewhere in the back out of sight of the showroom. Mentioning it in class one day, Martone learned from his students about the battle tuxes that were part of their wardrobe—cheap formal party dress that could suffer the excesses of the students' celebrations, a spontaneous dive into a nearby pool for instance. Martone ended up buying several battle tuxes for himself. To the one commencement he attended, he wore a dinner jacket designed by Bill Blass who was from Martone's hometown of Fort Wayne, Indiana. Martone took to dressing in a tux for the first day of his classes. He had inherited a blue paisley tie and cummerbund from his Uncle Wayne, which lent a jaunty and ironic flavor to the get-up. In one of the last first classes, during the introductions where the students shared what houses they were from, a young woman asked him if Sallie Gouverneur was his agent. This surprised Martone as he never talked about his business with his students. How would any of them know who his literary agent was? It turned out that this student had interned for Sallie who was a graduate of Radcliffe herself and this intern had seen and sent out Martone's stories the previous summer with cover letters she had composed herself. Another student in the same class reported that she too had interned in the summer at *The Atlantic Monthly* where she received from her fellow student Martone's manuscripts sent to the magazine to be considered. Martone remained silent as his students talked a while about the business of writing and publishing, trying to recall just which of his stories he had sent to Sallie that summer. The next year Martone took a job teaching in the creative writing program of Syracuse University. He moved from the Boston area heading north with a box of several tuxedoes that he never had the occasion to wear again.

ABOUT

by Jacques Roubaud

It has long been known that poets don't know what they're saying. They say one thing then they say the opposite.

You can't count on them, a fact that Socrates pointed out years ago, one that even school children know, and that I've been able to confirm by experience.

I practice a particular artistic discipline, not really plastic, not really musical, although it has its similarities with music, yet also occasionally comprises visual and graphic investigations: it is *poetry*, a modest sector and, let's be honest, somewhat neglected in the contemporary world of the LANGUAGE ARTS. On this account I'd like to relate the personal experience of a meeting between a practitioner of poetry, myself and a class in a Parisian elementary school.

A few years ago, I wrote a little book of poems intended for a public of all ages (but children in particular) called *Everybody's Animals* (and published, with illustrations by Marie Borel and Jean-Yves Cousseau, by Seghers). Each poem was about a more or less familiar animal, one that pretty much everybody knew—the dormouse, the hedgehog, the otter, the duck, the (pink) elephant, the junebug, the giraffe, the snail—beginning with the cat (but without the dog).

A little later, once the book had made its way into bookstores and reached a few schools, I received a letter from a young man of 7 or 8 years of age, a third grade student, if my memory serves me right, which began something like this:

Hello Jacques Roubaud,

My name is Etienne and I'm learnin some of your poems in
my school. The teacher has already taught us: The poem of the
cat, the rhinosceros, the dinosaurs, the snaile (an e, crossed out, I
respect the spelling of the letter-J.R.) the marmot and that's all.
Last week my dad told me that he went somewhere
wher you read some poems with your friend Pierre l'artigue
(he's his friend too). I didn't believe him cause I thought you
lived at the same time as Victor Hugo.

Having learned from his father that I was a living poet,
an endangered species, as we know, one that he thought had
disappeared from the face of the earth like dinosaurs and dodos,
young Etienne had an idea. His letter went on more or less like
this: If you are (really) alive (in spite of his father's affirmation
to the contrary, he had a lingering doubt, which could only
be dispelled, in accordance with the sound doctrine of the
experimental sciences, in one way: by verification of fact), so
if you are alive, Etienne L. wrote me, come to my school, my
teacher, Miss S., says it's O.K. I'll be waiting for you.

He added the address of his school and, as a precaution,
already dubious of the practical abilities of poets, indicated that
when I got to the school I was to press a button that would open
the door, that I should cross the courtyard, go up two flights of
stairs, take the corridor to the left (or was it to the right, I don't
recall exactly), and go to the third class. That would be the one.

Having made an appointment with the teacher, I went to
Etienne's school, answered questions from the little girls and
boys in the class, and read the poems they wanted to hear.
One of the poems was about the pigeons of Paris, an unsavory
bunch. I hesitated and asked them why they wanted me to
read that particular poem; after a quick glance at Miss S., one

boy said, "Because it has 'bad words.'" The poem, which I read with the permission of Miss S. (who assured me that she was making an exception in my case) did in fact begin like this:

The pigeons that shit on Paris
Its trees, its benches, its automobiles
Can't wait 'til the Hotel de Ville
is clean so they can cover it with piss.

Later in our meeting I had, on reading a poem dedicated to the cow (and I shall reproduce it here in its entirety), a very interesting lexical and zoological discussion which will serve as the moral to this little experiment in the contact of two spheres: the didactic sphere, and the far removed sphere of the irresponsible inventor of poetry.

The Cow

The
Cow
Is
An

Animal
That
Has
About

Four
Legs
That

Reach
To
The Ground.

Having read the poem (it's a sonnet), I sensed that something in the portrait of this particular animal bothered some of my listeners. It turned out to be the word "about." We discussed (with the aid of Miss S.) the meaning of this word for a time, and when it was clear for every one, their disapproval was unanimous: "Why do you say 'about,' Jacques?" they said to me (it didn't take long for them to call me by my first name), "a cow's got four legs!" "Really," I responded, "how do you know, have you counted them?" Certain children had. I told them that since I hadn't counted the legs of each and every cow, I couldn't be sure that they all had the same number of legs. Maybe somewhere, in Savoy for example, there were some with five, or even three legs. I told them that cows were big animals and that you couldn't always see all their legs together at the same time and that, as a result, it was difficult to count them; that's why, as a precaution, not to say something wrong, I had written "about." They still couldn't agree: a cow's got four legs and that's that! We discussed it further but couldn't come to a conclusion. And finally, seeing my lack of obstination and lack of precision they turned to Miss S. and said: "How many legs does a cow have?" "Four," answered Miss S... "Told you so!" they said.

Translated from the French by Guy Bennett.

EXCERPT: *THE GOLDEN TRIANGLE*

by Susan Daitch

From her hotel window in Semarang, Minou had a view of a square where vendors sold coconuts, mangoes, soda, rice, and goat wrapped in banana leaves. It was very hot and at street level the air smelled of motorbike exhaust and clove cigarettes. Sometimes the calls to prayer from a nearby mosque woke her early, and staring at the ceiling covered in bamboo mats, she went over his lines in the dark. Locations were still being scouted, last minute revisions were being made on the script, and shooting was therefore behind schedule. The film was a thriller, but only a small number of cast members were needed for the parts being shot in Indonesia. There were scenes in the jungle, on wharves, the sultan's palace, in kampungs in Semarang where contacts were made and liaisons uncovered. The leading character in these scenes was a Burmese drug smuggler working out of the Golden Triangle. Abducted and beaten, he whispered his confession to the shards of his platinum watch lying on the ground beside him in a cell which was only a jute covered set.

The actor who played him was Hawaiian, and in an adopted accent he revealed the identities of his international connections: an American vice president, an evangelical talk radio host, and some other characters in various positions of authority. Terry, the actor who played this role, was a loud, happy man who did imitations of a Chinese Mr. Ed excerpted from a comedy routine he used to do in hotels in Honolulu. In his combination of brashness and bonhomie he stood close enough so that one could always identify his smell of mouthwash and chlorinated water from the pool. They were supposed to practice Kung Fu scenes together which he was very enthusiastic about. Minou punched and kicked the air as if she were actually leveling Mr. Ed.

Her character, Flora Chang, was from Hong Kong, half-English, half-Chinese, and in this part she had many costume changes which reflected the protean nature of her role. European clothing meant to be severely business-like (about power) but tight and sexy at the same time, jungle combat fatigues, tattered sarongs of the kampungs all hung in a trailer waiting for her. Flora Chang occupied a universe of conundrums easily solved by daring, nerves of steel, and physical prowess. She was able to defy gravity in every possible sense of the word, but an undefined longing gnawed at the edge of her character. She was in love with a man who appeared only in scenes not yet shot, and even then he didn't have much of a part. From the script Minou had trouble figuring out much about him except that he was a painful memory for Flora. The man was stuck wasting away in jail, wrongly accused of murdering his former partner. She tried to give him a personality, because avenging his honor and getting him out of prison were part of Flora's motivation in the movie, but it wasn't really working out. Schemes for plumbing the persona of men she actually knew in order to give her interpretation of Flora Chang more life was one technique, but these images somehow resisted being superimposed over the idea of Flora's jailed boyfriend. He was not like the sound man she had briefly lived with, a strict vegetarian who smoked only organic cigarettes. She tried thinking about her neighbor in Brooklyn, a high school basketball coach who was dedicated to his job, and addicted to watching sports on television. They had conversations in the hall and at the mailboxes about martial arts. He was an admirer of the skill and level of concentration required and recommended what he called "Eastern training" to his students. Minou knew a little about Kung Fu, enough to talk to her sports-addicted neighbor (although she could summon no passion for him) and enough to get the job as Flora Chang. Her character was from Hong Kong, supposedly half-English, half-Chinese, and because of her origin she was able to pass as many things she was not, just like Minou herself.

64

Terry, on the other hand, had been doing ethnic character parts for years and made jokes about as many stereotypes as he could get his hands on. Charlie Chan, of course, was his stock in trade. Once when Minou was preparing for her part, trying to get into character, he made fun of her in front of the director, the crew, everyone.

"So, you Lady of Shanghai who feels as at home in the gambling dens of the Tong as in corporate towers. You jockey for power with dealers of financial abstractions. You speak of honorable derivatives and futures, but you meet violent death, missy, if not careful."

Everyone laughed except Minou.

"Minou," he said, "what's eating you?"

After this Terry tried even harder to include her in his carousing. He bragged to her about drinking snake blood from a stand in a market, watching impassively as the snake's throat was cut, and its blood gushed into a small glass while still writhing to free itself from the merchant's grasp.

"Cool, huh?" He said casually undoing and retying his sarong in front of everyone as if he were changing trousers in a dressing room somewhere.

She believed he really had drunk snake's blood, but in the telling the strangeness, what he meant to vaunt as the foreignness of the act was reduced to something carnivalish, a kind of pumping iron display, like surfing a particularly deadly beach.

The Americans had hotel rooms with working ceiling fans, or they congregated in clusters beside the outdoor pool. Frogs found their way into it at night, and when the pool was drained dead animals and flakes of turquoise paint drifted to its bottom, collecting in corners until it was filled again. Few of the guests saw this. During the day it was a magnet for the American cast and crew who put every possible desire on the film company tab.

"Come, join us!" They shouted from beside the pool. Drinks without ice were raised in a gesture of inclusion, but

Minou shook her head, and left them to their gossip and their boredom with the heat, rain, and fear of amoebas. They listened to the radio, or read newspapers, but Minou concentrated on Flora Chang. Unlike Flora Chang who defied corporate power, Minou had recently performed in a Dunkin' Donut commercial because it paid well, and she wasn't in a position to turn down any work. It was easy to smile behind the counter and hand an invisible customer an empty Styrofoam cup and bag. She had also performed in basement clubs standing on aluminum buckets, balancing on the backs of sewing machines saying lines which at first seemed to have no relation to the props that surrounded her. When she described her previous jobs to Terry, his only comment was, "You have to live."

Another film crew moved into the hotel. They had been shooting a documentary about the disappearance of the rain forest in Kalimantan and were on their way back to London. Their film equipment filled the space that functioned as a hotel lobby, but before the sleek black-and-silver cases were sent somewhere else, the men could be seen leaning on their stacks of equipment talking amongst themselves. During the stopover in Semarang they planned to shoot some footage outside an office building belonging to Pertamina, the national oil company. Just exteriors, it was no big deal. Minou tried to talk to one of them, but he was dismissive as if he knew instantly that she who wore a lot of gold jewelry wouldn't understand the need to protect the ozone layer. They were big guys with ponytails who occasionally wore sarongs as they drove into the town or jungle, and in subtle ways made the actors from the action-thriller (especially Terry, Minou, the Chinese supporting cast) feel like pleasure seekers tramping from one tropical inlet to the next, a small mob whose hands were used only for rubbing one another's oiled body parts. The two groups generally avoided conversation, only nodding in recognition at the hotel desk.

66

On a day off Minou learned her way around the city's dirt roads, wandering past tailors, metalworkers, motorbike repairs, food stalls set up one after the next in uneven rows. She walked down a narrow street beside the Java Sea where prostitutes gathered, and into kampungs where raw sewage ran in ditches, and motorbikes, becaks, chickens, and dogs filled the streets. Down one dead end she saw a few men from the documentary gathered in one spot, bargaining over the price of some gamelon tapes. The young man squatting behind a bamboo basket shrugged off their haggling as if he didn't understand the amount they thought a reasonable sum to pay. He rummaged around in it, pulled one or two recordings out, held them above his head, then stuck one in a battered cassette player. In her aimlessness Minou was drawn toward the loud voices haggling in a combination of Indonesian and English which carried above other sounds. "Man" this and "man" that. Although they ignored her, she blatantly eavesdropped on their transaction standing almost at the elbow of one of the Englishmen who, his sarong slipping towards the mud, described a ceremony he'd attended on a distant island in which he'd gone into a trance stepping on live embers but feeling no burning, no pain, nothing at all. The tape seller smiled broadly as if he understood and was interested in this feat. In the middle of the trance monologue barefoot children in tattered T-shirts approached Minou, little boys saying in English hey, lady, where are you from? The Brit who'd shut his eyes in imitation of his trance turned around and looked at her, annoyed at the disruption. His friends stuffed their gamelon tapes into their bags and moved away from her as if she were an embarrassment to them. Her sunglasses were too big, her skirt too short and her arms were bare. Minou smiled stupidly, arms crossed over her stomach and stared at them as they got into their jeep and prepared to drive away.

The men reminded her of an incident during an anti-nuclear march she'd gone to when she was in high school in

Brooklyn. It was an enormous event, people flew into the city from all over the world to attend, marching from Wall Street to the United Nations. Minou marched for a while with her friends, but feeling like she was going to throw up, she stepped out of her group and sat on the grass near the UN, drinking from a bottle of water. When the German delegation passed her, a big blond man made faces at her, as if to say she could loll on the grass drinking while others engaged in more serious pursuits. She had walked over to the man and screamed at him, who the fuck did he think he was to make fun of her, but he continued to parrot her drinking from an invisible bottle. She wanted to tell the documentary crew to fuck off, too, but their dismissal of her was more elusive and the kick in the jaw she wanted to deliver remained a gesture restricted to Mr. Ed.

The small boys had no interest in the men who had documented the erosion of the rainforest on an island they didn't even know existed, but the jeep was a miracle of creation. There was little space to drive it in a kampung designed for bicycles and people on foot, and it had to be maneuvered slowly, a dinosaur lumbering between warungs and repair stands. The boys followed Minou for a while as she turned down another road, asking her questions in as many languages as they knew bits and pieces of: Dutch, French, English. They tried to sell her things, to carry her bag, to steer her towards warungs that sold drinks, fruit, cigarettes. She had imagined that because of her face, she wouldn't stand out at all, and that it would be possible for her to blend in with everyone else in the city, knowing at the same time this feeling of inclusion was entirely false. The rainforest crew, big men in their sarongs and backpacks, exuded an enviable confidence. She wondered how many rupiah she should give the boy who was shouldering her bag. She had enough money to pay for anything she wanted, but didn't know what her next job would be when she returned to New York.

At night Minou found herself in an area of kampung bars which were no more than a table set up in the street, covered by tarpaulin and separated from the other identical bars by partitions made of flattened tin drums, cardboard boxes, or bamboo screens. Loud Indonesian pop music blared out of radios or tapes, each song blending into the next as she walked past. Stopping at one to watch a woman jaipung dancing, she saw two men from the film crew, local Javanese hired to set lights in place, enter the bar and order beers. A woman in a blue skirt and T-shirt put her arms around the neck and shoulders of one of them, then he got up and went behind the curtain with her. Two other women approached the second man, but he shook his head repeatedly. He didn't seem to want to go behind the curtain with either of them, and they stared blankly at him not comprehending that he might want to sit by himself. One sat in his lap anyway, and so trapped he finally stood up and danced with her. Goats with faces like pit bulls wandered by while the two danced together around the table.

"I like girls," the man said to Minou as he danced past her, then they moved off, only to return a few minutes later.

"I like girls," he repeated.

Minou finally understood that he hadn't enough money to pay for the prostitutes. She gave them 10,000 rupiah so he could go behind the curtain. That was the price for the two women, about $6.25. As soon as money changed hands everyone disappeared, and Minou sat alone, thinking about what Flora Chang would do in this situation. What would her lines have been?

When the women emerged, they were wearing different clothes, other T-shirts with American cartoons on them. She didn't know the name of the characters, some kind of bird like a penguin, some kind of dog colored sky blue. Long ago she had probably spent a torpid morning watching them, falling asleep in front of a television, dry cereal toppling to the floor. The women looked out into the street barely visible in the light of the petromaks. A few people stopped to talk to them.

Although night had fallen she identified Terry as he walked past on the far side of the dirt road. Since the bar was open to the street there was no less visible place for her to move from her chair, and so she could do nothing when he beckoned in delight at seeing her. He crossed the road in a hurry, grinning broadly. At the same time a man approached Minou.

"Not her, she's mine." Terry said in Bahasi Indonesian. Her toes curled inside drenched running shoes. Terry flashed an imitation Rolex and a gold tooth. He was in character, although the square emerald in his ear, he told her, was fake. The women in the dog and penguin T-shirts, the men who lit the petromaks behind pictures of the President, or who sat in tiny warungs splitting fruit and smoking clove cigarettes— on whatever terms they imagined she left with Terry all of them must have thought the two of them were from the same country, spoke the same language so it made sense that they would leave together.

Terry said something about lucky breaks as they caught a bemo back to the hotel. He was happy to work in a serious film after doing so much comedy. The van was nearly empty apart from a woman who clutched her son between her knees.

"Our business is fooling people. There's so little work out back home. This is a lucky break coming here." He rubbed his hands on his bare knees.

Minou felt no one was fooled, but she didn't know how to say this to Terry. On her first day in the city she had stopped at a market run entirely by women who sold stacks of round bamboo hats, bell-shaped cages for transport of chickens and roosters, piles of tiny chili peppers, and bright pink soupy coconut sweets. Minou bought a meal of rice and goat paddled into a cone made of banana leaves. Stopping in the shade of a banyan tree in order to eat it with her hands, the taste of hot chilies burned her lips and the ends of her fingers with a lingering heat. She had thought she could eat anything hot and laced with any amount of chili and spice but had been fooling herself. The film, on the other hand, contained no surprise heat buried in the rice.

Torrential rain further delayed shooting. Kampungs and rice paddies were flooded, even the surly documentary crew were stuck in the hotel. A few of them climbed into their jeep only to become mired in the mud road. Minou asked them where they were going as she walked past, thinking the environmentalists must have known the villages were only connected by pathways, but they were too busy pushing to answer her.

Terry found a man who, for a large fee, would make the rain stop, but the production manager turned him down, shaking his head and rolling his eyes as if to say what next? This was interpreted as a maybe, not a no, so the man lowered his price. Again the manager turned him down saying that he was fed up, gesturing impatience, running his hands through his hair. Terry shrugged, his Bahasa Indonesian not up the task of completely translating refusal. Disappointment hung in the air. The sound of rain hitting the tin roof felt comforting to Minou as she watched the negotiations back and forth. Finally the production manager asked if the man would pay them if his spell failed and the rain continued. Besides doubting the man would have any effect on the rainy season, the manager suspected someone in the crew would get a cut from the conjurer's commission and he said so in a loud voice but Terry did not translate this last comment.

"We don't need the show stopped for a bunch of hocus pocus," the production manager said.

"It might be interesting to see what kinds of incantations or prayers might clear the clouds even if the spell doesn't work." Minou said. She felt sorry for Terry who seemed to have a lot riding on the idea of bringing the man in, but the overworked production manager wanted no part of him or his schemes.

The rain continued. They shot interiors: bugged telephones, love scenes, scenes with the informer who rats from a jail cell. For a scene in a restaurant Minou was served steaming prawns sprinkled with red, green, and black pepper which she would never be able to eat because she would be shot at and the table would be overturned. As usual the scene had to be shot several times. A pile of prawns lay waiting to be served and another heap, swept up from the floor, was put out the back door of the restaurant. She practiced her accent.

Why shouldn't I be suspicious of you? I'm suspicious of the waiter. I'm suspicious of the cook. I'm suspicious of these prawns here, you know, the mouths and ears might still be attached. They might only be playing dead.

Despite the occasional moment of hesitation and reflection when a crescent of sunlight entered a dark room, Flora Chang was a woman of authority. Minou wasn't always convincing in eliciting fear in the hearts of those she encountered in the movie. She felt her fellow actors kept seeing in her the voice of Terry's imitations and no one could even imagine being afraid of her. A chance encounter with a soldier gave her a small window into the kind of fear an ordinary person can summon.

The scene had been simple and fast. Minou watched two men drive up to a warung on a motorbike, parking beside the stand. She couldn't make out much of their faces, but the rider was wearing a green and yellow striped T-shirt similar to the one the electrician always wore. Once he came to a stop the driver walked away, down the street, and into a shop. The soldier approached but did nothing, standing by motionless while the rider who had just gotten off the back of the motorbike went up to the warung and bought a soda

72

and cigarettes. The man in uniform was very short, had a tight narrow waist, a moustache, and very short hair, but his authority was small potatoes. Not small potatoes intended to blend in like the beleaguered nice guy cops from the movie, men who sat behind cluttered desks drinking coffee out of Styrofoam cups not available on the island, but the small authority with the power to put you in jail on a whim nonetheless, the power to make you disappear. When he did approach the motorcyclist it was sudden, as if acting on an unknown signal, coming up behind him and pushing him against a wall. Soda bottle shattered when it hit the ground, cigarettes were strewn all over the road from the force of blows. The face of the soldier registered signs of exertion in the heat, but little more, and as far as Minou could tell he remained almost expressionless throughout the short struggle. No one from the market crossed the road. Minou walked a little closer to the warung, close enough to see the man shoved into a car, but not close enough to identify him. In her next scene instead of imagining a tall, long Flora Chang, she was small, wound tightly like a spring. Terry saw her walking towards the set and said, "Hey, here comes Bruce Lee."

Have you ever seen this man before? Minou spoke harshly to Terry. Flora Chang knew when she was being lied to.

What makes you think I would tell you if I had? Terry looked cocky, blatantly folding the papers from the puppet and stuffing them into his shirt.

The choreography of their fight took hours. Circling kicks and jabs came close but never touched flesh or bone. Stunt doubles did the more difficult flips. Terry and Minou had a lot of close-ups. Finally Terry lay on the floor, looking at the electrical cord snaking its way around the room. It didn't take much for him to break down, to blurt out everything he was supposed to keep to himself. The scene took place in a set that was made to look like one of the kampungs outside Semarang.

73

Okay, okay, he was trying on masks, and I remembered him because he had an American car.

Like that one?

Yes.

For this scene in a shop full of masks, puppets, and Indonesian carvings, the props department had constructed large puppets equipped with elaborate headpieces. The puppet heads split into two halves, front and back. After splitting one, Minou would find papers hidden between the two parts. When released from the masks and held up to the light the papers retained the shape of faces: nose and eye sockets in shadow, mouth fixed in a smile. Writing, allegedly in code, ran across the cheekbones. Minou's character thought the man who had disappeared, the one Terry claimed he had no knowledge of, might have been what was called a Cadillac communist. In an era before Minou was born, American advisors had evacuated Indonesia in a hurry, leaving their cars which were taken up, in turn, by the Communists. The Props Department had trouble finding such an old Cadillac. There were none left, and they were too expensive to import, even with Terry on the phone making deals with someone in Honolulu. Nothing came from his calls and faxes sent out as a favor to the director so the car was referred to but never seen.

The next day the electrician she had seen that night in the kampung approached her again. The rain had let up briefly and for a day shooting moved outside the city to an easily accessible part of the jungle. They were sitting above the deserted ruins of an abandoned village where Minou was due to find Terry hiding the papers discovered inside the mask. They would have another fantastic fight. Minou practiced her moves, kicking and punching the air. She had to wear a rubber catsuit for this scene. It had been specially made, molded to her body.

"I have something to ask you," the electrician said, pulling

74

a Statue of Liberty paperweight from a basket. I ♥ N.Y. was written on its base.

"What does this mean?" He shook the glass ball so snow fell inside it.

Minou tried to translate, pointing to herself, to her heart, then she pulled out her address book and pointed to her address.

"You are from Wall Street. I understand. America," the electrician said, "superpower."

Minou tried to explain that she wasn't from Wall Street. She lived in an apartment in Brooklyn with a view of the Gowanus Canal.

"I live in rooms in another part of the same city." She shoved the little book in a shirt pocket. The documentary film crew would say, of course, Wall Street, even here everyone knows Wall Street is the center of the universe, and they might be right, but she wanted, in the middle of the rain forest, to say something about the futuristic machinery that lined the canal making it look like a bit of post-industrial Mars. Why she felt this impulse she had no idea.

The electrician shook the paperweight, watching plastic snow fall as if something unexpected might take place in it. Minou tried to explain snow, but she didn't know the word for crystals, only ice, "es." She made gestures with her hands to indicate falling snow or ice while huge brown and white snails crawled up bamboo trees and pineapple stalks, and a few yards away the crew moved lights and equipment into place. The electrician returned to the others busy hanging lights or squatting at the edge of the set, drinking tea and talking among themselves. He was pleased with her answer about ice falling on Wall Street. Minou rehearsed her lines.

You can never figure out when he's telling the truth. He has a long history of saying it's not him, and he knows nothing about whatever it is you're talking about, and then it turns out it was him all along. She didn't feel like Flora Chang. Her rubber catsuit was a form of torture. It stuck to her like a second skin, but water trickled down her neck and back as if all the liquid in her body had migrated to the space between her skin and the rubber. Maybe it didn't matter if she felt out of character, and the woman she played seemed so alien to her that her imagination, when she tried to be this woman, faltered. She recited her lines to the rain for the squawking sound of the words, not for their meaning.

EXCERPT: *LONG DAY, COUNTING TOMORROW*

by Jim Feast

November 12, 1998

Even if I were an advice giver, I don't think I'd tell anyone "Begin writing a diary the way I did: You start it on the day you are going to die."

Not that I cracked open the book as I ate my last meal on death row. That would be a little boneheaded, even for me. It's just that I was almost killed 3 hours ago, and the experience sobered me up. It made me realize it was time to set things straight. But let's go back to the beginning: my death.

The day started badly. At 10 a.m., I vomited blood in the bathroom of the Social Security Administration. In the afternoon I learned my T cells had dropped below 100. It was downhill from there, capped off when I was pushed in front of the R train at Union Square.

It's possible the man who knocked me off the platform was one of the cogless homeless who wander the city like hungry ghosts with nothing to do but decapitate citizens; but it's just as likely it was skullduggery fostered by the people at the Framing Institute, an AIDS hospice where I used to reside and many of whose secrets had come into my possession. If they were out to get me, driven by what would have been (a few hours ago) the groundless idea that I would expose their perfidy, then my best revenge will be to set out an account of their crimes. Their disservice to the PWA community must be revealed, for they have perverted their mission too long. Someone has got to correct this thing. Curse the God who said I, Raskin Hasp, must set it right.

Raskin stopped writing. There were things about today he wanted to add and things about yesterday that had to be brought up. Which should he tackle first?

He sat there stymied. It was a little early to admit defeat at this latest in a long list of aborted writing projects, but he was unsure how to proceed. He ended folding up on his bed, a narrow rollaway with stained sheets and a lumpy mattress. The only other piece of furniture in the room was a small icebox over which he'd built a shelf for his hats.

He had begun writing with high hopes of using this format to flesh out his dark forebodings; but now he realized a diary, because it concentrated on the present, might not be the ideal vehicle for telling a story that would delve so much into the past.

Perhaps he could modify the form. He would simply start the diary a week ago when his roommate died and his suspicions were awakened. It was in this last week that everything relevant had taken place. He could use negative quantities to keep track of things. Taking November 12 as the baseline, he could number the 13th as +2 and November 11 as -1. Thus he could rove freely through time.

Had it only been Monday a week ago (-7) that Yardley died? Like Raskin, Yardley Chu had been a person with AIDS, though having gone through 2 bouts of PCP, considerably the worse for wear. It was hardly a surprise that he never returned from the emergency room.

And yet Raskin felt there had been foul play. Why? Because Yardley, too, kept a diary, hidden under the book jacket of a Western, *Hard Dust*. After they carted Yardley off, Raskin spent all night paging through it, piercing together Yardley's

78

paranoid thoughts concerning how the treatment center was covering up deaths.

The notes broke off chillingly with Yardley's vow to confront the institute's administration with some computer data that backed up his contentions. What this data was and whether he actually did have a high noon showdown was not recorded, but it certainly was creepy that he died shortly after his scheduled confrontation.

And there was something else. The morning after he'd finished reading Yardley's diary, Rask demanded an audience with the Institute's director, the eccentric Dr. Vesuvius. Without mentioning Yardley's writing, Rask made some accusations.

No comment as his words bounced off the smooth surface of the doctor's domed forehead. The man quietly fingered the "medicine pouch" he wore around his neck and nodded benignly, promising he would look into Rask's charges. The next day Rask was discharged. Coincidence or…calculation? True enough, his expulsion didn't come out of the blue. Because of Rask's anemia, he hadn't been able to start on the new drug, and had been told if his condition didn't improve, he might be shifted out. Face it, he was occupying room others could more profitably use. Thus the catapult had already been primed to eject. Still, he couldn't help wondering if his inopportune questions hadn't speeded the process.

He picked up the pen.

Let's start at the beginning.

At 7:05 a.m., I pulled into "Ringmaster" Donuts, so nicknamed because it's the haunt of choice for retired circus performers, the ones who form a colony around 23rd and 8th Avenue.

Over the last few months—excluding the 2 weeks in the Framing Institute—I have gotten to know quite a few of these itinerants. It seems every time I turn around nowadays: rushing to the bus stop, buying a Lotto ticket, or entering the library, I'm combing one out of my hair.

I ordered the usual: one large coffee, an Aqua Vita, a bowtie and a large chocolate-covered cream-filled. With the water as booster, I downed vitamins, aspirin, and a fistful of AZT.

My neighbor addressed me with "Do I look like farm material?"

"What?"

"Am I someone who should be farmed out?"

"Listen, fellow," I told him, "I don't know what your story is, but it's too early in the morning."

"Hey, Rask, you know me: Jasper. I come in here all the time. I'm usually with my lady, Jackal Rose."

"Jackal? What kind of name is that?"

"She was a main-ring circus attraction. Trained jackals."

"What did these jackals do?"

"Spit fire. That was the big draw."

I coughed up some of my bowtie. "How can an animal spit fire?"

"Take it easy there, boy. It's just a trick, nothing more."

"How do they do it, though?"

"The trainer does it. The audience loves it. It's main ring.

"I was never main ring. Just a contortionist. That's what I was: a contortionist with stiff joints."

He seemed to be depressing himself. Jasper had been speaking expansively, but now he gradually grew distant and distracted as if he'd struck certain memories that, like subwater rocks, caused him to cascade down, a sunken vessel. He lost interest in me and drifted back to his cronies. God, I wish I could remember more about him.

Truth is, though, I was glad he left. He'd killed my day. Night, too. Let me explain. Sick people are dependent on omens. At least this one is. Usually the first unusual thing that happens to me after I get up, I take as symbolical of how the rest of the day will go.

So what kind of sign is a jackal? It's a vulture on four legs. The *rest of the day was going to be bad.*

And then there would be the night and my dreams. Before I became ill I had this idealized notion of a sick man's sleep. I imagined his dreams were terribly vivid and sexy. The idea went back to childhood; the time we were living in Fort Myers, Florida.

Our house was so low-lying that instead of having a lawn in our backyard, we had a swamp. And when I was sick, maybe with a fever, I'd lay on the porch on a trundle chair, watching the yard and letting my mom sponge me down. Dreams would come and go, intersecting with and disintegrating the wall between my surroundings and the subconscious. Looking into the house through the screen, I would see cattails growing around the kitchen table and jackdaws perched on cereal boxes. Back and forth I went between dreams and laying wakefulness as if swaying in a drifting dingy.

That was the image of sickness I had in my mind when I found myself HIV positive. It turned out to be a lie. My fever dreams were haunted with scary shards of reality, incidents or objects seen during the day taking flight as nightmares. And the worse the day, the spookier the dreams. This day had started out promising to be a real bell ringer of misery.

Thing is, Jasper says he knows me; we've talked before. Since I don't remember him maybe I also don't recall something important I said to him concerning Vesuvius' operation. Got to check that.

I walked over to SSI. I was already pooped, and had to sit for 10 minutes on the steps of the public library to get my breath.

The walk took longer than planned but eventually I got there. I went up to the clerk, identified myself and asked for Mrs. Saunders.

"She's not here yet," I was told by a chubby blonde woman who had either tinsel or streaks of gray in her hair.

"But I had an appointment a half hour ago," I said.

"Then how do you explain coming in so late? You'll have to reschedule. You can fill out this API to request a new date." She ended, handing me three pages of squares to be inked in.

"What are you a moron? The lady I'm supposed to see is not even here."

"You don't have to raise your voice, Mr. Hasp." She shook the form at me. "I was going to see about fitting you in today, but why should I do extra work for someone who's going to rag on me?"

I apologized as best I could, but she wouldn't relent. Then I had a coughing jag that went on for 2 or 3 minutes.

After I stopped, she said, "You shouldn't smoke."

I don't, but I let that go. She took pity on me, and let me have a 1 o'clock.

We settled on a better note than we had begun and I rushed off to the restroom. I had the runs again, what is called "Wet AIDS" Actually "runs" is a better term than "wet," cause when you have that condition, you're always racing to the nearest facility.

Missing my appointment meant I could go earlier to the Cancer Ward, where I overheard something slip, a definite clue.

Most of my consultation was the usual story of what happened in Deadwood when the Cancer Quacks faced the AIDS Honchos at high noon at the corner of Health and Barely Surviving.

But it hadn't always been like that. The cancer guys at first convinced everyone I must take chemotherapy. In chemo, they pour red schnapps in you and it circulates through your blood, killing cancer cells. They had everything arranged for my visit, but they overlooked one minor technicality: I don't have any blood.

That's an exaggeration. But everyone knows the AZT in the cocktail screws up the tissue in the bone marrow where blood cells are reproduced and results in low blood rates. So, at this meeting the doctors were arguing over the whole thing.

However, the significant thing was what was said, supposedly, out of my hearing.

Let's get some background.

Back in the good old days, before they found out I had cancer and were only worrying about AIDS, my entourage of physicians, counselors, social workers and so on made shift to all row together in coming to a consensus on how I should live my "life," using that last word loosely. The only disagreement then was on whether I would do better under aggressive or less aggressive therapy.

AIDS is such a favorite subject nowadays that when I tell people about even the more esoteric quirks of my regimen, they pretty much know what I'm talking about. Even you, dear diary, know that aggressive AIDS therapy entails ladling out the drugs to the PWA as soon as there's any signal of the disease's presence, even before the glands swell, to try and nip that HIV sucker in the bud.

The problem is, well, 1) that little vitamin cocktail of AZT, ddI or whatever analogs or terminators you prefer itself kills you; slightly slower than the disease, admittedly, but in a way that makes you wish you were dead. Then, 2) there's the danger that drug resistant strains will arise.

NEWS FLASH! In AIDS, it's the mutations that kill you! At least that's current theory. It used to be thought that because there's a long time between initial infection and crash that HIV was like a winter mammal that laid up in caves (the lymph nodes) for ten years, before it woke up and began marauding. But with more sophisticated tests that could detect smaller concentrations of the retrovirus in the blood tests—the PCR which checks for the existence of viral proteins—it was seen that there was a fluctuating presence of HIV throughout the body during the latency period when it was fighting a generally losing battle against the white blood cells.

If it can't beat the body for 10 years, you might ask, where does it get its second wind? HIV is a volatile so-and-so. It keeps altering its genes until it develops a strain that the human antibody system can't deal with and you go down.

The thing was Vesuvius' new max-aggressive therapy claims to push back HIV count and hinder its mutation rate.

When I got early to the hospital clinic, I could hear through the dovetail door to the waiting room and they were discussing this very thing. Then, one said this, "But Vesuvius is coming under more and more fire about the reliability of his early studies."

Must have been three physicians talking. Another said, "How's that? They're small controls, but—"

A third, "They had to have small controls."

"Yes, but the question is whether he was sloppy."

83

"Fudging?"

"No, not at all, but sloppy."

A nurse came in and shut down the conversation, but it got me thinking. Was it coming out that he was lying about the efficacy of his whizbang treatment? Did Chu learn something about it?

Raskin had been writing fast, his hand like a shuttle flying over the page, and just as his narrative was beginning to get interesting, he began to deflate. It was part of his condition. He was crisscrossed by these patterns of sudden frenzy and sudden collapse.

He lay back, wilting on his bed, hearing the tin whistle of the radiator in the background. He still had so much to describe: his return to SSI, where'd he heard about the possibility of a one-shot paying gig as a specimen; the writers' get-together at the Bull and Shamrock, the one where he'd heard more interesting rumors, then gotten drunk and fought with Mac. All events bulging with clues.

"Where will I get the strength to finish this?" he thought. "Maybe if I didn't go into so many details." But that would more or less annul the very reason for writing this diary.

Rask had a theory about detective stories. He believed the crime emerged as they wrote. Think of Dame Agatha writing the quarry scene in *Hall'een Eve*. In fleshing out the background, describing the hooded woods, the half-effaced trails, she weighs which landscape features to include. Mentally assaying the possibilities, she sees each in the light of a place to lay a clue. This is how she plotted. Later, she would work backward and revise earlier patches to lead up to this clue.

Rask would do the inverse. He would write down a very circumstantial record of what had been happening to him (what he had seen without noticing while they were plotting against Chu, and now him). Suddenly, jutting out of the material like a red flag tied to a shark fin would be an unmistakable clue. All he needed to go to the police, he calculated, was one shred of evidence.

Rask was going through all this groggily as he slipped near sleep. The pen slipped from between his fingers and dive-bombed to the bed.

But for the present, he still had to create memories: he had to do things that would provoke clues to spring forth. If he still held the pen, he would jot them down, a few that occurred.

1) talk to the ACT UP characters that Yardley always had visiting around his bed. Perhaps they knew something.
2) read *Hard Dust* looking for more "dirt"
3) break into the offices of the Framing Institute

On serious reflection, only the last possibility sounded reasonable. Or least would be if he had something he was missing, a tentacle.

The office floor was closed on weekends. Knowing the procedures, he could probably get upstairs and to the entry door. In it, there was a mail slot through which a bone-thin arm might be able to reach and lever it open. There had to be a way, he thought, laying further back so the diary slipped to the floor, uncovering the "Think Positive: Happy Thoughts Calendar for People with AIDS." It was a present from his girlfriend.

He looked at today's message. "I never knew how much my Father loved me until I read his will…on his face." His father. He thought of him tenderly. That had been the last person in his family Rask had alienated.

His sister had broken contact when he was arrested for drugs. Next went his mother's affection when he came down with AIDS. He said he was infected via blood transfusion, but she still refused to speak with him. Father drew the line upon learning Rask admitted to a few homosexual dalliances. He was really bisexual, but his family couldn't grasp the distinction. He wasn't sure if his father maintained their relationship so long out of love or due to being out of touch, due to his itinerant lifestyle, managing carnivals.

Sprawled on his bed, near the choppy waters of sleep, Rask remembered one spring day when his father happened in town. He woke Rask at 5:30 a.m., saying he was pulling out in an hour. Rask was going to Midlothian College, a small school in a Chicago suburb, where a mildly famous poet he adored was teaching, and Dad was scouting locations en route to an Iowa state fair.

Dad and son went down to Lake Michigan to watch the dawn. Pop took the car right down to the beach, driving along the shore where they could watch the water drifting in, its waves as regular as the lines on corrugated cardboard. The tires made a hissing sound and, over the lake, a single bird pitched across the near horizon.

They went to a local diner. He recalled his father, usually a master of inept, impoverished phrases, as if he didn't have a poetic bone in his body, looking at four or five freshly poured styrofoam cups of coffee, lined up on the counter for a construction crew order, and saying they reminded him of "a row of smudgepots in an orange grove." He was struck and moved by the sense that his father did have some of the feeling for language and metaphor Rask did. Maybe, after all, there was a half-disguised affinity between his rough-housing dad and his lumbering but effete son, that might some day mature into real, mutual, and even family-wide, respect.

That never-realized hope, perhaps, was still playing itself out in the background of Raskin's uncharacteristic foray into crime fighting. He had this uncanny feeling that if he could work out the riddle of Chu's death, it would be by forming a set of connections linking together all the people he knew, from his friends to the biddies at Social Services to Ringmaster Donut denizens to his family, including those people, like Mac, who said he was a worthless pile. As he was falling asleep, he was thinking, "If I could tie all my friends and enemies into one long link, then a pipeline will exist to a solution and a home."

CONVERSION IN CONNECTICUT

by Martha King

It was only eleven in the morning, and it was a school day, but there were groups of high school kids at the bay beach. With cans of beer, with tape decks and car radios turned up loud; with pimples on their mouths, and expensive cars, and the drifting intermittent scent of reefer. It was only May but the day was hot enough to foreshadow the summer, and it was all old hat to the kids—the dust, the sun, the little waves quietly crunching last summer's beach glass, even the hallucinatory towers of New York City in the distance across the water. This was a town of power boats and private docks, houses with live-in maids and glassed-in patios. The kids were leaning or sitting on their cars, covertly watching us. Their faces proffered boredom, exclusion, and scorn.

The water was blue but what lapped on the shore was soiled and laced with bits of trash. Still, off shore it was very blue and glittering, and a few people already had their sailboats out. Despite the stale smell of the water and the thump-thump music from the parked cars, Bergman and I were feeling all the fine things cooped-in city dwellers feel on the first really warm day of the year when you're magically out of town.

We had parked near a jetty built of red rocks; Berg said the stones were native to the mountains of New Hampshire. Mike walked out and picked one up for us.

I'll clue you in: I don't always get it. That's being as fair as a rattlesnake. When I'm the reader, I don't like having someone who doesn't know me lying in wait. Some damn writer who pulled the rug out from under me two pages earlier and I didn't get it. I offer my heart, damn it. I always start reading without suspicion; I expect to be told the whole story, and a subsequent discovery otherwise is just too much like real life. Reading isn't real life. The writer's figuring this out and telling you, and the writer is always the one who has the most time.

Mike, Bergman, Mike's wife Roxanne, and I were in Mike's car. It was a lot older than anything those kids were driving and had something wrong inside that made it sound like a washing machine. Mike talked about how terrific it was to live out here in this clean, well-cared-for suburb. On the way to the bay, he had driven us to see a grotesque imitation English country house. It had seven chimneys, a four-car garage, and stood on a hill with a golf-course perfect sweep of lawn running down to the road. I thought it looked like a Publishers' Clearinghouse sweepstake prize.

"Isn't that a house, man? Whaja think?" Mike had nudged Roxanne. "If we score with the new book, should we go for it?" He wasn't kidding, and she looked thrilled.

Mike had lately joined A.A., the latest in a lifetime of cures. He was here after many years in Los Angeles. Roxanne, also an A.A. member, was very concerned about the kids' beer.

"Fairfield County has more alcoholics per square foot than any place else in the *world*," she said, glaring back at the sullen looks she was getting.

Her daughter Tessie, who was not Mike's daughter, was the same age as these kids. Tessie was going out with a boy who drives his own Lincoln Continental, Roxanne told us.

"What will *come* from giving a car like that to a drunken boy?" Her voice rose and her face was pink as she said this, but earlier her tone had been unnervingly calm as she informed

Bergman and me that her daughter was twenty pounds overweight, had a liver infection, probably drug-related, and carried a bottle of mint-flavored vodka in her school bag. Tessie's problems were Tessie's to contend with, she had said.

"Does she have any idea what she wants to do after high school?" I had asked.

"Act. She wants to be an actress. I'm afraid she thinks she can make a life for herself by having people admire her." Again, Roxanne's tone was matter of fact. She and Mike would not be able to send Tessie to college. Money was far too tight. But that wasn't a problem because, at this point, Tessie could hardly be expected to get into a college, her grades were so poor. So she, Tessie, would just have to "work it out."

She and I had this part of the conversation in Roxanne's kitchen, away from the men. I was drinking coffee, which she made for me. She had cured herself of a fifteen-cup-a-day habit, she said as she handed me the cup. Coffee was just one more item on the long list of things she had had to learn to do without. "I'm a classic addict," she said. "Soon, I'll have to do something about my eating. That's *really* hard."

Roxanne was not overweight. She was huge. She rolled as she moved under her tent-like dress. Her wrists were creased like a baby's, her face was encircled in excess, her eyes forced into a squint by the size of her cheeks. Still I could make out even features, a classic nose, and delicately curved eyebrows. There *was* another woman inside. Her rapid-fire deadpan personal revelations made me a little queasy. I had met her for the first time at ten-thirty that morning.

I first met Mike, which is not his name, years before. He was married to another woman then, but she had left him and I never saw her or the two kids. I heard they lived somewhere in New Jersey. In those days, the world beyond lower Manhattan hardly seemed to exist for us.

Bergman and I still live together on the Lower East Side. Bergman is still writing, I still teach, and we still don't have much money, but almost everything else about us is different these days. Not that we've turned peaceful exactly, but we're purposeful. The neighborhood has changed too. People now pay thousands to live in those dumbbell tenements, which actually became smaller once the bathtub wasn't in the kitchen. NYU has taken over most of the larger buildings along Second Avenue, and the tastes of college students now mold the shops and eateries.

Back then, when Mike had a railroad flat on Sixth, green trees were rarities and bright colors were confined to an occasional neon sign. Going up to Mike's place with him was an ordeal. It was five flights, six if you counted the flight of steps up the stoop, and Mike talked as he climbed. His wheezing would get louder and his talk crazier as he went. No, resting was not the way he did things. "Rest! You wanna kill me?" By the time we were on the risers between the fourth and fifth floors, I'd be shaking with fear and he'd be screaming and wheezing. Then he'd undo the locks on his apartment door and disappear into the bathroom.

"I sent a lotta money up my arm in those days." He smiled peacefully at Berg and me. "Almost everything I made from my first book. You know, heroin has a wonderfully organizing effect on your life. Ya never without something to do. You're as single-minded as a monk." He was wistfully lyric. "Lovely," he said, "Deep blue calm." Heroin was easy on the body, he maintained. "Horse won't give you ulcers, heart strain, vitamin deficiencies," he said. "I owe what's left of my fuckin' liver to being a junkie, praise Jesus. You think I'a survived this long if I'd been boozing the whole time?" He wheezed a little as he laughed in his Fairfield County living room.

These days, Mike's publisher has stopped putting new photographs on the backs of his books. They use the old one. His books are all variations on the same theme, which is *not* an artistic fault the way I think about it, but he's not the darling of the people who write criticism for the *New York Review of Books* any more. There is now a sense of routine—another novel, the same photograph, quotations on the cover from the old rave reviews. The cover always says "Author of…" under or over his name.

Out in the rest of the world, beyond America, he's still a culture hero. Mike showed us a shelf crammed full of his foreign editions, all his books, not just his first one—and not just Italian, French, or German editions. He was gleeful: Polish, Japanese, Indian, *Croatian*! Some were modest paperbacks, but many had fancy jackets with ghoulish full-color cover art. I was shocked at the comic-book violence. But I've already warned you about my naïve views.

"Yeah, well mosta the money from these things goes to the publisher," Mike said. "No matter what I do, I don't seem to get on top of those *contracts*. There's always a new day, though. Praise Jesus."

A fall like Mike's is a well-worn cliché in American intellectual life. A lot of critical ink is spilled on why, usually some long disquisition on the psychic assault of success, losing touch with one's roots, blah, blah, blah. For Mike, at any rate, the critics could be advised instead to analyze the aesthetic and practical problems of managing ecstasy, but most critics prefer ironic detachment anyway. They see disengagement as minimalism—and minimalism as the glory of our day.

Sometimes I wonder if the motive isn't practical, if it isn't, at bottom, *commercial*. Writers who avoid passionate engagement never risk disappointing an audience hot for a bigger thrill the next go-round. The naïve narrator strategy could be called good risk management. Flat affect easily makes the sentimental and nostalgic appear sophisticated and ironic. Well, there was never anything sentimental about Mike's writing.

Mike and Roxanne told us they married ten years ago in a Las Vegas wedding chapel, a week after they met. He'd just picked up a $50,000 movie option for one of his books, and he was partying nonstop in anticipation of the sweet life to come. But the studio never made the movie.

"That's when I found out they buy things just to lock 'em up. Just in case somebody else might be crazy enough to want 'em. They think *I'm* nuts! I been living on money I get for selling stuff that's lying in vaults just so nobody else can get at it."

He wasn't laughing as he said this. His voice resonated with passion, but he was smiling benignly, his eyes as deep blue as a prairie sky. "It's all part of God's plan," he said.

Bergman and I had lost touch with Mike months before he left the Lower East Side for Hollywood. As it looks now, he was at the height of his fame then, in those first years after his first book had been published. As the money rolled in and the phone rang and rang, he was spending his time with April, a high-school girl he'd picked up somewhere. She was too awed and too slow and too stoned to have any idea what was happening to her as Mike relentlessly switched from egging her on to humiliating her. One night Berg and I had a screaming fight with Mike and severed our ties.

Was this one of those art world fights? Was Mike shucking us off so he could move on to the big time? Were Berg and I so righteous about April because we were too jealous to keep Mike in our lives? He took *her* with him to such uptown literary parties as he was willing to attend—not us. Were we ticked off? The truth isn't what it's cracked up to be. I really don't really know the truth. I do remember how glad I was it was over and I wouldn't have to see April scratching her track scabs and Mike eyeing her like a snake does a bird.

"This is one of Mike's good days," Roxanne told me in the kitchen. My offer to help her with lunch was declined. There were procedures that had to be followed precisely because of Mike's multiple allergies.

"He's been eating and writing, praise Jesus. There are days when he can't tolerate food and he writes anyway," she said. "The drain on his energy is so devastating, he goes into terrible rages. Mike is even worse on the days when he doesn't eat and doesn't write. Then he just lies wherever he is. And he's cold."

"Do you have a good doctor here?" I asked.

"Doctors don't know why he isn't dead," she said. "Take fillings. Do they listen?"

"Fillings?" I said.

"It's just a question of time before the mercury leaks out. You don't know about that!"

Tessie and a girlfriend wandered in through the kitchen

door. They were acknowledged with a kind of nod by Roxanne. The telephone rang. Roxanne had an enormously long corkscrew extension cord which followed her as she walked around the kitchen, gathering lunch plates, glasses, silverware. Talking, she carried them through to the big dinner table at the back of the living room. Bergman and Mike looked up. Still holding the receiver wedged into her fleshy chin, she deftly set the table, mouthing the name "Barbara" to Mike. It was an A.A. call.

Back in the kitchen, she listened while she chopped. She chopped peppers, cabbage, zucchini, yellow squash, green beans, bean sprouts, peanuts, celery, endive, walnuts, and eye-watering amounts of fresh ginger. Everything was rinsed in filtered water and drained in a stainless steel colander. She chopped methodically until she had filled an enormous china basin with dense, finely shredded multicolored stuff.

On the other end of the phone a woman was crying. After a bit Roxanne told her that some things are just too strong, too hard for any one person and that no one can get through things like that alone. It was wrong of her to think she was supposed to.

I wondered if the woman on the phone would mind if she knew that Roxanne considered her misery so normal that she could listen without missing a beat in her lunch chores? Dancers and athletes grow casual to the point of indifference about being naked in company, I thought.

"We'll just keep talking no matter how long it takes," Roxanne told her gently.

I went into the bathroom. If was full of back issues of *Prevention* and comic books about the life of Christ. Mike had always been a Christian, of his own particular sort. I thought he took malicious, very unchristian comfort from his faith that god was going to sizzle all the slobs and assholes who crowd the world. He used to say he was so pleased at the prospect of apocalypse that he didn't give a tinker's damn that he would be one of the fried. Mike knows the bible as only a regular bible reader can, and sometimes quotes it prodigiously.

In this house, he and Roxanne praised Jesus as routinely as other people say hi or thanks. At lunch, he began with a grace. "Holy father, divine mother, universal friend" he said. He asked a special blessing on "this gathering of friends." Tessie and her girlfriend were not among us. They had disappeared into another room, taking their aura of discontent and defensiveness with them.

Mike stopped his grace just short of giving Bergman a personal blessing. All of us could see from Berg's neck that—as Mike and Roxanne might have put it—he just wasn't in the right place for it. Of course that was okay. Because everything was okay, no problem, praise Jesus.

Okay. Bergman laughed. It was good to see Mike again. It was good to melt down the estranged stiffness that had clogged up the place where an old, old friendship had once been. The atmosphere of mutual forgiveness was so comforting that Roxanne's cold vegetables went down like soufflé. While we ate, Mike spoke about how anger and bitterness have to be avoided. "They create negative energy," he said with an air of cheerful right reason.

Bromides like this suck up my oxygen, and I began to argue on behalf of the devil: "Mike, don't you believe there's a real world out there, a world beyond personal self?" I asked. "It's not just a question of anger being useful personally. Which it certainly is. But, damn it, unless you refuse to look at the world or you murder your feelings about it, anger is just plain unavoidable. The world's *real* and it's a fucked-up mess!"

"Oh, there's something beyond self," Mike agreed. He began talking about the source of energy he has learned to lean on. How it, and it alone, had helped him transmute his rage into forgiveness.

"You don't have to call this process prayer if you don't want to. But believe me, you can tap into it." His eyes were like blue sparklers on the Fourth of July. Devilishly merry.

Mike looked clear and energetic—ravaged face and caved-in chest notwithstanding. Compared to the old days, he hardly wheezed. In fact, I thought, he wasn't nearly as thin as he had been when he lived on dope, cigarettes, and junk food. If vegetables, and twelve steps, and Jesus Christ can keep him this way, well, what, except for the grating praise-Jesus stuff, is so objectionable? He probably *would* be dead in a reasonable world.

Money not health seemed to be Mike and Roxanne's most pressing problem. I couldn't stop myself from ticking up their expenses and wondering what their income was. The house they had rented was luxury property, all cedar and polished brick, with window walls cantilevered over a woodland stream. The muted furniture had the kind of solidity that only money buys. None of it was theirs. Their belongings—except for Mike's books—were in cartons stacked up in the garage. Mike said they hadn't unpacked because they were going to move again, "when I have time to buy a house." Roxanne said they hadn't unpacked because their things were mostly shitty anyhow. Their talk was packed with allusions to a coming change. Money was out there somewhere, gathering itself, due to arrive.

Tessie and her friend came out of her bedroom and said they had to go. After the front door closed Mike said, "She going back to school?" This was the first interest in her he'd displayed. Roxanne didn't reply. It seemed unlikely. I could see the two of them out on the grass near the sidewalk going through their shoulder bags. They were comparing something. Both girls wore deeply scuffed espadrilles tied up their bare legs and long tent-like tee shirts, under which their haunches moved in tick-tock, fuck-you rhythm as they moved off down the street together.

"I wouldn't be alive now if I hadn't been so sick," Mike was telling Berg when I plopped into the oversized sofa next to him. It was a familiar story. Mike had always been sick. He used to brag about the number of times a priest had been sent for, "to get me when I couldn't defend myself." His first serious illness had earned him his very first shot of morphine. "They say it doesn't make ya high when ya get it for pain, but, man, I had that first rush and I knew *this* is for me!"

"I was dying last winter," he said. "There's nothing like a crisis to teach you time. You don't own it, you can't keep it, it carries you like a cork on a wave. Nothing mystical about it, Berg. You could say that it's *time* that connects you to everything. That being so, it's my convenience to call it grace. I feel that way."

Bergman had a look on his face that I knew meant he was dying for a cigarette. We had promised Roxanne not to smoke even outside in the yard. A single whiff could trigger Mike into allergic shock, she'd warned. Roxanne leaned against the wall near the kitchen entrance, resting her shoulders and smiling.

"Negative ions," she said. "They're killers. Another few months of California, and we might have lost him!"

Then two of them began telling "my bad life" stories—laughing about car wrecks, apartment fires, midnight move-outs to duck bill collectors and repo men. The high point was a tale in which they were both so drunk they forgot Christmas day and woke to watch eight-year-old Tessie in tears searching the house for gifts. "We felt so fuckin' bad, we got drunk again," Mike said.

People in Mike's books torture cats, murder prostitutes, thrash their kids with belt buckles, then weep and dream of the power their cruelty never gives them. People in Mike's books are loved by their author. By Mike. It's his love that infuses the rank unsparing language. Have I made it clear that Mike is an artist?

Roxanne went back into the kitchen and I followed.

"I've got to get his supplement together," she said, peeling apples swiftly and expertly. "The regimen works best if he gets it every three hours."

"But you haven't sat down."

"It's the only thing keeps him alive. This food and the healer up in Stockbridge. Wonderful woman. Praise Jesus." She began feeding apple pieces into her electric juice extractor. The back of the counter and the underside of the overhanging cabinet were crusty with spattered food pulp. The phone rang. Soon she was detailing her earlier phone call.

"I shop every day," she told me as she replaced the receiver. "It's the only way to be sure I get him food that's truly fresh." The only organic supplier she trusted was thirty miles away. She was going again, later this afternoon,

It had taken me 'til now to see how wired she was. She'd eaten no lunch; she hadn't stopped kitchen work for two hours. The phone rang again. This time it seemed to be something about the bank. She said, "No problem. I'll deal with it later." "I'll deal with it later," she repeated firmly. "It's in the hands of a higher power," she said to me.

I got Berg and me out of there by quarter past two; his energy runs out, I told Berg on the quiet; Roxanne will absolutely bug out if she thinks he's overdoing.

We've kept the red rock Mike took from the bay; it's on the kitchen table. Roxanne sent us a card with flowers and leaves twining around the word "Peace." Inside, she told us what a blessing our visit had been and how we must come again soon and that Mike loved us both very much.

I meant to phone her but couldn't make myself.

Two months later another card arrived. This one was embossed "Bless Our House" and carried a return address in the poor northwestern corner of Connecticut. This one said it was wonderful to get Mike away from that high-pressured Fairfield County town. Here, life was simpler. The neighbors were "real people." Mike was deep into a new book. Praise Jesus.

A few weeks later, Bergman rang the phone number Roxanne had enclosed, but it had been disconnected.

Mike's new book had come and gone; I had glimpsed the paperback on a stand at LaGuardia when I was catching a plane for a conference. I was running for the gate and hadn't had time to stop. The neighborhood bookstores never had a copy. We never saw a review. Like a wink or a shadow, it was gone. To the Croats? To the publishers of the Tamil translation?

To the 99-cent bins in suburban discount stores?

So what's happened here? A man who has lived disastrously, a gifted man—who is as busy as I am at making a story out of himself and changing everyone around him to fit the needs of his words—after binges, bloody hemorrhages, midnight arrests, after jars too numerous to list, turns to Alcoholics Anonymous and Jesus. Is there a point in this?

Praise Jesus.

After our visit, Berg and I talked about our own anxieties, and we again remade some of our own history. Why we live as we do. The wreck of our socialist dreams and our mutual pledge to retain humor, without blindness.

I also learned from Berg that Mike hadn't brought his troubled family to live in one of the city's most expensive suburbs on pure faith alone. He had persuaded his eighty-five-year-old mother to sign her insurance policy over to him. That was what funded their half-year stay in that cantilevered house.

"I wish you'd told me," the naïve narrator complained.

"So you could look shocked, the way you do now? So you could say, oh no, you must be wrong?"

I didn't answer.

"Don't you know Mike yet?"

"But the food allergies! All that stuff Roxanne had to do everyday."

Berg just looked at me.

"Things that are too much for you *are* too much for you, and that's the very thing folks like us refuse to believe," Mike said that day. "We're always rejecting what we know. You *can't* do it alone. Accepting that's not so bad. It's just bein' like everyone else on earth."

"How can you say that? All artists work alone. That's so very *not* like everyone else," said naïve narrator.

Benevolent Buddha was twinkly clear. "I don't know what I'm doing," he lied, smiling that loving smile of his.

Six months later we got a postcard from Los Angeles. It said, "My heart is broken." It said, "I'm in a furnished room and Tessie is pregnant. We are happy, praise Jesus, except for bastard welfare paperwork. Neither of us can ever forgive that bitch Roxanne. Warning, if you see her: protect yourself. She is **evil**. Blessings." There was no signature, no return address.

The card came three years ago, but it's finally clear the story isn't written yet. Think of the changes in a Mozart symphony. Think of the displacements in Beckett. The conversions of van Gogh. These are not very nice people, these great lovers. To move on, they will always mean never what they say.

FORTIFICATION RESORT

by Lynn Crawford

A Sestina for Peter Williams

Fortification Resort counts on guests to respect our specially designed bylaws, and to engage in periodic personal exile. For self-repair. Some of what we provide: nourishing food, body creams, seaside views, organ protection. On each bedside table, a basket containing complimentary wrap-around, UV ray glasses and tubes of sun defense oil. Rays pass on Vitamin D, but so does a safer choice: oral tablets—even casual solar exposure brings danger. Cancer, premature aging, infertility.

Visitors approach their stay here as an investment in physical and cerebral productivity. Our mission is to provide healthy pleasure: polite, informed staff; well-ventilated rooms with balconies; cooked or raw meals with and without animal ingredients; prohibition of unprotected sunbathing; state of the art gym equipment and movement classes (pounding exercises—in demand last decade—have been replaced with vigorous low-jolt forms of motion). In the beginning, beach checkers—assigned to verify that skin has been properly defended and peak hour bathing takes place under an umbrella or cabana—create a bit of an outrage. But over time, feedback turns positive; consumers appreciate the fact that they can leave Fortification Resort without any damaged skin to peel, inject, reconstruct. Our most recent bylaw (close the beach completely during peak sun hours until we build more sun shielding structures) meets with little resistance since it reinforces our missive of protection and allows us to offer special workshops on regulation observance and organ (particularly skin) lubrication.

Temporarily revised beach hours (early evening to mid-morning) bolster daytime indoor activity (fitness center, board and table games, film and book library, special seminars); because we are a multi-windowed structure on a prime piece of property with panoramic beachfront views, time spent indoors still gives one the sense of being out in weather.

We are realists, accepting—for example—that at a certain stage of everyone's life, only technology makes skin glow a prospect. Still, even with creams, injections, surgeries, good habits are crucial for health: positive self-image, frequent physical activity; ability to spend time alone, ambition to achieve.

Meals here are eye-popping; Chef accommodates food preferences and allergies, while maintaining devotion to health and pleasure (he relies heavily on the Omega-3 oils found in fish like salmon, tuna, anchovies and in the almond, walnut, avocado).

Walks alone on the beach, time spent on an (enclosed) balcony, or in one's room are examples of periodic personal exile, more extreme is our one-night "Solo." Following a map with clear directions, a customer backpacks to a spot several miles from our hub where we've set up a well- equipped tent (lanterns, charged-up laptop, cooler), there, the guest spends an afternoon, night and morning alone to achieve what we call Personal Fix. Inside the cooler is a six pack of water, a bottle of wine, and exciting meals prepared by Chef according to the individual's specific needs; toiletries are backpacked in by the participant.

In case something goes awry, we have a video camera installed inside the tent and at various points around the camp, each guest carries a cell phone for the same reason, these measures eliminate any true threat of madness or danger.

This element of charade—necessary for customer safety and our insurance. The laptop allows the participant to chronicle the range of emotions experienced while approaching the challenges of Solo, the blend of exhilaration, fear, solitude, anger. Rescue vehicles at Fortification Resort are gassed up and fully prepared to speed to the spot within minutes, should an individual in fact need assistance.

We attract a hardy kind of visitor; whining or complaining—for example—would wind a guest up in social exile. Sturdy would describe the culture created here at Fortification Resort; we use the term *personal fix* (rather than, say, *self help*) and do not encourage late night confessionals, or direct guests to save calories by cutting out sugar or oil.

Guests who frequent Fortification Resort are comfortable in a spa environment: hair and nail treatments; body waxes and oils. Attentive grooming offsets the stress of the furiously paced work and personal lives they tend to lead. Our reviving treatments make customers feel better, and do not require long periods of time away from professional or social circulation.

We provide a structured setting, without the extensive services of a medical or spiritual center; guests report that they leave Fortification Resort with lighter moods and worldviews. We are not geared toward the disturbed, depressed, infertile. Our repeat visitors come for casual, not serious, assistance.

We have no beef with those in need of more detailed repair. The opposite is true; we direct needy guests to places that focus on heavy-duty physical, professional, emotional reconstruction free of charge. Just this morning we transferred a customer who broke down during cocktail hour (late enough in the day to be held out, unprotected, on the beach) after revealing a distressing set of personal problems. We responded by driving him—teary-eyed—to a nearby center outfitted to confront and contain such suffering. We believe he will function well in that particular placement, where difficulties are expressed under the supervision of an expertly trained staff. We took a different tack with a younger guest who stayed in her room for two days because she admitted to not being able to decide on the right color polish for her nails and toes. We invited her to view beauty and repair treatments in our spa. Inspired by what, at that time, was our latest rage (a topical ointment that moisturizes, protects from the sun, and increases fertility), she emerged permanently from self-imposed exile and is now our daytime spa manager.

OUTSIDE BOSTON

by Lewis Warsh

"You look just like your father."

A man reaches out and pats the top of my head; the gesture accompanies the words, a disembodied hand parting the curtains of air. The words are spoken to please my father, of course, who stands alongside me, a firm hand on my shoulder to emphasize possession, but I don't know what it feels like to feel proud—is this it? I don't feel I've done anything to deserve the compliment.

Sometimes, if my father isn't standing nearby, the stranger presses a folded five dollar bill into my palm.

"You look just like your old man," he says, closing my fingers over the bill.

Then he shakes his head in disbelief and turns away. The assumption is that I'm going to tell my father the identity of the person who gave me the money, that I'm going to put in a good word for him. It's like I'm the middle person in some secret adult game where strange barrel-chested men with square jaws and receding hairlines give me money in order to get something from my father. The only problem is I have a hard time remembering names. "Tell your dad Jim Somebody says hello," and I forget the name immediately. I forget when I want to forget, and even if I could remember the name I would never dream of telling my father. I unfold the bill to check the denomination and then add it to the roll in my shirt pocket. It's my money now, the less anyone knows the better.

It's the last memory of my father, but the most insistent one. The anonymous stranger mouthing the words: "You look just like..." and then wandering away. The ritual of slipping me the money as if it was something I deserved. My father drapes his arm around my shoulder and looks proudly into my face as if he can't believe I'm his son, that after he's gone strangers will approach me and say: "I remember your father..."

The scene of this memory, this glimpse of the past, is a roadside bar called Eugene's outside Boston or the house my father rented after he and my mother split up, or a larger party at someone else's house, where different people, both women and men, all say the same thing, every sentence begins "You look..." and then they present me with money, especially if they're drunk. My work is done. I've played the role of my father's son, I've watched my father play the role of the proud parent, his hand on my head as if he were a ventriloquist working the strings, mouthing the response (but I never say anything) without ever moving his lips. I feel like I'm at the mercy of what other people choose to say, that if I go up to my room or leave the bar unnoticed and stand in the parking lot watching the lights on the highway, my father will be angry with me, and nothing is worth that. Someone will approach him and he'll say "I want you to meet my son" and I won't be there when he needs me. Even now, fifteen years after he died, I can stare into his photograph and compare it to my own face in the mirror, or to a photo of myself taken at the same time, and there is nothing, not the slightest hint of resemblance.

"Maybe," I once told Angela, a woman I lived with for a year after graduating from college, "maybe they were just saying it to be polite. But if that's the reason it wasn't me they were talking about. I could have been anyone. The whole point was to kiss my father's ass by playing on my vanity. They'd say

108

anything to me whether I looked like him or not."

It'll go on forever, this memory, outlasting all the silences, another myth of childhood, last glimpse of dad blowing smoke in my face as I look up into the eyes of a man with pink jowls and a handkerchief folded neatly in lapel pocket, some strange oily substance coating his fat pink lips, this friend of my father, this colleague whom I was supposed to call uncle, Al or Fred.

"Shake on it partner," the guy said. "Did anyone tell you you look like your dad?"

The spitting image: that's the expression they used. It was the last time I saw my father though I wasn't aware of it then. He was being honored for something in a nightclub in Boston and had to make a speech. But beforehand, everyone mingled around drinking and shaking his hand, and shaking my hand. So I remember his face that night as a blur of smoke and I remember the women in short dresses and long hair entering the sphere of his conversation as he sat on the edge of a barstool, a drink in his hand, a cigarette, while people dropped out of the immediate circle and others stood in the background waiting to be introduced, while still others just shook his hand, said "Congratulations," and moved on. And I was there beside him, he had a hand on my shoulder at all times, while the other hand never stopped moving, lifting a cigarette or the glass to his lips, as he talked and smoked and drank simultaneously: was anyone listening? Two men stood behind him at all times like bodyguards who did nothing but nod their heads in encouragement and laugh in the right places. He was talking about nothing. Every few words he said "fuck" and then apologized, squeezing my shoulder. All of the men, and even some of the women, as if he had given them permission, used the same word to punctuate their various responses. Even the women with their permed hair and their perfume that smelled like lilacs used the word "fuck" as a hinge at the end of their sentences. Possibly they would use this same word later in the night in another context, as in "do you want to fuck?", initiating the idea that anything was possible. Yet it was the first time I ever heard a woman speak this way. The woman who perched on the barstool near my father smiled at me lovingly with the hope (the same hope as the men who offered me money) that I might play favorites and put in a good word with my father. As if it were up to me to choose a new mate for him, a new sleeping companion. One woman with silver lipstick even kissed me on the mouth. I watched my father's hand disappear beneath her skirt as she threw back her head and exhaled the words "Fuck him!" to describe a mutual friend, her boyfriend or husband whom she would leave in a minute to be with my father.

After awhile, he was so drunk I don't even think that he realized I was there. Someone drove us home, eventually, my father in the front seat, dozing off, me in the back between two women, the windows wide open so no one would get sick. I was aware of their thighs and legs pressing against me and I held my hands in my lap for fear that I might reach out and touch them, put my hands between their legs (I was a step away from believing they wouldn't stop me if I did), and when the car stopped suddenly I would feel their breasts push against my shoulders, and one of them said "Fuck" again, because that's what we were doing, in a way, and no one cared. I was happy that when we arrived at my father's house my mother wouldn't be there, that they lived separately, since I knew how angry she would be if she saw him drunk, unable to walk. I knew that my mother, who hated being alone for even one minute of the day, had left my father because he wouldn't stop drinking, because he went out every night, because he slept with other women and because he did all of these things openly, as if he purposely wanted to hurt her. It was logical that they should separate. At least now I didn't have to lie in bed listening to them fight at three in the morning.

But before we went home he made a quick speech to his constituents. He pontificated drunkenly into a microphone about labor unions and strikes and the relationships between management and workers and the laws, the "fucking laws," that allowed management to hire replacements when the workers went on strike. I can't imagine that anyone was listening. I stood in a corner, trying to make myself invisible, frightened that he would call me up to the platform with him (as if the fact that I existed somehow validated his principles), drape his arm over my shoulder, as he sometimes did, and introduce me once again to all his cronies. The last thing I wanted was for anyone to mistake me for him.

"He got drunk again, I bet," my mother said. Those were her first words when I called her the next morning. Followed by a sigh. My parents lived all of ten blocks away from each other. Two weekends a month and special occasions like this one I slept over at my father's.

"I bet he brought someone home with him," she said.

Before calling her, I looked into my father's bedroom, which was empty of furniture except for a king sized bed, and he was alone, lying on his bloated stomach in a white undershirt, one arm hanging over the side. I knew the women who had accompanied us on the ride home, either one of whom would have been willing to spend the night with my father whether he was drunk or sober, had stayed in the car while the driver carried him in the house and dumped him onto the bed. That was really the last time I saw him. When my mother came to pick me up, though I insisted I could walk home alone, was the last time. My mother never came inside when she picked me up. She was certain, if she ever crossed the threshold, that a strange woman in a short red nightgown would appear, my father's latest "piece of fluff," and question her right to be there. Before I left I went into his room, said "Goodbye Dad," but he didn't hear. Then I put on my jacket and closed the door behind me.

THE LULLABYE MOTEL

by Pat MacEnulty

Cara looked out the office window at the black wrought iron fence surrounding the cemetery. A female cardinal with red-brown wings perched there, head tilted up as if she were waiting for someone. Cara was 19 years old and trying not to feel bored. Her job had some uneventful interludes, but she had learned to love it for the moments in between the boredom.

At first she had hated working at the Lullabye Motel and Burial Service Center. Her cheerleader smile seemed to rub the customers wrong or else they were simply impervious to her youthfulness and charm. But she was a quick study and she had learned from Ms. Wickham how to treat their patrons. Seriously, but not solemnly. There was a difference and Ms. Wickham with her calm voice, short pink-polished fingernails and crisp linen suits knew how to convey the perfect balance. Their customers were special people, she had said, pay attention to the nuances.

A grey rental car pulled into the driveway and parked outside the office. The man waited for a few minutes before getting out of his car. Cara could see him looking around at the place. When he stepped out, she saw that he was handsome—tan, smooth faced, with thick sun-bleached hair. His good looks became even more apparent as he came inside. His face was perfectly featured, except for his nose, which canted toward the left. His eyes were gentle, almost curious, and green.

"Good afternoon," Cara said. It was important to give the customer a feeling of normalcy, Ms. Wickham always said, and Cara sensed that with this man it was especially important.

His blue button-down shirt and grey slacks spoke of his utter craving for the ordinary. Not like the last guy who came in wearing one of those tank tops where you could see inside. She had winced involuntarily upon seeing the little gold hoop hanging from his dark aureole.

The man did not answer her immediately. He glanced quickly around the room. It was an ordinary looking motel office in nearly every way. But behind the counter there was a desk for registration and a computer; it looked more like some place you might sit to apply for a home loan.

"I heard that…" he began and then changed course. "Do you have any rooms?"

"Yes," Cara answered. "I have a very quiet room in the back." She paused and then added, "Each room is equipped with gas jets."

"Gas?" he asked.

"It's painless and it's clean. We don't allow any firearms in the rooms," Cara said. Some people thought they could use a gun, but if they wanted to do that they might as well go to an ordinary motel. Cara wondered if the violence of a gunshot was more satisfying to some of them. There were those, she had discovered, who did not want to simply end their lives. They wanted to murder someone and the person they wanted to murder was themselves. Murder was messy business. Suicide did not have to be. This job had brought her wisdom.

"No, I didn't bring any firearms," he said. "I thought maybe someone administered poison or something."

"An overdose carries complications. At least that's what Ms. Wickham says," Cara answered. "Would you like to come around and register?"

The man cracked his knuckles nervously before nodding. Then he followed her around the counter and sat down in the leather chair opposite her. Cara had learned to modulate her voice in gentle tones the way Ms. Wickham did.

"Now, this is the form we ask you to fill out," Cara said. "It will take a few minutes for me to verify all your information on the computer. Then we're all done."

The man looked into her eyes, and she felt his sudden gratitude. The voice modulations were extremely comforting.

"We need a next of kin or the name of someone you would like us to notify," she said gently. "Or you can just put down the I.R.S. if there is no one you have in mind."

She watched his strong hands as he wrote down the information. He was left-handed, she noticed, and did not wear a wedding ring.

"What about the rental car?" he asked, staring at the paper.

"Just put down the name of the company and they'll send someone to retrieve it," she said. She cleared her throat and straightened up in the chair, felt the desk beneath her arms as she folded her hands together.

"Now, we do offer burial services and cremation services. If you do not choose one of ours, you must show a receipt from your preferred funeral home or whatever." She'd forgotten exactly how Ms. Wickham worded that part.

"The cremation service is quite reasonable," she continued, showing him a brochure with the rates listed on it. "And we offer other services all the way to the ten thousand dollar deluxe package which includes a satin-lined casket and a funeral service."

Some people loved this part of the explanation. They were extremely attentive to the details of their burial. Others didn't want to think about it.

"Just put me down for the cremation," the man said.

"Where shall we send the ashes?" Cara asked.

"Can't you just dispose of them?" he asked with a trace of irritation.

"Yes, we can do that." She placed a check mark on another form and scratched her temple.

"The gas jets can't be turned on for two hours. We do that to ensure the customer feels secure in his or her choice. There is also a tape you can watch on the VCR, a phone for making any phone calls. We have a chaplain on call at all times. The suicide hotline number is posted by the phone if you care to avail yourself of that service." She said the above in a rote voice, so as not to imply any kind of judgment. Most people were not interested in watching the tape—a presentation of alternative solutions—or calling a chaplain or anyone else. By the time they checked into the Lullabye, they had made up their minds what they were going to do.

Cara took the completed application form from him. She checked to make sure he had put down his social security number and then she used her computer program to verify the phone number matched the name that he had given for notification. Most people were pretty forthright at this point. There was not much left to hide. But if someone really wanted to be anonymous they could be without much trouble. At the bottom of the form there was a line that said: Reason (optional). Most people wrote something like "Tired of it all" or "Can't go on." They rarely used the word "I" as if they had already erased themselves. There were paper and pens in the rooms if they wanted to leave a more in-depth explanation for a family member or for friends. Few of them did. Sometimes they wrote poems or drew a picture.

In the space under reason, this man had written in black ballpoint letters, "Too many reaons to list them all. Suffice to say, I have had enough."

"If you change your mind," she said, clicking off her computer, "we can always refund your money for the crematory services. Some people find that just coming here is enough."

"Does anyone ever change their mind and then come back later?" he asked.

"Yes, that does happen sometimes. We charge more for each visit because we want people to understand this is not a regular motel. This is an important decision," Cara said, quoting Ms. Wickham verbatim. Then she eased into her own voice. "It's only happened once since I've been working here. One woman came back four times. The fourth was her last."

"How long have you been working here?" he asked, tilting

117

his head to the side as if he had seen her for the first time.

Cara felt her skin flush. She was not used to having the attention turned toward her.

"Almost a year," she said. "Ms. Wickham was the same age when she first started. She says some of us just have the calling."

The man smiled—grim but a smile all the same. She didn't like the smile. It told her that he would carry out his plan, that he had no doubts. He was the type of person the Lullabye Motel had been made for. Cara wondered briefly if perhaps she really had the calling after all.

The man took the key in his palm. If the customers were drunk or deranged, they were sent to the rooms where the gas jets did not work. More than once a person had woken up the next morning sober and delighted to be alive. But this man was neither drunk nor crazy. At least he didn't appear to be.

"It's the last building," she said. "We do have a pool if you want to take a swim. There's a liquor store next door, too."

He looked out the window at the liquor store and said thanks he would probably stop by there.

"You can turn on the jets any time after the two hours that you like," she added. "Some people wait until the morning. I don't know why. They just do."

"Thank you," the man said, shoving the key into his pocket. He walked out the door.

"God go with you," Cara said as the door slowly fell

back into place. She had never been religious before this job, but this somehow felt like a holy mission and the customers seemed like saints instead of the desperate sick people she had once imagined suicides to be.

Mark stopped to gaze at the cardinals that swooped by his car. Now that he'd made the decision, his depression had lifted. He could encounter people—like that pretty black-haired girl in the office—and converse with them. He knew he could not change his mind. If he did, that which made it impossible to function would return.

He kept his thoughts centered on the immediate situation—get out of the car, take the key, open the door. Look. Room with one double bed, a dresser with television and VCR, blue walls. Why blue, he wondered. He was proud of the way he could keep his mind firmly grounded. It wasn't that he was crazy, he never had been, and he knew all about crazy. But now he didn't have to think about the future— bleak and fruitless—or the broken picture of the past.

But as soon as he thought about not thinking about the past, he began to remember his mother. He always had to fight the anger he felt for her. She couldn't help her illness or the things it made her do, but what would have happened if she had just eliminated herself when the schizophrenia first began? Would he be here right now? No wonder his dad had found refuge in the beds of other women but that wasn't exactly an option for an 8-year-old boy. Who knows, he thought, perhaps his life would have turned out this empty and hopeless even without her constant insanity. The rest of the family had been able to desert her, get unlisted phone numbers, move across the country, why not he?

When he felt his mind picking up the pace, delivering the

same old information to itself like a basketball player throwing the same orange ball over and over into the hoop, he forced himself to stop thinking. He went to the window and opened the curtain. A pool. Some pine trees. A cardinal at a bird feeder. A woman in a white suit, not a nurse's uniform, but a business-like tailored outfit and high heels. Ms. Wickham?

He looked down beside him at the air conditioning unit. There was a red knob on the very end. Above the knob, the word "gas." He tested the knob. When he turned it, nothing happened. Two hours. What would he do for two hours? He looked outside again. The woman was gone. It was warm out; the swimming pool looked inviting, almost as inviting as death. What was this feeling? Light-heartedness? Was his impending death such a relief that he could actually feel something that was not anxiety or despair? He couldn't go swimming. He hadn't brought a swimsuit. He hadn't brought anything really.

He sat down on the bed. He didn't want to be alone with his thoughts, but this could be the last time. He thought about Ruth, the one truly good woman he'd ever been involved with. He'd broken up with her because something about her just wasn't enough. Enough what he didn't know. Pretty enough? Exciting enough? Cold enough? His doing this would probably hurt Ruth more than anyone. But she was a strong woman. She took things—her father's cancer, for one—in stride. After four years of living together, he'd left Ruth for Lisa. Auburn-haired, fashion-model tall, tequila-drinking Lisa. She'd stolen two hundred dollars and broken every window in his house before she left for Key West on the back of a Harley. The thought of Lisa no longer made his skin ache. He imagined them both in the room with him—Ruth and Lisa. Suzanne would be next. But even though she was the most recent, she was the one he had the most difficulty remembering. Studious, intelligent, sober. And critical. Now he remembered. That stiff look that came over her face whenever his mother called, which was always in the middle of one of her episodes, never in those few periods when she was relatively normal. Episodes which lasted months. Mother would call seven times a day—or night. The last time he'd seen his mother she had weighed 280 pounds and had a house full of items she ordered from the television—lawn gnomes, exercise machines still in the box, a dozen set of kitchen knives, ugly jewelry, diet programs, videos from PBS that she would never watch, rooms full of useless stuff. He had finally cut up her credit cards with a pair of orange-handled scissors from a set of nine.

The motel room grew darker, and the air stifled him. He stood up and opened the door. No one was outside. A few fireflies danced above the lawn. He wondered if there were a god, and if so, would this god welcome him to the other side, or would his essence just disintegrate like one of those fuzzy flowers you blow in springtime. He shut the door.

He studied the phone on the nightstand by the bed. It suddenly occurred to him that he didn't have to stay here. He could do this thing somewhere else. Or not at all. Then he noticed a word scratched into the wood of the headboard. He bent down and looked closely. It said "Angie." He wondered who Angie was and why she had come here. He looked at the bed, brown bedspread, soft pillows. Did Angie turn on the gas as soon as the two hours were up or did she wait? Did she lie here with her head imprinting these pillows until something told her to turn the knob? He felt tears rolling down his face for this woman he had never known as if she'd been a lover, a friend or perhaps a sister. Then the feeling subsided.

He lay down and dozed a bit, then he heard a sound, a metal clinking. The gas had been turned on. Was it two hours already? He could turn the knob any time now. He did not go over to the air conditioning unit. Instead he turned on

121

the television. There it was—the twenty-first century in all its glory, glimmering from a 19-inch screen. Commercials, canned laughter, facsimile people who were paid enormous amounts of money to distract us, he thought. They didn't care if they made everyone crazy.

He watched the television shows one after the other until midnight, not thinking anything. There was nothing left to think about. And now he did not feel alone. At midnight he turned off the television and sat in the dark. Such an empty world like the inside of a balloon. He turned on the light by the bed. Suddenly, he saw the room as if he hadn't seen it before—the walls, the yellow and white curtains, the pillows now freed from the covers of the bed. And he knew he had prepared his whole life for this night in this room. He stood up, walked over to the air conditioner and turned the red knob. Then he lay down on the bed and rested his fingers on Angie's name as he drifted off toward a quiet sleep.

When Cara came in to work the next day, she noticed the gray rental car at the far end of the lot. The cardinals were already up and chirping on the other side of the wrought iron fence. Cara unlocked the door to the office. The door stuck slightly from the humidity. She shoved it open and automatically flicked the light switch. Then she walked into the kitchen to turn on the coffee pot. She didn't want to check the gas valves right away. No reason to know or even care about the man with sun-bleached hair. And yet as she sat at her desk with the hot coffee in a white mug, she glanced over at the meters in the corner. Well, he'd gone ahead and done it, after all. She'd known that he would. Now she would need to call the rental car company to come get his car. She adjusted the sleeves of her flower-print jacket as she gazed out of the window. Ms. Wickham would disapprove of the cheery colors of her clothing today, but it was spring, after all.

THIS IS IT

by Will Fleming

I'm on line at a check-cashing store, the ghetto bank, as they call it up here in Spanish Harlem, up here on 103rd and Lex, waiting for the money I convinced my mother to wire me so I could get some laundry done, buy a few packs of smokes and get a decent meal before I go in. Before I call it quits. Before I throw in the proverbial towel. But what I'm really planning on doing is running right up to the nickel spot on 105th and First and filling my veins one last time before I admit myself into another detox unit. One last time before I'm forced to face King Heroin's withdrawal from my addicted little cells.

If all goes as planned, sometime after four o'clock this afternoon I should be strapped to a bed, pumped full of methadone, Tylenol, Prozac and Virasept, and be answering questions about my mother and my father, why I hate myself, why I'm trying to commit suicide, and from where I think this behavior stems. And if all goes as planned, I'll shrug and tell them I don't know. And then they'll ask me how long I've been shooting heroin, drinking methadone, and shooting cocaine. And me, always the class clown, I'll shrug again and say something like, too long, I guess. And when they ask me when my last fix was, if all goes as planned, I'll get to tell them, just now.

I went halves on a nickel-and-nickel speedball this morning up on 110th with a Spanish guy they call Frenchie. But already it's wearing thin, the jones stealing back in like a cold hand against my skin.

I step up to a bulletproof glass window and yell to the woman on the other side that I'm expecting a very important

Western Union delivery. I tell her my name, and she tells me to wait and that there's no need to shout. Then she thumbs through a stack of thin, pink receipts and says, "Nothing here."

I ask her if she's sure and, trying only to be helpful, add, "It's coming from Baltimore. From a Carol Foster. I mean Larson. I mean, Larson's her maiden name now, but she might have used her married name because it's the same as mine and all."

The woman throws me an irritated glare and then barks, "Like I said, it ain't here yet." Then she says, because maybe she feels a little guilty for shouting after just having told me not to, "If you want, you can have a seat right over there and wait," pointing to a window ledge at the front of the store.

Why I do this, I'm not quite sure, but I tell her that I'm not some white boy who just moved to New York because he's been watching *Friends* and thought it might be fun. I tell her I've been here for years. "Don't mistake me for one of them," I say, gesturing out the window at no one in particular.

But she just ignores me and again tells me to go sit down.

Then I tell her I'm sorry and give the truth a try. "It's just that I'm ill and I'm going into this place this afternoon and my mom said she'd send me this money, and I don't know what I'm gonna do if she doesn't."

"Listen, honey," she says, "you go on and sit over there, and I'll let you know when it comes. Okay? Okay," she answers for me.

I fall out of line and excuse myself as I cut between two older men and fold down onto a window ledge that looks out at Lexington Avenue. Over my head the words CHECKS CASHED hum white noise, and then my own voice chimes in saying, "Not today, Mom. Please. Not on my last day."

And then, to no one in particular, I'm saying, "She told me she'd send forty. Said it would be here by ten this morning. And she's usually pretty good about things like this. Unless," I'm telling no one at all, "unless she's been going to those Al-anon meetings again. Unless this is another one of those tough love lessons."

I walk outside and step into a payphone booth to call my mother collect at work. And when she finally picks up, I try to sound as innocent and as clean as possible. Try to sound the way she'd like me to be, the way I once was. I tell her I'm fine, that I'm still going in, that I'm doing it for myself this time, and that, overall, I've been feeling pretty good. And when that's finally all out of the way, I hit her with, "I was just wondering if you were able to send that money we spoke about last night."

After a pause, a pause that feels like it could have been an hour, she tells me she hasn't and that she doesn't understand why I need it.

"I told you, Mom," I say. "I just need to take care of a few things before I go in. You know, like, all my clothes are dirty, and I need to eat and get some smokes for my stay and all that."

There's another pause, so I jump in and add, "And, you know, I just wanted to have a few bucks while I'm in there. For, like, toiletries and stuff."

Then she hits me back, asking me point blank if I'm going to get high with it. I tell her no, of course not. But at this point in our relationship, I think we both know better.

And then I think about telling her that I'm going to get it one or way or another, and that it would be much easier if she just gave it to me. But instead I tell her I'm sorry and that I'm really going to do it this time. "For real," I add.

Then the next sound I hear is of my mother trying to hide the fact that she's crying. Then she's telling me she loves me and that she really hopes it's for real this time.

"It is," I tell her. "This is it for me."

And just when I'm thinking I'm losing, just when I'm thinking I'm going to be hustling change the rest of the morning and picking up last night's beer cans from the gutters and the garbage cans of the Upper East Side, she caves and agrees to send me twenty, saying, "That should be more than enough."

Pinching the skin and pulling the hairs on my leg through my pants pocket, I thank her and tell her I love her and that I'm going to get it together. Then I hang up the phone and smile as I picture a new twenty-dollar bill shooting through the underground glass tube that runs like a giant syringe from Baltimore to New York to the pockmarked ditch in the bend of my arm.

I step back inside the ghetto bank, smile at the woman behind the glass and sit down under the buzzing sign. Trying to relax, trying to regain my earlier high, I cross my legs at the knee and close my eyes.

"C'mon, Mom," I'm saying aloud, folding my arms and knocking the back of my head against the window. Sitting here waiting for it to come, it's like watching a pot that never boils.

If I've learned anything it's that you can't think too much about it. You can't think about how you're never again going to get to chase down ten bucks, cop a couple dimes or a few nickels, gun them all at once, and then disappear into a nod. You can't think about how you'll never again get to run those old streets in those old neighborhoods. Or how you'll never again get to taste the kerosene-like fumes of an East Baltimore coke shot. Or feel the spreading warmth of an East Harlem dime bag on a winter's morning. You can't think about the death sentence that managed to get mixed up with your shot one day. You can't keep turning over all the regrets, or thinking about how much of a failure you are in everyone's eyes. If you want to get clean and stay clean, you have to push all that away. If you don't, what I've learned is that you end up right back where you left off.

You end up right back here.

I was clean once. For almost five months. After a three-month stint in the world's largest correctional facility, a judge mandated me to a two-year residential rehabilitation program as an alternative to sentencing. No problem, I thought. Anything's better than jail or the cold streets, I thought.

The place was called a therapeutic community, but it wasn't the friendly, loving, or nurturing recovery environment the name suggests. It wasn't that at all. Instead, it was one of those military-type break-you-down, build-you-back-up rehabs, one of those leftover treatment models from the sixties where they shave your head and scream at you all the time about how you're a piece of shit because you're addicted to drugs, just in case you weren't already fully aware of that. Just in case the fact that you lived on the street, ate out of trash cans behind bagel stores and bakeries, begged for change on East 86th Street until you had enough for a nickel shot from

127

103rd, and shared needles with just about anyone who would give you ten on the hype isn't enough to break down your ego, they take care of the rest.

For nearly five months I stuck it out, shouldering the screaming confrontation groups, having to wear sandwich-board signs informing my fellow junk- and crack-addicted brothers and sisters that I didn't know how to follow directions or didn't know how to listen, and having to scrub the building's East 10th Street brick facade with a toothbrush and a cup of water as part of what they called addicts' learning experience. I stuck it out, every day harder than the one before. I stuck it out because I thought it was what I needed to get clean, because I was afraid of going back to jail, and because I didn't want to go back to this. I stuck it out in spite of the fact that each and every one of those 140 days I thought about riding the crest of a dime shot of coke and parachuting back down on a three- or four-bag shot of dope.

After a few months, after I'd gained back some weight, after the gray in my eyes had lifted and the blue had returned, they let me have a visit with my mom. And since I seemed to be doing so well, since I looked so good, since it seemed like I was finally getting myself together, she took me shopping and bought me some new clothes, a new pair of shoes, a Walkman, and a tape.

The next day I left.

The next day the weather finally broke and spring had hit the city, and all I could think about was getting high. And when a counselor put me on another learning experience for asking for a cigarette when it wasn't a designated smoking time, I decided I couldn't take it anymore. And before I knew what I had done, all my new stuff had been pawned off on the streets of Spanish Harlem, and I was banging a twenty-and-twenty speedball in a crack house up on 117th Street.

Because I couldn't stop thinking about it. I couldn't push it away.

That was three months ago.

"Sign right here," the money lady tells me.

I sign my name, and she reaches into the drawer and removes two tens. And then a twenty. And that's why I love my mom.

"Thank you," I say, but again the woman ignores me. But I could care less, because my pockets are fat and I'm already out the door and heading up to the spot.

Now I'm at the First Avenue entrance of the Metropolitan Hospital Center, enough coke and dope in my pockets for two solid blasts. For two good last shots.

The automatic door slides open and I step inside.

The trick to getting a fix on in a public place is to stroll right in like you're supposed to be there. Walk right through that diner door and head straight for the bathroom in the rear as if you do it every day. Walk into that corner bar in the middle of the afternoon, smile at the bartender, maybe even offer a hello, and then just amble straight on back to the stall and do your thing. Or, like I just did, cruise right through the sliding doors of your local hospital emergency room, go right past the security desk, and right over to the public bathroom.

This particular bathroom has been my spot since I've

been out here this last time. It's been like an old friend. This particular bathroom is a two-man job with a sliding bolt lock on the stall door, which, when you're used to trying to fix behind parked cars, in project stairwells, or on floors of abandoned buildings with about five other junkies all vying for your kickback, is almost like having your own place again. Plus the main lobby has three color TVs where you can watch CNN or catch a soap opera or a talk show while you're settling into your nod.

The best part is that it's only three blocks to the nearest nickel spot.

And nobody ever says a word.

I got caught once in another hospital doing this. Last summer I shot four dimes in the Beth Israel lobby bathroom and fell out with the hype still clinging to the bend in my arm. A few hours had gone by before a security guard—this big black guy— unlocked the door and woke me up. When I opened my eyes and my brain finally processed what was happening, rather than trying to run, rather than risking a chase and losing my high, I forced myself to cry. And it worked. Instead of calling the police or even throwing me out of the building, the guy brings me into his office, gives me coffee and donuts, and tells me how he had been a junkie years ago and that if I was ready for help, he could help me. I say, "Sure, yeah, I can use some help. Like a twenty or something should do it." But all he does is hand me a small piece of paper with his number on it and tells me it's way more valuable than any amount of money.

I slide the bolt lock into place, drop my pants, and let loose. I do this because once the smack hits your system, you can't, and until all your coke's gone, you'll have to. And it's best to get it out while you can, while you're in a bathroom.

I gently put the four bags and the four vials, my spoon, my works, and a piece of cotton on the top of the toilet paper dispenser. Gently because my hands are shaking and because just about the worst thing I can think of right now would be to drop my shit on a wet bathroom floor when I'm about to get busy. When I'm about to get busy for the second-to-last time. I flush the toilet, wait for it to refill with clean water, and dip the needle in.

Squeezing toilet water into the spoon, two coke nickels and two dope nickels go from powder to liquid, and I'm already sweating. I drop in a piece of cotton, stick it, and pull back until the solution races up the neck of the syringe. And despite the fact that it's a myth and no one's ever really died from an air bubble in the vein, I give the hype three firm flicks.

I lean back.

I slap awake my veins.

Sometimes I wish one of these shots would just put me in the Big Nod and let me leave all this behind. Just let me sleep. Sometimes I wonder if I would have died had that security not found me on the toilet.

I pull my sleeve up to the shoulder, slide the needle in at the bicep, and fish around until I get a vein. Blood shoots into the neck of the hype and everything fuses into a red cloud. A red cloud of blood and drugs, of life and death. I gun it and then pull back. It leaves. It comes back in. It goes back out. Back in. Back out. In and out. In and out, like something pornographic. And then I slam it home, watching it leave the syringe and feeling it flare through the blue cords of my arm.

Sometimes I wish I could just stop remembering things.

I inhale and hold it.

My needle is dull, and dull needles hurt when they penetrate. They hurt even more when you're fishing for a vein, like trying to draw your own blood with an old nail.

My friends in Baltimore used to call me Doc because I could hit just about any vein in any arm, as long as there was still blood flowing through it. No one calls me anything here.

I hook a vein that seems too tired to put up much of a fight.

They say junkies are just as hooked on the needle as they are on the dope they shoot. They say it's a manifestation of self-hatred. They say it's self-mutilation.

Once, when I was clean for about three months, I used to punch myself in the face. It started by putting soap in my eyes until they were red and burning and tearing. When that wasn't enough, I wrapped my hand in a damp washcloth and punched myself in the face as hard as I could in front of the mirror. When that wasn't enough, I started bashing a shaving cream can against my face until my eyes were all black and blue.

I guess it was like picking up where someone else left off.

My blood starts to jelly in the hype, so I slam the shot. The last shot. The last hoorah.

The coke hits first, and I'm paralyzed. I'm sweating. My ears are ringing. And I feel like I could shit myself.

I'm holding my breath. I'm underwater, and rays of light splash down from the surface.

In my last rehab they made me talk a lot about my childhood. They made me talk about things like how my father used to hit me and how my mother was invisible. One time my father beat me so badly that my sides and back were all full of bruises and handprints. But nothing was visible with a shirt on, so I went to my room and smashed a dumbbell weight against my face to try and break my nose. I don't think I broke it, but it swelled up enough that my father felt bad the next day when he saw me.

The dope rolls in, and I'm easing back down.

All I can see is my own reflection in the stainless steel walls. My reflection, all distorted and muddy. "This is it, you know," I tell the reflection. "It's all over."

Over 56,000 soldiers died in the Vietnam War, but my father wasn't one of them.

I pick up the needle and start poking myself with it until I find a vein. I pull out some blood. I let it hang for a moment and then plunge it back in my vein before it coagulates. Then I fill the syringe and start spraying lines of blood on the white floor and on my shoes. Then I fill it again and spray my reflection until my own blood runs down the walls. Then I fill it again and splatter the walls around me until the stall is a murder scene, a battlefield.

Then I fill it up again, cap it and put it in my pocket, just in case. Just in case someone wants to fuck with me.

I lie back against the toilet and let the dope flow through me, let it crest and flow. I try to forget. But I can't stop trying

133

to figure out which one it was. Which shot in which city with which fiend?

Right now I'm thinking that if I had a gun I might kill myself. Or maybe I would go out into the lobby and kill a bunch of people, sit down and watch some TV, and then take myself out.

But I'd probably just kill myself. They say turning around the figurative gun is the hardest thing to do. They say once you pull it out of your own mouth and point it at the right people, you're getting healthier.

I close my fist and punch my reflection. Then I do it again. And then again, until the wall warps and my knuckles hurt too much to do it a fourth time.

Maybe once I'm clean my mom will buy me another new pair of shoes. But this time I won't have to sell them.

I spread my syringe, cooker, empty dope bags, and coke vials out on the floor with the lines of sprayed blood, because I'm hoping someone will find them. Because maybe someone will understand. Maybe someone will grasp what happened in here today. And maybe they'll start being a little more careful with this bathroom.

"It's time to go," I tell my muddy reflection. And then I'm back in the lobby. And then I'm back out in the world.

Picking up a half-smoked cigarette on the ground and lighting it up, I tell myself this is it.

Then, waving at nothing, I say, "This is it. This is definitely it."

THE FARCE

by Carmen Firan

I had come to an understanding of sorts with life. All things seemed settled for the foreseeable future. I had even come to terms with the business of surviving. I had my own alliances, having found a way to communicate in a crooked, topsy-turvy world, in which little was being communicated and even that was in code. I had determined to put up with the conspiracies and the conflicts, and was by now even amenable to certain compromises, as long as I could enjoy certain liberties in exchange. I thought I had a good handle on any states of exultation. There wasn't much I could expect from outside, since events were so predictable; while on the inside I was putting on a front of calmness and indifference for what should have been real poise and equilibrium. In short, things were neither here nor there.

Times had become sort of neutral to me. The children were by now college students; my wife had stopped tormenting me with her fits of jealousy. I was working as an editor in one of the Capital's dailies, and prided myself on having deftly avoided landing any management position which would have required a much too heavy dose of involvement in politics, which, in turn, would have entailed all sorts of shameful, humiliating compromises. I was more and more resigned to just age nicely, putting off as long as I could, as best I could, any serious attempt to answer life's hard-nosed questions. I opposed nothing and no one. I made sure I never stepped out of line. I was a dutiful aspirant to the commonplace, a nostalgic seeker of normality. And at that very moment, just when I thought I had it all down pat, madness broke out.

I was living in one of those relatively "good" districts of the Capital, neither too central, nor too peripheral. An area with prevailing tall, gray buildings, with ugly rundown balconies that were far too narrow, which had been built during the years of socialism with the express purpose of herding as many similar people as possible into standard, one-size-fits-all tiny apartments appropriately nicknamed "matchboxes." The ground floor of these buildings invariably housed all sorts of stores, mostly of a useless variety. In fact, in those days many of them were almost always empty or stocked with unappealing, shoddy products nobody ever wanted. Their grimy, dingy windows displayed only spinach jars and tomato cans.

For two years we had had no lights after ten p.m., due to the authorities' supposed need to conserve energy. Naturally, we had found a way to cope even with this inconvenience, by acquiring tons of candles, which came in very handy in those days, when our eyes could hardly penetrate the thick darkness on the streets, on the staircase and practically everywhere else. Kerosene lamps, formerly discarded by the stores, now made a triumphant comeback; and if one had the right connections in an electrical appliance store, one could get, for a price and almost always under the table, Russian-made flashlights and electric rings from Czechoslovakia. Needless to say, when the lights went out, the water and heat supplies were also cut, as well as the natural gas.

We were experimenting with a glorious "Back to Nature" movement! During the summer nights I could do a bit of reading by the candlelight, but in winter this was almost always impossible. We would all go to bed very early, quite fed up with everything. Water was heated on the electric ring. Then we washed ourselves as best we could in a washbowl, put on warm socks, a track suit, donned a ski cap, and slid under the covers, numb with cold. All these things were going on in the waning years of the eighties, when the world outside was abuzz with all kinds of wonderful high tech gadgets, with news of great breakthroughs in outer space exploration, and with so many other out-of-this-world wonders, which nevertheless left us—in our sad, cold, forlorn corner of the earth—quite indifferent.

Bundled up like this, needless to say there were few, if any, romantic stirrings in us. Whatever passionate desires might have reared up in us would have been quickly stifled under these harsh circumstances. The birth rate in our country was steadily declining, in sharp contrast to mortality, which peaked among young women who were trying to abort their fetuses in their own homes, either by themselves or aided by some old woman, skilled in such matters, through the use of knitting needles, corkscrews, clothes hangers and other such unconventional instruments. The woman would consent to go to the hospital only at the very last minute, after desperation had overcome her fear of the authorities. Once there, next to the doctor, waiting for her would be the stern-faced secret police officer and the unmerciful prosecutor. An emergency curettage would ensue, followed by prosecution or rapid death.

My job at this daily had its well-set routines, running, as it were, on automatic pilot. Mostly I was in charge of the miscellaneous news page. I would dig up some "true stories" that would pass muster with the government censors, in an attempt to give the unhappy, sensation-hungry readers at least the illusion they were being informed about what was really going on in the country. The least I could do was to spice these stories up a little, employing as lively and attractive a style as I could, while at other times resorting to a dry, ironical tone, to describe what were really quite ordinary affairs— petty crimes that brought disproportionately heavy sentences on their perpetrators, traffic accidents, maybe an avalanche or two in winter, insignificant losses and ideologically-sweetened dramas. Nothing of the real social traumas ever made it into print. None of the on-the-job accidents, resulting in the death of scores of workers, was reported, not a word was written about the murders that occurred or the abysmal conditions children in orphanages, in hospitals, or in schools, lived under. And certainly not even a passing comment was allowed about the corruption permeating the leading political and economic circles. Not a word was breathed about these things, for, after all, such horrible things "only happened in the West," right?

Here's what a typical item in the miscellaneous news section would have sounded like: *A woman employed by the Red Ear of Grain was caught, upon getting out of her shift, with three loaves of bread, concealed under her padded parka. She was sentenced today to three months imprisonment. Angela Balaci is the mother of three children, this being her first offense of the kind.*

Everything was highly centralized, run by a handful of incapable political leaders, who tailored the laws to their own taste, changing them at will or, as the case might be, breaking them if it suited their purposes.

The days wore on, long and boring. The sensational, the unusual, the out-of-the-ordinary always happened somewhere else, never here. What never happened was exactly the kind of events we desired fervently and knew in our hearts we badly needed for any good change to occur in our country. After a while we even ran out of conflicts. As for failures, for depressions, we had no time for such sentimental nonsense! Both radio and television were triumphantly spouting stories about our supposed victories, achievements, quotas met and exceeded, bumper crops in agriculture, incredibly high industrial outputs, in our exports and, above all, in our birth rate.

Happiness and triumph were rolling out in waves over the heads of the country's inhabitants, over the happy-go-lucky, grateful beneficiaries of tons and tons of pig iron, coal and other natural assets. All graphs showed unusually high values, shooting up vertically, while we went on living our miserable lives, half-buried underground! And yet, when it came to sports championships and artistic events, we always came out on top.

Our children were the best. They crammed all day—what else could they do? They invariably won the highest places in the science competitions. And, of course, if by some miracle they were allowed to go abroad to attend international competitions, they always fetched first- or second-place prizes.

Our old folks were dying decent deaths, many of them still in their prime, having had but a few years in which to enjoy the ridiculously low pensions allotted to them, with which there wasn't much to buy anyway. They spent most of their time waiting in lines, grim, silent, and determined, dragging their feet through the dusty parks or playing rummy on the benches in front of the dilapidated apartment buildings.

Our women would get up very early in the morning, and throughout the day they kept cooking, and washing—by hand— the household's dishes and laundry. Their natural beauty was rapidly fading, as they didn't have time to look after themselves, soured as they were by life's hardships, with unkempt, disheveled appearances, embittered by hard labor and the absence of any basic comforts. Wherever they went, they carried with them their ubiquitous plastic bags, humiliating us when they got home with the display of their meager contents, acquired after much effort and at ridiculously high prices. Because abortion was illegal and contraceptives almost impossible to come by, they hated their husbands and had sullenly consented to include sex among those unavoidable, risky sacrifices that simply had to be put up with, in which all pleasure had long since given way to revulsion.

No one committed suicide. Officially there were no murders, no robberies, no sabotages, and no strikes. Come to think of it, in every town there was but one basic newspaper, coming out in two or three slightly modified variations, but all written in the same drag, hollow, and artificially pumped-up style—just like the paper I was working for. People were buying these papers mainly for the classified ads or for the obituaries page, which they were watching feverishly every morning, in the vain hope that one day they would wake up and discover, with delirious joy, right there on page one, framed in a heavy black border, the official announcement about the death of the most beloved son of the nation.

Like everybody else, I would sometimes mumble some incoherent, barely audible criticism against the regime, but only within the confines of my close-knit circle of friends. I managed to keep my humor, quite convinced that we were not what we imagined ourselves to be. It was quite an exuberant, lively kind of humor. There was no shortage of jokes in those days, which acted as some sort of a safety valve, another survival mechanism. We seemed to be a surreal country that could not stop laughing, even while it was slowly dying!

The jokes covered a wide range, from the political to the social realm. Some wag came up with the idea that even these jokes were being concocted and deliberately spread by the dreaded *secret police* in its clever attempt to inculcate a certain illusion of freedom in us, to allow us the cheap privilege of a few harmless liberties. It should not come as a surprise then that this led to the development of a unique genre of science-fiction-like, surrealist, absurd literature so prevalent at the time.

Naturally, political jokes topped the list, being told with gusto, in a wide variety of situations. Example: On page one of the main daily there appeared, framed in black, the following obituary: "The family of the head of state is deeply saddened to announce the passing, after a prolonged illness, of the entire nation."

We repressed our feelings as best we could, while they were fine-tuning their experiment on us, the hapless guinea pigs, cynically resorting to psychology and to the so-called "national specificity" concept. I once had the privilege of getting hold of a copy of a report written by a foreign observer from the West at the end of his two-month stay in our country: *A talented but lazy people, wavering between the ridiculous and the hyperbolic. Suspicious when prosperous, resigned when in trouble. Easy to manipulate, prone to going with the crowd, forever practicing the art of survival at the crossroads of empires, systems and religions. Oscillating between excessive praise and self-deprecation, between lamentation and victimization, now living 'under the times,' now beside them.*

At first I got quite mad at this no-holds-barred, unvarnished description of us, but later had to admit the reporter was right. After all, things are much clearer when viewed from afar, through cool, detached eyes.

I hated the political system in a passive but unrelenting manner. I was totally convinced nothing would ever change in my lifetime, not a thing would stir in the political arena. I foresaw no reversal of the status quo, in spite of the constant message I was getting from the foreign broadcasts, that communism's days were numbered.

Eastern Europe was going through unprecedented turmoil. However, to me these convulsions seemed quite laborious and somewhat contrived. Still, whatever they did in the rest of the region, I said to myself, for us there was no hope. For we were, in my opinion, an enclave, a cage deeply entrenched in totalitarianism, with no one capable or willing to pull apart its heavy bars.

True, the East was beginning to groan and shake, but I could have sworn the wave would lose its momentum by the time it reached us, that is, if they hadn't first nipped in the bud even the passing thought of a revolt. We had become quite good at being stuck in our isolationism. Terror reigned supreme in our country. The infernal oppression machine—finely-tuned and driven daily by the contribution each of us, pliable puppets, were making, whether we realized it or not, to the triumph of the seemingly never-ending nightmare—was running on quite nicely, thank you.

However, I did not make the mistake of attributing all failures to our all-pervasive cowardice. I knew there were people who thought deeply, who conspired, albeit at a purely intellectual level, but all these forms of personal resistance were unable to trigger any meaningful, lasting change. It was a silent resistance, relevant only to the cultural space, extended as a compensation for the official political obscurantism.

We were like some individual oases in a vast desert, our only solidarity manifesting itself through our obstinacy to be different from what we looked like as a nation. As if viewed from an imaging space satellite, hovering over a dark area of the earth, we must have appeared as isolated pinpoints of light, in the blackness of the vast surrounding night, thereby intensifying our sad plight.

We were living a paradoxical existence. While barely above the poverty or, should I say, subsistence line, our artistic and cultural lives more than made up for our material destitution. On Saturdays we would stand in line for hours to buy tickets for all the shows that would be played in the city's playhouses during the following week. We had our own talented actors, our own skilled directors—at least the ones that hadn't yet emigrated. The censorship was again laying down its weapons before such texts as those composed by Pirandello, Shakespeare, Bulgakov or Chekhov and turned a blind eye to references to the underground, to political allusions and to directorial ironies. To be sure, we were permitted certain liberties. But these could not provide the heat we needed to keep from freezing in our apartments, nor did they satisfy our hunger. They could not cause the communist bloc to crack, but they did vindicate us to a certain extent.

In the concert hall where the symphony orchestra played it was so cold that the players had to perform with gloved hands, while the conductor had a heavy sheepskin hat pulled over his head.

While national writers had to do battle with the censorship apparatus, translations from world literature were curiously enough permitted. The top communist rulers simply did not care one way or another about this kind of literature. What the decadent imperialists were writing was not their business. Theirs was to watch over the national values. And so there were plenty of court poets, committed writers, slavish servants of the regime who, year after year, published, especially on the supreme leader's birthday, thick volumes of sickeningly obsequious poetry, paeans filled with incredibly low-taste high praise addressed to him. Everybody was happy. After all, everybody had to live, one way or another, and every one coped the best they could. For the system did not appear to us in a hurry to expire. In fact, I was convinced it would survive me.

In those years, a friend of mine, a journalist with a daily in the south of France, came to visit me. He had been sent to write a sensational piece about the Dracula castle, the only real attraction we could offer the West. So he took advantage of this trip and he stopped by. I took him home, assuming not a few risks, given the government's strict laws against any contacts with foreigners. And should the latter just happen to drop by unannounced, we were under orders to immediately notify the authorities and report to the militia all pertinent information about them. My French friend was quite impressed with my large library. Like the rest of my family, I read whatever copy I could get my hands on of the latest books and magazines published in the West that made their way to us. We always seemed able to somehow watch the latest films produced in the West and seemed unaccountably well informed in all matters of culture. All this in spite of our precarious material conditions, which did not take my distinguished friend long to notice.

On that particular Sunday, I was not allowed to drive my car. Again, because of the alleged need to save energy, the authorities had instituted a system of gasoline distribution, based on the alternating odd/even number of the vehicle's registration plate. To insure plentiful supplies for those Sundays I did have permission to drive, in our bathroom I kept two spare cans always filled to the brim with fuel. Naturally gasoline was another rationed product, so I had to save it up for trips we would take to the mountains, perhaps once a month, or for our annual family vacation.

So we hopped in a cab, and I was thus able to show him the city. The old, beautifully ornate housing districts alternated with areas filled with horrible, ugly apartment buildings which, although new, looked already old and falling apart.

At that time, acting on the orders of the *dictator*, they began bulldozing quite a few churches, and other historic buildings included on the National Trust list, all of this with a vigorous socialistic *élan* which filled my friend with disgust and dread. He could not understand anything from all that aberrant architecture and I had nothing to offer by way of an explanation. Filled with patriotic zeal, they were building an absurd universe. My friend was shocked to see on the streets the same make of car, multiplied *ad infinitum*. He was bewildered by the empty stores and intrigued by the interminable lines in front of bookstores and theaters!

"You have nothing to eat, yet there you are, standing in line to buy books?!"

I explained to him that we lived in a world of "dependencies." Books were our hard currency. One could exchange them for milk for one's children, or with them one could get special, personalized treatment from a doctor who was going to operate on one's wife. No one would look at you unless you had something to give him. Whiskey, cigarettes, books, cheese, or chickens sent over by one's relatives in the provinces. You could find nothing in the stores. It was quite an adventure to raise a child. I would sometimes buy a ticket for the Orient Express, which ran through our capital, simply because I wanted to buy various goods from the traveling foreign tourists—maybe a little chocolate, a box of cookies and candy for our children. I would then get off at the nearest station and return by way of a dirty cold slow train, whose doors were sometimes off their hinges and the cushions on the seats all torn up.

Like everybody else, in addition to the refrigerator, I had a freezer box, which I had bought with lots of money through special connections, out of a batch destined for export. In this freezer we would place for long-term storage whatever food we had been able to garner through strenuous efforts, whenever we could.

145

Every fall my wife would spend a considerable amount of time canning vegetables, making zakuska, various juices, fruit preserves, syrups and tomato juice. She would place in the freezer plastic bags filled with green peppers and ripe eggplant, with all kinds of vegetables and semi-preserved fruit, to provide us with sustenance during the winter. Then the freezer had special compartments for cheeses and meats. These were the most prized, usually reserved for our children. Adults were banned from using these delicacies.

The meat, obtained through all kinds of complicated, ingenious rituals, after waiting in line for hours, was carefully portioned for steaks, for soups, for minced meat, or for schnitzel. My wife would label each plastic bag, writing with an imported, felt-tipped pen its intended use. In addition, we had a ration card, but, alas, it was so low in value! We could only buy ten eggs a month with it, one packet of butter, a kilo of sugar and one liter of cooking oil. Card or no card, in some months these food items could not be found in any store.

In certain cities one could still use one's ration card to buy flour, corn meal and two scrawny chickens, so tiny they could fit quite nicely into one small plastic bag. No wonder they had been nicknamed "sneakers," for they were nothing but legs! No one used the phrase "they are selling" this and that, but only "they are giving" or "they are introducing" these items. I was 48 when I saw my first banana.

One evening my wife and the children were out, leaving me alone in the apartment. Suddenly I felt an irresistible urge to eat a steak and drink a glass of red wine. I paced around the freezer, until I could take it no longer. Guiltily I pulled out a little bag on which my wife had clearly written "for grilled meat." I lit the grill and when the steak was done, I wolfed it down greedily, only to be later tormented by guilt not unlike that of a criminal. A guilt my wife exacerbated when she got home. Smelling the aroma of grilled meat, she quickly opened the freezer, pulling out the now empty incriminating meat drawer and voicing the forbidding, dreaded words:

"I simply can't believe it! You have taken food from the children's mouths!"

I saw my friend fidgeting uncomfortably, while I helplessly looked on, deeply embarrassed. Only when I began to explain to him the rules of our complicated survival game, did I realize what an absurd world we lived in, what grinding poverty we were sinking into!

Whatever exciting sensations the Dracula myth might have aroused in him, what he saw in our family's living conditions that evening must have produced a far greater impression than anything he had seen in the rest of his trip. The next day they called me in to the *secret police* office, where they interrogated me for six hours straight. They wanted to know who he was, how I got to know him, why he had come, and what we had discussed.

Translated from Romanian by Dorin Motz.

MANIFEST DESTINY

by Bart Cameron

I've been working steady now for two years, since I finished high school. I throw tires at Klemen's Tire Wholesale. I work in the warehouse where used tires are dropped off, and we decide which ones are at all salvageable and put them in containers based on make and level of wear, and the others we throw in bins for trains to take to a recycling factory in Indiana. The tires that are to be recycled are also subdivided by content—whether or not they have steel, how much steel they have in them, etc. I took the job because I thought it would be funny to pitch tires around and because, truthfully, I didn't have any other offers. I worked hard enough in my first year that now I don't have anyone check up on me.

My mom is waiting on her Irish citizenship papers and she's dying—she's got ovarian cancer, like her mom. I live with her on Cicero in a one-bedroom, and I walk to work. I sleep on the couch, and she gets the bed.

Her duplex went after her hospital stay, as did her car, a new-looking '84 Reliant. In one month, she used up all her medical insurance. She was very sick from the get go, and the hospital knew they couldn't do much. They insist that she knew she had cancer long before she finally asked me to bring her to the emergency room. She couldn't take the hospital after a while, and she asked me if she could live at my apartment for as long as I could manage. She's been living with me for three months now.

I work with this American Indian, that's what he tells me to call him, named Russell Means Greening. He's named after some activist, the Indian equivalent to Malcom X, he says.

He talks more than I do, about a lot of things: Ford cars, he knows everything about every model; rap music; and he talks about history a little. Not Columbus and George Washington, he talks about what Sioux really means, and how the Lakota were killed off for no reason, just as, he says, the Irish were killed off before my grandfather came over. He even says Indians gave the Irish the potato.

Russ doesn't get hurtful when he talks. He isn't speaking to get at you, like my uncle. He never gets loud or distant, so I like his stories. I take more of his load when he talks, and I try to push him to tell more. He gets going on how Crazy Horse was set up, and I'm tossing the steel-belted into the bins, and our shift ends nicely. I go home to my mom, and my body aches at the joints. Something about that tired pain lets me think about running around in canyons, or fighting for Russ's ancestors. After a good day, I've got three movies going through my head to get me through the night. I can cook for my mom—always some canned soup and buttered dark bread; help her with her shots, and even help her write letters to Ireland without feeling bad. Without even being there.

The way Russ talks, I wish I could speak like that. I wish everywhere people were talking like him: low, relaxed, taking time to breathe, but pushing out these little points. "Custer really started the scalping," he might say. "Do you know Custer had lice and the clap? Every day of his life he burned and itched. His eyebrows were loaded with them. You can understand why he got so full of hate."

I never have to answer his questions if I don't want, but if I do, he turns and follows where I'm coming from. "Shay," he says. Really my name would be spelled Sea, for Seamus, but even I write Shay so no one gets confused. "People have to keep the US powerful, so they put the details where they want," he says, when I say I was told that the Irish brought lice to America during the famine.

The doctor from the clinic explains cancer to me. He says that the lump on mom's inside starts like a colony and grows and grows. Then, he says, if the lump is malignant, or bad, the lump sends things into the blood stream and attacks her whole body. Mom's lump is bad, he says. She gets more pain medication, and the doctor says I should think about putting her in the hospital for good. "Just admit her into the emergency room at Northwestern Memorial," he says. "They can't reject her, and you're too broke for them to go after money from you. At least then she'll be able to go easy."

I really appreciate the doctor helping me, but Mom doesn't want to go to any hospital for a while. It costs me more to keep her at home, because I have to pay twenty-five dollars for every prescription with my mom's insurance, whereas at the hospital they'd have to provide it.

So after Mom's cancer spreads, and I have to carry her to the bathroom when she's in pain and when the pills to take the pain away make her sick, Russ has a cold streak and stops telling stories at work. Part of it is because we have a heavy load in the winter—this happens every winter because people ditch their tires for snow tires, and the dealers convince them their old tires won't be any good after winter.

Part of it is because one day he says my mom should get a divorce.

"We're Catholic," I say.

He looks me straight in the face and says, "Does that mean you have to act like you're brain-damaged?" I tell him that we'll be Johnsons instead of Murphys for the rest of our lives. And I tell him if he talks about the church I'll kill him. I only go to mass, haven't been to confession in a long while, but I know my mom needs the church, and I can't let anything get in the way of that. In any case, Russ hardly tells any stories, and I need something to help me when I carry my mom around, or when I have to send another letter to "Immigration Services, Dublin, Ireland." That's the whole address. In Ireland they don't use zip codes and things like that.

Russ is pissed at me, for good reason. I can't stand how quiet it gets at the warehouse and how quiet it is overall. My mom has my TV in the bedroom, but she's at the point where she can't stand very much light or noise.

I start reading comic books and listening to Kiss, like I did before everything got bad. Mom doesn't like the noise, and she thinks the church would have a problem with some of my comics, but now that she's really sick, I need something to help me along. I once brought home a bottle of whiskey to help me get to sleep and to keep me busy, but Mom cried through her tight throat. She can't smell enough to taste the difference between tomato soup and beef broth, and yet she can smell the whiskey on my breath after one drink. No booze has been allowed in my house since my dad left, since I was six, and I have to observe that until Mom's gone, and even then I know she'll cry if I take a drink in the house.

When I'm at home now, I turn the stereo on quiet; I have to hear if Mom gets choked up. But if I keep the level low, I can make out all of the music that I want and hear most of the lyrics, and I can still hear Mom's wheezing: slow when sleeping; high pitched and quick when awake; high pitched and loud when she's gonna throw up or she's in really bad pain. Conan and Thor, both by Marvel Comics, are the only comics

151

I get into. I go to a shop that sells comics, baseball cards, and alcohol, and is between the train station and my place, and I buy the old Conans, which are the only comics there that get cheaper the older they get. When I get a big stack collected, I bring them in and trade for new ones. The owner of the store is a heavyset black guy who always tries to talk about comics, but I feel guilty being away from home and not working, so I can never listen to what he says. I know that he gives me a deal on the comics; every old Conan and Thor that he's taken from me on trade ends up going in the ten cent box, even though he gives me a lot better price.

Comics aren't that stupid, especially Conan. He's from an ancient country, Cimmeria, where there aren't any green trees, and there aren't newspapers and buses like in the other comics—even Thor, which I like, always has some reference to newspaper reporters or alter-egos. If you look through the issues, what I'm saying about Conan really being different holds true.

I have one issue that I'll never sell back, where Conan has to save this really old guy from a pack of mystic wolves. The Watcher, he's the guy that tells Conan's stories, explains that the old in Conan's world aren't worth saving, but Conan is too stubborn to let this guy get eaten. The comic actually shows the blood that the wolves get out of Conan, but he fights it out, until, eventually, he strangles every one of them—his sword couldn't cut them.

Mom finally can't leave the bed. The cancer is all over her body, and she has to take so many pain pills that she just can't move. I have to put a bed pan under her, but I get worried about her throwing up when I go off to work. She won't go to the hospital, though. She says she wants to stay where she's wanted. Uncle Dan offers to come and check up on her while

I'm at work. He makes a deal with mom that she'll go to the hospital if life at home is too difficult. He takes me aside and says I'm wrong for letting her stay home, and I should live my own life. He says I shouldn't sleep on the couch like a bum, but he'll help out for a little while.

I really hate having my uncle around. He does anything to get a rise out of people. One of the things he talks about is how all the rest of the family got their citizenship papers years ago, and how I probably messed up the applications. But he pays for the medication, now, and he really takes good care of Mom, his sister.

Russ starts to talk a little more as the load lightens at work. I tell him I don't like my uncle, and that my uncle said I was probably a Viking.

"Everybody's a Viking," Russ says. "Those fuckers raped everyone. They were like the American government going after Indians. Nothing to get that upset about. I'm even part Viking." Then he explains how Vikings were from a place with no trees and not much sun. The way he describes their home, it sounds just like the place in Conan. He says that being so far from any natural life, they didn't have any perspective.

"Hey Russ," I say. I carry a fresh load of tires to the bin without checking if the tires even have any wear. "Was Conan a Viking?"

"Probably," he says. "He was a big dumb-ass white rapist wasn't he?"

"I don't think he was a rapist," I say.

"Then he was a fag. That's the way the big white heroes

go. Rapists or fags. Like Alexander the Great was a fag and Thomas Jefferson and Columbus were rapists."

"Columbus?" I ask.

I get home late because I buy a few new comics. When I get there, Uncle Dan's sitting in a chair next to the bed. I can tell he's been there a while. Mom's breathing is slow and heavy.

He gets up, holding a letter, and walks out to the couch. "Your mom's ready to go to the hospital," he says. I thought eventually she would decide to go, but I expected Uncle Dan would be happy about it. He's not. "She got a letter from Dublin."

"Yeah?" I say.

"She didn't get citizenship yet," he says.

I feel like I want to break something. I know I messed up the letters somehow. "What'd I do wrong?" I say.

"You did everything right. They're just changing the rules on you. They're only going to take so many a year now."

I nod my head.

I have to take Mom to the hospital, because my uncle doesn't want them to notice she has any relatives with money. The only reason she can get good care is because there's nothing more anyone can take from me. The nurse at the hospital knows what's going on, but she's really nice to Mom.

"Maybe Conan was a rapist," I say the next day at work. When I first started reading the comics, I would imagine my work area was Cimmeria, and the tires were loose rocks or hunks of enemies or anything that might be part of a story. I can't get myself to imagine today, though. When I pick up the tires, I always get my hand jabbed by a piece of wire.

"No," says Russ. "I was thinking about this. Where was he from?"

"Cimmeria," I say.

"Where's he really supposed to be from. Well, never mind. I think he was probably one of those people from the Russian mountains. A Cossack. Which means he's not white, and may not be that bad."

"So he's not a Viking like me," I say.

Russ laughs at me. "No, he's probably one of my great-great-grandfathers." I'm carrying four tires to the recycle bin for all-rubber, and he struts up beside me and lifts two tires up above his head. "You see," he says. "I'm definitely part Conan."

I go to the comic store after work. I know I have to go to the hospital, as my uncle and I have figured out that tonight will be the hardest night for my mom.

"You know what you want, you want the Red Sonja comics," the owner at the store says. "It's like Conan only the bitch has got a nice set of tits."

Every day before I have ignored whatever he has said and replied that I only want Conan or Thor, which spooks him a bit. Now I say, "I want something about a place outside of the city and without any tits. And I want something without any white hero," I say.

He smiles. "Are you trying to start shit? Is that what's going on?"

I smile back.

"I guess the Silver Surfer's not white. Someone just brought in a whole bunch of those. They're not as cheap as Conan. I'll sell you them for a buck a piece."

I spend fourteen dollars on comics, which is more than I've spent in a while on just myself. On the train in to the hospital, I open up the Silver Surfer and I forget all about my mom and anything unpleasant. The first page is full-color—deep greens and purples and yellows make up this huge planet which is the backdrop, and in front is this tall, naked, chrome, bald man on an old-style surf board. The words in the upper right say "Silver Surfer, once Herald of Doom, now Explorer."

There isn't anyplace in Chicago where I've seen this light purple set against the deep green that makes up the planet in the background. The areas in the Conan comics always reminded me of the places I walked through, they made me imagine myself in an area more dangerous than it really was, but Silver Surfer, coasting past planets with intense colors and taking on clouds of men or machines or his old boss, an enormous god-like thing called Galactus, those are completely outside what I've ever seen. I flip through six comic books on the ride to see my mom.

I wait for her to wake up for three hours. While I'm waiting, I keep the comics out of her view, just in case she does open her eyes for a second. Finally, at ten o'clock, the nurse tells me that, even if I'm family, the hospital prefers that visitors only stay until nine. She points at the curtain, behind which is another woman a few years older than my mother who has been talking to her TV.

When I get home, I realize that I can't sleep without hearing my mom's breathing. Every time I start to lose consciousness, I dream that my mom has stopped breathing. I wake up and it takes me a while to realize that she's in the hospital now. I spend all night reading the Silver Surfers.

Issues number eight and nine contain the origin of the Silver Surfer. He is from a planet called Zenn-La, which is on the other side of another galaxy. An enormous being comes to his planet and says that he must consume it, make the planet a part of him. One man, Norrin Radd, steps up and tells the being, Galactus, that his planet is beautiful and peace-loving and shouldn't be put to waste. Galactus agrees to spare the planet, as long as Norrin will work for him, touring the universe in search of planets that can be consumed. Galactus takes the full-grown, white man, Norrin, and blasts him until he is completely chromed and bald and naked. Galactus says, "It's a fair trade. You can see worlds you've never imagined, you just can't come back to your home again. And I will spare Zenn-La."

"Have you ever lived anywhere outside of Chicago," I say to Russ the next day at work. I have been looking at the green lines on the 84-89 all terrain tires—it's the same green that is in the background in some of the planets that the Surfer cruises by.

"I used to visit my grandparents in Minneapolis," he says. "I decided that I've got the best chances in Chicago. Either that, or I'll push East. I'm going the opposite direction that the US wants me to go." He's already told me about Jackson's attacks and the marches West, but he goes on anyway.

My arms are completely exhausted by noon. There's no way I can get through another four hours of carrying tires. When our lunch break is over, I don't get up from the edge of the bin where I sat to eat.

Russ is quiet for a while. He carries tires at double speed, trying to make up for the fact that I'm not doing any work. After an hour of doing both my work and his, he sits down next to me.

"Maybe you should tell the office you're sick. I don't know if I can make it look like both of us were working," he says.

I go into the office and tell the secretary I'm sick for the day. She says she can see that. On the walk home, I'm so tired that it feels as though I'm coasting by the Dominick's supermarket and the six blocks of duplexes before I get to my apartment building. I fall asleep on the couch and dream that I am standing on a massive tractor tire, gliding past my mom's hospital and past Ireland and up into space where I can see the Earth as a perfect circle with neat blotches of light blue and red. Still, as distant from the Earth as I am, I see a tiny white dot over the blurb that looks like the United States. It grows and erases, slowly, first the East part of the country, and then it heads West. In my tractor tire, I take off past the Earth. I hear Chicago get sucked up by the white mass, but I don't turn around. I am able to imagine, as I ride in my tractor tire across a swirl of purple dust in the middle of space, that my home in Chicago is bright and alive, as long as I don't turn around.

I am holding the phone when I wake up. It is the nurse who threw me out last night. She says she's sorry and that I should come down with arrangements for what to do with the rest of my mother.

MYRIAM'S REVENGE

by Constanza Jaramillo Cathcart

I lived with Cristina in Duke Dormitory, one of the best addresses of our college campus. The rooms were spacious. We could wake up five minutes before class and rush on the soft grass through the magnolia trees to the Chambers building, where most of the lectures took place. In the spring time the air was humid and the pale flowers seemed to go perfectly with the student's pressed pastel shirts. Smiling, they would wave from afar in this landscape, which begged for a "Hallmark Special" title panning across the Carolina blue sky.

Living with Cristina entailed many benefits for me: Cuban coffee daily, 30 pairs of shoes in my size, and sharing my days with a florid soul who sprinkled herself copiously with the contents of an enormous crystal bottle sculpted with the silhouettes of bees.

I almost cannot remember her wearing something not starched, her round cheeks without rouge, her retroussé nose, powderless. She never left the room without disentangling a knot of her jewelry, which she kept in a little black leather box with her embossed golden initials, next to her bed.

Come the spring, she would iron her linen dresses religiously on a foldout board, and wear straw hats. During the second semester of our living together she was dedicated to the study of José Martí, and to acting in the Black Box Theater, where the experimental troupe to which she belonged would improvise, guided by a stern teacher of Japanese training. To their shows she contributed a dark version of Martí's *La Niña de Guatemala*.

We fixed the room as an open venue, an airy smoking boudoir framed by blue and white flowers printed on contact paper from the "Roses" store, where the international student van would take us on bimonthly trips. In the corner between the beds stood a clandestine single stove from which flowed Cuban coffee and rice and beans. We would eat our "moros y cristianos" on these fat cushions printed with enormous flowers, a gift from her bejeweled and golden haired aunt from Charlotte.

I had lived with Cristina for a few months, however, without even suspecting the prime benefit of being her roommate: the boxes sent by her sister-in-law. Brenda, named as the villain in a certain soap opera, was a most elegant Cuban from Miami's crème, gifted with boundless generosity. Cristina's older brother had fallen for her volatile temper, and possibly because she looked like a Latin Snow White. She seemed to walk too fast for her perfume or for fashion itself to catch up with her.

Needless to say, Brenda would quickly bore of her things. When this happened, she would place them all in a box the size of, say, one where an enormous television would be stored. This box would arrive in our room on the backs of several men. We had just received a big one—even by Brenda's standards—when we started seeing the flyers of this "Tacky Party" all over campus.

Before opening the box, Cristina arranged two baskets side by side. The first one was labeled "Formal" and the second, "Costumes." "Those go in the second," I said, motioning to a white linen ensemble, a vest with Bermuda shorts decorated with golden buttons and a parrot green hem. Cristina looked at me with distrust. Then she agreed to throw them in the "Costumes" basket. The shirt, however, remained in the "will decide later" corner and it seemed to want to crawl out, with its line of shiny buttons, which gave it a certain military air.

Some days, through the light green pastures, the dogwoods and the magnolia trees, which perfumed the air with a sweetness capable of making one forget everything, we would see some of our classmates perform military maneuvers in their camouflage fatigues. They would practice different formations and sometimes they could be seen going from tree to tree, hanging from ropes.

Little by little, we got used to the echoes of their songs under our window, early in the morning. So much, that we almost stopped noticing them. But we never lacked reasons to look out: from herds of naked students galloping in the night, to a Jesus of Nazareth, cross on his shoulders, with a following of Romans in plastic soled sandals, hurling insults in contemporary English.

This university, campus without any noticeable danger, not only had its own student army, but a most benevolent security force, which transported itself in these three-wheeled carts. They were supposed to escort young ladies around town at a moment's notice. I had never felt such a small risk of being mugged in my life, as I did in the streets of Davidson, but I got used to the free rides, until one day, the driver inhaled, and using his clearest diction, indicated that they were not a taxi service.

Cristina didn't take advantage of this in-campus transportation except when semesters were coming to an end. Her sleepless cycles of inspiration resulted in plays sometimes written in languages she did not speak, analyses of tango's political effects, and studies of the edible plants which grew on the university's fields. During her end of term delirium,

161

she would not go out on the street except in the most absolute discretion in order to avoid undesirable encounters with professors to whom she owed work. For some reason, in this pastoral paradise, time flew at unexpected speeds. We would try to stop it in any way we could to no avail.

Sometimes, during these clandestine outings she would make out the approaching silhouette of a galloping small dog, choking on its collar, trying to reach the runner it was attached to, a professor who once had declared she was "Part of the Class That Was Part of the Problem in Guatemala."

The divisions outlined by this studious athlete were, however, not comparable to a certain corner of Chambers, home to a Latin-style cold war. On one side, Guatemalan work union posters, whose owner considered our scholarships as a dirty trick from the Right. Across the hall, a newspaper clipping: Castro standing by Kadafi with a by-line saying: "Devil creates them and they get together."

This office contained the idiomatic treasures of Spain, the Andes and the Caribbean as well as a Cuban professor who taught without haste, in conversations which none of its parts dared to interrupt. Professor H had dedicated his life to the study of alchemy and he had managed to divide the universe in two: the Baroque and the Neoclassical. He would draw lists on the board, which resulted in our own never-ending mental ones. The Baroque: Latin America. The Neoclassic: Developed countries. The Baroque: irony, nostalgia, Catholic guilt, Latin American traffic, the young lady's shoes, yes, yours, Lorca's verses, perennial vines, Mambo trumpets, most soap operas, Piaf's "Rien de Rien" and Celia Cruz's relationship with her wigs. The Neoclassical: sarcasm, Protestant honesty, Excel sheets, ballet, minimalist art, functional design, Hemingway's clean and powerful prose, bow and arrow, Pink

Floyd and schools of sardines. Every time we went to his office we would secretly swear lifelong loyalty to list number one, while we dusted the books with a yellow plumero of synthetic plumes.

But, if not on these premises, which offered a Latin America for every taste, the continent remained one, represented by the school's three Latins. If one of us came from Cubans exiled in Guatemala, another lived childhood under the iron clasp of a Southern Cone dictatorship and another, from a city in that time under siege by drug terrorism, in this school we embodied Latin America, the one and only.

One afternoon Cristina returned from classes to find out I had agreed for both of us to speak about our beloved continent at a Charlotte school. The invitation wasn't so easy to decline, and we knew the Antipodesque speech by heart: near the center of the world leaves never fell, snow never melted, rain didn't stop and the sun always shone, depending where one stood. And this happened when one was on the world's navel: Earth could dance on her axel all she wanted without being noticed by the landscape, except of course on the Southern tip, where people sunbathed during Christmas.

When we arrived to "World Day," a full theater and not a classroom awaited us. The program said: "Welcome to World Day: Latin America: Our names." Once we had reached the podium, out of nervousness I presented Cristina as an expert on all Latin American matters, able to answer "any of your questions" to which she replied with a "Whatever" that resonated on the loudspeakers. I don't think she could ever completely forgive me for that.

For the long-awaited party, we prepared with the same tranquility as we had for "World Day." If we weren't completely in the wrong, "tacky" was a universal concept, and we had so many materials to spare, enough "to throw with an slingshot" as Guatemalans say. "Tacky, lobo, mañé, grasa, cholero." We assembled terms from Cuba to Patagonia and got to work on a Saturday afternoon.

I opted for an outfit that my social studies teacher from elementary school would favor: Myriam was a most Cartesian being, prone to order and classifications of all kinds, but her chromatic freedom was remarkable. A pair of fuchsia wool pants and a purple shirt with puffy sleeves seemed adequate. I did my hair up until it wouldn't move. Cristina mainly wore golden Mardi Gras beads over a lycra top, in the fashion of a soldier from the Mexican Revolution: rows of beads instead of bullets, crossed over her heart. It took a while before we could leave the room. Cristina's beads kept falling off of her shoulders as she performed each of her rituals: the cologne, the pearls, the packing of the purse, the blush, as she sucked her cushiony cheeks in, and her minuscule torero ponytail.

Finally Social Studies Teacher and New Orleans Insurrectionist left the room and went off to the party. There, they soon realized what "tacky" meant in the United States. No one had come out in a gigantic sweater embroidered with rabbits and eggs, for example. They all wore clothes from the 1970s. We saw only Barbarellas, Princess Leias and Bee Gees: belly buttons and a lot of fur.

It was as if we had entered the wrong movie. This one seemed like the old American midnight specials invariably dubbed by the same three Mexican voices. Something truly grandiose. (How "great" was always translated.)

A drunken Chewbacca came to us. "You look so nice," he said to me, bowing with reverence. "So dressed up," he added, his simian eyes full of the most sincere admiration. "And you, Cristina, you look so sexy. Hot momma!" We stared at him.

"Alma de Dios," said Cristina, as she slipped the beads back on her shoulder: Poor Innocent Soul of God. There were a lot of these types of spirits on campus, according to her.

"Let's go," I snapped to her, after a nasal lull punctuated by a Bee Gees song. I was indignant, just as Myriam had been when she couldn't stand our mischief in her class, as she drew her graphs on the board.

"No," my friend said. "Better yet, let's light up a cigarette." We lit up two Marlboro 120s and drank beers in XXL red glasses better fitted for a giant's birthday party.

While covered in polyester, our hosts acted very courteous. They were paying their tuition for a reason, to learn about other cultures. By the end of the night, Myriam had smoked a good meter and a half of 120s. She had also updated her disco routines. As for Lycra and Beads, she found herself kissing furiously with a friend of Chewbacca's, her golden guirlande hanging from her arched back. The next day, as we recovered, feeling introspective and with our hair reeking of cigarette smoke, we tried to get through piles of reading and overdue work. It was a long Sunday night.

The parrot green-lined shirt waited, hanging from the basket, to be reclassified later on.

LA VENGANZA DE MYRIAM

by Constanza Jaramillo Cathcart

Vivía con Cristina en una de las mejores direcciones del campus: Duke Dormitory. Los cuartos eran espaciosos y uno se podía despertar cinco minutos antes de clase y llegar a tiempo, corriendo por entre magnolios. En primavera, el aire era húmedo y las flores pálidas hacían eco a las camisas de los estudiantes. Sonrientes nos saludaban de lejos y sólo faltaba que sus nombres aparecieran en el cielo azul de las Carolinas, como títulos de una película de matiné.

Nuestra cohabitación resultaba en un sinnúmero de beneficios para mí: café cubano a diario, unos treinta pares de zapatos en mi talla y un inmenso frasco de abejas esculpidas sobre cristal, lleno de una colonia con la que Cristina se rociaba copiosamente.

Casi no logro recordarla en algo que no fuera almidonado, sin polvos en su nariz respingada, sin colorete en sus mejillas redondas. Jamás salía de su cuarto antes de soltar un manojo de cadenas y aretes que guardaba en una cajita de cuero azul, con sus iniciales repujadas en dorado.

Cuando llegaban los meses cálidos, planchaba religiosamente sus vestidos de lino en una mesita portátil y usaba sombreros de paja. Al correr mi segundo año, se dedicaba al estudio de Martí y a un grupo de teatro experimental dirigido al estilo japonés, al que aportaba una versión dark del poema "La Niña de Guatemala."

Habíamos arreglado el cuarto como un salón abierto y propicio a las humaredas de cigarrillos y de una estufa clandestina en donde se preparaban café cubano y moros y cristianos para festivales folclóricos implícitos en nuestras becas. Una franja autoadhesiva de flores azules daba la vuelta al cuarto y unos cojines de flores muy, muy grandes, regalos de una tía rubia y alhajada residente de la ciudad de Charlotte, reposaban sobre el piso.

Viví varios meses con ella sin sospechar siquiera el beneficio mayor de ser su compañera de cuarto: las cajas que mandaba su cuñada, una dama llamada como cierta heroína de Televisa, dueña de una generosidad sin límites. Brenda era una cubana elegantísima de lo más exquisito de Miami, con un carácter volátil del cual el hermano mayor de Cristina se había enamorado. Brenda era bonita al estilo de una muñeca. Tenía los labios muy bien delineados y pintados de rojo y le gustaban las cosas de pepas. Como una Blanca Nieves cubana.

Brenda caminaba demasiado rápido como para ser alcanzada por su perfume o por la moda en general y se aburría rápido de las cosas. Entonces las metía en una gran caja y las mandaba por correo. La caja llegaba hasta nuestro cuarto en espaldas de varios hombres. Nos acababa de llegar una bastante grande cuando comenzamos a ver los volantes de la última fiesta de disfraces, llamada *Tacky Party*.

Antes de abrir la caja, Cristina dispuso dos canastas para echar lo que iba sacando. La división se hacía bajo los criterios "formal" y "de disfraz."

Un conjuntito blanco de lino con botones dorados y bordes verde loro vacilaba entre canastas. La blusa quedó en "formal," pero en la esquina de "queda por verse" con su fila de botones brillantes queriéndose salir, con un cierto aire militar.

Algunos días, por entre los pastizales verde claro, los magnolios y los cerezos silvestres, que daban flores en varias gamas de rosado, y perfumaban el aire de una dulzura que lo hacía a uno olvidar de todo, veíamos a algunos de nuestros compañeros ensayar maniobras militares en uniformes camuflados. Practicaban varias formaciones y a veces se les veía transportarse de árbol en árbol por cuerdas.

Poco a poco nos fuimos acostumbrando a oír los ecos de sus canciones bajo nuestra ventana a horas tempranas de la madrugada, y hasta casi dejamos de notarlos. Pero razones para asomarnos por la ventana nunca faltaban. Desde manadas nudistas al galope, hasta un Jesús de Nazaret con la cruz a cuestas, perseguido por romanos y romanas en sandalias de goma, gritándole oprobios en inglés contemporáneo.

Y tal universidad, campus sin mayor peligro, no sólo tenía estudiantes del ejército que a veces iban a clase en uniforme, sino una benévola fuerza de seguridad que se desplazaba en carritos de tres ruedas por entre las praderas. Los oficiales tenían orden de transportar a los alumnos de un lugar a otro, a cualquier hora.

Jamás había yo sentido tan poco riesgo de atraco como en las pequeñas calles del pueblo de Davidson, pero me acostumbré al servicio, hasta que un día, el conductor tomó aire, y me indicó con su mejor dicción que ellos no eran ningún servicio de taxi.

Cristina no aprovechaba el transporte intrauniversitario sino en la semana de trabajos finales, cuando entraba en ciclos de trasnocho e inspiración de varios días. Estos resultaban en obras de teatro—a veces en lenguas que no hablaba—análisis de los efectos políticos del tango, o estudios de las plantas comestibles que se daban en los jardines de la universidad. En su delirio de fin de semestre, no salía a la calle sino en la más absoluta discreción para evitar encuentros indeseados con profesores a los que les debía trabajo. Vaya uno a saber por qué, en este paraíso pastoril, el tiempo corría a unas velocidades nunca antes sospechadas. Tratábamos de detenerlo de todas las maneras posibles sin éxito alguno.

A veces en esas salidas clandestinas divisaba a un pequeño perro ahogado en su collar, al galope tendido tras un profesor, atlético estudioso que alguna vez había declarado a Cristina "parte de la clase que era parte del problema de Guatemala."

Sin embargo, las divisiones trazadas por éste no eran nada en comparación con cierta esquina del edificio de clases, sede de una guerra fría a la latinoamericana. De un lado, afiches huelguistas guatemaltecos, cuya dueña consideraba nuestras becas como una jugada sucia de la derecha. Al frente, una foto de Castro con Kadafi con la siguiente leyenda: "El Diablo los crea y ellos se juntan."

La segunda oficina albergaba los tesoros idiomáticos de España, los andes y el Caribe y a un profesor cubano que enseñaba sin afán, en unas conversaciones que ninguna de sus partes se atrevía a terminar. El profesor H había dedicado su vida al estudio de la alquimia y tenía el universo entero dividido en dos: lo barroco y lo neoclásico. Pintaba listas en el tablero, listas que seguimos alargando de por vida. La del barroco empezaba con "América latina" y la de "lo neoclásico," con el mundo desarrollado. Y continuaba lo barroco: la ironía, la nostalgia, la culpa católica, el tráfico latinoamericano, los zapatos de la señorita, las enredaderas perennes y las telenovelas. Seguía lo neoclásico: el sarcasmo, la honestidad protestante, la lógica, las tablas de Excel, el ballet, la elegancia minimalista, lo funcional, la prosa limpia y poderosa de Hemingway, Pink Floyd y los cardúmenes de sardinas. Cada vez que íbamos a su oficina jurábamos lealtad vitalicia e incondicional a la primera lista, mientras desempolvábamos los libros con un plumero amarillo de plumas sintéticas.

No obstante, por fuera de estos recovecos ofrecedores de Latinoaméricas para todos los gustos, el continente, representado por las tres alumnas latinas de la universidad, no se dividía. Si una de nosotras era hija de exilados cubanos en Guatemala, otra venía de una primera infancia bajo una férrea dictadura del Cono Sur, y una tercera, de una ciudad atacada en esa época por el terrorismo apolítico de las drogas, en esta universidad, fuera del segundo piso, éramos el continente mismo.

Una tarde Cristina había vuelto de clases y yo le informé que había aceptado por las dos ir a un colegio privado de Charlotte para hablar de nuestro querido continente. No era tan fácil decir que no, y el discurso del clima ecuatorial nos lo sabíamos a la perfección: cerca del centro del mundo las hojas no se caían, la nieve jamás se derretía, la lluvia no paraba, y el sol no dejaba de brillar, eso sí, dependiendo de donde uno estuviera parado. Y que eso pasaba cuando uno estaba en el ombligo del mundo: la tierra podía bailar en su eje todo lo que quisiera, sin ser capaz de marcar el paso del tiempo en el paisaje. Y, para terminar, cuando la tierra sacaba el pecho al sol, metía la cadera y por eso a los del sur les daba frío en agosto.

Cuando llegamos al "Día Mundial" de un colegio privado de Charlotte, no nos esperaba un salón de clase, sino un teatro entero. El programa decía "Bienvenidos al Día Mundial"— Por América Latina: Nuestros nombres. Una vez que las dos estuvimos en el podio, yo, de los nervios, presenté a Cristina como una experta en todos los asuntos relacionados con Latinoamérica, capaz de contestar "a cualquiera de sus preguntas," a lo que ella respondió con un *Whatever* que retumbó por los altoparlantes. Creo que por esta mala pasada nunca me logró perdonar del todo.

Para la muy esperada fiesta nos preparamos con la misma tranquilidad que para el "Día Mundial." Si mal no estábamos, lo *tacky* era un concepto universal, y nosotras teníamos material de sobra, "para tirar con onda," como se dice en Guatemala.

"*Tacky*, lobo, mañé, grasa, cholero," juntamos palabras de varios países y pusimos manos a la obra un sábado por la tarde. Yo opté por un atuendo que se pondría Myriam, la estrictísima profesora de sociales de mi colegio, un ser absolutamente cartesiano, muy dado al orden y a la clasificación, pero de una libertad cromática impresionante: pantalón de paño fucsia, camisa morada de unas mangas que nacían fruncidas en los hombros y seguían pegadas por el antebrazo. Completé el atuendo con un enredo de pelo considerable, y un maquillaje que me añadía unos buenos quince años de edad. Cristina se forró en lycra y se cruzó un collar de pepas de Mardi Gras en el pecho, muy a lo revolucionaria mexicana, con pepas en vez de balas.

Profesora de sociales e insurgente de Nueva Orléans empacaron cigarrillos, pintalabios y salieron para la fiesta. Allí comenzaron a darse cuenta de lo que era ser tacky en los Estados Unidos. Nadie salió con un suéter de conejos y huevos gigantes, por ejemplo. Sólo veíamos salir a las Barbarellas, las princesas Leia, los afros, las chaquetas de peluche y los pantalones bota campana. Era como si hubiéramos entrado a la película equivocada. Esta parecía de esos especiales americanos de media noche, cuyo doblaje siempre hacen las mismas voces mexicanas. Algo verdaderamente *grandioso*.

Se nos acercó un Chewbacca ebrio, seguramente alguno de nuestros alumnos de español.

—Te ves muy bien—me dijo—qué elegancia, como te viniste de arreglada. Y me abrió unos ojos simiescos demasiado sinceros y llenos de admiración.

171

—Y tú Cristina, te ves tan, tan sexy.

Este representante de la era del disco nos había dejado frías. Nos quedamos mirándolo.

—Alma de Dios—declaró Cristina. Para ella, el campus estaba lleno de tales espíritus.

—Vámonos—le dije—indignadísima, como cuando Myriam ya no resistía el desorden que le hacíamos en clase mientras nos daba la espalda y pintaba sus cuadros sinópticos.

—No, no—me contestó mi amiga. Mejor ten un cigarrillo. Prendimos unos Malboro 120 de esos de tallo largo que duran y duran, y nos bebimos dos cervezas tibias en unos vasos de colores, que parecían haber sobrado de la fiesta de cumpleaños de un gigante.

Todos nuestros amigos forrados en poliéster se portaron muy corteses. Para algo les estaban pagando esa universidad: para aprender de otras culturas. Al final de la noche, Myriam se fumó medio paquete y aprendió varias coreografías disco y Cristina se agarró a besos con un amigo de Chewbacca. Al otro día nos recuperamos introspectivas y olorosas a nicotina, dispuestas a leer todo lo que nos faltaba para llegar al lunes. La noche fue larga y la camisa con bordes verde loro tuvo que esperar, colgando de la canasta formal, para ser reclasificada más adelante.

FAMILY LIFE

by Aaron Zimmerman

They all gather together over dinner. Eat as much as possible, as fast as possible. The youngest, the baby sister, doesn't eat as fast as the father and the two brothers, no one does, except for maybe some forms of wildlife. She misses out on seconds, on snacks, on Yodels; she was saving that one, she didn't want it yet and now she won't ever get it. One of many things none of them will ever get.

The older son loves spaghetti and meatballs, can eat sickening amounts of it. The mother makes a pound for him, a pound for the rest of them. This makes the middle son hate spaghetti even though he likes it and he complains to the mother that they have it all the time. He starts to hate the wormy pasta almost as much as he hates green beans and the smell of Cheerios, two foods his brother likes. The only two foods the middle son dislikes. He pukes up the red strands one day, not quite digested, and leaves them to bake under the sun in a gravelly gray supermarket parking lot.

The father is done eating first and quickly starts clearing the table, the one job around the house he does. The two sons take turns setting the table and the father cleans it well before the others are finished eating. Everyone holds on to the food and drinks and glasses and plates they still want, or else the things will be gone. The baby sister sits there long after everyone else is finished and sometimes the middle son stays with her.

The father goes into the living room, sits on the couch. The TV goes on loudly. He is in charge of what they watch. It's still early, they eat as soon as the father gets home and changes out of his clothes, so prime time is still a ways away. The father watches reruns of *Quincy*, of *Dragnet*, every night—shows he rushes to, shows he sits on the couch for, not really even watching, newspaper in front of him or hands down his pants, legs flipping while he stares off into space.

The mother sits there too, or calls one of her relatives from the kitchen, so she too can see the TV. If she's not on the phone, she occasionally says how stupid the show is. This annoys the father; he takes it personally. He takes everything personally. Whatever the father says, everyone always automatically disagrees with, without bothering to think of it. The father is always wrong. The mother has taught everyone that very well.

This goes on night after night, week after week, year after year. Every three years, the father changes jobs and the family moves. Every few days or so, the father comes home in a bad mood or has a headache and things are even quieter. Only the older son is stubborn enough to speak to the father then.

Everyone hates each other, but no one hates the baby sister. Except the father, he seems to hate her too, teases her and starts fights with her. She is not as quick-witted as the others, she is not sarcastic like the mother and doesn't point out how stupid the father is. She just gets mad and upset and storms out of the room. She cries. She says she hates him. The father is bewildered. He doesn't understand what the baby sister's problem is. Doesn't know why everyone picks on him. He says this, says no one listens to him. He is right. No one does.

When the baby sister gets married, the family gets together again. They go out to dinner. They play board games while the father watches TV. They play Taboo. The older brother gulps beer and yells at his wife when she can't get any clues.

The older son has a daughter. The granddaughter. She watches tapes of Winnie the Pooh, of Mickey Mouse. Everything stops when the tapes are on, her body limp, eyes focused as they pick her up and put her in front of food. She cries, has a fit when it's turned off. She can recite the lines. She's very smart. The older brother's wife, her mother, is nervous. She's afraid of the dog. She's afraid to leave the granddaughter with the rest of the family. When she realizes her daughter is not by her side, she panics. She asks where the child is. The middle son asks if she's checked the bottom of the pool. Nobody thinks it's funny.

The older son and the baby sister's new husband drink tequila at the wedding, lots of it. They spin the bride and groom on chairs. The baby sister doesn't feel so good. She doesn't want the DJ to stay overtime. She goes up to her room. Her husband needs to get out of his tuxedo so it can be returned. He's very drunk. He goes in the glass elevator, the one the bride came down in, to the middle son's room, to change. The middle son and a friend of the new husband undress him. They want to put him in the glass elevator in his underwear, but don't. The baby sister is in her room and feels ill. She throws up. Her husband, still in the middle son's room, can't move. He throws up. The middle son puts a wet cloth on the new husband's head and goes down to the bar. The baby sister doesn't care. She is not feeling well either.

The next morning everyone laughs about it. The new husband and the baby sister are going on a plane, then a cruise. The baby sister is pissed, because the new husband is hung over, pukes in the fake bushes in the hotel atrium after breakfast, near where they were married. They pack and they are off.

The middle son goes back to the parents' house, where the older son and his family also stays. Nobody really wants to talk to each other. The granddaughter holds the TV captive, watching video after video. The father roams the too large house, nothing to focus on, nothing to say to anyone.

They are saved later in the day when more relatives come to see the granddaughter. They play with her. The father regains possession of the TV and he stares at it, surrounded by the mother's aunts and uncles and cousins. They speak Spanish. The father doesn't understand Spanish. That doesn't matter, if they spoke English he still wouldn't understand. He never understands why people have to talk about things all the time.

The relatives eventually leave. The mother and father go to sleep. The granddaughter sleeps. All that's left are the older son, his wife and the middle son. The middle son sleeps in the living room, where the TV is. The granddaughter gets one room, the older son and his wife the other. The older son has rented a movie, a bad movie, starring Barbra Streisand. He and his wife watch while the middle son tries to read. The middle son is sleepy. He is angry. He hates the movie. He hates Barbra Streisand. He hates the older brother. All he wants to do is sleep. All he wants to do is punch the older brother in the head. He wants to beat him up in front of his wife. Make him cry out, beg the middle son to stop. Instead, the middle son gets up, goes to the kitchen and takes out the leftovers. He wants to eat until he nearly explodes.

The leftovers are all wrapped in Saran Wrap. The middle son spreads them all out on the breakfast bar. The TV is still blaring. He opens up everything, takes out chicken parts, rice, beans, sandwiches and just starts eating. The older son comes in, picks up a chicken breast, holds it in his mouth and carries another one in his hand back into the living room. The middle son hopes the older son chokes to death. He knows he won't. None of the horrible things he wishes for ever happen.

The middle son eats until he has to unbutton the top button of his jeans. He wants to crawl into bed, but he doesn't have a bed. He has a sofa, a sofa that the older son wipes the chicken grease from his hands onto.

The movie is almost over, but the middle son can't take it. He asks the older son and the wife to leave, tells them he needs to go to sleep. They don't leave. The movie is almost over, they say. The middle son curls his fist in a ball. The older son is surprised when the punch lands right on his throat. The usually nervous wife gets more nervous. In a voice raspy from the punch, the older son tells the middle son he's crazy. The middle son says nothing, just stares back at the older son, arms at his side, fists clenched. He wants the older son to try to retaliate.

The older son has a way of punching the middle son, right in the center of the back. It makes a loud hollow thudding sound. The older son loves that sound. He doesn't feel one way or another about the sound of crying that always follows, but he could listen to the punching sound over and over again. Usually he only gets to hear it once or twice at a time. One or two good solid punches.

The best time to do this is when the father isn't home. The father hits hard too. He is strong and if he is not in a good mood or of he gets woken up for any reason, he forgets how big he is. The mother stands nearby, watching, arms folded. Later, she tells the middle son how wrong the father is. Everyone knows that, even the father. The older son has all kinds of tricks to get to hear that thud. They all involve getting the middle son angry enough to take a swing. The older son always sees it coming and easily turns the middle son around. The older son punches and hears the sound. The baby sister cries when she sees this. She doesn't want any part of this at all. The mother wonders how this became her life. She doesn't know why the middle son gets a baseball bat one day and threatens the older son.

That night, as soon as dinner is over the TV goes on. The middle son goes to the baby sister's room. She wants to play a game. She wants to play with her dolls. She wants to play Candyland. The middle son does whatever she wants. She's the baby. The father comes by the room and stands in the doorway and watches. He doesn't understand why they don't come out to the living room. He doesn't understand why the middle son would want to play Candyland. He goes back to the TV show. He doesn't understand it. The baby sister goes to sleep. The middle son goes back to the living room. He sits next to the father, rests his head against him. The father absentmindedly scratches the middle son's head, almost like a dog. The middle son likes the scritch scritch scritch sound. He likes the way the father's hand smells, sweaty, meaty.

The father gets up to go to bed. His pants are practically falling down, pushed by his overhanging belly. The father holds on to them with one hand so he doesn't lose them.

In the morning, the older son tells the mother that the middle son is crazy. He shows her the mark on his throat. The wife stands by his side. The middle son watches the granddaughter watching TV. He chases the dog around the living room. The dog chases the middle son. The wife sees the dog running near the granddaughter. She is nervous. She opens the sliding glass door to the backyard. She yells at the dog, afraid it will step on or bite the granddaughter. The dog stops playing but just stares at the wife. She grabs the dog's rear quarter. The middle son says nothing. He knows what is about to happen. The dog turns and bites the wife. The skin is broken. She is bleeding. The mother comes in. She yells at the dog. The dog hangs her head. The mother whacks the dog and drags the dog outside by the collar and slams the door shut. The dog puts her nose against the glass and lies down, looking in from outside and whimpering. She knows she has been bad. The older son says he'd put the dog to sleep if it were his. The mother and wife and older son get in the car to take the wife to the doctor. The middle son lets the dog back in, goes to the cabinet and gives her a treat.

Whenever the family goes to a restaurant, the middle son throws up. It might happen as soon as he gets there. It might happen right when the food comes. It might happen just as he's finishing the last bite. It might happens as they are all leaving the house. Every time the family is going to go to a restaurant, they know one thing: the middle son will throw up. They pretend they don't know it will happen. They all get ready, wash up, put on their shoes. If the middle son knows in advance they will go out to eat that night, he doesn't eat all day. He doesn't want to have anything in his stomach to throw up. If he finds out at the last minute that the family is going to a restaurant, he is sure he will vomit. Sometimes he pretends that he is really tired and gets into bed and says he doesn't want to go. It doesn't matter. He always has to go anyway.

He throws up at the table. He throws up in the bathroom. He throws up waiting on line to be seated. It could be anywhere. The father doesn't understand why. The mother pretends she understands, but she doesn't. The older son doesn't try to understand. He just wants to have chicken parmigiana and spaghetti without someone throwing up. He tells the middle son that he ruins everything for everyone.

The middle son doesn't know what's wrong with him. He just knows something is. He doesn't understand why the family always makes him go out to eat. He likes restaurants.

He doesn't want to throw up.

The baby sister doesn't seem to notice, but she does. In a few years, after the middle son goes off to college, she catches it. She throws up every time the family goes to a restaurant. The father doesn't understand. The baby sister doesn't want to go to school. She runs off into the backyard one morning, into the small woods behind the house. The father runs out after her, still in his underwear. He yells and screams. The middle son hears about this at college. He feels bad. He can't help her. He doesn't throw up in restaurants anymore. Once in a while he throws up when he goes out with friends to a bar. But he knows when it's coming and knows how to hide it.

The father has large red pustules on his back and shoulders. The mother squeezes them. The children watch. It's painful. The father hates doctors. He refuses to go to them under any circumstance. He has an ironclad stomach and can eat anything without getting sick. The mother has a sensitive stomach. She often doesn't feel well. She's in bed a lot. The older son breaks his bones. He falls down the stairs and breaks his arm. He breaks his clavicle playing football. He breaks his wrist running into a car on his bike. The middle son and the baby sister inherit the mother's stomach.

The middle son's face is covered in acne. Large oily pimples mask his face. The family ignores it until the mother finally takes him to a doctor. The doctor shines a bright light into the middle son's face. He takes a metal instrument and jabs it into the middle son's face. The baby sister and mother watch. The baby sister thinks it's kind of funny, the blood spurting, the brother's clenched fist, the way he holds onto the side of the exam table, white paper crinkling under his sweaty hands. His face is bloody. He doesn't go back, doesn't get better.

The father is fat. He puts his hand down his pants when he watches TV. He sits and he stares and his hand moves around under his jeans. His legs flap open and closed. The middle son walks into the older son's room. He doesn't knock. The older son's pants are down, *Three's Company* on his TV. He looks very surprised to be caught stroking himself. The middle son closes the door quickly and leaves. The middle son comes into his underwear when he jerks off. He throws them into the laundry basket. The mother does the family's wash. The baby sister lies on the couch, hands tucked underneath her. She moves her butt up and down. If asked what she's doing, she'll say, "Exercising."

Soon after the baby sister's wedding, the father's company is sold. The father gets laid off. He gets a year's salary. All the children are jealous. They'd kill for a year off with pay. The mother works. She has gone back to school and gotten a degree in family studies. She helps teach others how to be parents.

The father is miserable. He doesn't go out. He has no friends. He mows the lawn and cleans the pool. He looks on the internet for jobs. He goes on interviews for jobs he doesn't want and won't get. He thinks about becoming a real estate agent. He thinks about working at Wal-Mart. A year passes and still no job. He will never get one.

The older brother lives far away, with his nervous wife and the granddaughter. The older son calls the father and mother every Sunday. He tells them what the granddaughter did and said. He tells them what stocks he bought over the internet. The baby sister and the new husband live near the mother and father. The baby sister calls the mother everyday. They talk about their jobs, their houses, their illnesses, what they are cooking. They see each other often. They go out to dinner together. Then they all go back to their nice houses.

The baby sister gets a water softener, a hammock, a couch and a bedroom set from Rooms To Go. It all looks very nice.

The middle son lives far away. He doesn't have a wife. The middle son calls the father and mother about once a month. They talk about the weather, their jobs, sports. The middle son gets off the phone as quickly as he can. He wants to forget that he has a family. He is happy that there will be no more weddings.

REVENGE

by Sharon Mesmer

And all along I had thought *she* was *my* project.

And who was I? In the beginning, a eunuch among eunuchs—an academic. Distinguished Professor of Something-or-other (quite often I honestly couldn't recall) with a complexion like Dresden after the war and a genius for meaningless language: *The serial modes of organized mass aggregates capture the pure experience of modulated discourse and flow it through tropes of self-imposed identity structures, the result being the unhinging of secure disciplinary backing and a releasing of the unbounded potential of linguistic form as disruptive and excessive pleasure.* That, from my highly regarded *Epistles of Accidental Exile: Selected Essays.* To my colleagues I, Herbert P. Bell, was the Kaaba of pure linguistic sensation. But, as is often the case, my prowess in the magic kingdom of Academe did not extend past the ivy-covered walls of the quad. My problem? *I was projecting a composite speaker vacillating between traditional images and deformations of accepted gender-based reflexes.* In other words, while I flirted and paid lip service within the established guidelines, I didn't find the Girls of Academia appealing. Appalling was more like it. How many tales of rank Connecticut can one man listen to, I ask you? But by the same token, how many nights did I waste chatting up blowsy women glistening like Italian salads in the garish lights of cheap saloons in blue collar neighborhoods? Outside those ivy-covered walls I was nothing—a big pink man in worn corduroy, flaky about the scalp, obtuse in speech and manner. I had pretty much accepted that I was doomed to merely dream of laying paws on a pair of common gee-gaws. And then outside those walls I found *her,* on a rainy night perfect as if sent out from the mythic source of all rainy nights.

It all started when, drunk at home, I knocked over a lamp. No damage to the lamp, but the bulb had shattered and I was out of extras. Luckily, the K-Mart was only a short sprint away—how easy life could be once quality and beauty were sacrificed to convenience! As I made my way across the garish agora, my hair lank and plastered to my forehead, she stamped past me in tight pants and jacket, stuffing a hot dog into her mouth, her eyes fixed on the distance, contemptuous, defiant. How many women with that same inscrutable look (but minus the hot dog) had I stared at on subways and never dared to approach? But this time something, maybe a sodden resignation to Fate, made me brave. This time, I would say something! But something that would confound her, confuse her (and hopefully reveal her low mind to her—female vulgarians need a lesson like that). Dubious manhood be damned! And so, with breath suspended like a feather on the air of failure, I uttered:

"Excuse me, but you seem to be hatching an alien *doppelgänger*. Oh, I'm sorry—that's your head!"

To my utter shock she stopped, turned, fixed me with her dark, suspiring eyes and...laughed! Had she actually understood? If not, she was at least playing it right, her head cocked sweetly to the side, the planes of her face reflecting the fluorescence in a way that conveyed a feeling of Alexandrine jalousies at evening. Or the daytime moon at high noon. Or maybe the frustrations of small town auto repair. Or maybe a haunted landscape of naked suburbanites smearing human waste on holy statues. My refined mind, as you can see, was reeling. And in that reeling my initiation into the Mysteries began.

What happened that night? A whirlwind of things. I remember teeth, a flushed feeling, and cheeks suffused with moonlight. The next day, still reeling, I cancelled class and ventured to collect her at the address she'd given me, which turned out to be an abandoned, half-collapsed American Can warehouse in the used car district—not what I'd expected (five-floor walk-up off a wide, dull boulevard, packed with squalling kids and sprawling grandparents). In the fashion of people of her station, I yelled up for her—no doorbell. She breezed to the door smiling and flinging a long scarf across her shoulders—also not what I'd expected: the trademark look of the Bryn Mawr mafia? No, not her! Glowing, she smelled of tuberose, and I pulled out all the stops: took her to sample freshly-made patés in the back room café of an otherwise disregarded bakery; for mussels and butter, *gratis*, at the Spanish-style bar of a swanky old place sequestered high above downtown where my favorite wizened waiter brought me my usual (which impressed her more than anything that day, I think); and finally, at her request, to slobber down tacos at her favorite ramshackle joint in back of the factories. I learned that she was actually educated, and had in fact finished college, although her choice of college communicated class status alas. But to her credit her style of dress reflected an innate, intelligent embrace of fashion's temporary zeitgeist: a tight white t-shirt with black satin pants, Beatle boots (or what looked like), and of course that anomalous scarf. Her eyebrows were unplucked. She wasn't wearing rouge. She didn't need to; her complexion was clear, smooth. In fact, I became a bit obsessed with the planes of her face, and how her beauty imparted a deeper elegance to the elegant places we visited that day.

She continually surprised me, as we got to know each other over time. But at the same time, her pretentiousness started to grate: sweeping into a room, shaking Florida water onto her hand, she'd declaim some discovery concerning "text modules" (whatever that was); daubing her face and neck with white cream from a flat blue jar she'd mutter something about…something. Her favorite gesture seemed to be waving a cigarette around her head, gleeful eyes raised, and making some grand statement about…oh, who knew (her quotes were always erroneous, but I never corrected her; after all, I wanted to sleep with her). Even the placement of objects on her dresser was designed to further the image of artistic integrity and inquiry that she was attempting to project: an Art Deco gold compact resting atop a first edition of Reisling's *Faith and Fear* (had she actually read it? I certainly hadn't); Egyptian "depilatories" (I suspected they were just drugstore cold creams) in green glass jars; and this, scribbled in lipstick on her mirror:

What I want. What I want now. What I want to devour. I'm just a little black stone, tiny little cold stone. You don't notice me, at least not right away. You may think I don't feel, because I don't say. Because I just wait. But don't be fooled. I'm watching and waiting. For you. For the right moment to destroy you. And create you anew.

Her laughable lines were as empty as the moments she felt they occupied and defined. She was a self-defined "master of moments." She had done a study: every day, every hour, every second, had its own angel. For instance, for the first twelve hours of Sunday it was Michael, Anael, Raphael, Gabriel, Cassiel, Sachiel, Samael, Michael, Anael, Raphael, Gabriel, Cassiel. And so on, in a slightly different order, for the subsequent twelve hours. And each angel embodied some emotional idea. Once, when we were in bed and watching *Columbo* she suddenly announced, "Oh—we've switched to Raphael. Can you feel it?" There were also angels of the four seasons, angels of the altitudes, angels who ruled the twenty-eight mansions of the moon, the watchers, the sixty-four angelic wardens of the seven celestial halls, and seventy amulet angels invoked at time of childbirth. She used the information to ponder her place and role in the harmony of the spheres, which seemingly shifted from moment to moment. And oh, those moments: the changes, the transformations, the little invisible victories and defeats in the arrivals and departures of thoughts...maddening intricacies! Even the slight shift of light when walking through automatic doors into a department store revealed something of Eternity to her.

I soon accepted that she occupied a realm where profound gifts and fatal flaws held sway, a place where herculean strength is demanded and only the strong survive. To merely appease the weakness one hated in oneself was not enough because it would just grow into something else, something worse. It became clear to me that she believed it was necessary to feed one's weaknesses to someone else and then devour the person because that way you were also taking into yourself what was good as well—in essence, turning every good and bad thing into one's own sustenance, thus transcending dualities.

By late September we were sleeping together. Sex with her was not what I'd guessed it would be—a roil in realms of invictive (and thus instructive) pleasure. It was less a descent into her delicious flesh than me feeling like I was staring down the length of a long industrial corridor at a pathetically decorated Christmas tree. But soon after that our denouement began, at her hands, and as expected. It didn't mean much to me. She was inconsequential. It was the experience I was interested in. I was outside pain because this was my experiment, my project.

She "achieved" my destruction in four stages. First stage: every argument was made to seem like it emanated from me, from my failure to perform according to her tastes and needs. Mundane stuff: she didn't like my loafers, and the way my feet turned out and scuffed the wooden floors of sales basements in old department stores; she hated the cashew chicken I cooked

187

in the wok; she made fun of the PBS shows I watched. It was cute at first, but then I noticed that I was actually beginning to doubt myself. And then the doubts piled up, so that just getting dressed to meet her became a theatre of pain. I couldn't tell how I felt after awhile—did I even want to be with her? I feared the "with her" as much as the "without her." As a reaction to that, I began to derive comfort from my own kitchen utensils, those serene sentries of a solitary weekend. I was surrounded by the frumpy things that defined me, and they demarcated a blessed hour without emotion. I suppose I could've used the pain as a way of revelation, my response instructing me in my own mediocrity and its remedy, but then the subsequent moment would bring another revelation: the beauty of the utensils could not replace the fact that she'd been sleeping with some admirer "out of necessity." Oh yeah, believe it: she was sleeping around, and I accepted it! (The precedent for my attraction to women given to creating disturbing situations was set long ago, when I witnessed my young female cousin's frenzied sex with a slow-witted farmhand atop corn husks.) And that led to the second stage of her campaign: describing her triumphs to me.

"So-and-so's got a rich family. They support him and he throws the extra dough my way. But it don't come easy, honey—I gotta get down on my fuckin' *knees*!"

"You'd be shocked to see what he brings to the party. You'd never let any girl see your tiny little penis again! *Shiiit*, I should be paying *him*!"

"I told him like I told you: I sleep with people out of necessity because I need money. Living is expensive for the disenfranchised—something you'll never know anything about. You have a position. And you look down on me from the great distance that your *position* grants you, and you figure

I'm going to clubs all the time, or parties, but sometimes I just hang out by the Tastee-Freez. You can always find a bunch of guys showin' their money around. That's where I met...Tsk! Check it out, I almost just told you one of my secrets! Just forget I mentioned the Tastee-Freez, okay? Don't come and rescue me, okay?"

Soon we were at stage three: revealing the base knowledge from which all thoughts about her had to come, and the only valid perspective from which she could be judged: she'd been violated by her childhood. Stories of blows delivered to her head behind the shed by some fake cowboy boyfriend of her mother's, and then having to watch while the fake cowboy fucked her mother in the tub, then having to pee in his hand while the mother watched, blah blah blah...And then I was made to wait, sometimes days, for those moments when she could leave it all behind and just *be*, for me. Usually it would come after a bitter fight, the ensuing sex, and then the long palaver about growing up in the backroom of the hillbilly bar, making a bed in the beer boxes, and then breaking away and maintaining the exhilarating free-fall of life in orbit through sleeping with people "out of necessity." All the while she'd speak in a deep pretentious tone, as if she were speaking against a red velvet backdrop:

"I never knew my real father. My mother was an Andalusian gypsy by way of Mexico. She met my father while working as a 'hostess' in an underworld club. She had no experience with real dating, real love, and so she couldn't see that he was really the *one*. Then she dumped him and took up with a string of men who abused her and then abused me and she was complicit in it. My memories of her are framed by the smell of cheap perfume and cooking grease filtering into the backroom of the hillbilly bar where she worked night and day as a waitress. She occupied a world of innuendo and suggestion, vicious machinations and outright lies where the

189

enemy was always just beyond her vengeance, hiding and seeking, utilizing seemingly endless snares. No one could be trusted—*especially* one's family. I can't blame her, really, despite what she did to me. I mean, she just didn't realize…"

She stored those memories up to buttress her sadness with a vision of revenge, her crepuscular voice whispering memories of humiliations and ill-gained satisfactions, the wash of background into foreground, the shrinking depth of field…Was any of it true? Who knew. By then she'd be lying back on the bed, a glint of streetlight from the little window shrinking down to a refracted apple in her right eye. We'd both be exhausted. And so we'd sleep, wasting the next day and sometimes part of the next week, on that mossy mattress. Then came the languor with which we'd awaken, bathe, order more liquor. Then a brilliant sunset would come, brighter than the light of noon—a sign that The Angel of Illumination had finally arrived. And so we'd rouse ourselves and throw open the door to the roof; the sudden flight of white pigeons, also dazed by that hour least easy to deal with, dazzled us.

A whole month passed that way once. Then it seemed to me that all of existence became stilted toward those long moments, the times in between being recovery from the last, and preparation for the next. That's when I learned I could ready her: by nourishing and cultivating her soul, already rich with sickness, toward divulging its secrets to me, for my own purposes. I would stir up both battle and resolution, at the expense of my own self-confidence, just to break her. I matched the stages of her destruction with stages of re-creation. I got a purchase on her shallowness by bringing up something sure to infuriate her: "Um, about that new poem you showed me, the one that goes, *'Everything I ever held dear is gone…I am nothing, and so I am innocence, destroyed and created anew…I will never go back to the old ways again…I thank you,'* "blah, blah, blah…I'm sorry, but do you really think you have the proper background to be attempting to work that field of inquiry? I mean, it's easy to see from the books you read that there are gaps in your education…"

That instigated the initial battle. Her answer: "Oh yeah? Well, maybe I should lick toilet floors for a year so I can work my way up—*in your estimation*—to a proper field of inquiry, whatever the hell that's supposed to mean. I don't think you even know what it means. Gaps in my education…fuck you! You know, I don't need you; there are other talents around! You don't have enough money anyway!"

Her voice like sandpaper scraping my brainpans. But I knew now that in a day or two I'd feel the predictable effects of her displeasure: she'd hang up on me when I called, letters would go unanswered, messages sent through mutual friends would be ignored, etc. Then, the mutual friends through whom I'd sent messages were no longer my friends: she'd close ranks to exclude me, freeze me out. But I just laughed as I saw this happening.

(However, as time wore on, the efficacy of the *imagined effects* of her anger was as destructive as ever: had she managed to fuck her way into my school and was she *at that moment* meeting with my dean over martinis? Did she connect with a colleague via sex and was she *at that moment* poisoning his mind? They were weak people, those rum-dums of academe, and a person like her could easily worm her way…ooh, that fiend! I could just see her, eating dinner with the dean, or the chair, or whoever, cocking her head back on her shoulder and laughing in that Valentine's Day way, so free, then opening her eyes wide, real innocent-like, crooning her concern about my instability over her plate of seafood like a eunuch crooning over another eunuch's jewelry: *"nooo, I'm sooo worried about him, I've knooown him a long time and I think he's coming ungloooed…"*

That maddening panorama of possibilities. I'd wake up in the morning and remain shivering in bed all day, my panic assuming a progression of different forms with the day's progression of moments. Every five seconds I seemed to receive from the ether another image, and I became exhausted by the streaming, like a film continuously looping. It was as if my punishment was to experience viscerally the knowlege that I would never be able to completely rid my system of her. Then, finally, I realized: this was stage four!)

I had allowed myself to drown. Which was interesting, but I had to move on. And so I surfaced, and drove everything toward my own satisfaction: when we had the inevitable "summit meeting" at some hole-in-the-wall Indian restaurant, I blindsided her with a brilliantly written letter ending our relationship. Suddenly her eyes got wet and her breath smelled like a church and she appeared as her true self, tawdry as the bad wood-paneling behind her. She never really wanted separation; she needed the classic, cliché dynamic of predator and prey to be maintained because she maintained her connections through tension, and the tension through pain. But now I was finally about to mine that rich, sick vein for my own purposes, my final triumph over her, in the world she had no control over—the world of intellect. So with her still sobbing we cabbed it back home and there, after sex, the sign of my triumph appeared: her pretentious drone:

"...back when I wanted to become a nun because I was in love with Jesus..."

Oh, brother. But she didn't know I'd turned a tape recorder on! She didn't know I was taking notes, building a narrative, constructing a character around her adventures! My stealing of her story and making it my own would be my final triumph. Was that wrong of me? Maybe, but let's be honest: she didn't know her own worth, didn't know how to use the opportunities existence consistently presented to fuel her so-called "art." Again, like I said, she was no poet. She was just stuck in the past, misled by echoes. For her, her life was like a favorite book she'd read over and over but could never remember, and which would become my project to capture. Language—written language, where my genius resided—was the only medium adequately unstable enough to capture her. Music's not like that—too much like math—and painting's too static. Language, and language alone, was for her, and so I'd use her own improperly wielded medium against her. She deserved it, for demeaning language. For demeaning *me*.

So I removed myself from her and her influence (stopped calling, stopped answering calls—oh, I was such a cad!) and realigned myself with the academic arena. I freshened contacts with those eunuchs and bluestockings who'd deified me in the first place. They were mighty glad to have me back, and eager to know where I'd been for so long and why I'd been there. I explained I'd embarked on a systematic derangement of the senses for the sake of art, and would soon produce a *magnum opus* that would make my name a household word—beyond the households of the quad! Ah, I was back at home...

And then, finally, as expected, she began pursuing me! And I just couldn't shake her! The more I ran from her, the quicker she'd appear. I fled from one milieu to another. As soon as I'd ingratiate myself with one group, there she'd be, at their local bar, fresh meat for them to fête. The more I tried to rid myself of her, the quicker she'd assume top cat status. If I found some loser poetry group that met monthly at the library to discuss their odes to halitosis, a week later she'd show up there, a featured reader, adored and simpered over as if they'd known her forever. I knew she'd mimic my moves, but how did she mimic them so quickly? Was she stalking me?

Did she have detectives trailing me? She had, in fact, access to "lots of money," from all her "sleeping with people out of necessity"—hell, she had more assets than me! However she managed it, the starry magnitude of her anger radiated out in all directions, penetrating the fleshiest of bodies to find me. It was a marvel, really, because now that she loved me I didn't give a rat's ass about her. I had just what I wanted: true psychic distance from her, in the service of story. Everything was ready for my final conquest.

Her desperation, her beast of burden routine, was a beautiful thing to see. Her once-lovely and delicate porcelain back was now as broad and strong as a horse's, broad enough to bear the baggage of her bad karma. But I wasn't through with her; the vindication was coming. I decided I needed travel. Didn't Rimbaud say that travel was the key? (And charity. Okay, so I'd let her down easy: she'd learn of my leaving from my answering machine.) Of course my colleagues were baffled and saddened: I'd just returned to them, and now I was ready to flee them again? How could it be? Was this a coda to my *dérèglement des tous les sens*? Well, yes, I said; how did you know? Of course this made me the most admired man on campus, as I was the only one bucking responsibilities to run down a dream. My superiors were seeing themselves as the slaves they were; my inferiors were inspired: I was the hero of my own imagination—and theirs. My idiot chair was in tears, I swear.

In a year of travel I did no writing, but had faith that language would surely return. At least I'd been free of her. Or so I thought: there were times when I swore I saw her trailing me, in various disguises: carrying on her head a wet earthenware jar, or a bundle of sticks, or a Selectric typewriter. Once she was a leper in tatters, prostrate at the side of a busy intersection; another time a woman with bratty children boarding a train. I had vivid thoughts that she had

194

somehow entered whatever country I happened to be in for cultural purposes and was at the moment the toast of some artistic circle, and her project was to trail me and write about my movements—a documentary of a sad, failed man bent on escape from a phantom of his own making.

And at the end of that year I realized that I'd never for one day not thought about her. In fact, I was more in love with her than ever, and our love had the possibility of being forever. Oh, I was elated at the prospect of regaining her. We would meet again in the K-Mart Café. I sent her a letter, suggesting same...

Returning to the campus I was greeted by my chair with a slap on the back and a sarcastic congratulations: it was certainly brilliant, it would make my name, but not in the way I wanted my name to be made, har-har! What was he talking about? He steered me into his office, told me to sit, offered me a drink—"You'll need it"—then proferred a magazine that I'd been regularly publishing in for years. He opened it and pointed to a story bearing my name:

"*And all along I had thought* she *was* my *project.*"

"And who was I? In the beginning, a eunuch among eunuchs—an academic."

It was quite brave, he crowed, especially the descriptions of my colleagues. But I hadn't written it, I assured him. He laughed again, and I read on, in a state of disbelief. Yes, there was my inimitable voice, syntax, and rhythm, communicating the most intimate details of my time with *her*. Absolutely amazing—the stamina and discipline required of this *doppelgänger* author: my history, the events of the recent past...*this very scene that both you and I are reading!*

195

And now, as I come to this ending, as I read these final lines that you, reader, are also reading, my mind is reeling. How could this be? The only person who had access to this story was...*her*!

BLADDER BUSTER

by Jeremy Sigler

In order for everything to run on schedule, it was important for me to be numbed seconds before the surgeon arrived. The anesthesiologist had already given me a shot in the spine, left, and come back to see if I was ready. Every few minutes he would touch my knee and ask if I could feel it. "Yes," I said repeatedly, "I can feel it"—though I was beginning to think that I should lie to him.

In my pre-operative anxiety, it had occurred to me that I might be causing a hospital traffic jam. Maybe I was already costing insurance companies millions. Or, I panicked, if nothing else, maybe I was causing some person in need of a doctor somewhere in the world to get rerouted to an HMO automated phone service. Perhaps, I thought, I should just brave the surgery without total anesthesia.

The anesthesiologist left the room once more and returned shortly. Again he put his hand to my knee and softly tapped it. *Yes, I could feel it.* And I was also beginning to feel more accountable for my unfortunate condition, as the operating room started filling up with surgical assistants and medical students, who were intimidating in their identical light blue scrubs and masks. I imagined, with a growing sense of guilt, that if the internationally acclaimed surgeon were made to wait, his schedule would become backlogged for the rest of the month.

Knowing that his timing was now off, the anesthesiologist decided to drug me up even more, rather than wait any longer to see if the drugs he had already administered were going to kick in. With a second sting to my lower back, he hit me with a double dose. The fact that I could have become paralyzed, gone into cardiac arrest, or fallen into a coma, didn't seem to concern him. Given the value of the surgeon's time, it was obviously worth the risk.

The anesthesiologist left the room yet again, giving me a third chance to go numb, while two nurses began to prepare my knee. I could feel everything they were doing as they applied a creamy lather to my leg and shaved me. I felt them lay a light sheet over my tingling leg, centering it so that my kneecap protruded through a small cut-away circle. I felt a chill on my kneecap as the nurses used sponge-brushes to coat my kneecap with a mysterious syrupy liquid.

A few minutes later, back came the anesthesiologist. Once more, he asked if I could feel it, as he gently massaged the skin on my kneecap. "Yep," I said, more ambivalently. "I still can."

"You're sure?"

"Yes, I'm sure," I answered in a monotone.

"Can you feel this?" he asked, pinching my knee harder.

"Ouch." I guessed he had forgotten that was the knee I had just injured.

The anesthesiologist looked at me in disbelief. Was I the type who could drink a case of beer and still talk without a slur? We both knew he had shot me with enough drugs to deep-freeze me for the next five years. So why was my leg still sober? I began to wonder if he had missed the spinal cord altogether. But was it possible that he could botch the spinal twice?

Whatever had gone wrong, there wasn't any more time to hypothesize, because at that moment the double door swung open and in came the famous, dopey looking, wall-eyed surgeon. He was the kind of guy who had learned to do one thing in life, and to do it well. He wasn't simply an orthopedic surgeon, nor would he have been referred to as a simple knee specialist. Dr. Voekler was an all-out, self-proclaimed "meniscus man." Every day for the past thirty years his job had been to cut, sew, and sometimes remove a single two-inch piece of cartilage from the human knee joint. That was all he did.

The surgeon gave me a wink, and wished me well. I stammered back a reply, but before I could address the fact that my knee was still sensitive to the touch, the anesthesiologist had snuck up behind me and placed a soft cloth over my nose and mouth. "Breathe in," he whispered in my ear—and I instantly felt my eyelids sag and my head tilt back. What was happening? Was I being kidnapped? It didn't seem right to get mugged on the operating table, yet it didn't seem to matter so much at the moment. For suddenly the operating room had the warmest velvety glow, and I could tell I was in good hands. I couldn't see a thing below my chin, but that didn't seem to bother me either.

I relaxed and enjoyed feeling my cotton hospital gown being lifted up over my baby-shaven knee and past my waist. I supposed it was necessary to pull back my garment in order to get the extra, messy fabric out of the surgeon's way. Though I felt embarrassed for a moment, fearing that I might have an erection down there in full view, I reminded myself that the doctor and nurses, and even the med school students who were my age, were surely accustomed to involuntary patient arousals. Just to be on the safe side though, I decided to give myself a quick check. I lifted my heavy skull from the padded table enough to glance out past my shoulder. I couldn't raise my head high enough to see over my chest, but I was suddenly able to see the television monitor to my right.

And there they stood—a little gathering of people wearing scrubs, all peering gleefully into the monitor's shifting blue glow. It reminded me of an Academy Awards party I had recently attended. Earlier, one of the nurses had mentioned that the monitor would be used to televise a close-up interior view of my knee's herniated meniscus cartilage, which would make it possible for the surgeon to view his microscopic handiwork on the enlarged screen via a tiny fiber-optic lens. I felt proud to be on display to this friendly group of voyeurs, all of whom, seemed at the moment to be entirely entertained. I looked more closely. There was the surgeon, guru-like, right in the center of the adoring group! I was doing great.

I strained harder to get a glimpse of the monitor, and finally I was able to lift my head enough to get a view. To my surprise the image was not of my knee's interior. Upon the screen, I saw what appeared to be amateur video of a deer scurrying around the interior of a thick forest. "See it?" Dr. Voekler shouted. "Right there... THERE. That was the deer we were tracking." To my silent amazement, I intuited that everyone was actually watching Dr. Voekler's weekend hunting trip—as he held the crowd's attention with a sort of play-by-play!

Bambi, I thought, happily. That deer looks like Bambi. I watched the vulnerable creature dart about from tree to tree, innocently looking for a way to slip into the instant camouflage of the forest as the group waited for me to go numb...or was I in mid-operation already? Was it possible that Bambi was actually my meniscus?

• • •

When I awakened in the recovery room there was a cheerful staff of people on hand to care for me. I was hooked

200

to an IV, and my hospital gown lay flat across my lap—no
pitched tent, thank god. The nurse came over to check on me
and told me that the operation had gone well. Dr. Voekler, she
informed me, thought I'd be walking on my own in a week. I
wasn't to worry about the fact that I had no feeling below my
chest. I had gotten a rather large dose of Spinal, and it would
take a little longer than usual for it to wear off. As she told me
this, she removed my empty IV bag and hooked on another
full one. She explained that my bladder should be full, having
taken an entire bag already, and that as soon as I was ready to
relieve myself, I should feel free to crutch over to the men's
room. Once I released my bladder, I would be free to leave
the hospital. However, until then, it was regulation that I stick
around the recovery room.

After lying in bed for a few minutes, I realized the ball was
in my court. So I awkwardly threw my numb legs over the
edge of the bed and grabbed the crutches. I felt my hospital
gown part slightly, and had the by-now familiar sensation that
my penis had jumped out. But this semi-erotic fantasy was
immediately interrupted by reality. I was putting pressure on
a freshly probed, diced, and sewn meniscus, propped up on a
slippery floor, on crutches which I didn't know how to use, in
a robe half-open, in front of a room of strangers. It occurred
to me that if I fell, I would be in worse shape than I'd been in
before the injury.

So I wobbled with the best coordination I could muster
towards the bathroom across the room. Once there, I stood
in front of the toilet and pulled my gown open. Looking
down at my penis, I whispered to myself, "There it is... but
I can't feel it." I then looked straight ahead at the tiled wall.
"It's OK," I reassured myself, "the piss will come on its own.
I'm sure it will." When nothing happened, I reminded myself
that such delays were very common. Then I remembered Dr.

201

Voekler's Bambi video. Did that really happen? I got caught up in the erotic memory, until, after about five minutes of waiting without a drop of pee, I just gave up. Slightly dizzy, I trekked back across the recovery room to my bed, pulled myself under the sheets, and promptly went to sleep.

When I awoke the second time, there was a small wet mark forming on my blue gown right around where the tip of my penis would be. Although, surprisingly, feeling disconnected from the lower half of my body made it tough to pinpoint the spot of origin. I understood that the slowly expanding wet mark was a sign that I was, indeed, peeing. In seconds, the stain reached five inches in diameter. I reached for my crutches and got myself up into a standing position.

Suddenly I was in motion—as if paddling fast in an inflatable raft—my hospital gown hanging down in front of me. The stain had grown to an 18-inch, slightly irregular oval with a small tinkle arching out from its wet center. I was pissing on, and through, my gown, and all over the floor—and I still *wasn't able to feel it.*

My pissing muscles were still anesthetized, which meant that I didn't have the ability to flex my bladder. Instead the piss leaked out on its own, like a water fountain that continues to run. When I finally reached the bathroom, I simply aimed my penis at the toilet. It wasn't a strong explosive geyser of urination. It wasn't the kind of piss that makes a loud noise in the water and proves one's masculinity by pitch and octave. It was just a steady, mechanical, un-filling of the bladder. It went on, and on, and on. After several minutes I finally had an inspiration. I pushed my stomach with my hand, and sure enough, the stream got harder at my penis. I kept clutching and squeezing. I was a piss-filled bagpipe with a deer in my knee. And I was just beginning to feel it.

MY PORTRAIT

by Jill Magi

"Come over, I'll make you some spaghetti." I had no money when I got back from Mexico. "It would be an honor for me to paint your picture." For hours, you're looking, finding the blue in the skin under my eyes, and while I was doing nothing, nothing but sitting, I had to look at you. "Include me in your prayers, Edward." You wore a red flannel shirt and blue jeans every day. You shaved your head. "The eyes are the hardest, most important." "The eyes, the eyes," you would softly repeat. I was begging for you to take off my clothes, without saying anything. You pulled up a chair, used it to lean on, to pray. I still think I see you on street corners. You had candles, a crucifix, the rosary in your fingers. "I'll pay you for every hour you pose. That's how you can pay me back." In October after that summer I went to Mexico I couldn't make rent. You wrote me a check for two hundred dollars. "It's nothing, Jill Magi." You would say my full name. We had broken up four months earlier. I had brown boots that year and wore them in every season. "Wear your green sweater. Bring over the red one just in case I need you to change." We were not supposed to make love but it was too late for me to go home. The warmth in your bed, there, next to you after sitting for my portrait, it was impossible not to embrace. I teased you: "You've got yourself an apartment in Bushwick; the realtor told you Williamsburg; the boy from Edmonton gets bamboozled" and I laughed. Your basement, filled with canvases, a desk piled high with sketches, paper stiff with gesso. The charcoal let in only candlelight. "Remember Vermont?" You watched me swim. You watched me dance on the porch. That picture you snapped with my camera; my open face. But you looked concerned. You were plotting our break-up, weren't you? "Just let me hold you." Sitting for an hour, thinking, am I beautiful? I hope you have made me beautiful. We both hated *The Piano*, the movie. Our kissing was automatic on that first night. It was too late for me to go home. "You would have moved to Edmonton for me? You would have converted?" "Yes." The Lucien Freud show, we go and you are shaking your head at the paintings. "There's so much depravity, Jill Magi." "The misuse of the body, Jill Magi." Until I pay back the debt, these visits, these sittings go on. "Call in sick, Jill Magi. Stay with me today." "When you paint someone the truth is sometimes unbearable." "I'll stay, Edward." That November day we walked around the city and said good-bye at the subway. The hours ran out, the debt was paid, I never saw you again and I never saw my portrait.

ROY AND BELINDA

by Blake Radcliffe

On the shoulder of a two-lane road through the woods, there was a bar that had once been a garage. After the mechanics left it, for a few years in the seventies, it was just the stripped hulk of a building. A junk crew took down the chrome trim and sold it for smelting. They left the garage a yellow cube at the end of a stained gray concrete lot. The county sold the property at auction in 1980 and got eight thousand dollars for it. The new owner, Richard Laney, put an awning around the building. It was supposed to look like a thatched roof hut. The workers quit halfway through because their checks were always late. Finally Richard left the project undone. He couldn't change the bank's mind and that didn't really matter to him and it didn't matter to the patrons. The local bikers flocked to the pool table at the ugly oasis on the road and everybody else could go fuck themselves. Richard ran it that way until 1988, when he started blacking out. In the waiting room of the university hospital where he got the news that he was already done, that tumors had spread through his entire body, he took his only son, Roy, for a walk to the drink machine. They walked past the T.V. mounted to the wall, where it was just one short trial after the other. They split a can of fizzly orangeade, and Richard told Roy to take over the bar.

Roy sat in the swivel chair in front of the cash register. He shared his pitcher with a cackling woman in tight jeans. He thought that would be a good way to warm her up for a walk outside with him, but she wouldn't shut up. He pretended to watch a dart game. A farmhand in overalls and a pressed short-sleeved shirt asked him for a cigarette. Roy got a loose pack from behind the bar and handed it to him. "What's the matter boss." "Was working o'er yonder for Mister Henessy. Lost my job for no goddamned reason at all." "I hear you." "Not one goddamned reason." "Sumbitches." "Son of a bitch." "There oughta be a way to teach some people a lesson." "Damn straight." "Show some people you won't never take their shit." In the far corner, a twelve-year-old pool crackerjack propped his left arm on the felt to shoot. He was wearing a cast. The hard elbow made the felt crease. The trucker from California who showed up every few months with a dozen ounces of weed played him. He told the kid, "Watch not to tear it. Or I'll break your other bones." The drunk Swedish woman who could never get laid stroked the man's ass and said "Say it again about the boning."

Richard Laney died in 1993. Two months later Roy and Belinda got married at the courthouse in Charlotte. Belinda was the statewide roller skating champion in 1981. Roy'd been engaged to her five years.

Random drunk-driving checkpoints started setting up on the county limits. Then Roy spent five hundred dollars for a May Day fish-fry. They didn't do any advertising for it, though. Roy wasn't going to be bothered by making photocopies and posters. Belinda thought he would take care of it. Fourteen people showed up. Three weeks later, as they ate catfish from the giant freezer full of filets, she tried to be optimistic.

The death of his father left Roy morose, weak and easily panicked. He was too tired to go out anywhere for weeks, even to the bar. He sat around on his living room couch and let his mind drift like a fog. One night, with sudden urgency, he ran into the yard. He walked down the road to the bar and checked the air conditioners in the back. He remembered one time how he changed the freon tubes. It was like the soldiers who put their rifles together blindfolded. Only Roy didn't lift a finger and his eyes were open. He took it apart in his head and put it back together. Like solving a Rubik's cube.

He looked at the back of the building and felt invisible.

"It don't have to be this way forever," Belinda said. They were at home. She stood in front of the microwave. She picked up a can of low calorie, homestyle cooking spray and fired it at a large iron skillet on the range. The pan sizzled. She clicked the stop button on the microwave, pulled out a thawed piece of fish and threw it in the pan.

Roy sat at the table. It was a wooden picnic table from a kit. Over it, a red and white checked plastic tablecloth was spread. Grape jelly stains dotted the cover from breakfast. He twirled a drink mixer, a tiny orange plastic sword, in his fingers and scratched at the spots. "Say again?"

"We gotta get on."

Roy said nothing.

"It don't have a mortgage on it. But every month the take home gets littler."

"What do you mean to say?"

"There ain't no shame to sellin' it. We could have a plenty good life."

Roy tossed the drink mixer onto the table. "What in the hell am I supposed to do without a job?"

"We could take it easy. Buy some trailers. Be landlords. You fixed up this place into a dream castle," Belinda said.

She flipped the catfish in the pan, leaned and turned around to look at him. She lifted her eyebrow. She was talking about the three-car garage Roy added onto the house. The automatic doors glided up and down like water ballet dancers.

"How long until dinner?" he asked.

"Fifteen or twenty minutes."

He walked outside and looked around. He had also built the back porch, redone the roof and put plastic siding around the house. He came back into the kitchen and asked her how she'd like a pool.

Their last night as the owners, they had a private party for the regulars. Everyone dressed up. Roy ironed his jeans, polished his boots and buttoned his turquoise Western collar shirt to the top. They ate buffalo wings and played poker until the cards stuck together. They drank until their toes were drunk in their shitkickers. At dawn Roy and Belinda walked down the street to their house with the framed collage of fading snapshots they took in the bar.

A lawyer, an accountant, a real estate agent and a safety inspector examined the plumbing, the roof, the floor, the parking lot, the drainage ditches, the property lines and the ventilation. They walked away with a hundred and fifty thousand dollar quote.

Belinda hung the picture in their den. They hadn't decided if they wanted to buy trailers or a house to rent. They figured they'd realize which idea was better after they got through all their projects at home. He planned on putting together an above ground pool, a deep one with a six-foot wall around it. She bought three cookbooks to try out all of the recipes. They were going to have their second honeymoon, on time for their first anniversary.

"What the fuck," Roy muttered to himself. He was in his truck on the way home from buying a case of beer. He revved the engine and honked at the bar, but when one of the workers looked up, Roy kept driving. At home, he sat on the back porch and drank alone. Belinda was out somewhere. She didn't leave a note. He felt a buzz aready. The lightning bugs came out.

At the bar, workers tore down the awning and hammered together a wide platform for an elevated deck in the parking lot. They struck at the floor and ripped the linoleum off it. They dismantled the mirror taped over with cartoons behind the bar. Lit ceiling fans replaced the low hanging lamps that floated over the pool tables. Finally, the new sign came up by the side of the road. Beside a red silhouette of a palm tree were blue letters in scattered sizes that read "Tropicana."

A truck came out to their house to deliver the pool kit in a couple of crates. Roy said to leave the boxes in the back yard. They sat diagonally in the grass for weeks. He spent just about every morning watching television without following it. By the time Belinda would prod him to get to work, he'd say it was too hot to work and he'd get started tomorrow. When she called him to eat, he complained that her recipes were fancy, that he couldn't eat high class food. "Is all you cook for me now food for stuck-up bastards?" he said. "It's fettucini alfredo. It's Italian. It ain't special." "I-talian. What in the goddamned hell am I supposed to eat if all I ever get is Italian food that ain't even a goddamned pizza?" She told him to get out of the house. He had to drive out near the highway to find fried chicken and biscuits.

Roy had been drinking since noon. The heat and the constant drone of alcohol gave him a headache. When he saw the melted cheese baked brown across the top of the glass tray filled with lasagna that Belinda brought out of the oven, he said, "Jesus Christ. How many times am I gonna eat one of your experiments?"

"You kissed your mother with that mouth?" Belinda shouted.

"What? What did you just say?"

"I'll show you what you deserve," Belinda said. She put the oven mits back on and picked up the lasagna. She walked into the bathroom and shook the tray into the toilet. Steam rose into her face. She threw the rest into the bathtub. When she hit the latch to flush it, the lasagna clogged the pipes. Rosy water gushed over the rim of the seat. She picked up the plunger and walked back into the kitchen. "Here," she shouted, holding out the plunger to him. "Take this plunger and eat shit for all I care."

Roy held a watermelon and a large cutting knife. The fruit lay slashed open. He stared at her while he sucked the seeds from the pink meat. He spit them into his palm and asked, "What did you say I am supposed to do with what?"

"Nothing. Do nothing with it. That's all you're good for, anyway."

"This was all your idea, wasn't it?"

"It wasn't my idea for you to turn lazier than hell."

Roy slung the watermelon across the tablecloth. He pushed open the screen door and slammed it behind him. He crossed the yard. Then he heard her scream at him. He turned around. A piece of the watermelon landed at his feet.

Belinda'd got out a blanket she bought at the farmer's market. She got a real good price on it since it was summertime, and it was handmade. She turned on the a.c., put the fan on high, and set the temperature meter down to fifty eight. She spread the quilt out, and stroked the corners on her bed.

"Godamnit's fucking chilly." Roy burst into the bedroom.

"Tryin' out my blanket. I put the air all the way down to get warm under the blanket," Belinda held the covers up to welcome him.

"You did what?" Roy went to check the thermostat. "Fifty fucking degrees?" he yelled. "How we gonna pay the sonofabitching power bill?"

"You mean to scold me for using up too much of your hundred and fifty thousand dollars? You can kiss my ass."

At the foot of the bed, he grinned at her, plucked his boots off and crept around the side of the bed.

Roy took the edge of the quilt and started to lift it up. Belinda swatted it down.

"You're not sleeping with me you foulmouth."

"What're you mad at me for?"

"Go to hell. As long as it's out of my sight."

"You make me sick."

"You take that back, woman."

"You're afraid of your own damn self," she shouted. "It's been this way ever since… It's the thing keeping us from movin' on. You cain't give it up. It's gone kill you. You got to do something about this. You got to get rid of that place inside of you. You got to do it yourself."

He stomped out of the room barefoot.

He flicked the cooking spray nozzle. He heard the kissing sound in the dark. He flipped open his bald eagle Zippo. It went out and he had to strike the flint one more time, hold it, work the right hand and not blow out the flame but start slowly, and then a mighty shush of flame and he held it like a flaming sword that's right in his hand and swooped it down across the vents, watching how it split up and ran through the slits in the metal just like it was cutting straight through it until it caught. It smelled like eggs frying in a pan.

In the woods, he could feel the wet clay soil sucking at his feet. Red feet. He was going to cross over barefoot. He knelt down to watch what he started. It was just glowing now, and then he heard it crackle through the tap of the wet leaves. Now it was all done, and it was going down blazing. It was what he had always wanted to get done with. It was like a jail being torn apart by angels. Before he couldn't get rid of remembering. And it was her idea. Say fuck it all. When he slipped across the asphalt, his feet didn't make a sound, just the rush of the air against his clothes.

Daybreak he sat in the yard watching the haze from over the forest. It made a dark gray spot in the clouds moving across. Putting it together reflexively in the dark. Starting in the air conditioners. Vents carried it. Foil stringers. The fire was roiling inside and it took most of the building down in a half hour. Somebody drove by, then another twenty minutes later firemen begin to show up in their own cars. They finally got a truck out there, as the flames burst out of the windows. The blaze was so bright it made the sky pink.

They drove past the blackened frame. One of the walls had collapsed. They could see inside. It looked likes piles of black leaves with smoke rising out of them. They kept driving, not stopping to talk. The police were marking the place off.

At the Baptist church, the point on top of the steeple looked naked in the clearing air. Nobody was there. The pews were empty. He took her hand and they marched up the aisle together. At the foot of the altar, they sat on a red carpet. The edges were stapled to the corners of the steps. He knelt down and took her hand.

"Do you forgive me darlin'?"

She sat down on the step. "You done forgave yourself. You understand me?"

"I do," he said.

"I do, too."

She took her old skates out of the top of the closet, put new laces in she'd bought at the hardware store, and sprayed WD-40 on the wheels. At the counter of the roller skating rink, he rented a pair for himself. They were drinking Cheerwine and having smokes in the parking lot, gliding in circles in the rink, taking one another hand in hand, rotating around each other, moonwalking and winding counterclockwise.

"I want you to turn around and look at me." The six of tall boys bounced in the water.

"You're an outlaw."

A purple float slid over them. He thrashed it into the yard, where it landed standing up against the ladder into the pool.

"Look now. Can you see me now?"

EXCERPT: *MR. DYNAMITE*

by Meredith Brosnan

Well Sean I'm back at Firewaters—It's Friday around 7 in the evening though I imagine the days of the week/hours of the day don't mean much to you in your present condition—well they do to me: Maude Privette's coming home today so I'm officially no longer welcome Chez Ken—I'm still locked out of my studio—Olegarkis hasn't returned any of my calls—I had a nasty hangover all day and work was horrible: Vincent the bossman is gradually morphing into a full blown psycho— "Jarleth! JARLETH!! Did I or did I not tell you yesterday to put toner in machine number 2? I did tell you. Are you drunk? Well? Are you on drugs? Well? Welllll?"—it's all right—I shall be released… Yesterday Sean we started on a trip down Memory Lane—it was a big mistake—there's obviously nothing to be gained by raking up the past but as Magnus the Grand Inquisitor on Mastermind used to say I've begun so I'll finish: Amelia—that whole period of my life—is water under the bridge—that said I feel a FLASH BACK coming on: If this was a movie Sean there'd be a close-up of my face with the screen blurring and rippling to underwater harps and strings as we dissolve back to the early '90s a scene of domestic violence in a rundown apt. on Rivington St. starring Hurricane Martha and a cornered cowering Prendy—a scene identical in many respects to Martha's recent atomic explosion re Raptor except the Otto hiding under the bed was still a kitten—he hadn't yet swelled into the big furry football of today—Flashback Action Highlight: a black army boot connects with Jarleth's testes as the boot's owner screams:

—You son of a BITCH!! Why don't you FUCK the little cunt if you love her so much?

The answer is: I would if I could. I would if I could. I

215

would if I could if she'd let me ("let me let me let me…" a heartrending echo fading into the cold blue distance)

The little cunt = Amelia Jane Francesca Garrity (saint & martyr)

All right Sean you inquisitive spectre you twisted my arm—I'll take you back further—back to The Night It All Began back to the fateful hour when The Little Freak shot me in the groin with her poison arrow—it was a night in late September—we were drinking a huge gang of us in some downtown bar—I was in the middle of recounting some totally fabricated escapade starring me and Bono and Philo and Steve Jones from the Pistols + a ton of coke and a bevy of European supermodels hijinks and bijinks blemming round the Wicklow hills at 4 in the morning in our Porsches and Beamers—not a care in the world drunk as a lord I let my gaze stray down that long wooden table into the trap of Amelia's waiting eyes—a breeze blew out of heaven or hell or both and Prendergast found himself borne aloft by hosts of singing cherubim—a Mystic Curtain was lifted and I was allowed to glimpse the world as a glorious place full of endless possibilities—then the curtain came down the cherubs let go and I fell—down down down into Ye Deepe Darke Poole of Desyre—in other words Sean I fell in love with the little psychopath—I know I know: "little" sounds patronizing and God in Her Infinite Mercy will shrivel my bollocks to useless flaps of seaweed if I don't retract—but the fact remains she was little—only 4 foot 8—125 lbs. (9 stone to you)—even wearing 6 inch platforms and a man's overcoat she was minuscule—she had grey eyes Sean terrible amoral grey eyes and a mocking smile—it was a leer really—tiny hands like a child's tiny breasts tiny cunt full of magic doorways into secret universes not that I was ever vouchsafed more than a glimpse

oh yes it's all coming out now

PADDYSPULSINGPURPLEPENISPADDYSPULSING PURPLEPENIS

I loved her madly

I loved her madly yet she sank

down into the cold ground

Singing (all together now):

Toi qui mets dans les yeux et dans le coeur des filles
Le culte de la plaie et l'amour des guenilles

(Thou who puttest in the eyes and the heart of girls the cult of wounds and the love of rags o Satan)

I can't hear you

Fuck off so

Miss—another pint please and a shot of your best sorrow

Firesnorters—1 in the morning—yes I'm still here—you know Sean I really like this bar—it doesn't pretend to be more than what it is which is a long dark room with a low nicotine-stained tin ceiling half a doz. tables and chairs one pool table in the back and tucked away in one corner a really good jukebox—I finally got a hold of Olegarkis the absentee landlord half an hour ago—he said he was busy and he'd call me back—who knows if he will or not—meanwhile Crooklyn's favourite punk rock saloon is getting mighty crowded—some citizens just walked in with foot tall mohawks— always a cheerful sight—brings me back to 1978 and my glue sniffing days on The Old Kent Rd—a moment

ago Cindy the looney with the dog popped her head in—I
hid behind my *Daily News*—when I peeped out she'd gone
thank god—no sign of the woof woof—I'm sitting by myself
in a dark corner—I'm pretty drunk Sean—I've had 4 pints of
India Pale Ale plus a Guinness 3 Irish whiskeys and a pint of
the house's special bounce-me-off-the wall supercider—Be
prepared: I'm in a grey velour leisure suit Michel LeGrand
Windmills of Your Mind Scott Walker Walk On By sort of
mood—it's Amelia—I haven't talked to anyone about her for
ages—when I used to vent to Privette he always said the same
thing: she's crazy—she'll mess you up—break off all contact
immediately—thanks Ken you're a bottomless pool of karmic
wisdom—cue Scott crooning Windmills:

when she stole your movie camera were you suddenly aware
that the autumn leaves were turning to the colour of her hair?

The colour of her hair!—that was a sore point later on—
but first I want to tell you about Our First Date: the first time
Amelia and Prendy walked out together—it was the 16th of
June 1904 no it wasn't—we went to see *Touch of Evil* at the
Film Forum—we bought popcorn and Raisinets and snuck
in a hip flask of rum—we jeered at the trailers—we laughed
out loud at Charleton Heston's outlandish appearance (it's
Black Moses!)—I tried to cop a feel during the Janet Leigh
and the bikers orgy scene but Amelia grabbed my paw and bit
it—she drew blood too—oh we were both in high spirits that
night!—I was deliriously happy Sean incredibly happy—I'd
dreamt of being alone with her for months and months—I
kept stealing reverent glances at the side of her face—her
haunting profile—yes I was happy happy happy but at the
same time incredibly nervous—Martha was out of town—she
was up in the Catskills at a teachers' conference—my rational
mind kept saying "You have nothing to fear" but the rest of
me wasn't buying it—I was waiting for my wife to appear—

to burst into the theatre and come stomping down the aisle in her black army boots and trap the pair of us in the beam of a powerful flashlight or—my god—a far more plausible scenario—what if someone in the audience recognized me!?—I hadn't thought of that—so I sat in the dark seesawing between the agony and the ecstasy—at last bad cop Hank Quinlan's great bloated bulk toppled backwards into the filthy water—pull back—music—The End—lights up—so soon?—No no no I want to stay here in dark with Amelia and watch *Touch of Evil* over and over and over again till judgment break excellent and fair—I knew Martha was waiting for us out in the lobby—or if not Martha-in-person then a stand-in-for-Martha one of her crunchy granola teacher pals—born informers every man jack o' them—oh yes they'd be only too delighted to report back that they spotted Prendergast out and about with a pint-sized sex bomb dressed in thigh high red leather boots and a fake fur jacket—I was fool enough to confide these fears to Amelia—she laughed nastily and called me a coward and headed for the exit—at the door she turned around and shouted

—fucking come on Prendergast I'm thirsty!

Torn between desire and trepidation I sidled towards her crabwise up the aisle—she stood there leering at me and mockingly grinding her hips like a burlesque dancer—which of course she was—I just had time to pull my scarf up and pull my hat down as she pulled me out into the lobby's glare—we repaired to a bar on Houston St. and drank some whiskey and later back at her place we did the business—or about 41 % of it—I woke up during the night and heard her crying out in the living room—of course thinking back it's easy to see I should have gone out to her and comforted her but the fact is I didn't—it's too late baby it's too late now and the rest is autumn leaves—autumn leaves and auburn hair—Time out: a moment ago a grinning mohawk dropped a shot glass of schnapps into my pint of cider—he claims to know me—says that 6 years ago I was his AD on a music video!!??—it's clearly a case of mistaken identity but I've accepted Jimbo or Jumbo's invitation to join him and his mates up at the bar for a round of submarine shots—it looks like I'm in for a night of serious networking Sean so slan leat agus adios amigo for the mo

Sunday Morning—Well Sean I finally got in—The 2 padlocks turned out to be the result of a silly misunderstanding: because I haven't been using it much lately Olegarkis assumed I'd let the place go—he claims I owe him 8 months back rent!!!—at our meeting yesterday I disputed this hotly but in the end to avoid aggro I promised to pay him the arrears ASAP—of course I didn't let on about my present homeless crisis—"OK Jar-a-leet. I give you da keys when you give me da money"—Easier said than done Christos my old flower—but I didn't say that—Instead we shook hands and I tiptoed back here at 2 o'clock this morning armed with my bag of tools jimmied off the locks no problem they don't call me Jock Genet for nothing—so I'm presently curled up in my sleeping bag on the hard slightly damp concrete floor wearing fisherman's socks and my old Peruvian shepherd's cap reading John Buchan by a combination of dawn's early light and flashlight—There's an oil heater here that wasn't here before—no idea where it came from but never look a gift horse etc.—Of course Olegarkis and his brothers won't be happy if they find out I'm squatting in their space—By the way I should point out that this isn't one of your chic sundrenched hardwood floor 150000+ sq. ft. former factory spaces so popular with the gentleman carpenter class— no this is basically a garage that a candy wholesaler used to keep his van in—2 years ago he went bust and Olegarkis rented it to me—from the outside everything looks the same—except now those are MY padlocks—I actually don't think there's going to be a problem staying here—Olegarkis lives in Queens and he's normally never out this way—If I watch my exits and entrances I think I'll be OK for a week or 2 maybe longer—In the meantime all my worldly possessions are still with Ken on E. 5th (Maude's hopping mad about it)—Prendy's future is tray uncertain: a month from now I might be living in Jersey City or Yonkers or—a horrible thought—Staten Island!!!—You never know—You never did know—which brings to mind My Favourite Poem of All Time:

Down life's random path we all
stumble as strangers...
You never know though...
You never did know...
You never will know...
So what though...

One day, one day though
whoop whoop, boom-boom,
1-2-3 yer number's up...

...straight back to the House of
Strangers, for your meeting with the
Big Guy with the Beard...
the original God though...
then you sit back and listen to the
wind forever...

brr brr whoo whoo
nothing but wind, forever

Nice isn't it? One night at the open mike on Stanton St. I used to frequent this gorgeous drunk-off-her-ass Middle Eastern woman was handing out flyers with that poem printed on it—the poet is George Rubin—he was an old New York guy who died in '87—the flyer said his friends and neighbours were collecting

221

money to put up a plaque in his memory outside the house on East 6th Street where he lived—well Sean I walked down 6th the other day and there's no plaque—I've noticed dogooder schemes like that have a tendency to start strong and then fizzle out—and of course one has to wonder: when the time comes who's going to shake the can and put up a plaque for Trendy Prendy?

Well Sean so far so good—This is my 3rd night here—The Brothers Oleg. are none the wiser—I popped over to Ken's earlier to pick up a few odds and ends—I was just walking out when Maude appeared out of nowhere and pounced on me: when was I going to take the rest of my stuff? This isn't a storage space I feel that you're taking unfair advantage of us etc.—Chill out Elvira (Maude looks like Elvira Mistress of the Dark but without the bust)—Anyway I danced around her and escaped with my CDs my tapes my boom box and my headphones—I was experiencing terrible cravings for my Scott Walker my Léo Ferré *Boy George's Greatest Hits* Duke & Trane etc.—seeing as I'm going to be here for a while I'm trying to make the studio feel like home: to this end I've hung my photo of the Fleischer Brothers beside the little round window (you DO know the Fleischer Brothers = Betty Boop - Popeye - Koko - *Gulliver's Travels*)—There they are Max and Dave standing outside 1600 Broadway c. 1924 in their shirt sleeves Max grinning Dave not—I must say it's great to have the little heater—of course this being originally a garage there IS a lingering petrol smell not that I'm bothered by it I actually like it—The main thing is I'm having no trouble slipping in and out—I'm on a very quiet side street and there's never anybody around—Had a bit of a close shave the other night or it might have been nothing: c. 3 in the morning I heard somebody poking around outside—I held my breath—after a few minutes they went away—One of the definite pros about living here is that I seem to have given Raptor the slip—She tracked me down to Ken's of course—I hid in the toilet while he talked to her out in the hall—Last week she turned up twice at the copy shop but I saw her coming both times and ducked—I got one of the zombies to tell her I out sick while I hid behind the big Minolta in the back—Let me state in no uncertain terms that I have come to my senses at last: I intend to erase Raptor from my life once and for all—The woman has been nothing but trouble from day one—in other words she's all yours Seamus—"Begorrah! At last!" cried Seamus O'Shem the Leprechaun Detective and Part-Time Pimp. And in the wink of an eye sure hadn't the cunning little man unzipped his emerald green tights and pulled them down: "Behold o mortal dame my candy cane of power!" "Oooooh!" gasped Gwyneth and promptly swooned (To Be Continued)

I'm sure you'll be pleased to hear Sean I took the bull by the horns this morning and called your former employer Aiden McGrath (please note that just because you're dead I don't jump to the conclusion that you know everything!)—anyway I asked him straight out about a cash advance—would he front me a couple of grand?—He told me straight he wouldn't—Fair enough—At least it was a manly exchange and none of that namby pamby legal fuckology—no offense Sean—I asked if there was any chance of getting my inheritance before February—Who said February? he said—Mr. Reynolds I said—Oh no says he I'm afraid Mr. Reynolds was being unduly optimistic. I should think we're looking at April at the earliest and then he launched into some bullshit explanation—I couldn't listen to him—I hung up—Which showed amazing restraint because what I really wanted to do was extrude myself along 3 thousand miles of transatlantic cable like Mr. Fantastic of the Fantastic 4 to pop out the other end and smash the phone down on his head—I mean he's REALLY trying my patience—I know the loot is coming I know it's just a matter of time but come on Sean I can't go on like this forfuckingever!!

Atelier Jar-a-leet Night the 4th

From time to time the thought does pop into my head: "I wonder what Martha's doing right at this moment?"—Of course I know what she's doing: she's lying on the couch under the anglepoise in her black turtleneck and her red sweat pants smoking a Gitane correcting a stack of Spanish compositions—Otto is hovering around trying to hump her leg and she has to keep pushing him away—don't give up old son friction is your birthright—for the first week I know she was on the blower day and night blackening my name across the world's continents—she called her mother in San Isidro and her father in Barcelona and her halfwit brother the sculptor in San Fran and soul sister brown sugar Gabriella in Caracas and I've no doubt they all said the same thing: what a no-good rotten bastard I am and how they always knew I'd fuck her over again how they tried to warn her and she's better off without me—that Suarez family Sean: a bunch of stick-up-the-arse parvenu dago customs inspectors spoilt priests and back street abortionists—not one of them with any breeding sensitivity table manners or couth except maybe Fernando the queer uncle who sadly had his mickey mangled by Fidel's boys on the Isle of Pines—Nana the Bent Banana he was the only one who liked me

Firewaters—2 A.M.—I'm drunk—You're dead—where does that get us?—NOWHERE—all right Sean stop lapping the waters of Lethe and pay attention—it's time for another exciting episode of...

MY LIFE AS AMELIA'S DOG

Where was I?—oh yes I remember: me and Amelia became an item—Martha found out about the affair went ballistic and booted me out—I stayed for a couple of weeks with Ken and his then girlfriend Pippa (a very nice woman—a painter—10,000 times nicer than Maude)—after that I

224

lived for a month in an SRO up on 97th and B'way—the less said about that the better: stepping over junkies every night to get in my door— paper thin walls—nosey psycho neighbours—the whole Hubert Selby trip—at the start of March Amelia got kicked out of where she was living—moving in together seemed a logical step—we found a rundown little one bedroom on 9th between A and B—it was relatively cheap by the standards of the day—for a while I think we were actually quite happy—of course we had our fights—all the usual domestic shit plus she was stripping again and I didn't want her to strip but she told me to fuck off and mind my own business—"If you don't like it move out" etc.—so there was tension and moodiness and a good bit of shouting and door slamming but generally things were OK or Okish—one night Martha rang up and left a nasty phone message calling down the 7 plagues of Egypt on me and my "little white whore"—fortunately there was no follow through and after that she more or less left us alone—we ate a lot of takeout: Chinese Vietnamese Thai Mexican—in the evenings we'd load the bong and watch Hollywood classics on the VCR—Charles Laugton as Dr. Moreau in his spiffy white three piece cracking the whip—see the hedgehog-faced mutants cower and cringe!—Lugosi playing the pan pipes!—Basil Rathbone glaring at him!—make him well Frankenstein—bone stuck in throat—wonderful stuff—we'd go to bars to check out bands and get stinking drunk and shout The Cum Jerks Totally Rule Everybody Else Totally Sucks—we'd go for walks in the park at 3 in the morning and feed the squirrels potato chips—Saturday mornings were spent shopping in Chinatown midtown uptown maxing out the last of the Prendian plastic—yes Sean it was all rather idyllic in a downtown sort of way—and in a downtown sort of way it fell apart—One Fateful Night we were in bed: Amelia started getting frisky—putting her tongue in my ear biting my neck feeling me up etc.—it was great but at the same time almost

225

shocking—it wasn't like her at all: she usually just lay there in her ice queen trance and let me do all the work—anyway just as I was starting to really get into it she pulled away and sat down at the end of the bed and lit a fag—She said you're probably wondering why I don't do that stuff—What stuff I said?—Like why I never go down on you for example—Yes I said I had wondered—I can't she said—Why not?—Because I was raped when I was 13. A friend of the family raped me repeatedly over a 2 year period. He made me suck his dick that's why I can't suck yours and I can't do any of the other things you'd like me to do. I'm sorry Prendergast—I wonder Sean if you can imagine how I felt—An immediate insane flaming hatred for this man this total stranger exploded in my chest—I wanted to kill him—I actually decided there and then that I WOULD kill him—It took me 2 weeks to get her to tell me his first name—Peter—What's his last name?—She shook her head—I kept at her tell me his last name—Peter what?—she kept shaking her head no Prendergast it's not your problem which of course only made me all the more determined to escort the bastard down the primrose path and heave him on to the everlasting bonfire—I kept at her: What's his last name? Tell me his last name—I thought I could wear her down I thought if I kept the pressure up she'd eventually cave in—one night I came home and there was a note taped to the fridge door: GOODBYE PRENDERGAST—she's taken all her stuff Sean and cleared out—evidently I'd pushed too hard—I legged it round to the strip bar where she was working—the Fuzz Box up on 44th—they told me she hadn't shown up for work and because she hadn't phoned in she was probably going to get fired—one of the managers accosted me on my way out—dark blue suit big oily grin—he told me she was staying with a pal of hers up in Harlem this woman called Cheryl another stripper—you can picture it I'm sure: Prendy's visit to the rundown semi-tenement building off Lex. Ave.—Prendy pounding on the door of the apt—Amelia open up! I know you're in there!—old ladies in curlers peering down at me through the banisters—waiting—listening—then the depressing retreat down the dark hall—and next day my 20 second phone interview with friend Cheryl: Listen man she doesn't want to see you. She doesn't want you in her life. She's doing fine now. Don't call here again OK?—click— Next scene: I show up at the Harlem address with a huge bunch of violets only to be told that 'the ballet dancers' had moved!—no forwarding address—I made the rounds of the strip joints all the places she'd worked and a few she hadn't— my attempts to question les girls/pass around her snapshot led to several violent clashes with fascist pig bouncers—Prendy grabbed by the scruff of the neck Prendy sent flying through the air to kiss the concrete—Boris the Bouncer at Flutterbyes: And the next time you show your face in here sir not only am I going to kick the living shit out of you I'm going to make you eat it. Do I make myself clear?—as a bell Boris—the long and the short of it was that Amelia had vanished.

HOUSING DIFFICULTIES

by Evan Harris

I first met Cinderella at a party exactly like this one, a number of seasons ago. The invitation had been slipped under my door in a red envelope with a note penned over the seal: *Your secret is safe*, it read, punctuated by a chipper little smiley face.

It was a big affair with catered waiter proffered trays of elaborately cut crudite and an anything you can think of bar. I stationed myself in a corner, between a potted palm and a cluster of visibly up and coming guests. Somebody's girlfriend, somebody's cousin, somebody's ex. I'd just gotten a comfortable hold on my whiskey sour when the hostess bubbled over with Cinderella in tow, and introduced us. *Not as he seems, Dear,* she said to Cinderella, then turned to me and winked. *Unattached,* she mouthed, her face right up in my face so that Cinderella couldn't see. Then, wiggling the lacquered tips of her fingers toward a guest recently arrived, our hostess left us.

And there I was, looking like a walking glitch on the guest list. Rumple, slouch. That secret alter ego identity nondescript nice guy routine. A practiced persona held over from my days in the Superhero racket. Which I quit. Bye bye Captain Implosion. I was a generalist, making the world safe through destruction, exploding the dangerous inward. Upon itself. Bad guys, speeding bullets, plummeting safes: Zap—Pow. Let's just say I couldn't take the fallout. Weary of ducking, I walked in favor of full time obscurity in my cubicle at the DMV. Hello to the 40 hour week of petty bureaucracy.

So that was me.

But Cinderella. Wow. She was a real star. All shine and mystique.

The crush was instantaneous.

She was wearing a blue halter dress and silver lamé heels. She had a cluster of multi-colored spring crocus in her thick honey hair, and in her hand, a cranberry-colored drink decorated with a yellow twist. Delicately fishing, Cinderella hooked an ice cube, drew it out of the glass, and tossed it in the air. She tipped her head back jaw ajar, adjusted with her shoulders, and caught it neatly in her mouth.

Heads turned in the cluster beside us. Cinderella didn't notice.

She cracked. Demurcly, she let the fractured ice cube slip back into the glass. Then, she held her drink up as if to propose a toast.

"Ask me anything," she said.

I broke out into a cold sweat. Could she? Ever? Longing with a question mark stabbed on the end. Hope cut jagged and raw by the saw of clumsy desire. Impossible; impossible to frame.

I produced a hankie and mopped my brow.

All I could never ask. All I might never know.

But there are, always, the fallbacks. Where do you live, what do you do?

In response to the usual questions, Cinderella told me she

was renting a glass house on the West Side and working on her marksmanship—perfecting it—by throwing stones.

I worried for her safety.

Cinderella laughed and gestured with her drink. She spilled a small amount, wetting a well tailored sleeve in the cluster beside us. Up and coming eyebrows raised. Somebody's girlfriend made a whispered assumption; somebody's cousin presumed it true; somebody's ex nodded knowingly.

Cinderella didn't care. She inclined toward me confidentially.

"Don't worry, You. It's shatterproof," she said.

I made a note there and then to re-read her story, to check for the presence of foreshadowing.

• • •

Several months after that first encounter, I was returning after a day's work to my apartment. Four walls, a square of floor. The window with its graying shade drawn shut against the unseemly view of a narrow air shaft, brick wall broken by a window that gives into the lives of two fat, ruined women. Their voices pierce glass in shrill tones of antipathy for one another, blame for all, and complaint of swollen feet. I was loath, that evening, to return to my dreary little box. I was taking the long way through the warm twilight, wondering: Should I make something more of my claim to humanity? Throw myself into a renovation project, improve my posture, spruce up the old act.

Get a girl. Give glamour another whirl?

That's when I spotted her.

Cinderella was wearing a strapless white taffeta dress and those same silver lamé heels. She had a delicate rhinestone tiara perched atop the intricate coif of her up-done hair and a transparent chiffon scarf in her hand. Poised to step off the curb, she froze when I called her name, then wheeled around, the skirt of her dress swirling out.

"You again," she said. Then, rising up on silver lamé tippy toes, arms held gracefully out at her sides, she executed three perfect traveling pirouettes that landed her on the pavement less than an arm's length before me. Cinderella studied me thoughtfully. "Tell me anything," she said.

A declaration rose from my gut through my heart and into my mouth; it shifted lightly on the tip of my tongue, tickled, sent threads of itch back down toward my throat.

Cinderella glimmered in the blue gray dusk, out already, a precocious star waiting to be wished upon.

My lips opened.

The declaration would find its home!

But actually, no. Tender and totally unrealistic, my poor unfortunate declaration was stricken by the acid of self consciousness, broken down, dissolved. I swallowed. Down the hatch.

All that I cannot say. All that passes into the sink.

But there are always, always the fallbacks. Fine weather we're having, followed by the usual questions.

Cinderella reported that the glass house had gone up for sale. She'd put in a bid, which was accepted, and she was meeting mortgage payments by performing an act in which she walked barefoot on broken glass.

Her safety?

Cinderella let loose with a giggle like the sound of ice tinkling in a glass.

"Don't worry, You. I'm a professional."

Her training?

"I practice on eggshells," she told me, "Or the bits and pieces of any old fragile thing."

Cinderella turned from me. She stepped away, off the curb and into the street. She fluttered her scarf above her head, and a Northbound taxi with out-of-issue plates swept up to a stop in front of her. The rear passenger door swung open. Cinderella looked back at me, and gestured with a tilt of her head. "Come on, You. Spot me for a dress rehearsal," she said.

It was not Cinderella that was the one in danger of falling, not she in need of a safety net...

On the front step of her house of glass, Cinderella paused, reached up behind her tiara, removed a hair pin, slid it neatly into the keyhole, and unlocked the door.

She lead me through the foyer and to the entrance of a sunken living room.

"Break something, will you," Cinderella said, "I'll be back in a sec."

She descended the steps and crossed the room. Her heels clicked lightly over the glass floor. She moved through a see through door in the far wall, then turned a right angle into a corridor. Through the layers of glass, I watched as she trailed her fingers along the wall. Then, she passed into an invisible place; some sheltered space unexposed by transparency. A trick in the floor plan, perhaps.

Break something?

The room was completely bare. I scanned the sheet glass walls, looked up at the seamless glass ceiling, looked down at the spotless glass floor. A riddle? A test? A code I was meant to crack?

I pondered the problem, nervous for her return. Anxious to provide her with something upon which to practice her art.

And then, in the still of that room, in some convolution of a preemptive strike, I took my old ready stance. The pressure began to build. That blue white power began to lash through me, molecules bonding, synapses compressing, concentration honing inward, inward to a target I'd never tried. Then the close in, the box off, the freeze. A final jolt of blue white focus and Zap—Pow—

I reeled back.

Comeback performance complete, and there it was, in a heap of shards on the floor: My imploded heart, the splintered ruin of it, chambers collapsed, beat blown to bits, ready to be walked upon.

"That was spectacular. And very resourceful," Cinderella said, addressing me from the far side of the room where she was leaning against the door jamb. She'd changed into a pair of cut-off jeans and a white tee shirt with a silver C decaled on the chest. Her hair was loose and she had a pair of fuzzy purple bedroom slippers on her feet. "But you know what," Cinderella continued, "false alarm. I'm sort of not in the mood, and to tell you the truth it's a pretty stupid act. Not nearly as professional as yours. But the finale's not bad," she said, "We could just skip to that."

Whatever you want, is what I told her.

Cinderella gave me a dazzling smile.

"Wish anything," she said.

I shut my eyes. Envisioned it: A whole true night. A whole, true night with her.

The room went staticy silver. I lost equilibrium, surrendered all balance in favor of weightless suspension within the bubble of a blown glass world. Sweet gusting heat, the exhale of an exquisite myth gone real.

By dawn, the glass house was gone. Cinderella, too. Vanished.

I reappeared alone, on the unfamiliar corner of two unfamiliar streets. A dense smoke clung to my clothes. I was hot all over and dizzy; sick.

The yawning emptiness in my chest.

Of all the chances to take.

A fool humored with a one night stand. A fool in the

aftermath of a foolish wish.

All I could think of to think was fuck her and fuck this.

And my fractured self sustained a new split.

• • •

Tonight, the hostess greeted me with a kiss aimed at the air near my left ear and a rush of italics. *"Welcome back, Darling,"* she said, *"rumor rumor I hear you've been ever so busy breaking hearts."*

She's right, in a gossipy kind of way. I am back in the game these days. A rogue force for breakdown, crack up, collapse within. State of the art demolition. I don't stick around to take the credit. Ditto the blame. Isn't every one always on the verge anyway?

I scan the room, looking for my mark.

The up-and-coming cluster, pinch cocktail napkins around glasses, pick crudite from silver trays. Somebody's girlfriend turns on the charm. Somebody's cousin embellishes. Somebody's ex bores even the potted palm.

And Cinderella looks like hell.

She's in a dark wrinkled trench coat and scoffed brown boots. Her hair is a dirty blond straggle, her hands disappear into the depths of her pockets.

I've got her cornered now. Ready stance for heartless revenge. But at close range I can see it's no use. Something has beaten me to the punch. She is claimed by change. She's a wreck. A ruin.

She has closed her eyes for longer than is normal in a crowded room.

But wait. Cinderella begins to whisper:

The glass house melted as the result of a wild conflagration—it was arson—arson, she is sure: Her ex-husband, a prince with an aquiline nose, a shoe fetish, and an empty dance card crept into the house that night while we slept. He found his way to the attic, and lit a match to the feathery, iridescent stores of hope she kept laid away in a trunk with out-of-season outfits. The place went up quick as a stepmother's ire to rise. So much for the durability of avant-garde construction. She waked in a choke, wished me to safety, and barely got out with her life, much less her wardrobe or her nascent future. She knows the prince holds a grudge from the split-up—a nasty all-out fight during which he accused her of transparency and claimed he could read her like an insipid children's book, every line right down to her destiny. She countered with a revision of the story. He threatened to sue for the rights to her dance steps, her footgear, her beauty, her eventuality. Obviously absurd, and he knew it, knew that he would never win in a court of law, so he took what he could steal via low-ball bottom-feeding connivance, and paid a footman double holiday overtime to impersonate a high-end cobbler running a special on crack-proof souls. Duped, she brought the glass slippers in, returned in a week with her ticket, and was given a pair of well-heeled counterfeits. As if. As if perfect fit can be faked. But she took no action, let it pass, let it go, moved on, wore silver lamé and never complained. Yet the prince is bitter still, jealous and deranged—deranged, she is sure, sitting at home in that stupid penthouse castle compulsively windexing those slippers when he's not out setting vengeful fires.

And now, there's no house and no hope and nothing decent to wear.

Cinderella has declared bankruptcy. She's subleasing a mouse hole on the South Side down near the tracks, collecting bottles for redemption and barely scraping by.

She reaches up to her throat and buttons the top button of her coat.

"There's a wedge of cheese in my pocket," she tells me, "I'm going to take it home."

STATE OF THE NATION

by Douglas Glover

We in the Republic are exhausted.

Our enemies have lain down their arms, leaving us suddenly without a national purpose.

Brown people are pouring over the border to take up work we heedlessly relinquish in our pursuit of leisure and sexual gratification.

Nights I drive down the coast road to the marshes at the mouth of the Tijuana River and park and watch them crawling across the border like insects.

The country is awash in brown people and perverts of all kinds.

The fat woman across the street (we are four storeys up) has pushed her bed to the window and lolls there naked, exposing herself, masturbating shamelessly with an assortment of household objects: salamis, broom handles, cat brushes, vacuum cleaner attachments, bits of broken furniture, aerosol cans, stereo albums, pizza cutters and cork screws.

Sometimes she simply lies with her head thrown back in ecstasy, holding the lips of her vulva open.

This is an electrifying development, let me tell you.

All of a sudden, I have an attention span again.

Prior to this, I often couldn't think of a reason to go out

or stay in (except at night when the sewagy, rotting smell of the Tijuana wafted me southwards along the coast road). Occasionally, I have stood before the door for hours on end, trying to decide what to do.

Now I race to get up before she does, shower and comb my hair, then dash down the stairs for a box of week-old raspberry Danish pastries, five pounds of salted peanuts and a dozen Mexican beers. Usually I am in position, stretched on my Naugahyde recliner in front of the window, before she stirs, before she thrusts the first dainty foot from beneath her soiled pink sheets.

Sometimes she waves.

On one hand, I keep a cooler for the beer, a carton of Marlboros, a slab of Irish butter, my pastries and peanuts. On the other, I have a large steel garbage can (I am a firm believer in design efficiency). I throw the trash—bottles, rinds, husks, butts, packaging, spent matches—into the garbage can, which occasionally leads to minor fires that annoy the neighbours but cause no more harm than a little localized air pollution and a mark like a storm cloud on my ceiling.

Once I woke up to find the hair on the left side of my head blazing like a fatwood torch.

One day we meet accidentally in the greeting card shop at the corner (I go there to read—I can't get through a whole book anymore).

I'm abashed. I have nothing to say.

She says, Are you the guy with the telescope?

I nod. I am wearing a leather World War I aviator's helmet with goggles, a white silk scarf, yellow shorts printed with nodding palm fronds and Birkenstocks.

I don't want to fuck you, she says. I want things to go on just as they are. You understand? Only I want to see you too. Everything. I have binoculars. I'll watch.

A purulent musk assails my nostrils. Sweat pools in deltas under her arms, slides down the side of her nose like translucent snails.

Her eyes roll up in terror.

She flails the air with her arms, then tilts backward into an array of comic wedding anniversary cards and crashes to the floor.

I can see what effort this terse communication has cost her. This access of vulnerability has its own peculiar allure.

And I rush away in a panic, fearing nothing so much as love and the loss of love, worried above all else that, having revealed herself, she will now retreat into the spell of anonymity by which we all protect ourselves from hurt.

But things go on just as before.

Except that now I strip off and parade myself in front of the window from time to time and wave.

She no longer waves back. Engrossed as she is in her pleasure, she rarely has a hand to spare.

Then she tries to kill herself. She lets me watch the whole

thing, ripping up sheets to tie off her arms, slicing her wrists vertically instead of horizontally in order to avoid severing the tendons, then letting the blood spurt in a decreasing trajectory over her thighs and sheets.

After a while, I call 911 and save her life.

One of the EMS guys vomits when he enters her apartment. From what I can see, she is not much of a neatness freak.

In the hospital, she mistakes me for someone else, someone named Buddy.

From internal evidence, I conclude that Buddy is her brother, that he disappeared twenty-two years ago after accidentally shooting a boy named Natrone Hales to death in the family garage. The boys were twelve at the time.

I have brought her a spring posy from a gift shop downstairs operated by a blind person who reads the money with his fingers. I got eighty-two dollars in change from a ten-dollar bill.

Presently, she begins to yell at me for going off like that, for never sending a postcard.

I say I called twice, both times on her birthday, and both times I hung up when she answered.

She looks at me. Her features soften. She says I called more than twice like that.

I say, yeah.

241

You look about the same, she says.

I tell her about the man who held me in a closet for eight years against my will, the time in the hospital, the girl I loved who died of anthrax, the accident with the car when I had no insurance and had to pay off the kid's medical bills holding down three jobs and how he used to come around in that custom wheelchair and taunt me, about my time in Nam, my self-esteem problems, the hole in my nose from drugs, my bladder spasms.

What happened to your hair?

A fire, I say.

I say, I don't think you really know me.

Oh, Buddy, Buddy, Buddy, she says.

I try to lie down beside her on the bed, but there is no beside her. I end up on the floor.

Why did you do that? she asks. You haven't changed.

Who will you want me to be tomorrow? I think, as I leave, realizing that there is a mystery here, a truth about the nature of love, that we are always falling in love with some picture, that the real person eludes us, though he is always jumping up and down in the background, waving his arms and shouting for attention—someone has turned off the sound.

Mostly, I am afraid that with my luck the real Buddy will walk through the door at any minute now.

In *Time* magazine, I read that the Buddhists call this place the hungry-ghost world.

On the way out of the hospital, I ask the blind guy at the gift shop for change for a twenty. I give him a five and get forty-nine dollars back.

You made a mistake, I say.

He gives me another ten.

I don't get down to the hospital for a week because I can't figure out who I think she is, maybe just one of those multiple-personality sluts you meet in the bars these days, women who give you five percent of their souls and take no responsibility.

When I do go, she is sitting up in bed with a food tray. She has combed her hair, she's wearing a pink nightgown, she's lost weight.

Ominously, they have untied her hands.

She smiles and says, I'm glad you stopped by.

The voice of total insanity, I think.

I got something for you, she says, handing me a gift-wrapped parcel.

It's a new universal remote for my TV and entertainment centre.

I nearly weep with gratitude. No one has ever given me a present before.

Then I recall that I'm not sure who I am supposed to be today.

She says, A year ago I was a nurse in Arizona. One day, an old prospector drove down out of the Two Heads mountains to drop off a ten-year-old Apache girl he'd bought and got pregnant.

He said we could do what we wanted with her. He just couldn't use her now that she was pregnant. He'd have to go and get another.

The Apache girl didn't even know she was pregnant. The doctors delivered her, then put both of them up for adoption—without ever telling the girl what had really happened to her.

I kept thinking about her, that this important thing had occurred without her knowing it, that somewhere there was another person closer to her than life, without either of them being aware of it. I imagined she must have been haunted by a feeling of something just out of reach, a mystery without a name.

I asked myself, What if, later on, she were to meet her child in the street? Would she just pass by? Or would she feel tugged toward him?

She stops talking for a moment, looks a little frightened.

I say, That's exactly the relationship I have with reality most days.

She smiles again and says, I guess I cracked up. I believe drugs and alcohol were involved. They are most of the time.

You mean you're normal now? I ask.

You're not Buddy, are you?

I am out of there, a crushing weight on my chest—heartburn or love, I can't tell which.

The blind guy at the gift shop is watching the local news on TV with the volume on high torque. A band of Yuma Indians on the border near Nogales has just sold its tribal land to the city of San Diego for a landfill and plans to use the money to start a casino.

We should put 'em on a boat and send 'em back where they came from, he says.

I ask for a Snickers bar and give him a five.

He gives me back four Jacksons and change.

I say, I can't take this. You counted wrong.

Oh boy, he says. Just checking. I got burned twice last week. Called the cops. Eight of them got the place staked out right now, waiting for my signal.

Don't die, I think, suddenly fearful.

I click back to CNN and catch the news from the Republic of Paranoia, where only victims are citizens with rights.

Hell, our army won't even consider fighting a country where the people can afford shoes anymore.

I knew a woman once who said love is nothing but a mechanism for heat exchange.

She said, We are just roadkill on the highway to nowhere.

I click the remote and see myself as a slim young man with a future. I see my country, violent and innocent again, like a flash of sheet lightning in history. I see her cradling a child to her breast, the child feeling absolutely safe and unafraid.

I think, Sadness, sadness, sadness.

OUTSIDE

by Johannah Rodgers

Eliza leaned back and yawned. The sunlight played on the drops of water remaining on the porch from last night's rain. Eric wondered how well he knew this person as he lifted his glass. "You will never understand." Ants were crawling over the tight buds of the pink and white peonies, which looked like a child's drawing of lollipops lined up in a row. It was 10:45. A car pulled into the neighbor's driveway and a faint smell of exhaust was left in the air; the neighbor waved. In the middle of the backyard there was a tree with fern-like leaves. She brushed away some crumbs that had fallen on her shirt from the piece of toast she was eating and took a sip of coffee. "I wish you wouldn't say things like that."

The sunlight played on the drops of water remaining on the porch from last night's rain. Eric wondered how well he knew this person as he lifted his glass. "You will never understand." Ants were crawling over the tight buds of the pink and white peonies, which looked like a child's drawing of lollipops lined up in a row. It was 10:45. A car pulled into the neighbor's driveway and a faint smell of exhaust was left in the air; the neighbor waved. In the middle of the backyard there was a tree with fern-like leaves. She brushed away some crumbs that had fallen on her shirt from the piece of toast she was eating and took a sip of coffee. "I wish you wouldn't say things like that." Eliza leaned back and yawned.

Eric wondered how well he knew this person as he lifted his glass. "You will never understand." Ants were crawling over the tight buds of the pink and white peonies, which looked like a child's drawing of lollipops lined up in a row. It was 10:45. A car pulled into the neighbor's driveway and a

247

faint smell of exhaust was left in the air; the neighbor waved. In the middle of the backyard there was a tree with fern-like leaves. She brushed away some crumbs that had fallen on her shirt from the piece of toast she was eating and took a sip of coffee. "I wish you wouldn't say things like that." Eliza leaned back and yawned. The sunlight played on the drops of water remaining on the porch from last night's rain.

"You will never understand." Ants were crawling over the tight buds of the pink and white peonies, which looked like a child's drawing of lollipops lined up in a row. It was 10:45. A car pulled into the neighbor's driveway and a faint smell of exhaust was left in the air; the neighbor waved. In the middle of the backyard there was a tree with fern-like leaves. She brushed away some crumbs that had fallen on her shirt from the piece of toast she was eating and took a sip of coffee. "I wish you wouldn't say things like that." Eliza leaned back and yawned. The sunlight played on the drops of water remaining on the porch from last night's rain. Eric wondered how well he knew this person as he lifted his glass.

Ants were crawling over the tight buds of the pink and white peonies, which looked like a child's drawing of lollipops lined up in a row. It was 10:45. A car pulled into the neighbor's driveway and a faint smell of exhaust was left in the air; the neighbor waved. In the middle of the backyard there was a tree with fern-like leaves. She brushed away some crumbs that had fallen on her shirt from the piece of toast she was eating and took a sip of coffee. "I wish you wouldn't say things like that." Eliza leaned back and yawned. The sunlight played on the drops of water remaining on the porch from last night's rain. Eric wondered how well he knew this person as he lifted his glass. "You will never understand."

It was 10:45. A car pulled into the neighbor's driveway and

a faint smell of exhaust was left in the air; the neighbor waved. In the middle of the backyard there was a tree with fern-like leaves. She brushed away some crumbs that had fallen on her shirt from the piece of toast she was eating and took a sip of coffee. "I wish you wouldn't say things like that." Eliza leaned back and yawned. The sunlight played on the drops of water remaining on the porch from last night's rain. Eric wondered how well he knew this person as he lifted his glass. "You will never understand." Ants were crawling over the tight buds of the pink and white peonies, which looked like a child's drawing of lollipops lined up in a row.

A car pulled into the neighbor's driveway and a faint smell of exhaust was left in the air; the neighbor waved. In the middle of the backyard there was a tree with fern-like leaves She brushed away some crumbs that had fallen on her shirt from the piece of toast she was eating and took a sip of coffee. "I wish you wouldn't say things like that." Eliza leaned back and yawned. The sunlight played on the drops of water remaining on the porch from last night's rain. Eric wondered how well he knew this person as he lifted his glass. "You will never understand." Ants were crawling over the tight buds of the pink and white peonies, which looked like a child's drawing of lollipops lined up in a row. It was 10:45.

In the middle of the backyard there was a tree with fern-like leaves. She brushed away some crumbs that had fallen on her shirt from the piece of toast she was eating and took a sip of coffee. "I wish you wouldn't say things like that." Eliza leaned back and yawned. The sunlight played on the drops of water remaining on the porch from last night's rain. Eric wondered how well he knew this person as he lifted his glass. "You will never understand." Ants were crawling over the tight buds of the pink and white peonies, which looked like a child's drawing of lollipops lined up in a row. It was 10:45.

A car pulled into the neighbor's driveway and a faint smell of exhaust was left in the air; the neighbor waved.

She brushed away some crumbs that had fallen on her shirt from the piece of toast she was eating and took a sip of coffee. "I wish you wouldn't say things like that." Eliza leaned back and yawned. The sunlight played on the drops of water remaining on the porch from last night's rain. Eric wondered how well he knew this person as he lifted his glass. "You will never understand." Ants were crawling over the tight buds of the pink and white peonies, which looked like a child's drawing of lollipops lined up in a row. It was 10:45. A car pulled into the neighbor's driveway and a faint smell of exhaust was left in the air; the neighbor waved. In the middle of the backyard there was a tree with fern-like leaves.

"I wish you wouldn't say things like that." Eliza leaned back and yawned. The sunlight played on the drops of water remaining on the porch from last night's rain. Eric wondered how well he knew this person as he lifted his glass. "You will never understand." Ants were crawling over the tight buds of the pink and white peonies, which looked like a child's drawing of lollipops lined up in a row. It was 10:45. A car pulled into the neighbor's driveway and a faint smell of exhaust was left in the air; the neighbor waved. In the middle of the backyard there was a tree with fern-like leaves. She brushed away some crumbs that had fallen on her shirt from the piece of toast she was eating and took a sip of coffee.

APPETITE

by Jonathan Baumbach

First of all, don't believe what you've heard about me. Given the stories circulating, you would think I was some kind of retrograde chauvinist but unless I'm suffering from amnesia or have been in a psychotic state for the past month, I know I've done nothing to warrant the current fuss. My lapses, such as they are, proceed from what might best be described as passionate excess.

When people refer to me as "larger than life." I don't think it's size alone they're referring to, though I am well over six feet and tend to weigh between 250 and 300 pounds depending on a nexus of variables. I have an oversized personality and an immense appetite, the one having only incidental connection with the other. This may sound like a rationalization but I try to strike a balance between my needs—I am no stranger to restraint—and my personal sense of decency.

Most women find me charming and that gets me in trouble. Four years ago, I was pressed to give up a tenured position at the University of Washington for having "inappropriate relations" with several of my women students. In fact, I never pursued a woman who hadn't made herself available to me first. The first of the women who complained about me to the authorities did so after I called an end to the affair. And though she lied about much of what happened between us, she never said I forced myself on her. One of the others—they came out of the woodwork like dust bunnies to testify against me—one of the more shameless others, said I had imposed myself on her against her will. It was her testimony and not the original complaint that turned me into a pariah. They gave me the opportunity to resign with the promise that my

251

stigmatized behavior would not be broadcast elsewhere. I had no choice, my craven lawyer insisted, but to accept their terms. Anyway, even if I hadn't been pushed out, I was ready to leave Seattle, which was like living in the afterlife.

After the Seattle debacle, I took a slightly less prestigious job at one of the city colleges in New York.

• • •

There was this woman in my Life Drawing class, who tended to hang around my desk after the bell chatting me up. An instinctive diplomat myself, I distrusted flattery in others, though this child-woman, Octavia, quite sexy in an unassuming way, and probably the most gifted student in the group, had circumvented my alarm system. In fact, she reminded me of myself some years back when I was starting out.

With Nora away for ten days, visiting her parents in Vancouver, I felt lonely and a tad deprived. Still (and I insist on this), I had absolutely no intention of getting involved with a student again.

On the other hand, I am an impulsive person and one Friday when the saucy Octavia showed up at my office ostensibly to discuss her progress in the course, I found myself inviting her to a weekend party at my country house, recently purchased and still in the process of renovation.

—That sounds fun, she said. Is there some kind of bus that goes there?

—You can ride up with me, I said. I'll come by and pick you up at 9 on Saturday if that's agreeable.

She accepted my offer with undisguised pleasure. It was only after she got into the car and discovered she was my only passenger that she asked who else would be there.

—Sam and Annie, I said, both of whom Octavia had met.

—They're driving up later in the day. Nora, unfortunately, is visiting her parents on the left coast and won't be able to join us.

I should mention that Nora and I, though not actually married, have been living together for 12 years.

Octavia rolled her eyes charmingly, withheld whatever rude remark passed like a shadow across her face.

—Anyway, small parties are the best, don't you think.

She glanced slyly at me as if taking my measure and I smiled back reassuringly.

She was mostly silent for the rest of the trip, and occasionally surly, preoccupied with whatever, so I told her some jokes, one of which provoked a laugh.

—You're impossible, she said.

—Yes, I said, and isn't that a good thing, which provoked further giddiness, all of which seemed a positive sign. In matters of the heart (or hard-on), I've always been a partisan of the implicit.

When we got to the house, we were the only ones there actually. Sam and Annie were not expected until much later

(I was beginning to hope they wouldn't show up at all) and noting Octavia's uneasiness, I made a point of being reassuring. I said that unlike some of my fellow shmearers in the Art Department, I was not the kind of man who sought affairs with his attractive female students. I let her know that the main bedroom was hers for the night and that I would put up in the airless guest room above the garage.

In the makeshift scenario of my imaginary movie, she would have said, Don't put yourself out on my account, but Octavia defeated expectation, thanking me in her sassy way for being a gentleman. I could understand that she didn't want to seem too available.

The house was a mess—we had left in a hurry the previous weekend—and Octavia seemed put out by the disorder. The first thing she did after checking out her room and changing into her bathing suit was wash the dirty dishes that had been left in the sink. I would have dried, but I couldn't find a dish towel so I stomped about impatiently in the living room, cleaning off the couch, rearranging the clutter.

—You're very domestic, I said, but you're here to enjoy yourself. That's the point, isn't it? So let's have a swim and then we'll go to town for lunch.

—I can cook, she said, if you want to bring food in. Is there a dish towel somewhere?

—Just leave them in the drainer please, I said.

When I could finally get her away from the sink, we walked through a wooded area to the pond, which is at the far end of the property.

254

—How can I be sure you're not leading me down the garden path, said my witty flower.

—Is that what you think of me, I said, playing at being offended.

—I never know what's expected of me, she said. You'll have to tell me.

And that was my cue (and didn't I know it), but I let the moment pass. I could tell from her expression that the pond, perhaps smaller and murkier than my description suggested, did not live up to expectations. She sat down on her towel and opened a book she had brought with her while I launched myself with a rather graceful, I will say, surface dive.

When I came up for air, I waved to her to join me.

—When I'm ready, she said, lying on her side on a skimpy towel in a provocative pose. I need to get some sun first.

There was of course no sun out, which I was discreet enough not to mention.

I did a few self-conscious, show-offy laps, imagined her watching my performance, then returned to her side. —The water's perfect, I said.

—I am getting hungry, she said, looking up from her book.

—Then let's go to town and get something to eat, I said.

—I want to finish the chapter first, she said.

I sat down on the grass next to her towel. If I were the author of that book, I said, I'd be terribly pleased at your devotion.

—If I were the pond, she said, I'd probably ask you not to be so rough with me.

—If you were the pond, I said, offering a mock sigh, letting the completion of the thought remain implicit.

At lunch she was again sullen and uncommunicative and it crossed my mind that there was something a little off with the disconcertingly variable Octavia. After I finished my burger, she was still picking at hers. Ultimately, she left more than half on her plate and it was all I could do not to ask for her leavings. The charmer anticipated me. —Would you like the rest of mine? she asked.

—Thank you, no, the hungry man said, averting his eyes, but when she insisted a second and third time, I yielded to her seduction. Her burger was still warm from her touch when I picked it up.

• • •

We had just returned to the pond when Sam and Annie drove up in their black Chevy Blazer. Sam is a former MFA student and Annie, who I had a brief involvement with myself, was a life model in one of the classes he took with me. Usually the models don't mix with the students but these two were living together with my blessing before the term was over. Octavia had met them both before and seemed pleased and even surprised by their arrival. Sam said they wanted to walk around town and invited Octavia to join them, an offer she accepted with more enthusiasm than seemed warranted.

So I had the house to myself for the next several hours and I whited out a painting whose solution persisted in eluding me, then I took a nap on one of the chaises on the deck. I must have been very tired because I didn't hear them drive up.

—Do you know you have snakes on your property, Annie was saying to me when I opened my eyes. Her remark embarrassed me. I had a hard-on when I woke from some unremembered erotic dream and her snake comment I somehow thought referenced my condition.

Sam and Annie had brought back two six packs of the aptly named Pete's Wicked Lager, which we took over to the pond with us. For the rest of the afternoon, we drank beer and lolled in the water. Octavia kept her distance in Sam and Annie's presence, which I read as a form of discretion. I asked her once as an aside if she were enjoying herself and she said—I'm doing my best.

After dinner, which was barbecued trout and vegetable kebobs, Sam and I went into town to get some more beer and we ended up at this pub that had a pool table and what with Sam bragging at how good he was, there was nothing to do but teach him a lesson. It took five games for me to assert my superiority.

When we got back—we had been missing for several hours—Octavia had retired for the night and Annie was on a couch in the living room dozing over a magazine. She was angry with Sam when she woke and she insisted on going outside with him to discuss the matter. —It's all my fault, I said.

In any event, Sam and Annie were planning to spend the night outside (under the stars, said Annie) in a sleeping bag they had brought for the occasion. My pajamas, which I rarely wore in warm weather anyway, were still in the bedroom and

I considered retrieving them. I had second thoughts about disturbing Octavia and besides the eight beers I had put away had diluted my appetite for sex. So I moved my bulk to the room above the garage and fell immediately asleep in my underwear on a sheetless cot. I slept for about forty minutes, then found myself rolling from back to side, the small room even with the one window propped open without the courtesy of a breeze, and of course I had to pee. I had to pee with maniacal urgency. So I hurried down the stairs in my skivvies into the starless night and let loose my waterfall against the side of the garage. Assuming myself alone, I sighed with pleasure as I peed.

I wasn't aware of another creature coming up behind me until I turned around.

It was very dark and I actually picked out her scent in the torpid air before I could make out who she was.

—Sam and I had a fight, she whispered.

—I'm so sorry, I said.

—It's all your fault, you know, she said.

—Yes, I said, I think I admitted to that.

—Oh not tonight, she said, not the drinking particularly, though having a drunk boy friend does not make me happy, but the whole thing, the getting together with him was your fault.

Although there was hardly more than six inches separating us, I could barely read her face in the dim light.—That's the moment's disappointment talking, I said.

She laughed and I realized from the sound of the laugh that she had also been crying.—You once said... she said, and the next thing I knew she was up against me, her head against my cheek.—You once said the moment was the only thing.

So we went up to my room–for–the–night above the garage to continue whatever had started of its own accord. The sex part was Annie's idea, though I will not deny that I did not offer much resistance. She gave me head and, a gentleman in my fashion, I followed suit. To the best of my recollection that's all we did. When I woke again at first light I was alone in the room and could almost believe that I had dreamt the encounter with Annie.

I put on the baggy Bermuda shorts I had worn the day before and went down the stairs and into the house to brew a pot of coffee. Octavia and Annie were already there, squeezing oranges for juice and making pancakes on the electric griddle. There was no sign of Sam.—You can take a shower now if you like, Octavia said.

What I really wanted was to brush my teeth and get out of the underwear I had slept in, which I did. I also washed my face and splashed some water on my private parts.

When I glanced out the window, I registered that Sam's Blazer was not where he had left it.

When I returned to the kitchen, Sam was stuffing his face with pancakes and the two women were gone.

—Did the women go into town? I asked him.

—Oh, he said, Annie and I had a fight. I would have won that last pool game if I hadn't been drunk.

—Of course you would, I said.

—So, what's going on with the two of you? he asked.

—Nothing, I said…what are you talking about, Sam?

—Come on, you know what I'm talking about, he said.

—You have my word that nothing much happened, I said.

—You don't have to be defensive with me, he said. I'm not Octavia's guardian.

So it was not Annie we were talking about. I sensed from the glance Sam gave me that he had also picked up on the implications of our misunderstanding.

• • •

It wasn't until about noon on Sunday that I found myself alone with Octavia again—Sam and Annie were off somewhere in the Blazer. I was doing the crossword puzzle on the grass by the pond, distracted by her footsteps as she approached.

—How is it you're not off with Sam and Annie? I asked her.

—Are there any cunning country walks around here? she said.

—It depends on what you mean by cunning, I said, making a point of not looking up at her.

Have I done something to offend you? she asked. If I have,

I'm sorry. Her question pricked a nerve. —Why would you think you offended me?

—I don't know, she said after a moment's silence. I seem to have a way that I don't understand of getting people angry at me.

I looked up at her, trying to assess the ad hoc rules of the game she was playing. —Give me a few more minutes with the puzzle, I said, and then we'll go for a walk if you like.

—I really think you're angry at me, she said and made an event out of walking away.

I returned to the puzzle but her presence or absence, my irritation with her performance, distracted me. After some procrastination, I got to my feet and walked back toward the house.

I caught up with her on the wooded path, sitting on a tree stump, looking pleased with herself.

—Would you help me up? she said in a sulky voice, holding out her hand.

I should probably freeze frame the action here to comment on what was going on with me. I assumed that the hand dangled in my direction was a sexual offer, belated perhaps but nevertheless whole-hearted and undeniable. I had of course been waiting with Jobean patience for this moment so I was not about to turn her down. As I took her hand in my paw, my mind had already jumped two steps ahead and I was sorting out possible venues. At the same time, I was warning myself to stay in the moment—a sure indication that I had already lost it.

I can still see us, connected by our hands, Octavia moving toward me in mind-induced slow-motion.

I remember bending toward her because of the disparity of our respective heights, feeling the strain in my back, tasting her mouth for the barest of seconds.

Her voice interrupted whatever was happening.—I didn't ask you to do that, she said, did I? Did I?

—Of course you didn't, I said, and I lumbered away like some wounded bear.

She caught up with me at the end of the path and said she was sorry if I had thought she had led me on because that had not been her intention. She even made a convincing effort at looking regretful, though I was not impressed.

It was time for some truth. —Of course it was your intention, Octavia, I said. —It's what separates adults from children, taking responsibility for what they do.

—Wasn't my apology an indication of responsibility, she said. I thought it was.

—You might tell me what you had in mind when you asked me to take your hand, I said.

She smiled slyly, seemed about to explain herself then teared up, mumbled something unintelligible and sashayed off toward the house.

I was tempted to follow her but instead I returned to the pond to cool off, swimming with a kind of demonic purpose, feeling at once immensely reasonable and unreasonably angry.

Sam and Annie were holding hands when they appeared at the pond about an hour later. They were going to take a quick swim and then make their way back to the city taking scenic back roads. —When are you planning to leave? Annie asked me.

—I tend to leave as late as possible, I said. It's an easier trip if you wait.

—Sam needs to get back, Annie said. Sam was uncharacteristically silent.

I had no inkling that the sky was falling when I trailed after them to the house to see them off.

On my return to the house, Octavia was sitting on a chaise on the deck, a book open on her lap. Her backpack, I noticed, was conspicuously positioned alongside the chaise. She seemed packed to leave, which was just as well.

—Your wife called about an hour ago, she announced, not looking at me. Nora, that's her name isn't it, seemed surprised to hear a woman's voice and asked me who I was.

—Is that right? I said.

—I said, you know, that I was a student of yours, she said. I totally hope that was the right thing to say. I didn't want to get you in any kind of trouble.

—Not to worry, I said.

While Sam was packing the blazer, Annie sidled up to inform me that, in the spirit of being honest with each other, she told Sam about our late night encounter.

I merely nodded, feeling a bit stupefied. —Sam doesn't seem too put out by the news, I said.

—Don't be fooled by his manner, she whispered. He's actually furious. The reason we're leaving is because he feels compromised accepting your hospitality.

• • •

I was prepared for disaster when the following Tuesday the department head called me into her office for an unscheduled meeting.

The night before I had what was probably the most literal dream I'd ever had or could remember having in which, prophetically, I had also received an invitation to see the department head. In the dream, she showed me a hand-written letter including elegantly drawn illustrations ("elegantly drawn" were the head's words) from one of my students complaining about my behavior.—Before I bring you up on charges, she said, sticking her tongue out at me, I'd like to hear your response to the letter.

She pushed the document across the desk to me as if there were something so loathsome about it she could barely stand to touch it.

—Whatever's in the letter, I said, I want you to know that, given the situation, I behaved pretty well.

—Read the letter before you defend yourself, she said.

The handwriting was mostly illegible and I wondered as I read the letter, or tried to read it, how much of it the department head had actually deciphered.

What follows is what I remember of the document.

Dear Chairman Meow (the Head's name was Dr. Kittman):

I am writing to you out of gentile (perhaps genuine) concern
over (illegible} dis-something in our otherwise dis-something
deportment (probably department). One of your (illegible)
shmearers invited me to conjugate at his cunt-ry estate in the
Catskills. There was supposed to be some kind of {illegible} and
I believe, all things considered, I was inveigled (perhaps invited)
to be the final course. I am not a tart no matter what {illegible)
seems to think. He, the oppressor (professor perhaps), paints
us all with the same tart brush. Frankly, I was shocked and
offended to find myself in this man's crutches (surely clutches}
when I had every right to expect that I had let myself in for
no more than a peasant (no doubt pleasant} day in the woods.
Ask anyone, my own (illegible) was totally beyond reproach.
So what do you propose to do about this improprietus madder
(surely matter).

Yours truly,
Anonymous Annie

—This doesn't make any sense, I said.

—Okay, she said. I just wanted to hear your side of it.

—You have my word, Tess Kittman said, that whatever is
said here will go no further.

It was the heavy breathing quality of this statement that
put me on my guard.—You have the same assurance from
me, I said.

—During the decision-making process right before we

265

hired you, she said, we received an anonymous letter from Seattle advising us to turn you down because of certain imputed actions of yours at UW. As you see, we ignored the letter. You were otherwise such a strong candidate though the charges against you did give some of us pause. When you hire someone, no matter how impressive the vita, you never really know what you're getting. That's why we require a minimum of four years service before we consider someone for tenure.

—A more than reasonable safeguard, I said.

—Well, yes, she said, though some more established people like yourself tend to find our policy somewhat frustrating. You're in your fourth year and I should imagine you'd like to know whether the department plans to recommend you for early tenure.

—I hadn't given it a thought, I said.

Throughout this mostly one-sided conversation, I had been waiting for Tess Kittman to produce Octavia's damning illegible (dream) letter. Instead she nattered on about rumors passing her way about inappropriate behavior on my part but fortunately blah blah blah there had been no official complaints and the department (meaning Herself), otherwise pleased with my performance, was nevertheless prepared to recommend me for "early tenure."

And that was it.

But that was not it. My radar accessed some of the floating rumors Tess Kittman alluded to alleging sexual improprieties and I've had to deal with knowing smiles from a wide range of colleagues and students, some who had never even taken my classes. Octavia, herself, wore this sassy look on her face

266

whenever our paths happened to cross.

As a consequence of unacknowledged anxiety, I've gained fifteen pounds in the two weeks following Octavia's country weekend.

Without telling anyone, not the department, not Nora, I've looked into other job possibilities, but there are no openings so far at the places I'd been willing to consider. If my financial situation were stronger, I'd take some time off from teaching and do nothing but make art. Sleep has not been a friend for the longest time.

Whenever I go into the college to teach my classes, it is as if I am perpetually re-entering the landscape of my disgrace.

Look, if I don't know my own heart, who does?

If I were given to complaint, which I'm not, I would say circumstances have conspired unfairly against me. I will not say it, but I think it, I can't help thinking it, and this deep sense of injustice, which comes unbidden, which whispers itself, provides a kind of private consolation.

Second of all, there is no second of all.

ON THE OTHER SIDE

by Marie Carter

The airline refuses to take our money.

"You don't have to pay until you've arrived at your destination safely," says the woman at the desk, chewing on the ends of her ponytail between breaths. "That's how confident we are that you will enjoy flying with our airline."

Susan and I are going on the "holiday of a lifetime" to Elizabeth, New Jersey. We throw our suitcases into the overhead compartments. Our suitcases are stuffed with empty plastic bags that we will fill with all the things we buy in New Jersey.

"Good morning ladies and gentleman. This is your captain speaking. I have never flown a plane before, but it's been my boyhood ambition to become a pilot. Even though I only got 15 out of 100 answers right on my examination, I hope you'll all give me a chance because I bake cookies with my mother on the weekend and I'm wearing a yellow sweater."

Our fellow passengers seem rather calm, but Susan has gone blue in the face and is hyperventilating, tightly gripping the edge of her seat. "I think I'm going to throw up," she repeats every five minutes, but she doesn't reach for the sick bag or run to the bathroom.

The flight from JFK to Newark takes four hours and we are flying very low to the ground. We have almost reached the shores of New Jersey when suddenly the engine starts to stall.

"Don't worry!" the captain says over the loudspeakers. "I may have failed the first practical test, but I'm sure I can control the plane when under pressure." The plane makes a nose dive for the water. Suddenly we are *in* the water and everyone is swimming around, searching for their luggage.

"Just give me a chance!" the young captain pleads, bubbles blowing out his mouth. He is gradually sinking. "Get back in the plane and I'll make sure you reach the airport safely."

"He's got to be kidding," Susan says, her arms thrashing in the water. Everyone is bobbing up and down, craning their necks and trying to locate their soggy luggage. Underwear floats past my nose and slippers. People have packed lots of slippers.

"Let's give the poor guy a chance," I say. "He's just starting out and now the airline probably won't pay him because they won't get any money from their customers."

"Who cares," Susan says. "Life is hard. Deal with it."

"There's no harm done," I say. "At least you and I are able to swim."

We reach dry land, but before we can enter New Jersey, we encounter some fastidious immigration officers wearing dark-rimmed glasses and pink boiler suits with Irish wolfhounds. A young scallywag with spiky hair and bald patches is asking arrivals an assortment of questions and determining whether they should be allowed into the state or not.

He finally reaches Susan and me. "Do you have a favorite pebble that you like to play with on the beach?" he asks.

"Yes," I say, thinking up the best answer I can. "It's smooth with a grainy texture and it's pearl pink."

The young man chews on his biro considering my answer for a while. "I think you're lying," he says. "I don't believe such a pebble exists."

"How would you know?" I ask. "You don't even have a PhD in drawing."

The young man ignores me and goes to the next fellow. "Are you wearing the same suit as Arnold Schwarzenegger in *True Lies*?"

"Yes," the new arrival replies.

"Very good," says the immigration officer. "You can come on in."

EXCERPT: *NEVER AGAIN*

by Doug Nufer

When the racetrack closed forever I had to get a job. Want ads made wonderlands, founding systems barely imagined. Adventure's imperative ruled nothing could repeat. Redirections dictated rigorously, freely. Go anywhere new: telephone boiler-rooms, midnight grocery shooting galleries, prosthetic limb assembly plants, hazardous waste-removal sites; flower delivery, flour milling, million-dollar bunko schemes. Do anything once; then, best of all, never again.

No more gambling, horseplay, poker. Hyperordered strictures posit antipredictability, perhaps.

"References?" Herr Trollenberg interviews, cocked brow adjusting monocle glinting somber intent.

"Certainly."

Application blanks require plausibilities, employment doyens earnest applicants, fictions facts.

"William Henderson, Universal Export; Niles Whitehead, Schweppes Flypaper; Sneed Moot, Hunsuck/Moot/Flagwipe; Harley Bloom, Celibate Communuchations; Dr. Sydney Culpepper—"

"Mr. Raymond!"

"O.K."

Phony resume misrepresents George R., 39, divorced, remarried, kids; Foreign Legion, MBA Marketing, BS Economics, appropriated universities fronting posts commensurating mendacity.

"Fice-president, Vhales, Paratron Intercetational?"

"Cetations. Orca brokering. Aquaria, marine rodeos, Hollywood. Tremendous seller's market."

"Fending machinegunner, FoMoCo, Edsel Longdivision?"

"Common antiques. Dinosaur V-8 fossil-fueled premiums. Autoclubs, collectoral collages, gaspump themeparks."

"Mint?"

"Unused."

"Hmmm, caveat emptore," mumbling. "Porter, Vax Museum!"

Duties included mold preservation, mustache touch-up, anticandle eventuation, maniac proactionary vigils viz. sexdoll fetishisms, cathode monitoriums, lollipop fear-reassurance, hunchback impersonations.

Bigger lies fly hire? Entrenchantly fatuous ad-libs pique counterapplicationary formulae, inverting title-position hierarchical privileging. Heretically, lessened discomplishments premiere greaters, resisting progress. Troll deliberates. Protection's panic button? Applicant's attire connotes acquiescence, corporate-incorporation. Polite-toned conversing encodes dress. Well-spoken assertiveness forwards tempworker compliance, reallocating proportional cares. Tempagent's loyalty pinions: Das Ferm oder Der Vorkfarce?

Reliability commands responsibility. Trial ethics ideate intermixable tolerances. Businesses dun personnel, affording prognosticated risks.

"You vant vot?"

Forbidden kneejerks cue; free beer, instant gratification, effortless effort, monkey's paw nonbacklashing wish-fulfilled deliverances. Rather, employmentality affirms standardizational blubbering inre collar bleaching (white/blue), salary leashing (short/tight), benefit fleecing (bald/fuzzed). Backgrounding whitenoise annoys. Recession-minded exigencies pressurecook thought. Steely lips acclaim eye-lazered consequentiality, commanding reply.

"Opportunity."

Tilt? Nodded acceptance unclogs processional drainpipe. Headtalk gestures convey protodocuments: workpass, memo allocating stingy directional information.

"Report 8:30."

$6.50/hr answers unasked interrogative. Duration?

"Ve'll see. Veeks."

Among serious wackos, ordinary sober eccentrics hardly rate peremptory heave-ho. Handshaken thank-yous prestyle orderly's retreat. Deference uber alles.

Ratty glances deface waiting-room youngerlings learning hypocritical deceits enate magazines, sweating runaway apathy. Dressed, cleaned, cool-heeled musicians, artists, hacks, fuck-ups, Janes, Johns belong Paris, Kauii, Venice, SoHo because they'all're special.

Decades older, 39-year-old leapfrogs polywogs. Assignment: Overseer, Redline Abatement Vault, Transpacific National Bank. Objective: Burma. Entice Asians into dejunkied tenements via liponym (cull non-Asian surnames), purging loan-aps.

Yesterday's tomorrow todaybreaks, establishing management toady rank authority's half-assed accountableness, carelessness. Age's virtue installs otherwise-unqualified supervisor, but nonjob's cirrus-status desubstantiates task's resolution.

Samoan factor complicates mission. Teen gang profilings overshadow rival ethnic delinquencies, mixconstruing Filipino cannery syndicate mayhem, Chinese watertortures, opium tongs, postwar's abase vengeances interalienating Vietnamese, Laotians, Montagnards, Cambodians, Hmoung-others (essentially, non-Japanese orientals). Unstated jargon slates conquer/divide ghettoization modules platting African-American exile.

"Diversify," corrects apologist.

Provisional cullsquad scoutmaster briefing interjects clue-in terminology, public-address cistern's anti-giardial chlorine.

Russel Nakagawa, cleancut Nisei baseball fan, compassionately buttresses Charles Pickford's teamspeak. Superanglo exec-seminar cant swirls innocent corruptions justifying greed's underlying heartfelt paternalism. C.P. counterwinks Russel's admissive shucksing, humoristically ass-backing lest neo-employed tempster unpeel indiscriminatable civil right's facemask.

Underseated, toilers moil meanly. Para-employed placements file shufflings. Individualistic famines fantasize idling's idyl, waging workaday's lickspittle pittance.

Ordinarily, funds greenlight extrafunds; representatively, collateral's easysleaze guarantees rejection. Speedlabs, coca popstands, greenback laundryrooms, nefarial etcetera forebode sheriff's foreclosured posse. Mortgagors reshade black/white affluences denoting business-as-usual rubberstamp.

Overlapping instructions tether initiative, complicate supervising's easiness. Blurred accountability expresses month-old takeover confusion renominating TPNB (nee' Sasquatch Bancorp), currently B-o-A subsidiary. Triplicate stationery's letterheads confound drawers, self-inker hazards compel trialballoon blottering, phone-IDs splice trinomials. New-hires, tempists, unbenefited crewlings abound; retiring pension-treaded staffers rotate humanity spares. Pitbosses duck pendulum.

Namescanners scour barrio lien futures. Batteried Walkmen leak clashing Nirvanas' rhythmic poundings, avert authorizational muzaks. Henry Margashack, Cynthia Pugh, Christine Balder badgily number-name breastpasses. Henry's fingernails're longest. Guitarist tendoncies freakishly handsell narrow-gauged ring-sized digits. Cynthia's unbraed, spikey nipples symmetrate nosepins. Manlike crewcut crowns; midriff-bared navel encrusts lintal crud. Christi redheadedly flips ponytail, repeatedly backpushing hornrims ascrunch. Busy yawns yoke nonunion oxen.

Outputting's subaverage sag evokes substitute teacher hazing rituals. Intimidative slowdown's deceitful clumsiness charms, prolonging estrangement as tapes forestall conversation.

Pouting repulsers attractively invigorate casting-couchpotato mashering. Doubledate scenaralio satyricates. Backseat lap sitting apes Yule-logged office party's bacchanalian abandonings drunkly blundered ruts. Crashpad Romeo duel enscrews, sordid proximity reheating rawly wangled meatpie mincefillings fissured

275

amid filo-layered wallboard tympanically reverbing ruckus.

Realistically untransposed, cullions amass jerkloads. Dull chores sometimes cultivate flattering self-images, battle-ribboned fanciful cicatrixes demarcating angst. Naivete indemnifies foolish defiance.

Secretary sweeps out-basket.

Composing token burden, brevet corporal's minimalist hand-ins might also rankle esprit d'corps. Bossman's daydream off-fucking spurs nerve-ridden snits. Elsewhere-presided, martinet impersonation manages efficiently (goodguy persona's ineffective); herever, friendly manners, industrious attitude, businesslike wiseguy cracking succeeds.

Pee-bound self-excusing leavetaker HM saunters restroomward, savoring unsmoldered cigarette, cloth-bound *Cigarettes*. Midmorn addictions espressify adulthood's strapless privilege versus junior high's strap-on obedience.

Women continue.

"Coffee anyone?" disestablishes once-held pecker ordering.

He-man gofer?

"Double-short latte, pain au chocolate."

"Triple-creamed mocha, almond croissant."

Stuporvisor wobbles outward, passing cubicled blurs immuring hive-minded workerbees, uncrowned queens. Binged slid-shut elevator innocuously de-levitates, alighting downwind acrid steams, pastry-balanced butterings, almondian creams. Orders overlap unit's foursome (HM's unrequested portions appended), distending huge bag's protean comeuppance.

Retracing stirs bees. Swarm-drawn organizettes strop stingers, zingering impudence's cornucopia. Stylish audacity, panache, come-what-may spinners gyrate countertimeclockwise, defying roulette's revolvered gravity. Officious regulationists chowdown grease-nutted non-French doughs, industrially urned non-Italian java.

"Buncha feinschmackers," jabbers.

Feast-scale repast strews obliviously underneath capletters spelling offense: FOOD/DRINK/SMOKE PROHIBITED. Compu-copiers interdict room-shared snacking, superinvoking pristine environeeds. Liberties main office's papermates indulge're denied tempstaff, foreman comprehends. Delight pollutes guilt. Deficient wage's squandering ennobles unselfishness.

Solidarity enhances morale, reinstigates saltmine spelunkering.

"Harrumph!" toe-tapped designating.

Evidence condemns ex-post-facto: styrofoam beads, powdery fingerdust, fleshly smeared formica, breathable sweetened atmospherous particulata. Airblown contaminators doubtlessly windvade mechanisensors, altering delicate chemistries. She's correct. Wienerking's hotdogging endangers operational sensitivities.

"Sorry."

"Xerox specifically warned, contami—"

"Mea culpa."

Abject groveling unsettles wrath. Roiled angers displace, redouble, mysteriously reintensify. Glib contrition rings wrong? Passive-aggressive lassitude baits shark-attacked retaliation. Manpower-eater jaws self-righteously snap.

"Repairs cost thousands!"

"Heart bleeds," underbreaths.

Giggles unstifle, tempting shoutrage. Outnumbered spike-hceled toothcutter slinks offstage.

"Uhhh-ohhhh," milks yuks.

Gleanwhile, scurried wiping, trash concealments, grimescene fleck removals precomb Mac Arthurian beachlanding. Bag-crammed refuse eludes wastepaper's circularfile (disimplicating mess's transgression). Ingenues radiate productivity. Document-piled efficiency deletes antipathetic slackusations. Per-agreement compilative nomicultural investigations unstack in-basket, towerstack outgo.

Ogre, stormtrooper twintrude.

"Ready," perkily welcomes.

"Rules exist," stonetableheads preach, "preeminently—" goggled sniffing can't affirm sugar traces. Aimless fingerpointing merely visualizes refuse's prima-facie wastepapers.

"Problem?" rallies subchief.

"Eating's off-limits. Insubordination's categorically inappropriate."

"Pardon?"

"Miz Saludo observed four persons disobeying restrictions, stomached snickering insults—"

"Kindly give proof."

Grins freeze. Ballsy ploy knocks protocol, teetering King Charly's mountaintop hegemony.

Tattler lunges purseward.

"Scram toots," Christy stiff-arms.

Contact braces tableaux.

"Gotta warrant, babydoll?"

Sequestered allegements muddle vigilante moralists. Theft's casemaking disapplies. Marijuana smoke's likewise unwhiffable, defeating probable-causeways' paralegal contraband seizure. Satchels hide plunder, loot, narcotics? Garbage. Incineratable incriminations'd confirm caper. Napkin-wad inferences lie stashed: constitutionally protected.

Speciously espied gluttonies underpin emergent conflicts between corporationists, discorders. Clean-up's carpetbag rugsweep stashing waste renders accusations untenable.

Fish-hook extrication's easier. Unprovable charges damn accusers. Command-chain twistily chinks unlinkable apologies. Eagle-eye's knowledge complicitly echoes headman's proclivity: believe worst.

"Falsely" slandered noshers appear guilty unless charge's refuted. Deep-seated disaffections throb. Puny sin's inconsequentiality compounding contradictory Republican-held worldviews anent bill-of-rights privacy precedence emphasizes oppression. Suspended lectures forecheck lawyerly hockey defenseman reiterations. Eye-contact dominations emulate dogfight etiquettes. First-spoken interruption's weakening potentially registers wimphood?

"Apologize!," first-strike advantage's mine.

Adversaries harmonize ominously sucked-up breaths. Their departure chastens victory-minded rights advocates. Retributions'll appreciate exponentially, dwarfing normal rollovers.

Formerly committed sorters skitter carelessly, heaping willy-nilly yesses heeding shiftable confabulations respecting nomencultural numerology, concrete noun suggestions, fetched allusions, funny syllables, eeny-meeny-miney-mo. Minutes tumble lunchward.

Noon evacuates working-pooled secretarial strokers, suited mandarins. Errands untangle genders (brownbagger ladies, liquidlunch gents). Pre-fired jobsighter surveys alternatives illustrating optional choicelessness: cafe-carts, messengers, taxis, letterluggers, windowcleaners, leafblowers.

Comparatively, irony enlivens bankster drudgery. Mono-lithic institution's drab foilhood targetspots sportively fling-minded dart-throwers. Edgewalking stress recommends of-ficework, re: parasite interdependency breakdowns analyzing host/guest needs. Behemoth scratching plague-infested fleas romantifies mites' mightiness. Dumbo tasks institutionally insure hide-thickened surface.

Postnoon returner X-rays floorstaff's skeleton. Skullheaded executrix wields envelope's orthographic hatchetjob: Gorge Ramond.

"...decision, unfortunately, precludes continuance..." rejectionspits minced tidings.

Lowkey upperlackey, well-warned, tactfully ushers axed ex-supervisor closetward. Bricabrac's prepackaging de-necessitates reentry. Paperbacks (Perec's *Disparition*, Katchor's *Knipls*), soundtapes (Negativland, BikiniKill), combs, rattlings, material sundries underdefine quirk-sketched dogimpounded lost'n'found cohorts. Waiting hereabouts provokes impatience.

Gatekeeper's glanceblown acetylenes pantomime may-I-help-yous that'll tickerset tresspassing's countdown. Henchmen loiter nonchalantly.

Shrug countersigns impasse-word's unsaid "git!" Callbutton brings bingabonged elevator's all-aboard.

Lobby's desolate, excepting Buddhist securitygod. Benchless marble-lined temple stone propitiates riff-raff disaccommodations, excommunicating unsuitable humus beings. Freed bankculler exeunts.

Presently, gals upstride, unrecognizing co-worker herewithin sidewalk's chaotic context.

"We're canned," reintroduces.

281

Kaffe klatch kaputted livelihoods, however chinzy. Kiss-and-make-up's lascivity countercurrents commiseration.

We-word royally presumes this as-yet unconfirmed blanket firing; schmooze incorporating jingoistic anticorporate lingo effectively babbles, stymies cameraderie.

Credibility graduates. Misanthropic, disenchanted, re-signed, C&C agree upon powwow, should pink slips accost them.

THE FOREST IS IN THE EUPHRATES RIVER

by Leslie Scalapino

For the sculptor Petah Coyne, and for poet Judith Goldman

                    not a mirror
                    the forest is in the Euphrates River

          The outside   floor
                                         completely
                                         harmonious
     peoples on the rose desert
                    cruising Toyotas
                    break the delicate surface
     so the rose huge floor goes
     everywhere the rose floor of streets
                                         with people
               just the outside (word) is harmonious,
                                         though it is

Oarsmen/Eye/Forest—(Reading as Horizontal Sights)

Their looking from their eyes (theirs being plural) 'is' in
the middle. One's eye is in the middle. One's/they're in the
forest (thus silent words). One is walking. The floor of the

forest, black rose-sewage, floats then. Then black roses and fur grow floating, oarsmen row the forest. No sky is there.

Hospice did not allow treatment that would lead to remission, either chemotherapy or radiation. Knowing this, and hearing the mother state she wanted to live wanted to consider treatment, her youngest daughter arranged for hospice, without discussion with family and without the mother's knowledge or consent, to begin before the first meeting with the oncologist. The daughter announced this as a *fait accompli* to her next older sister who stuttered But we are seeking treatment... There will be no treatment, the younger sister declared.

The floor of the forest is the door (of the black train of roses). This isn't a dream but the rule is (it has a rule though it's not a dream, though it is free floating, undetermined): if black roses and fur grow, the oarsmen are rowing them there. Just seen. So they'd say this is nothing.

There aren't edges or periphery either. One's eye being in the middle sometimes sees the oarsmen but if they are close to blank eye they are invisible. Present they're oaring forest but *there they're* invisible. A word is still always.

The forest isn't black. Its train crusted black roses and fur. A face rose weeping. The face is seen only at random. It may be in blank eye still. Who is in the middle of the forest. Besides one. There aren't going to be any questions because the president has blinded them there.

But still and without there being a word one in the middle of the forest, therefore blank having only future, has that *then*. At the time.

One hasn't dreamed since her family, led by the third daughter suddenly assuming being its head, bullied her and their mother who had a brain tumor. Were also bullying the exhausted and frightened father, though sustaining him alone. It floats as a plate on the surface. When the mother is scanned and seen to have a brain tumor, the third daughter—unknown to the second daughter—has herself named as next in line to replace the father in determining the mother's care if he goes away. This should only take effect if the mother is unconscious, yet the third daughter acts as if the mother is unconscious now. The father keeps going away. The family concurs to oppose treatment of the elderly mother, who'd taken the treatments faithfully. Again. Earlier, unformed who'd turned into a minotaur intercedes insisting to the grieving father the mother is not in her right mind when she indicates intent to treat the illness, the unformed secretly securing a document giving herself authority over her mother's life, as if the mother were unconscious when she is not, should the father not be there. He keeps going away.

The father, without telling the second daughter and her lover about the existence of that document (is a forest of petals—no), asks them to arrange and draw up a document placing himself solely in charge, which would unseat the third daughter from this role without saying he is doing that to her. Because who could come up against her. Yet he relies on her to care for him daily in everything.

One goes against the unformed minotaur for the first time.

The hatchling minotaur can force because she is encouraged by Iago. The forest is the black-rose floor only. The hatchling, spewing, revved into another gear lies to the others—yet in front of one they appear not to even care if this is true—maintaining mother was being forced by one to be treated.

The others care about her mother. Are the elderly not listened to. Our—regarded as not there already. They conceive of her as elderly—It is in spring, it is spring.

One can't dream, yet later one dreams the woman who gored is sitting in a car as if planting herself in front of the house in which they'd grown up. The gorer is boasting to someone else—the same man who, with her, outside the dream, commented on the uniform process of all death, ascribing this to the mother, who lay listening and ceased to speak after this episode, either because the words had discouraged her or because she would have ceased to speak then anyway. The gorer's smug tone in the dream speaking to him in front of the house is usurping by condescension, the same tone she was using *outside* the dream of possessing and of being everything in a family in which devotion is central and one non-existent outside of expending that. So, it is the assumption of the dream also, which an outsider who 'saw' this dream occurring could not comprehend in it, that the family house is all. *As childhood.* (Though the people in the dream are adults.) The gorer having taken over the house of their childhood (from which the parents outside the dream had moved long before) occupies everything. At all. Not that she (one) wanted ever to be in childhood only, as does the gorer—but one's existing as it arises in childhood has to be *entirely* relinquished to someone else. Yet the second woman (one) is now not in either the family or in the outside. Why does she see that she is no longer in the outside.

There have been two contradictory directives outside the dream, which it is indicating: *Only being in the family.* (And thus non-existent otherwise.) And the simultaneous directive: *Only being outside.* (Not only is the outside the objective but the family hardly exists, in the second directive. One's reversed into the outside.)

The gorer has only one of these directives. She does not have the directive of one being *only* the outside. She 'lacked' it, a question as to the word 'lacked,' though there are no questions. For the gorer, in goring and in being blinded—by the president as we are—the outside does not exist.

A fine rose silt fills the air in day and night here. The Sahara is being broken down now by Toyota Cruisers used by everyone the nomads cruise the desert and break its delicate crust which disturbed enters huge sand storms that obscure the ball in space's atmosphere because the rose desert below as its floor is huge. The Toyotas cruising tearing the rose train, it is now everywhere. The rose train of those cruising causes illness in people's now rose lungs and in rivers of their eyes, black at night.

There's no way to directly articulate. A blind fascist having only personal life— that's what a fascist is *here*. The coercive hatchling minotaur shouted. The internal events occur while the second daughter is without words. How has the other one had only personal life here. A bully or fascist 'is' as if they were interchangeable because there aren't words here. They sneered as a pack as if they were expressing feeling and as if the other, in favoring treatment, were criminal in which the bully was sustained, speaking so that blank couldn't speak, speaking when one spoke.

One's family now hates her. The minotaur boasts to one that they all hate her, spoken as the minotaur traipses in front of her. Except the father, wanting treatment silently in front of the family in the midst of their actions to one. Yet not silent in that he agreed to treatment with the doctors and says this to *one. It doesn't matter what they think!*—about this—what they think about one—he takes her aside and says.

287

The ignorant bully knowing nothing of this illness, she thinks eating bananas fed by one is killing her mother, who'd have the mother die at once (yet mother had treatment which shrank the tumor to be a very small size—against the hatchling minotaur's will), and who aloud in front of the mother after which the mother becomes entirely silent says: Her skin is breaking down everywhere—pointing out process of all death where the mother had just said to one *Then we'll try!*—hates one in this, arising then, at the point of the start of the mother's illness. Now.

A man, clear, says people dying have to deal with things that happen when they're dying. Bad or good, it's what's occurred (now past), for that person. There isn't present seemingly: 'Too' is wordless. And is also. Now is folded over in space. There she flips her wild sides silently beside the family.

The shock hurts her. It appears that they don't have any sense of anybody being free.

For Iago, family is only tyranny which she (Iago) uses. Iago says to her (one), as if she were not, It is time to be mature, in the cold black desert.

Our insane maturity is—one is the outside as being, and one is 'the outside is entirely rejected.' Iago conflates these to one is only forced by the outside, one rejecting it therefore (which is oneself) but *being it* as *its convention only.*

        this is not bud. bud   is
        (lineage)
        unborn   is there at once
        a horizontal night.

If the mother can't be cured there is either only 'personal' or only 'being outside.' And family is not 'personal.' Outside the forest. Also. The sun goes down as one is walking, at dusk.

once. recurring. first
drones
floating
are killing the insurgents   who're
everyone   there
        the only thing to be is the insurgents
people cruising the rose desert surface is broken
by beside Toyota cruisers   also
                                        is rose black night also
black rose-sewage train so one's by   not from
roof sewage-forest

Therefore there's an empty spot where the eye which is her eye also at once is in the forest. Having entered, the red sun isn't visible there. She would walk anyway, at night also. Yet in the middle, one can't dream either. Seven doctors say the mother's pain would be alleviated by radiation though she will die only slightly later than if not treated. One doctor says No one knows when a person will die. Do it. Seeing the oarsmen is separate, has to be at the same time (that is, in the future only). Has to dream there, one feels. Dreams are only accessing one's own frame, which is stopped here, completely unlike.

C

Circe seduces others, charms without her sensation or touch there, other than her words, which flatter men in *their* hierarchies only. So she creates these in people who would not ordinarily do it. As if other women did not exist, the forest is in the Euphrates River. These two are not panels of each other. Some women are flattered by her but only to facilitate. Everyone facilitates her then. C gives them nothing else. Than their flattery. They don't see this. Feeling disgust for sensation, also wanting to have power (which seems the other part of not having sensation), in C, are invisible to these men, who also want power but as black roses fur furl in a flood in the thin forest, and there feel sensation. Fuel. In C's flattery, people seeing her only in their hierarchy turn: A man turns into a deer, or a white pooch, another man into a small owl. Thin on a green forest, they have simple features. Not flying or running. They're snubbed.

Seated on the dark, now hot forest rosefur-floor, the pooch appears to have a simple, flat body much smaller than C. How one wonders does C copulate with them. C is elderly almost. But these are lovers. Would C one wonders copulate with them before they've changed to be separate from her (in their being an owl or deer). Or before the separation in her being almost elderly. Yet before a small owl in the tree copulates with C's white, fooling with her flat, floating belly lying in the green shimmering forest pulls the long, heavy stem up in C and comes, it rose. From her belly, while C does nothing with or to the owl. C came on the heavy stem the small owl had been on her. There is a small space between that is ecstatic. One thinks the *action* only. In the future C comes, from the owl, maybe before it changed to be that, as a quiet man, but this is just in the future *here*. The small owl comes on her belly just in *their* future, known only to them. Under the wire.

At that same time, one is beside the deer-body of a man, lying beside her at night (lying beside *him* each night)—only his body projected as a deer as weight—mounting the brush leaping flames in their fleeing the forest-fire.

As a bulbous, blood-red sun lowering below the earth. There is a space that is not available to them, like the green meadow between, for example, but is between in spaces there.

One isn't being sarcastic. (Referring to C copulating.) Because it's a thin plate. Flesh and translucent something. A stretched cowhide with pierced, lashed wounds, which weeps occasionally, is there.

C asks to hire one to find someone, and asks her to do secretarial work. But one isn't a detective or secretary. C is imitating one. At a present moment she changes one's thoughts in what blank says to be something else—C imitating blank but altering it in front of others. Thus, for C, history is passive, without actions even. Always already altered. Yet C cannot change blank's body to be something else (such as a deer) in that one isn't a man. For C, men are separate, superior, though blank can't comprehend this as it makes no sense, isn't there. The moon squeezes. The ripple of the black night is before it, yet the round moon is before there was a black ripple. There's the sound of a crowd rushing, or swept into walls. Nearby. That is the black ripple on which or beside which vertically hangs and floats moon as a white iris sticking to the surface lens of one's eye. The pigment of blank's enflamed irises comes off in bright flecks on the walls of the eyes.

Concerned about the second's turmoil, seeing it and that it stemmed from herself dying, the ill mother had called out cautioning the second daughter who's leaving the house once, Enjoy being in your life. This is the instruction for this as well as to dream. Helplessly (may be—anyway, on one's own, with friends if one can *see* them—they're there).

It's called a black 'sea' of roses. For a black 'ocean' is weight. Ocean is rain. Ocean in rain *is* rain. C in the rain (the ocean that's coming down) is soundless too, her charm nullified in that that night no one is around, she's smoking a cigarette. Graceful dipping her legs stretched down from a chair in night. Rain 'at' night is that black ocean around blank with nothing but waves. The Euphrates River is the forest's choppy

291

black waves that are not in water.

Excruciating physical pain (when it had occurred) that is one's enflamed frame within one's skin, the spine a cord in the back—so it's neither inside nor outside anywhere—is at the same time (as the outside, in its being oneself) and is at once spring in that the trees blossoming everywhere are *then*, is there. One's formerly broken spine is outside then. Then the enflamed irises that are eyes are outside also. The blossoming trees outside them/the trees—seen have no pain. In the sense that they (the blossoming boughs, trees in them—a tree is in its blossoms then) have no feeling then, are not enflamed yet are the extreme in space present where nothing dies there. Oneself when it's excruciating pain is out alongside they're blossoming. It is not feeling there. Is to one. Is spring just then. Not outside that.

This happens now in one's enflamed eyes. The small, curled mother in the bed is alongside oneself in space. Speaking to her is there (is the inside) the only place in space in spring.

C is a civil servant. Doling out posts, she appears to have caused the future or control it in having many supplicants with no present existing. Thus no future is here either (it's described insolently), the president also at once (differently) turning the crowd into 'our' stupid, blind, gutted ones. There's no anarchy going on. But this is not visible here. Our soldiers in Fallujah where we live—no, we don't live—there now bomb and mow down the people demolishing the walls of the city. The streets are filled with the dead who are thrown into the Euphrates River because there are too many. Their stench and decomposition swam in the streets, in the rose-sewage. Everyone is an insurgent if they live. There. Yet they are to be invisible dead here.

The rose desert   is being
                                   torn up
  by
  floor
  the cruisers   the people cruise them on
                        the rose sand desert's surface
  in Toyotas
                                   break its surface
  which enters the ball in space's
                                            there
                                   with the desert

The Forest is in the Euphrates River

C does not think about this. Because I say/don't imagine so. She is flat, one-dimensional creamy lying in the forest with the owl: But she is *telling lies* also. Small posts are doled out by Circe to men who, being the only visible men, are easily turned by her. There's competition. Periphery not existing in space, visible men corrupted by sinecures (there is such a thing as 'corruption'—and perhaps C can't imagine this way of thinking) speak on their own periphery of hearing. C does not have much power, the posts being insignificant, if you ask me, yet the effect because of her being *without* force (outside of it, from the outside) is the change of another into a small, white, muted with simple features, pooch. Who may be at the same time a violent man. Or deer with dull, soft eyes on crafts of boat-bodies by which (their bodies) the deer are still, are seen from the oarsmen in the middle oaring the black-rose-sewage-floor-forest with no sky. Not by, *beside* the oarsmen. One's eye. They row by C perhaps (there are no questions asked—as our president blinded us). That is, *when* he did.

no sky. Not by, *beside* the oarsmen. They row by C perhaps (there are no questions

293

That lead-bully female appears, is translated, as a minotaur when in bullying (imagination), is utterly different from C by minotaur using savage force devoid of charm and by her being a different person. Who are the Brownshirts. Asks a man, dubious and suspicious, That this is real. Thinks it is. Mother is to be swept wordlessly away, she's swept wordlessly.

She stopped speaking. Yet utterly embraced, adored.

The minotaur female to possess father swivels on her bulging shoulders, there is to be no anarchism, anarchy. Her wild sides in bulk traipsing stalks pouring mouth shouting at one. Woman Iago holds an apple of discord to throw it in, shooting blank looks of hatred, one will not be speaking aloud, again. 'Not again' at all is anarchy. If this occurs in death. Of anyone, of anyone else. (Or anarchy if speaking does not occur again in their lives.) While father is silent, except in the background to one, favoring treatment for mother, and seemingly paired with third daughter, one is to take the hit. The minotaur traipsing bulges her face and shoulders pouring out from her mouth not from her head.

Repeating is a cold desert.

The humped hunched trotting and swiveling the huge shoulders and head which on the trunk with its rolls of fat tapers to spindling traipsing legs, each on a hoof—is extended in air shouting that's just in the mouth. Not in *one's* head either (in hearing), vitriolic spews in the air from the humped trotting. Whose only humped rage trots there. Back and forth in front of one.

The traipsing coiled rolls shouting had groomed her offspring to do this also—a daughter appears in the air, shouting over the phone that one advocating treatment to alleviate had *caused* mother's suffering, before the treatment begins.

But mother took treatment then.

Pulling back unrelated to anything, C is utterly successful, which is only irrelevant to one now. It *should* be irrelevant. A pooch waddles to C, only because transformed it has short legs.

This means there isn't anything as expression (here). Thus exposed as conflict how can this be anything (it can't be seen). For conflict is nothing, if only itself. We're taught. It is. The floor-forest is there fan of the oarsmen then. When. If it's only conflict, it's what we were doing always though. Apparently. There are just posts (positions) mirroring boards stuck in the desert floor. One hasn't a post, though she can't focus on it in this case. And are seen *from* the oarsmen (it's coming from them and from their or one being there). What are And. They're not blank but active space. And. And is rain, the ocean–floor with no floor. It's white rain, the snowing floor.

Whose conflict occurs in exactly the same way the outside is occurring. The violence of the minotaur with her swinging bulk body the sides traipsing shouting lies (she's lying in air) is to reverse her (minotaur's) own actions and behavior into being one in blank violence: That one is supposedly doing, has done, what the other in bullying is doing is interpreted to the others (their same family), never *'to'* though in front of one as if one had never existed. Therefore blank seeing this is not one doesn't matter. It's in Baghdad amid the US soldiers. Separately. In front of one, lying in air. One doesn't live then. Outside of this does doesn't.

Now nothing seems to move but the rose-black forest moves fast while everything is blank (at the sides).

Death doesn't exist. Mother'd said intensely Why can't *I* survive. *You've* had things happen to you and *you've* survived. My children have survived, why can't *I*. Or she said: My children have survived, yet *I* can't. She paused, then she said We just *have* to survive—that's all there is. There is no mortality. She didn't. Couldn't. Yet one has to alter this, but can't dream still yet.

They all meet in a room and silence one, speaking before I can speak. I'm not allowed to speak. After, the shaking, silent father takes me aside and when I cry They blame me for mother's suffering! who's alive lying in the next room, he exclaims *It doesn't matter what they think!*

The Circle on the Intestine

Their hatred coming from the lies uttered by the gorer, it is jealousy occurring at death. Around its time.

Her technique is to bottle up another and then attack. The woman who smirks. When mother was ill a circular incision formed from punctures of the minotaur's horns on one's belly.

Red liquid expands on the edges of the circle squirting the outside of one's abdomen and intestine. While horning, rolled minotaur smirking that everyone hates one derided blank if the latter rose from her chair during it.

Minotaur says to their father who was seated watching quietly there: You can see I'm being polite whereas she (one) is angry, when one rose from one's chair.

Claims jeering to blank that she kids herself— "You *think* everyone's against you"—as if it were her own deluding ego:

Whereas, the gorer condescends, no one's spoken of you with each other (supposedly)—while, nevertheless, everyone agrees they hate you, according to the mouth, which utters anything. Cruelty is polite, it thinks, it twists its floating hoof.

To lunge lying in air. Frightened the mother would live (it is one's theory now), the minotaur female had had to possess the ill one there in order to possess the father. Outside the boat-bodies float on the street of deer turned from men. Getting up in the dark at morning—though it's the green city during day—it's the day cold black desert.

The tsunami occurred at this time. A wave through one ocean after another. The wave withdrew the floor-ocean far back from a beach, then ascended over it curling fifty feet above in the air, drowning hundreds of thousands from countries, carried out to sea hanging on wreckage. Later, many hanging in mid-ocean were picked up by ships. Red Cross workers wrapped masses in blue plastic body bags. Later one thinks to the minotaur You think you possess the floating being (not dead, changeable)—who by that time has disappeared though he's there for the minotaur only—his the not dead changeable has something to do with forgiving, (him) later one thinks.

The mother watched the tsunami in the news. There's the desert in mourning after her death which seemed sudden. This is in the city at day, also at the same time the cold dark desert even in light at day it's clear dark with nothing there, people move around though, the boat-bodies of deer moving through the dark crystal light.

The gorer who had at first when the mother was diagnosed overwhelmed her sibling (one) with a lava of hatred, trying to push that other from the room to try to eliminate her, hovered presiding on their mother to possess her by sucking her from life, apparently. None of the arrangements are known to one. It's as if sealed. In one being excluded from this, sealed into it.

She maintained immediately the mother asking for treatment is not in her right mind (repeating is the cold desert now, despair). In order to prevent treatment, the third daughter says to the father What's the difference between a month and a year more of life. Eleven months, one thinks. The gorer moves in, nesting on the premises, strangely dictating *I'm—the—*daughter, she says into the phone. Iago's another daughter but tests by holding the apple of discord to throw it in from a distance in order to see what will happen, occasionally feeding the gorer (minotaur is more stupid than Iago) engineering on a flat plate her wild sides. They play with each other. They organize their offspring.

Blank had never had this thought of them before. Now, while it's going on, it won't go away.

It's like spawning though the offspring are born, are there. But on a mirror in dark crystal light.

Hops is the traipsing large bulk on a crystal dark clear plate in front of their father she's speaking any cruel words to one that have arisen in the mouth. She already gores but no scene like this has happened before, between the goring and blank. Before the mother was ill, this action hadn't been translated. Goring does not remember what she's said, or says in the same sentence apparently, in that there're no words.

Though Iago had exuded poison to both, to everyone. Her own offspring became Iago's ministrants. To be not in the stream of ministrants, ministering.

An Action

Gray rain was a straight falling ocean everywhere, the air horizontal inside it. The air that was is the falling ocean paused for a day or two. They went to the cemetery in the pause ocean between the horizontal air raining and itself vertically falling.

The burial occurred in a cold dewy green country cemetery. The others, not speaking to her as they were directed by their mothers, who were there (directed in everything—it would be a question but the president blinded us—everything *there*, what's seen), crowded to throw dirt on the coffin lowered into the ground. The father frail and trembling, helped by grandchildren, walked to the grave, a silent wail coming only visibly from him when they threw the dirt. They drove away. Driving on the ocean road, out-before-constricted other leaving mother there with dirt covering her! and T see that the others have turned on a mountain road, so they turn around to drive back and follow them. Is speaking about the burial to him. There is no one speaking inchoate yet is wild. At all, because of that. At a curve, which is a pull-off, on the winding road is a huge coyote standing.

They pull over, stop and look at it. The coyote eyes as if toward her using force crosses its front paws in front of itself and bows by dragging its thick neck down one leg with its neck twisted to look slanted eyes at her intensely while dragging the neck up against the other leg from the ground again—in a deep bow. The words occur to her *as* the coyote bows—presented [she thinks of] words "It *is* all right," words which are from, in the sense of in front of, or are beside the wild animal uttered by it yet as a weak translation occurring sarcastically transpiring to her.

The coyote comforted me. Then turning, yet it twists its head to look at her impression at first of sarcastically over its shoulder

299

again, it disappears off the ledge of the road into the forest.

Questioned, T says It bowed. Furthermore, you didn't know you were going that way (on the mountain road) and it was there when you came that way, for that. A friend who's a doctor, surprised, says It was your mother! Maybe she said meant It came from your mother! We're a second only. Second thinks It came from the coyote. That would be seen as a question except the president has blinded us. Or it comes at death from occurrence itself, like their jealousy.

Their jealousy is of her existence even, unrelated to her though overtime related to her nature, thus to her actions outside (apart, overtime, from any actions in relation to them).

How does it (the gesture) come from the coyote. If nothing moves. She's so stunned by her mother's death. Or from the dead. T says I stopped because I knew it had something to say to you, the way it looked. Because anyway it (the coyote's action) came from some other event, if only from the event of her perception from death. Whose perception. Is connected in space. Is its bowing not an accompanying event to hers. Or is its first, with the death.

Now she notes the fact that the coyote's action, evident and directed to her—from its facial expression—is in relation to it being outside the range of her personality (also! no), that she would not believe such a thing and therefore could not think to produce it.

Nor does she produce goring but she sees it though she's blinded in the enflamed irises. Days, going to take the mother to her radiation appointments she crazily slowly drives the car ahead of her irises, that are afire. Or rather, she is *behind* her irises. The enflamed irises are first.

300

Goring

Goring had transcribed in space: someone else is doing the thing (that actually *she* in goring was doing). The others hold in reference the transcribed version. But it is because they choose to.

The gorer had looked only at their father while she'd savaged the other, her mouth uttering whatever cruel word comes into it rather than the stream of words even first entering in her head.

And, as if to divert and thus convince him with lies even were success, her apparently having the sense that the occurrence (and the reaction of the one savaged) doesn't exist at all apart from his view, is only a reaction reflected in him which can be obliterated if he *shows* no reflection of it, he did not show any, seated. But he is elderly shaken. Then.

Like spring the event is not seen. Ever. Except by blank. By a second. Certainly the gorer is neither a boat-body nor a seducer like C, rather is gross force without intervention affecting her except fear. Iago had removed the hatchling minotaur's fear. That was new. Always has to have someone with the minotaur, someone accompanies her, to overwhelm any there.

Since one no longer has a family a thought arises first.

The other, blank in the sense that is spring, is exposed to an unavoidable, unbeatable thought. Both frightening and exciting. One friend phrases it, in regard to this situation: to be without the imagination. That thought is: the necessity to not have, by undoing all before in events outside in oneself, any authority retroactively *in* the outside before and in the present.

This thought had arisen before, but it occurs differently

301

now. What's important is to bring about seeing that difference by seeing its relation to this instant only. The nation is horizontal. The sky is. There are only present actions in that sense. So, anyone's actions are not behind anything. The minotaur uttering any cruel words coming into her mouth—and spring—are (in one) without any authority motivating them, there. Authority of any kind, one's creating, must be grasped and removed from anything.

Her particular instance of family authority is and has to be in the future foreseen as connected to people wading in rose-black sewage in the streets whose sewage-lines were to be restored by Halliburton, the US company that skims the cream of graft in Baghdad from the US government, for them and the US leaders who hold shares of Halliburton, the graft occurring as open intention on the US part unknown to us. There isn't authority in either—that is, not in any single of a pair, (of authority behind this, which is in her, isn't seen yet by her), or in (as) the two held together (any authority or basis, and that held in her), which would be imagination in respect to the sight she's to see of people wading in the sewage of their streets in spring now. Reads about it in the newspapers. The second (person) is the particular authority that is *in* both of these small and large (a family and the outside terrain) instances *at once*.

This does not mean there is not to be authority in the sense of: not restoring the sewage lines to clean use. There must be that. But no authority behind or after any, even at once *while* restoring the sewage system. Because there is the open fur door.

For this reason, one has to find authority linked and noticed in oneself in space that is to unrelated outside events. Dismantle this activity. As it *is*. In the outside, but not stemming in any way from one's family, as it does *not* stem from that.

In that sense the people wading in the rose-black sewage in the streets—there, the sewage-lines that are thought by our people, told this, to be being or to have been repaired—are thought first at this second.

Or a rose is thought first (not the rose-black sewage burst). Or the sewage *is* thought first.

The people wading in it are thought first. So the two coincide, both are thought first—before any other is this second.

Now.

This doesn't help them, Laura observes. Right. (That is, no, it doesn't.) Though we're not at this second.

When it comes to it, the other remembers that the father whom she'd thought was exactly the same as herself, a misperception that is a thorough illusion now, seen years earlier when she was at a young age, had been doing the same thing as now: In the intention to be 'even-handed' between the three daughters, he would erase her completely by her characteristics not being spoken of there as none of the qualities were *allowed* mention by him or them. Meaning, to observe by speaking of it would be unfair to the others. This is not on her part, it was strange on theirs.

This has nothing to do with authority in the outside, since she did not rely on this definition (of anything *from herself*). And the separation is part of their absorption.

Boat-Bodies

The problem is that the imagination is the way things are occurring. Or is *what's* occurring. In any case. Apparently this is obvious but she didn't know it until now.

It is only an illusion that men, except their father for the time of their looking at him, perhaps their father too, but except T, have turned and move by as boat-bodies of deer, or maybe the hopping owl rose off of C's belly.

The boat-bodies of deer who are the men move through, here and there, but they also begin to be distinguished as only seen that way. Now one/she sees she is a boat-body herself. It's a relief. She can rest, always. She thinks, for a minute.

It has nothing to do with C, C isn't around at the moment. That she turned one into a pooch, another into an owl floating on some emerald green dewy grass within the forest has no force. Anyway. Out ahead—boat-bodies are seen.

Though the man one knows, calm, kind—beside her the mysterious deer-body—floats walking, or at night lying in the dark between the red sun and the moon early—leaps over the enflamed brush everywhere when the forest catches fire.

It catches fire in winter, but he's very steady and clear, not cool dark crystal. While running, she sees a deer running appearing to be afire.

C's long slender legs curled around the waist of the quiet man or the violent man who's *then* a pooch or is *later* on the emerald hill only black at night. For it is childhood and elderly life at one time. For her. For both. There is never lack of memory. Of the senses, but how are events anywhere. Are animals who weren't people aware of making something else by their they're being together so everything is changed. Do they change everything so then it is different, or so events occur differently, far from them: from their being together.

And can they know this. Star is a hill at night but is a war evening. Plants do change each of the instants: is *their* authority outside—events *then* are different from what we're seeing making.

The use of time. Episodes that occur—as these occur in their consecutive 'order' (is now). The mother had had an inner life. Life (hers) through her imagination. Last night walking rain.

What I saw when I was walking through the city beside a main thoroughfare, a blue heron dipping its legs as trays in the air floating low slowly, almost touching the person with its legs when floating over in day—through the neighborhoods—it went right next to (in space, both frontal) the memory of the little girl with the other little girl, come home from school, told by their grandmother their dog Jet died hit by a car that day. This is beside the blue heron floating over one. The little girl bursting into tears puts next to it And we paid so much money for it! from the Pound. Petals are time, of years—only on blossoms on trees. One day or one time, the two girls together remember the dog, and the girl who'd burst out We'd paid money for it!, said to the other You said then: And we paid so much money for it! reversing them in the horizontal space. Because time and space have been compressed by her. No, it was not I who said that, *you* did. Yes, it brought out the worst in me! now the girl remembers. Petals are time but also a mirror in which side-by-side one thing is the other throughout, for her. Not for someone else maybe. Or: this wouldn't happen to anyone else.

In war, we have the leisure to remember anything.

A train in space clacking overpass over the city, seen at once through both rows of windows on either side, jolting as it hurls is in space by a phone call (next to it in horizontal space

305

though of eight years earlier than it) from the enraged little girl who pours out wrath that her mother having been asked by her to allow her (the daughter) to arrange the mother's things before her death, sort through her things before she died—that was eight years before she died—has refused. One asks the-consumed-with-wrath You said *that* in relation to her later death. There are no questions since the president has blinded us—so the wrathful is alerted to one hearing her. In a few days, the mother, who would not usually speak of another in the family to another, this time mentions, and almost weeps that she's been hurt by (the little girl) having asked to sort through her things before her death. An aside from one to Iago who fishes a few days later—finally leads one to say this event to Iago. And Iago says immediately She didn't say this! (the little girl didn't say she'd wanted to sort through the mother's things). But how could I know it if she hadn't said it—She called *me* (who was hearing) and said it—I'm saying it *after!* No: she *didn't say* it! Iago says on the phone, long distance. Wrathful here is then in rational actions. She's realigned. By herself and, at once, by someone else elsewhere. There meets a black butterfly that skims ahead wobbling and making the air. She *makes* everything. It is different from an inner life, there there is none.

Men who were supplicants to C. But the question is Why are only they changed. What is oneself—A boat-body too. You've been holding yourself in abeyance, separate in living not just in not dying yet. Concentrating on one thing separately. But one moves.

Others were hardly given time or attention (though they might not notice) to say a word while wrathful who seems jolly there talked in her deprivation uninterrupted in a loop without listening. To anyone. Any speaking would be omitted. Omitted that was outside, considered boring. Nothing returned (in the jolly one's [wrathful's] speaking), didn't speak of or admit the outside into the loop, sometimes speaking at the same time as others. Eventually, next to them all is a mesh that's a black butterfly that is rational action, unspoken. That is, speaking is being led by someone else—the butterfly is doing a rational act that is the same thing or instance there (the same as: that no one is allowed, by everyone, to speak except that one absorbing).

Two things begin to meet in the space. That itself. It is 'the' space, meaning 'anything there'—horizontal includes and subsumes vertical.

What's revealed is that one can think anything.'Concentrate on something else' is a tautology. That's what people are.

One cannot unravel a loop—there's nothing to unravel. It never touches itself.

It's also a tsunami wave reversed *in* to one and people. Because there are so many people.

Blank, oneself not identifying it, has been mystified by pop garbage spewed into other people, such as from talk shows. That were going on all this time, while she never watches television. But this phenomena is not tsunami wave, though it isn't surface either, in altering people. Their *behavior* is a tsunami wave.

A tsunami wave is people's behavior, which is also their speaking or thought [I'd thought], it has to have been *done*— has to be acted on space. Crowd running. Speaking to. After. After what.

Of course there aren't any rational actions.

Second is going to concentrate on something simple. One as a boat-body is submerged—but also loves (because one does) though one's eyes just see.

Still, a body is a jellyfish, a colored cape pumping in-place with no bone in it. They think.

While the boat-body is a deer banging in the forest with as against its sides, there is a part of one that doesn't have bone. Also the jellyfish pumps its cape held in the illumined there. The same body. But the deer anyway has an aspect that is boneless, humped flying with the legs drawn up to leap jumping over a bush, the moon standing on its one edge there. Before the deer, before its boat-body.

The soldiers are throwing the bodies into the Euphrates
she comes in says by mouth after hearing

it
the streets are choked stacked with the people's
corpses.
in that they won't allow people to leave the US soldiers
are throwing the bodies into the Euphrates
the US
to conceal the numbers
dead
saying only insurgents are killed. but more
than a 100,000 people
remained in Fallujah when before
the fighting
started starts
the president of Iraq says anyone there still is an
insurgent
the event wasn't spoken   *as occurrence*
no civilians
there   fore   are killed

308

                                              in the event
the difference and the relation between saying by mouth
                                              and
the (written phrase)
also event not spoken *as occurrence*   is

                                              in space
they   come

                                              out

   In this shape in space, or during it 'being'—after it—the
Second's mother passed away (in this instant of falling asleep, now,
remembering this burial had already happened, so she *must* have).
The words "passed away" rather than "died" seem to now (after
her 'going,' 'not being here') mean something, the words appear
not to be euphemism. But there's no relation except in that space
(a band or layer and time) between the people in Fallujah and the
one's elderly mother, apart from them 'going' then nor were all
the people killed there by fighting. The US soldiers demolished
the walls in the Fallujah citizens' space with them there. They
were there in it. It wasn't spoken (*as occurrence*). Nor was the
mother speaking (at the last).

   The young woman coming in speaking this, the phrasing
itself imitated an event in space. The words were a stream in a
shape that had come out of her mouth. They were a structure
in space in the room taking place in front of her mouth but
everywhere and perceived by a hearer only. Second became a
hearer also, in addition to seeing, things other, elsewhere.

   Only what one doesn't know happens. May include
mirror image reverse: Use of others only then they bound
there. One does also. Abandoning of the center occurs from
the people. The view that the father had abandoned one is
altered by him. We speak. He had attempted throughout to
move the others without abandoning them either. They the

others besides him don't move in her seeing. She is terrified
by death now.

                                      One's a wall to them bound
off of it to them there isn't day death doesn't exist
there both 'our'   *only* existing
(his) love is one isn't a wall then or rose desert's walls
                                      's walking one's
                        wall's 'walking' 'one's' 'wind' 'dusk' 'dusks'

Rule

A depression is a depression in space and it has
                                              no
                                      equivalent
            in authority
Depressed dusk walking. Rain is dusk *as occurrence then*. One
isn't event, except *as occurrence*. Though speaking wasn't *that*
event *as occurrence* ever.
They're coming to check-posts, if they
                              do not respond
            to the hand-signals   to slow
or to firing in the air   by the US soldiers
who say   they'd signaled
the Italian journalist kidnapped returned by the
                                      insurgents
                  they're being shot
                                              first
returned is shot speeding toward a check-post, the
                                              agent
in the car with her   who'd
freed her from the insurgents   is killed
                        all from this a train
by the US soldiers   bombs go off in the roads
everywhere

          black rose-sewage train   beside them
and night   everyday killing
civilians   and US soldiers
                          who say any
words after   first
          a family of five coming to the check-post is
                        day is beside them too at once
fired on the parents are killed   the newspapers say
the children were covered in the parents' blood they
live—a man deported from the US to Syria so
                                              they
                                              can
                                              torture him
                  push outside him
unlike the US   the relation to deportation
is
bursts of blossoming trees here   not in
                    black rose-sewage grounds
says everyday they beat him yet the Syrians say
                    he's no connection   to
                                        terrorists
now, is not related   after they
                                       tortured him
it's upheld in the US 'we'   *can*
                                deport
people who'll be tortured to be tortured *there* on
one side   is day   and a   night
on the other side   there is   horizontal
                                              here
this, on the level of black rose-sewage,
                                    hasn't authority
in order   that
not cycle   every event of any sort
                                    be first

311

This intrinsically, on the level of black rose-sewage, hasn't authority. But on other levels it does.

A dumb thought, which there aren't. Thoughts. But one has to flatten space in order that every event of any sort (eventually here) be first.

Depressed dusk walking—rain dusk walking alleviates death (of a mother—who not being there, the effect of that) slightly— the light and dark dusk is everywhere soft in pouring dusk rain—the buildings there that are also the vertically falling rain shafts, in them/the buildings, which they are (rain), and trees boughs in the dusk *are* the heavy rain first.

Precedes as rule with everybody dying a wave of every
thing dying yet first and   now mature
lovely woman major in the Marines   who's
Hawaiian   and lost
                                                          both
                  reversed into the outside   her legs
is a pilot of a helicopter that
                                    included   *was*
                                                          blown up
in Iraq
testifying seated
                                                              before
a committee on the needs of her soldiers   losing
both her legs
having happened right before the committee
one have to not be in either family or the outside not by
          (my/one's)   one's choice but by their
          (events')   occurrences
                              only
so both my choice and the events are the first occurrence
                  others first there her   and

312

floating above the people is the blossoming roof here

only once

At once Halliburton recipient of the US govt
contracts to

rebuild the bombed   and
wrecked Iraq   is paid ten billion, in that the
US vice president has shares in the company, over
charged by a hundred million for work not performed
while *their* streets swim in   black

rose-sewage
a split in one and blossoming trees
their civilians are arrested and removed   *on*
no charges   horizontal   to quell
discontent—while the contractors are not arrested
yet one is neither in the family nor in the outside why
does one see one is no longer in   the

outside
which opens *our*
actions   bound.
  so the city swims above and in the midst of it the
blossoming plum trees
have to not be in either, not by my/one's choice but by
their   occurrences

only
thus her choice and the events directing it are both first

there rose

A
m not either in the family or in the outside why
does she (I) see she is no longer in the

outside by
beside huge numbers peoples surface   cruising

313

                                                on
                                        the floor
                of the rose desert is broken floating
                                                one's
            the enflamed iris pushes out on   blossom
                                                ing trees roof
                    everywhere   rose
            surface   makes a hole in space's
            air   from their
                the old as rule the forest is in the Euphrates
                                                River
            Toyota cruisers river falcon enters space of fore
stalling people dying   silent
words   first
so, not   from it
plane there whose planes are invisible to birds
colliding with them   where birds
                                can see
the falcon   where is the surface of the rose
                            floor everywhere
drones floating killing the insurgents citizens
speaking separate   isn't
(the insurgents' speaking isn't)   first
nor is speaking the event's   as occurrence
these   .   (at) once

            _____

            is everything only lying   separate
                                            words
                                            one
lies 'night' also   of someone else everyone
                                (why is)
                                dawn
            the forest is in the Euphrates River
                                where

meeting the dead   occurs
only   asleep, in one
(words) in everyone   harmonious
do 'occur' in present wild friends here
      are their words also   once
in that they're (one's)   *as occurrence*
events   bound   'night'
only (separate) outside   yet no one is
     one isn't event, except *as occurrence*
in the outside (either) can't *be*   places
one's mind by from first beside any streams of is
          them once one's outside's
     events rose desert is everywhere in
        that peoples cruising their Toyotas on
                the huge floor
              break its surface
          black rose day first one

---

    horizontal bright space (words
                 at all)
           we have to *do*

Avril

           People cruising
Toyotas the rose desert   breaks
everywhere   because they are on its surface then
              only
a woman ignorant and from eyes blank gloating savaging
others   speaking only   no one speaks there they're
  not reflected in her eyes her
           either for her anywhere
tyranny of inverted in her/gloater's being defined as the
            social outside

their kindness   a train hurls on tiers seen in the sky

                    no sight admitted
into the gloating one savaging others then doesn't make
sights   cattle came to a blossom
                         in others
              so a man threw a ball
blank to everyone is inverted by her savaging speaking
                    only they cruise the
                    rose train surface
                              at
                              night
no reflection of anything on the rose floor everywhere
                    they leave the side

_____   _____

Authority or abandoning had to have been before
              so (one) is not outside either first
its/their weight is on (in) horizontal night as day also in
that   place 'trees' 'words'
         a man regards people as only to serve
                              him
sees nothing but matter   anyone   at the
requirement of someone else on the condition of *their*
                         slav   ery
to him   people given up are not slaves then
                              offed
abandoned
                              they
are set loose   black smoke comes out of a woman's
mouth   their black flowers there
              the soldiers walk
authority had to have been (before in one)   so (one) is not
                    outside either first
the roads to   see

316

          bombs hidden on the roads, a walking soldier may
be   blown in a road they make
the   invaded the living citizens arrested shot
                      coming to the soldiers
                            only driving
thin armor chicken-winged holding   it on
the soldiers' arms to their sides
                  at the side of night loose
everywhere
              there is no weight in or on it 'actually'
(it's only)   in one's occurrence
so they have 'imagined' 'one' is not there
after or first   no one   outside either
everywhere so   the 'flat' being of plants rose
trees   without their blooming   without
it bloom
she   a man who's kind a man threw a ball leaves
                                      the side

_____

     From the inside everything is matter   walking
                                      night
     rose   word
     'he'   re orders retroactively in having seen
                                      others
     only (?) to serve him existing economically there
     everything
     is no side   at the side
     of   night   rose   leaves
     the separation,
  which is joy   everything
     there first   to others,
     unseen retroactively
             there   (his)
     night   rose   leaves

                    ahead   (of people)
        no one so one not in the outside either while
                                                    there
                            while it is there

_____

As has to
be before crickets seethe sing are being the emerald hills that are
                            a dark blue
                                    day
no cobalt night can be there their singing at once is the emerald
                    hill alongside a dark blue
                                    day only one
's *seeing* its (seeing's) occurring at all is before it's pink clover
                                                    sea
            that authority only abandons and offs would have
to have been that authority's occurrence, (night isn't) the con
                            dition of slavery, *before*
is one
defined from that authority, both, seeing the definition of outside
                                    and not
            the people fan out cruising   the rose
                                    desert
    is not reflected in the pink clover sea on 'a' emerald sound
                                                    hills
        their having hearing is the social and 'night' cruising
                                                the floor
there   see and sea dawn   it's a sea
                    breaks stars them anyone can speak a man
                                                    threw
a ball

_____

318

One's a wall to them bound
off of itto them   there isn't day death doesn't exist
there both 'our'   *only* existing
(his) love is one isn't a wall then or rose desert's walls
                       's walking one's
that one is from language not in/from phenomenal night
                           ever that
(night) and
     their our there language *is* death in that 'our' having
made   that everything here stars
words a man says "expressivity" is forbidden by him in
people so he parts everyone   in their/its abaxial
leaf   separating is by beside his rules   regard
less of what every one any thing *is*   or from
                   soldiers rule
                   run
                   being
killed in (their they're) from phenomenal night *then*
only   he isn't yet
                 Alan saying Beckett's
"just personal" is by his figure's *being* an   Everyman
is it we're repeats every where people are thought
by Beckett to be mass that's of individuals   only
                     not as
                     if
they created side together 'one' being invisible then
oddly in   rose mud sole
                   the
other man's "no expressivist" anywhere is neither 'night'
nor   theirs
     that *'we're'* hasn't dawn
                 wall of
  rose walking
abattage suborbital eye one's theirs began outside the future
one's both   are outside one's suborbital eye   the

future itself separately is the present here is endless
the same action outside then   cyclists in black coming *to*
one for
ward in streams
ride by one after another to one on light day air they
jut black holes in its air
outside sole on suborbital eye rose desert rushes
to
trees
boats cycles horses bow in green that's
their there
cyclists ride bejeweled green on beside it every
where
jewel flowers strew that
outside green on flock of cyclists race there

Ex in cite ment of get ting up be fore dawn to be gin wh
at to
be gin a gain dawn
be gins from night, no   or oar be gins from that day
be fore it one night comes
for ward
birds sing ing are hid den fly ing by fly ing—we speak to
them the trees height waves e ve ry where yet the cars cruise the
rose
dawn be gin then two glis ten ing ly Ca na da Geese stood
on the cliff of
o cean th eyre honk ing on the o thers to come yet la ter
they come in
on   the men and wo men laugh ed
the air eir honk ing ar riv ing oar in honk ing in tan
dem *makes* eir fly ing see ing two days
the trees' si lence is sides thoughts edge
one's not in either the outside   or oar

320

rain pour s on red rose s and   a ny thing can't hear
plants si lence are   theirs

of the senses,   but how are events anywhere
eir in re verse is for ward if we don't make the out side
               drops out
if *we're* not   the outside oar a gain
are peo ple mass of in di vi du als then not mak ing that
la ter to ge ther for   then out side sole
first we're making *anything* 'ahead' future is itself and
separately in 'the present here is endless' do they and
do the birds make or are the
       out side s green on flock of cyclists race there
oar alter and make every thing out the side   *both*
                      birds do ing so that
      they jut in black air beside there their the oar
out side that's blue

EXCERPT: *BETWEEN FANTOINE AND AGAPA*[1]

By Robert Pinget

"...I was still very much under the influence of the surrealists, of attempts to approach the unconscious; in short of experiments made on language in what might be called its nascent state, that's to say: independent of any rational order. A gratuitous game with vocabulary—that was my passion. Logic seemed to me to be incapable of attaining the very special domain of literature, which in any case I still equate with that of poetry. And so it was a fascination with the possibilities, the absolute freedom of creation, an intense desire to abolish all the constraints of classical writing, that made me produce these exercises which neither the logician, nor philosopher, nor moralist, will find to his taste. That doesn't mean to say that the imaginative reader will not be able to find something in them to his taste. A reader in love with language and with the multifarious echoes that his emotions absorb when he is attuned to words. Hence, for him, a profusion of contradictory meanings, and the feeling of being released from the prisons of rationalizing reason." [2]
—Robert Pinget

Journal[3]
November 1
Ah those fingernail races! They're one of the great attractions of these parts. The whole world and his wife uproots himself with his family, his house, his terrain, and come and camps here for several months, for as long as the race lasts, in a special reserved

---

1   Originally published as *Entre Francoise et Agapa*, copyright © Les Éditions de Minuit, 1966. Copyright © this translation Barbara Wright, 1982. Published in the United States by Red Dust, Inc., 1982.

2   From the Preface to the American Edition.

3   These excerpts: November 1, 5, 7, December 2, 3, 18, March 18, 19 are taken from "Journal," the last chapter of *Between Fantoine and Agapa*.

site. Whatever his financial situation, everyone finds the means to perform this rite. The unemployed are rare, for a sizeable labor force is needed for the harvest. The collectors go to work a year in advance. They visit every residence, whether official or not, with sacks which they fill with clippings, with broken nails, with nails that have been extracted—they can acquire an inexhaustible supply of the latter in garrets, on account of the tortures. They've stopped bothering about animals' claws ever since the day they ran wild and pounced on the spectators. Once they've been collected, then, the nails are piled up in silos adjoining the racecourse. Usually there are only a few weeks to go before the start of the games. They are used for leveling the terrain and especially for stabilizing the atmosphere. This operation was delicate and even dangerous, only a few years ago. Today it is carried out with the aid of valves and giant compressors laid out along the track. The people who live in the neighborhood are warned when the stabilization is due to begin. They have to decamp within twelve hours. But there are always some hundred thousand laggards who get caught up in currents and torn to shreds. This provides some extra nails.

The inaugural day arrives. People can sit wherever they like, entrance is free. It may be said that in theory people prefer to be at a certain altitude, that of the silos, for instance, or one or two thousand meters up. The very sight of this multicolored crowd rising up in tiers several kilometers into the sky is magnificent enough. What can be said about the entrance of the nails into the arena? There is nothing with which it can be compared—unless it be a snowstorm. At the signal, they rush off towards the East.

November 5

In high summer, mauve placards are stuck up all over the country to announce that the leaf-picking is about to start. All the natives are mobilized for a week. The territory is transformed into a veritable parade ground. The State health services are entirely responsible for the transport, board and lodging of the workers. Given the density of the population, and that all private industries and businesses have to suspend their activities during this time, it is easy to imagine the extent of the task incumbent in the above-mentioned authorities.

At first I didn't quite understand the reasons for this transfer of the inhabitants from one province to another on the opposite side of the territory for this chore. It's a question of productivity. I had the honor of being introduced to one of the members of the top organizing committee. He is a morose little man who has spent his life in perfecting the administrative mechanism of the "leaves week."

When they have arrived at their destination, the groups (about a million souls) are divided up into squads of a thousand in the province to be stripped. These squads, commonly known as "the dryasdusts" set to work immediately. This has been going on for so long that men, women and children can climb trees like monkeys. Every native species of trees is a legal target.

Under this system, however, varieties tend to disappear in favor of one basic type of tree, which is something between an apple tree and a horse chestnut. Hedges, copses and the vegetation of the heathlands are similar targets. Every leaf must be picked without its peduncle; this requires great dexterity in the operators. The peduncles, which normally fall in the autumn, will be collected by private firms.

As the gathering proceeds, whole cartfuls of leaves are unloaded into the canals crisscrossing the country. They discharge their load into rivers. At the mouths of these rivers this fearsome accumulation is controlled by a system of dredgers and cranes along the bank, thus raising a vegetal bastion which, when the seadrift reaches it, slowly decomposes until the spring.

The exploitation of this huge, putrescent wall is begun in March.

November 7
The whole of their private life is autopsied in their eyes, even when they are lost in thought. When you walk down the street you are surrounded by decorticated beings. They present a spectacle of monstrous psychological division. I met almost none for whom the present had any importance. They project everything into the future. A future constituted of present and past preoccupations. Encumbered by this impossibility, they trudge from distress to downfall.

They are dangerously haunted by eternity.

As for the children, I think they resemble our own. They dream of buns, balloons and toy ducks. But they stagger under the weight of their anxieties, as heavy as planets.

December 2
The crowd didn't flinch at the sound of the leaves being torn off. It seemed as if it were being absorbed into an indiscernible, illocalizable object. This wasn't the first manifestation of the sort. The most celebrated one, so I was told, was that historically classified under the name of Good Friday. I made this comparison because a little girl by my side began to desiccate. First, her hair fell out like hay. Then her face, which had become fibrous, dropped down over her doll. With one hand the little girl hugged the fetish to her bosom, and with the other she tried to hold her head up. But her hands had become glued to her body, down to her pelvis. She took two more steps. Then her legs broke.

I had never before seen a mob immobilized. The place is usually so full of movement that you can only keep your eyes on an individual, or a couple, or at the very most a group. But at that moment one could only too easily take in the whole assembly. I had no need of proof, the spectacle was hypnotic. It was only when thinking about it later that I realized that the ease with which it could be seen confirmed its reality.

December 3
You ask your way, as a matter of habit, of a passerby. He doesn't answer. Right away, you are jerked out of your automatism because it's true, the way is there in front of you, almost on top of you.

The difficulty of fighting against your mania to understand is in proportion to your isolation. I am only now, thanks to a few friends, beginning to liberate myself to a certain extent.

One of my first experiences was buying my bread without leaving my house. It took me an hour of tension to relax; an hour to delimit the feeling of bread and to confine my desire to my teeth, my palate and my esophagus; an hour to evacuate the decision; an hour to abolish the time which had elapsed (I checked, later); and there we were, the bread was on my table, I was eating it.

All this was the result of an incalculable effort. They make no effort at all: they have never lost this astonishing faculty.

December 18
When they are trying to escape from shame, they are the most pitiable creatures I have ever seen. Since transparency of their souls is not merely constitutional but also an active function, a little like a walking windowpane which might go and shatter itself against an obstacle, no base action is the attribute of the person who commits it. It comes within the network of turpitudes that binds all these people together.

This kind of permanent link of omniconsciousness should, it would seem, exclude the feeling of the irremediable, which is egotistic, and substitute for it that of complicity, of collusion. But this is far from being the case; the sense of shame persists. I have seen poor wretches who were at odds with it perch up in the trees like owls and remain there sleepless for nights on end. The structure of sin and remorse, of their interpenetration and mutual influence, rose up, tangible and useless, in front of them, and up there on their perches they gave the impressions of being false meetings points, artificial intersections.

For their notions of the absolute are deficient. They have but a vague knowledge of divine mysteries and allegorical redemptions, whose disproportion to their wealth of emotion is such that the slightest lapse from honesty plunges them into dejection.

Oh, those trees, with their weight of suffering flesh...

March 18
Their artists work in isolation. They have no public. As they are recruited from common criminals, they are banned. Any kind of contact with them is a felony. Their penitentiaries are of a greater variety than ours and convicts may be placed in any artist's studio.

Far from being blunted, the sensitivities of this vermin increase in proportion to their guilt. When an interested observer, defying the risk of prosecution, goes to see them and admires one of their works, this feeling that the visitor is a kindred spirit is so unexpected that the criminals lose their heads. They whirl around, throw themselves on the work and trample it, lacerate it, pulverize it. Then they disappear into the walls, where for the rest of their lives they are racked by qualms of conscience at having deceived people.

327

March 19

If you lose a contour, or a segment, or one whole side of your body, the hachured surface is reduced by the same amount and your armpits are no longer included in it. You wander around with holes in you, carrying your charcoal-drawn silhouette satchel. Your cheek becomes emancipated. Your prominent jaw commutes between your neck and your glottis; the wings of your nose erupt in pharyngeal edemas; nauseating liquids ooze out down your apophyses. Your truncated sphincters flow back towards your nerve centers, your epigastrium becomes subdivided. The satchel finally drops, too, your hand becomes invaginated, and the sketch so carefully made the day before is stained with liquid manure. This is the result of a plasma deficiency. It frequently happens during country rambles. Several comrades have gone for a day's outing and come back unrecognizable.

Translated from the French by Barbara Wright

EXCERPT: *BEYOND HOPE*

by Elizabeth Reddin

This is the beginning of one hundred days. It is wrong, when to say no—nothing happens, yes nothing happens in the head of one building or one sidewalk. At the top of a generation all things fall over the edges and some will give each one a way of saying. It can't be you are missing, or that given a slope you react. You can't ask if we are wanting you; all of we is a silent tall. No one even broke these minutes but thanks and evening. You can't empty any minute. Stop the red wavering. That should be ablaze, you want to speak code vivid. Your mother is just old. She has come so far into this end, it is almost impossible to reach her now. This won't be a trick. I don't want to copy you by talking about my sex life, but ours are so different. Maybe you won't notice. Trucks and trailers all along the highway. That was a trip many families had taken. We passed them and the top was down. We were imagining we were alive.

I'm thinking it could all be starting now. This place is sitting and enough are behind you for you to go on. Don't bother those stories. The last time you attempted that, you fell face on. However, you might remember on the first day of being alive you didn't know it, and now you exist. All in the windows failing to be clear on the way. Someone said their mother was dying. You don't know which window she looked out of. Halt. Gain a circle and watch it all around. To fill anything up was well. To sit anything back was well when done. To be running to and from was lost. And losing is something you know less of tonight. Saddle is the color of a dark opening, to hear the keys rattling outside of the door could be a misunderstanding, a dread or a hopefulness. Any movement could be any of those things.

You reached across and laid your hands on both sides of me. That was our sex life for the time being. I wondering where you were and wanting the phone number of that place could be our sex life for the time being. Rattle. You were waiting for alone time to end. I was wishing I wouldn't have said I wanted anything. I said I wouldn't ask for anything, I spoke a lot and said I thought you were someone. Maybe you were in disagreement. Maybe having this facility is too easy. Maybe any mark would be laughed at. Maybe I shouldn't tell you about all of it . Maybe nothing bogus has happened. Or who knows what anyone thought or who would be able to tell you had forgot. Hell, how do you call the worth of it. Hell, blank, bawdy. There is no timeline to this. Not even then will you be able to skip ahead or go back to bed. Just now I want to go back to bed. But I'll wake up and I'll say to you, where is it. I know where you are and you can't take me with you. A crowd of people will stand all around watching you cry and it's possible they will get distracted or say, you aren't serious, your voice is too squeaky, and they might go looking for a new leader. How can you blame anyone for wanting a new leader. When someone takes the lead you can go back to bed, but in the morning there will be stories. You won't know them, you won't know what the stakes are. How can I tell a story of sitting in the same place for a long time. There is a story of staying in the same place for a long time. Where did you come from, Where to. You are not our leader when you are all the time asking directions. Stop looking around at other people's girlfriends. To be alive when they are dead. Going away from what I remember. I can't remember the day that was yesterday, it was Saturday you said, what did you do.

Should we be keeping secrets. With everything we're doing tucked slight and under until finally we punch out with all of it. Never say this would be curbed or flattened. Moving past all the houses we've lived in. Who's up there. Some of them were, when you were on the inside, looking in from off the low streets and down in from the high streets. We can lie in bed holding hands and not worry about how close we are. You are torching up my sides. I couldn't tell your story for you. Hold it, I can't be running out before I've gotten in. I have to get in. Get in here. Black night sees us walking all the way around this neighborhood. An old neighborhood can make me want to go back to bed or it wipes sometimes all the boards dry. Crossing the street in a white T-shirt. When you couldn't see the whole day you looked on and thought we were confused. It can't be directly from me or that would be too personal. Happen. Nothing isn't happening today, but is passing young, like I am compared to you, who are old like an old man's mother is dying somewhere. You stay young for me and never leave me. Agree to it. I will also agree to it. Around town you aren't known for being so removed. Tell me something about how you are now. What is this about.

I want to tell you not to say that. I want to tell you not to say your questions. This is a place for questions. Why are you such an asshole? Why did you waste yourself. How can you say someone has wasted themselves. How do you want it to look like. How do I look like. I have a pointy chin, I don't mind. I have wished for a covering that is smooth and new. Like something can last so smooth under water. Underwater your face is smooth for thousands of years, your alabaster face stays still under the water. Water bug in his house. A tall house a hundred feet tall. A pink house with pink wood. How many times have you said one hundred. With a lifted face you remember what it felt like so many times like it was the first. It was the first every time was it?

I have someone who I'm going away from for a while. What's it like. It's like everything disappearing long before it leaves. And when you don't know it's leaving before it leaves?

331

What's it like. It must be like everything disappears for a long time after, and keeps disappearing until everything is gone. And then do things come like a new set of teeth. Welcome. Years can pass before anything seems to leave. And all of a sudden. Close your eyes and say what you see.

When I close my eyes I see the Edward Hopper painting of all the young guys at the outside bar. And the yellow neon. I don't know if that's how the painting is but that's how I see it. I see James Dean leaning over. Isn't it scary when you close your eyes and you can't see anything. Isn't it scary when you close your eyes at night and you can't stop seeing things. Sometimes when I hate someone, I talk to them to myself, and I'm not hating them then when I'm talking to them, and I want to say, I never hated you, but it seems impossible. Isn't it hard to stop hating something once you've said you hated it. I don't like having to do that. Almost as much as beginning to hate at all. I hate the beginning of hating at all. Today I wasn't afraid of anything. Except for a minute I was afraid of a lie. Like when everything seems like one. I like a meal that has in it something starchy and something meaty, there should be something salty and something sweet like jam. In the meal there should also be something refreshing like a sprite, a juice, or lettuce because there should be something crisp. Also, there should be something to alter the state of mind like coffee, or wine, or a beer. Now we are not hungry. I see someone is coming.

There's no dread today. Just a fast flash of jealousy. I saw a girl out by the deli, and even though I barely saw her I thought about how you would want to have her. Maybe I wanted her. We want so much just on the surface of our skins. I listen to the music coming from the other room. So I feel crowded. And it sounds good coming from there. I am in the other room. Or on the surface of it. Pushed. The train passes. I want it to be quiet so I can hear you. But then I would always be alone. No. I can't think with this everywhere. Green hollow. I'm outside of the place where I can do this. I keep coming in and out and the music is too close.

Last night I had dreams about all the things I'd like to have. I was covetous and rejected. My aunt said, don't come visit me. We were on the phone but still I could see her face. And she looked mean and she said don't come visit. Someone's daughter that I'd known for a long time said, I don't recognize you. The other guy had small objects that I wanted. He had nice eye glasses and other small things. I stole one pair from him. Then I gave them back. I'm thinking about all the things I wanted to tell you about today when I was walking around alone. I like you. 9L95 is the number on the cab that was sitting at the red light outside the window. Now there are other cars passing through the green light. This gets off the ground sometimes and it's a place some nights. Sometimes a place isn't what it was last night and our voices aren't what they were when we were alone. Do you believe me. I said I would go a certain distance with you tonight, am I failing? I'm just here tonight. You'd say no if you were wanting to read a biography or if you were writing a biography or expecting one. Still, at this point I don't feel comfortable putting anyone's name in here and calling you seems strange. Will that change.

Maybe soon I will call you by your names. Many of the times I sing the songs to myself during the day that I heard you singing the night before and I rarely remember all the words unless I write them down and read them when I'm singing them or if I work really hard to remember them from off the paper. I can get real thin about being alone and when I am who knows, maybe I'll be stronger than I thought. Or maybe it will just be very quiet and I won't rewrite the letters but just put them down and send them. I might say, these are not me but they'll come to you anyway, and that might be a long time from now even though it's only a week away. What's it like, when you are going away alone. Maybe you are always alone. Who are you that I'm talking to. It seems like we haven't met. I fought with a kid today who said he couldn't understand why anyone would need to speak more than two languages. He got tears in his face and he wanted to blame me for everything. Everyone is in the room tonight. And after they go I'm sitting in everything that was said. Over in the brain that likes to go over and over again the sounds we make or the ones we say were mistakes. The loud sound mistakes make.

RETIREMENT PARTY

by Kenneth Bernard

Yesterday, esteemed colleague was ending his long labors and preparing to put himself out to green pastures. And we, his collaborators over the years, were joining with him in celebration. We plied him with food, drink, music, and thoughtful gift, and we were all a-smile. But, quite suddenly, when I tried to relax my smile, I could not, for it had become fixed, a look of pain. To avoid embarrassment, I looked out a window. And there, in the near and mid-distance, I saw the scene that awaited.

The grounds swept smoothly down to the shore. And there, an oarless, rudderless boat awaited. Laughingly we escorted esteemed colleague to the boat and with small jokes pushed him into the currents, waving and smiling the while. The boat at first seemed not to make headway, but soon esteemed colleague became smaller, his features pale and indistinct, as the boat zigged and zagged toward the further shore, which was the continent of death.

In its center was a Quickway, on which some few bent figures moved speedily to the buzzing interior. Some luxury vessels, on which a lucky few had booked passage, crested the waves easily, their occupants lolling at the rails with food and drink. But as the currents were treacherous, few boats, large or small, anchored at the foot of the Quickway. Some glided uneventfully to a sandy cove. Others were wrecked on rocks or shoals, and passengers scampered ashore as best they could. Some unlucky ones hit a steaming Arafura shore and were forced to brave sharp pestilence in the sucking mud.

But no part of the shore was free from danger. Although most arrivals immediately set forth for the interior, often leaving baggage behind, some few camped on the beach, oblivious of the crocodiles, scorpions, and snakes nearby. There they made model airplanes, planted seeds, prayed, sought partners for cards, or took out pen and pad. Even as they played or worked, worms crawled into their ears and laid eggs or oozed poisons. Occasionally an eye was plucked out in a sudden swoop or some reptilian creature darted into someone's rectum and fixed itself there with bloated spiky skin. From the dense interior, above the buzz, came screeches of larger creatures, whence the others had departed. Some few bodies were rolled up on the beach and contentiously consumed. The Quickway loomed in the distance but seemed unreachable.

One gaudy ship, full of fools, sailed unimpeded to the interior, its members feasting and rejoicing at the imminence of the realm of death, that lush land of the secret knowledge of all things. Their shrieks rang through the night, and as they madly danced and ripped off their clothes they shouted to the campers and trudgers—"We are eating our cancers! We are bleating our virgins! Kneel to the King of Worms!" We who have never lived in true cities, with their labyrinthine ways and their palimpsest depths upon depths— what ashes we have built on! What faces we have never seen! What lives we have never lived!

Gradually I felt my mouth loosen. I was able to abandon my smile and gain control over myself. Was no one else looking out the window, I wondered. What madness was afoot? I turned to speak to someone. And faced a sea of smiling masks. I looked out the window again. The former scene was gone. All was serene. But within, the rictus faces remained, rouged and smiling. Their arms were extended. In each hand was a glass. They were toasting me. Slowly I, too, smiled.

SUMMER (BEEN)

by Jean Frémon

Determined to leave, I had taken one of the lanes bordered with old timber-work houses which led to the banks of the river. A lively wind, coming from the East, had driven the clouds away and now again there was a cool breeze on the heights, which was soon to give away to the immobility of the growing heat: the drone of wasps would replace the trills of morning birds, the peonies' heads would plunge toward the ground, and later one would see swifts, like two-seaters of the past in an aerial skirmish, plunge down to the ground to seize midges, until the sun became overcast with a pallid haze. In the concerto which would serve as the musical illustration of this scene, the cello and the oboe, would take turns as soloists, the exchange of brass and strings keeping harmony. During the night, a violent storm, which the percussion would mimic, will beat down the bean poles in the low-walled vegetable garden, and the first drops of rain, at first heavy and slow, then suddenly more frequent and closer together, as the piano passes from solemn and slow to the leaping bitterness of pizzicato, will produce, through windows left open, a coolness in the bodies of the sleepers, who will tug the sheets a little over their naked bodies and turn over in their sleep, trying to continue their dream.

I had stopped a moment to follow a chess match in the village square. The chess board is made of alternating gray and white paving stones, slate and travertine, the shaped wooden pieces about the size of an eight-year-old child, the two adversaries moving about the surface of the board like generals among their armies.

Strange army whose forces seem defeated, dispersed to the four corners of an agreed-upon territory. Protected by a rook employed just in time, the King drowses under the

337

lone vigilance of two soldiers and a Tower, while the Queen, horses and bishops, rushing into the opening which initial moves will create, have already swept over the terrain many times, carried in the players' full arms. The soldiers, victims of these repeated assaults, lie to the side.

I thought, in watching them, of the way in which Tadeusz Kantor intervenes onstage during the performance of the plays for which he is at once author and stage manager. He wanders, absorbed in his thoughts, among his characters, puppets or simulacras of puppets, manipulating them to the point of exhaustion, indicating to them with a gesture, like the conductor of an orchestra, the start of a sequence, the tone wanted for a certain rejoinder, ordering stage business and changes of scene, imposing his rhythm on the whole. But, ridiculous conductor of a soon to be routed orchestra, he multiplies his less and less understandable instructions, runs desperately from the court to the garden to try to slow the coming disaster, like Ionesco's king limping from one arrow slit to the other within his besieged castle before theatrically dying.

From the low wall where I was seated, I overlooked the match and could believe myself the organizer of this little operatic war, which seemed to come straight out of a world where playing cards march past in cadence and where the Queen of Hearts plays croquet with a pink flamingo for a mallet and a rolled-up hedgehog for a ball, such as the Wonderland to which Charles Lutwigde Dodgson, mathematics professor and amateur photographer, had introduced the young Liddell Sisters after the growing heat of a summer afternoon, probably in every way similar to this one, had compelled them to interrupt their boat journey to go sit in a meadow, in the shadow of a haystack, where the little girls begged him insistently to tell them a story.

"Do you know how the fox manages to devour the hedgehog—one of the very finest foods, I'm told—without pricking his muzzle?" Dodgson might have managed to say.

"No, no."

"Oh! Oh!"

"Tell, tell," the young girls cried in the greatest confusion.

"By urinating copiously upon it. Trickling with foul urine, the sea urchin of the forests unrolls itself, allowing the cunning beast to take it by the throat."

I imagine Dodgson contemplating the growing fright in the eyes of the young girls with a strange smile. Later, he had them pose, in their slips, in the barn which served as his studio; he is already imagining the marvelous photos which gelatin will reveal.

"The form of the pink flamingo's beak," he continues, "takes the shape of a horrible rictus" (he seemed to take pleasure from making his r's roll while moving his bushy eyebrows as an ogre might do) "which gives this animal a stupid and naughty appearance" (he punctuates the phrase with a mimicry which returns uncertain smiles to the faces of the children). "Very happily," continues the storyteller, "the awkward winged creature is furnished with a neck so long that it is obliged to turn its head completely upside down when it dips it into the water to seize the slender minnows that it feeds on. Thus, viewed upside down, the rictus is changed into a smile, which no doubt is useful for not frightening the lovely pink shrimp which give its plumage its color as well as the name to the species, and for making, upside down, a lovely hedgehog mallet for the disagreeable Queen of Hearts."

Was it the heat, added to idleness, which led to dreaming? The match had ended in checkmate and the jousters had deserted the arena without my having noticed. Their undone armies lay in disorder: the pride of their starting order fallen into disarray. That king which had not been surrounded and enclosed by its opponent, was still sitting in state, alone and useless; the other was lying in the exact place of its undoing.

I again began walking toward the river whose cool currents I already felt. On the irregularly paved descent, I felt my feet pushing against the ends of my shoes. I had in my head simple phrases, descriptive and sonorous, modeled after those which swarm in the scholarly manuals from which one draws dictation passages for children. I walked along describing my acts or my thoughts as if I were engaged in drafting a "French composition." *The Promenade* or *A Summer's Day* would have been its title, and I saw myself as the principle character of a narration which, though unfolding in my head, was exterior to me, drew me into its circumvolutions, a narration which would have had the applied tone, the prudent rhythm, the preordained temperament of schoolwork.

Pawn which advances only a single square directly forward, bishop which sweeps back and forth along the diagonals, horse free to leap obstacles but never deviating from the angle which regulates its form: in what way was I different from these manipulated wooden tokens, even if I have been able to believe myself, for an instant, from the top of my little low wall, the commander of the players themselves; I who felt myself the subject of a phrase which seemed only a memory of reading, of a phrasing which parodied the teacher dictating to the student, taking care to make lightly audible not only the logical series which commas signal, but also the liaisons, the usual links of a plural to a vowel and those, more affected, which normally spoken language wouldn't have singled out and which were pronounced here only to try to warn the attentive listener to avoid a trap.

Divided between the familiar, although unsettling, feeling of *déjà-vu*, the impression of moving myself through a conventional world, the houses themselves with their coquettish little air and their potted, balconied geraniums seeming ready to collapse at the slightest nudge, and the haunting memory of not being there, of understanding nothing, of reading a book written in a language I didn't know; after having gone along the river at length and left behind me the houses clustered around the fountain, holding long in my head the familiar noise of the trickle of running water falling into the granite basin, I had gained a hill jutting over the village, and here I finally sat down on the grass and napped.

I saw in dream, from the top of my improvised observation post, the house of little Alice L., a child with whom I had been in love; spying on the comings and goings of the household, heart beating in the hope of seeing her blond hair appear in the sun, I saw successively and with emotion her father return a cart to the barn, her mother hang the wash on a line which crossed the garden between two poles, her brothers quarreling about a ball which finished its course in the neighbor's lettuce patch, and I concluded as a result of that strange logic of which only love is capable that she was in her room, busy sewing or more likely absorbed in fascinating reading, reading, for example, the book I had written for her, calligraphed and handsewn between two pieces of cardboard torn from a box of chocolates, and which I had secretly passed on to her during play.

In thought, I thus entered into the room where she in fact was. It sometimes happens that dreams thwart you, that a devil pulls the rug out from beneath your feet, that at the moment when what you want the most is about the occur, though it be in the unreal form of phantasm, the story forks without warning and leaves you flabbergasted, frustrated, deceived. This time, no—at least, not yet. She was stretched out on her bed, a little child's rosewood bed, and held my book in her hands. "I can't understand any of this," she says, when she sees me, "even though I'm a first-rate reader." "Naturally," I tell her, all proud of my discovery, "it is a mirror book, one can only read the reflection. And what's more, its title is a perfect palindrome, one of the four seasons in one direction, the past participle of the verb to be in the other, and inversely." [1]

But as I contemplate her naked legs and golden hair, the storm bursts at last and pulls me from my sleep, erasing this August day born at once from dream and from childhood.

Translated from the French by Brian Evenson.

---

1   *Frémon refers to the title of his own story, "Eté," which means at once "Summer" and "Been."*

EXCERPT: *UNTITLED*

by R. M. Berry

My voice is coming from inside this box. That's why it strikes
your ear askew. Brim full and empty, almost gone, its syllables
never sound, but resound merely. Or so I'm told. For myself
I can't speak, of course, having never been without it. The
box, I mean. Within, the sensations are pronounced, sonorous
as a shower stall, all reverberating surfaces, tile and porcelain,
if you know the echo I have in mind, but anyhow, a noise
like no other, the resonance, you could say, of its own name.
If names resounded, if bodies intoned them. My own name
is immaterial. The voice comes first, then this box, and only
later, if at all, the name, which makes for some frustration.
Once we're better acquainted, I hope you can ignore it, but
for now, you've probably got your hands full just trying to
hold your tongue. Anyway, the sound from the box isn't my
name, and at the start it's the box that occupies us.

Closets are something else. I've tried living in a closet,
passed my everlasting adolescence in one, groping through
strangers' pockets, lights out, mothballs corroding every sinus.
But a voice in a closet is muffled, gagged, the sound of its
stifling, and that sensation is another one, short-lived, less
hollow. Inside the box, by contrast, my voice is too replete,
chock-full, or just insufficiently farfetched, to smother. It stays
with you, like the flu. Let me tell you, before being boxed
I often rambled in my sleep and awoke more than once to
hear my gist rebound. My voice then struck me as outlandish,
the nasal mutterings of an exile. None of its clamor seemed
mine or, for that matter, anyone else's. Phrases returned like
bad pennies, familiar currency, little sense. Maybe they hadn't
been coined. Maybe I've forgotten to take my pill. Anyway, I
like the phrase, *his words hung in the air*, and would use it now,

I mean to describe this sensation in my box, if my box had air. Which I suppose it must. A vacuum is silent. I don't mean the carpet cleaners, which are, of course, very noisy. But outer space, the universe. A box is like that, no atmosphere, perfectly abandoned, emptiness filling all. That and the darkness are its most notable features, of which more presently.

The reason I'm boxed is I saw me happen. That is, though not exactly at peace, I can't really wish to flee, could only wish not to have seen, which I don't exactly do. What I wish is for whatever's to come and, in a manner of speaking, you, faceless at any account, but I'm rarely hopeful, having found this box too narrow for it. Which, of course, starts out all wrong, for being boxed isn't being anywhere, and wasn't hope always six-sided, always a suffocation? But I suppose I've got to start someplace, and if one day it happens…well, there you are! So. This box, my voice, what I've seen. Others have had more, but then I'm hardly them.

I saw me happen on a parched flat when strange humors oozed from my skin. I don't recall the circumstances, but I do recall the sensations. The light was unforgiving, but when isn't light unforgiving? I remember my face baking, heard tumors sizzle like rashers beneath the dermis. At any instant I was expecting my flesh to rupture, set this old heart free, when I noticed something forming on the back of my hand. There seemed to be globules, or not quite globules, where I'd never noticed not quite globules before. A glistening of hairs, watery beads, one rivulet. Who's this? I thought, putting my tongue to the place, tasting salt. Had I turned piquant, melted to a sauce? And then it occurred to me, exactly what it's impossible to say, in the merest whisper of wind. Oh, I'll never forget that coolness! I fell into a rapture, saw vapors rising. It was my bodily assumption. Whether the change was miraculous I still can't tell, but I immediately put aside former preoccupations. There was only afterwards now. What was happening had never happened to anyone before.

I surmise from your blankness that you're not amazed. It's to be understood. My voice rarely strikes anyone at first, or only in passing, and even then more often on reflection, like a comeback or belated rejoinder. Without this box the air could be torrid, as frantic as a sirocco, thoughts consumed in perfect incandescence, while these reverberations, regardless how fulsome, take an eternity to alight. Only silence could attune the ear to within, and who's to say if mere vibrations would amuse you? In the box all such assurances sound hollow. Not that I speak from experience, mind, but I've confused myself with this echo often enough, mistaken the dying of my own voice for others, and I know how prone I am to lie, or perhaps imagine things. If hordes were without would it be any different? I've dreamt of groans, children sobbing, and although I know it's just this box, the sound of myself recoiling, still it's no mean feat to keep all within. Why, even this now could be part of it! Let's be frank. Nothing I've recounted so far is anything you haven't been listening to forever. I could be utterly absent, my flesh a mirage, this box unbound, and how would either of us tell? See. What could be simpler? It's this that gives rise to my voice.

INSIDE-OUT

by Thomas D'Adamo

She arrives at my apartment more than forty-five minutes late, flushed and out of breath. She offers no explanation, nor do I ask for one—I never do—and I wonder if that bothers her. I make a move to kiss her and she offers me her cheek. This, I assume, is significant. I help her out of her coat and am surprised to see how she is dressed—neatly-pressed jeans and denim shirt, spotless tan work boots. What am I meant to infer from this getup?

She does a slow circuit around my living room in silence, pausing in feigned interest of, respectively, a lemur skull; antique obstetric calipers; an autographed picture of Professor Irwin Corey, *The World's Foremost Authority*; a jade Ganish incense holder; a Coxsackie State Correctional Facility ashtray; and a photograph of my twin sister Roberta, age eleven-and-a-half, doing a cartwheel beneath our grandfather's mimosa tree less than an hour before she died—all of which she has seen many times before without any of them, except, perhaps, for the calipers, having made the slightest impression on her.

She finally comes to rest in the entrance to my bedroom where she now stands in profile, absently studying the polished oak doorframe. Her utilitarian costume lends her a vaguely official air; and as I scrutinize her long, elegant form, I realize that all that's missing is a clipboard and the funk-steady throb of an electric bass behind a coy wa-wa Stratocaster. Gorgeous city inspector appears at home of reclusive, yet darkly handsome poet one golden Southern California afternoon to check for wood beetles, or asbestos fibers, perhaps. Meandering tour of premises replete with lame badinage:

346

MICHAEL

If I knew they'd send you I would've made a point
of getting beetles a long time ago.

GRETA

She stops at the bedroom door and leans against the doorframe.

*The camera slowly pans up her body, then over her shoulder into
the bedroom.*

Gee, nice bedroom; and I just love your canopy bed!

MICHAEL

*The camera pulls back to show GRETA as seen from his
perspective.*

*He enters the frame and presses in close behind her. He gently
moves the hair away from her right ear and speaks softly into the ear.*

Me too—it's where I do some of my best work.

*The camera cuts to them in the doorway as seen from the far side
of the bed.*

He slips his arm around her waist.

GRETA

She slides out of his embrace and enters the bedroom.

Cut to her as seen from MICHAEL'S perspective.

She flashes him a sly grin over her shoulder and treats him to the full booty shot as she slowly sashays over to the bed. She turns to face him and slowly runs her left hand up and down a bedpost.

Something tells me you're a huge talent.

The camera zooms in on her hand gliding up and down the bedpost.

The camera pulls back to show her from the neck up.

She moistens her right forefinger on her tongue then runs the finger across her bottom lip.

The camera pulls back to show her from over MICHAEL'S shoulder.

I'd love to see some of your work.

MICHAEL

I thought you'd never ask.

He comes up close to her and puts his right hand over hers, which is still clutching the bedpost, and his left arm around her waist…

"You're warped," she says with such bland matter-of-factness that it takes me a second to realize that she's addressing me and not the woodwork. Becoming more animated, she declares that my narcissism is impenetrable and the way I live obscene. There's such a horrible emptiness inside you, she says with tears welling up in her eyes—you think everything is just a big game and other people with all their messy feelings are just a bunch of dumb rubes. She tells me that I'm the Peter Pan from Hell and that my adolescent cynicism is rotting me from

348

the inside out and soon nobody will want to have anything to do with me. Her voice trailing off to a hoarse whisper, she mutters something with "all alone" and "rude awakening" in it followed by a long, shuddering sigh.

While anticipating Greta's needs is always a bit of a high-wire act, from the moment she arrived today I've sensed something special in the air, a stormy vehemence in her body language, that tells me I'll need the skill of a Wallenda just to keep up.

Putting on my best George-Sanders-as-Oscar-Wilde, I explain that emotionalism, dear girl, is simply a failure of imagination. And you know what Sartre said about Hell and other people. Besides, how could I ever feel alone, Greta darling, as long as I have you in my life?

"But that's exactly!..." she exclaims, her voice thick with emotion, while, like some silent screen diva, she brings the heels of her hands to her temples and pulls her unruly chestnut mane straight back with sufficient force to straighten every wave without uprooting a single follicle. Crying "Shit!" as if she's just struck herself in the thumb with a hammer, she falls back against the doorframe with sufficient force to evoke a thud without actually leaving a bruise. Following a mandatory four or five beats, *larghetto*, Greta now twists her cigarette out on the doorframe with sufficient force to bore a hole through my skull, sending a lovely shower of orange sparks cascading onto the carpet at her feet.

From a cloaked ship in stationary orbit high above the Earth I scan the smoldering carpet. Mission Log: Extraordinary performance. Quite perplexing. Nothing in my pre-mission briefing prepared me for this. Some sort of mating ritual perhaps? A curious species indeed—so much like ourselves, yet so different. The female is a particularly striking specimen. Based on what I have thus far observed on scanners, I believe it imperative that I bring her aboard immediately for close examination. I will begin by testing her responses to a variety of anal stimuli…Greta loudly clears her throat signaling that the ball is in my court.

A bit more tentatively now, I explain that, for me, aloneness is a problem only in relation to her, and it is only when I am parted from you for too long, my fiery vixen, that I experience a mild despair that might loosely be termed *loneliness*. Otherwise, I can't say that I miss what I've never desired. Don't get me wrong, it's not that I've *actively* shunned society. It's just that after so many years of invitations declined, greeting cards unacknowledged, and phone messages unanswered, society has learned to live without me. And maybe that's all for the best, since, at this stage of the game, a social life would only be a dangerous distraction.

During most of this speech Greta has been pacing in and out of the bedroom with the intensity of a caged predator. She keeps this up for some time after I've grown silent before coming to an abrupt halt in the doorway. For what seems like forever, she just stands there with a mean scowl on her face and her head cocked like a well-trained attack dog poised to strike. When she does move it is with startling alacrity, and for a split second it seems as if she's coming to slap me where I sit. Instead, she crosses to the window directly opposite the chair in which I am sitting, takes a cursory look down at Houston Street, then turns to face me.

Greta is resplendent in the late afternoon sunlight pouring in through the window, her eyes glow with a supernatural golden intensity. I can feel myself receding into the chair's blue plush beneath the weight of her scrutiny. Her gaze never wavering she fishes in her shirt pocket for a cigarette. After two or three attempts, she carefully withdraws a bent Virginia Slims Menthol with two fingers. She lights the cigarette with the black disposable lighter she has been passing nervously from hand to hand since she arrived and takes a long, angry drag while, with uncharacteristic gracelessness, plopping down onto the window seat. Siting down her long, well-muscled legs, she blows a steady stream of smoke through pursed lips which billows down all the way to the toes of her boots.

While I await her next move I do a quick tally in my head. Slouched in the window, shrouded in a numinous veil of smoke and dust motes, Greta is the bitch goddess *sans merci*. She also happens to be my one sure thing at the moment, and I suspect she knows it. If my suspicions are correct then the whole point of today's exercise has been to determine what that buys her. Clearly divinity has its attractions, but what are the added costs involved? Canny operator that she is, Greta must realize that in heaven truth is the only currency. Is she prepared to enter into a contract stipulating that she forfeit every pleasure to a new-found passion for "the truth?"

On the other hand, I could be totally off the mark and before arriving today she had already concluded that the time had come to sample other vendors' wares. In that case all the *sturm und drang* has been nothing but a depressingly clichéd buildup to a "clean break."

A slight panic sets in as I consider what a disaster it would be to lose Greta now, and I decide to wing it. Falteringly at first, but picking up steam as I go, I tell her that it is my work, you see, and yet...God knows, I have no illusions about...What I mean to say is that I'm sure there are plenty of more accomplished... but I'd always thought that my unwavering devotion to my art was as much a part of what made me attractive...But now, thanks

351

to you, I'm beginning to see how that same tenacity could have had a, um, a warping effect, and how in the process my, eh, my insides might have, you know…and how I could've mutated into some…thing…some kind of inside-out thing…That's it, Greta, that's what I am, I'm Inside-Out Man! Thank you, thank you my life, my light, my inspiration for opening my eyes to the truth of what I've become—I'm the Inside-Out Man—a freak of nurture who has allowed his portion of the abyss, his share of emptiness, if you will, to become inflamed to the point of prolapse. And it is from this grotesque eversion that you, along with the rest of the world now instinctively recoil like a bad smell. And who could blame you? Just as no one likes having the body's digestive processes described to them in graphic detail over lunch, nobody wants to be continually reminded of how their lives are being consumed in empty rituals with which they attempt to whitewash the shame and grinding sense of futility that necessarily accompanies sentience, or more specifically, consciousness of self, and that destroys every…uhhm, pleasure…

"You are *sooo* deep, Michael." Greta coos as she slides off the window seat and saunters toward me, the seductive lilt of her hips echoed in the pendulum-swing of the handcuffs dangling from her fingers. She places a hand on each of my shoulders and leans in for a long, rough kiss. Her lips moist and swollen, she straightens up and with a grinding motion of her hips, she slowly works her way down my lap until our pelvises connect. Her eyes roll in her head as she undoes her shirt buttons then peels back the stiff denim to reveal her magnificent breasts. She grabs a fistful of hair at the back of my head and hums as she buries my face between her tits. Low moans well up from deep within as she gropes blindly with her right hand until she achieves her target. Just as she is about to snap the cuff into place we are startled by an obnoxious beep-beep-beeping.

"Oh well, guess we know what that means," I whisper as I gently lift her from my lap and get up from the chair. Greta doesn't move, and for a long, uncomfortable moment we stand with our noses almost touching. Her breath is hot on my face.

Being only human, it is with great reluctance that I sidle out and leave her standing by the chair, breasts exposed, tousled waves framing an endearing moue. When I return a moment later, the flush has gone from her cheeks and she is looking as crisp and business-like as ever. I help her into her sable coat and with one arm around her waist I walk her to the door where she hands me an envelope.

"Here ya go. Thanks, it really was wonderful. So, same time Thursday?"

"Actually, I have a meeting with my agent on Thursday. Apparently a small Canadian publisher thinks my erotic prose poems are the bomb. How's 3:30 on Friday?"

"Friday, hmm, let's see…I'm meeting with a producer at 10:00, after that there's Pilates at 1:00, and then nothing until aroma therapy at 4:30. Can we make it 2:30 instead? I promise to get here on time."

"Aroma therapy—the rich really are different, aren't they? *Comme tu veux*, 2:30 it is."

"Oh, listen, sorry about the woodwork and your poor carpet—guess I got a little carried away."

"Not to worry, carried away is what it's all about, right? It's what I'm here for."

THE SAL MINEO PRESERVATION SOCIETY

by Albert Mobilio

A brutal cold had shouldered away any vestige of sunnier days as Mink hunkered down at what he judged to be the river's edge. Snow so deep, he couldn't tell. Holding a three-foot length of rusted pipe, a faucetless spigot at one end, he began spearing the base of a snowy crest. To cook up his blood, Mink imagined himself a Klondike prospector atop the motherlode, then for some rhythm he took on the bearing of a railroad pile driver. But neither proved an icebreaker, so he dug inside the skin of an Ice Age hunter desperate for a scrap of fish. He stabbed wildly at the same rust-streaked hole in the drift, his jagged, guttural howl quickly torn to whispers by the turbulent mountain draft.

When he finally punched through the ice, he flew forward to end up splayed out like a kid making a snow angel. A vigorous, unappetizing suck on the spigot drew water and, while his wet pants grew crisp, he watched the bucket fill. The bare trees stood motionless even though the wind blew steadily. It slipped down the river valley like a blade into an oiled sheath, its edge sharp enough to pare away the last of his imagined Neanderthal. Left alone to crawl back inside the husk of himself, the ordinary Minkovski, he found the fit no less strange than it was last night. That's when he, Jean, and Victor put on Popeye, Olive Oyl, and Brutus masks and kidnapped parking lot czar Eddie Zarg.

Chimney smoke curled through the evergreens making Victor's place look Christmas card quaint. It was his uncle's hunting hideaway but the old guy had stopped coming after he winged a surveyor pacing off lots for new summer homes.

"Goddamn frozen pipes," Mink cursed, a sloshing bucket in each hand as he pushed the door open with his head.

"Jesus, Mink, you go for a swim?" asked Jean from underneath the quilt she'd been cloaked in since they arrived in the middle of night. She was planted by the Franklin stove parceling coal with a hand shovel. "The beach is less crowded this time of year, I guess."

"Yeah, and you can't beat these off-season rates," Mink said, easing the buckets onto the picnic table by the sink. "It's zero-capital-Z degrees out there and you're snuggled so tight to the stove you've gotten a tan. Next time, call room service."

Outstretched arms spreading the quilt with regal flair, Jean came over and wrapped him inside her cocoon. "Welcome to the warm world," she purred, sliding her leg between his Popsicle limbs. An express train shivered uptown through his spine to smack flat against the back of his skull.

"Cut the *High Sierra*." He stiffly squirmed away. "You're not Ida Lupino and that movie don't end happy anyways."

"Oh, Mad Dog, my sociopath." Jean regained her hold and rocked him closer, her voice in a stage whisper, "Victor's upstairs with Zarg. It's you, me and a pail of coal."

Weeks ago she had floated all this as a joke, rang some changes on it, and then, when the boys got glassy-eyed watching her watch Sal Mineo in *Exodus,* she rode the plot home as inevitable—they would kidnap the developer who was about to tear down a brownstone where Mineo had *maybe* lived in the Fifties while playing Yul Brenner's son

355

in a Broadway production of *The King and I*. They would convince him—somehow—not to tear the building down. While advancing this cute piece of deranged ideation, she had vamped Mink with work-a-day earnestness while free-styling a caustic affection for Victor. Right off, Mink saw it plain. He knew Jean felt her jittery best riding some disaster's serrated edge.

Last outing she teamed up with an Israeli guy who made a living card-counting at the blackjack tables in Atlantic City, a micro-computer taped beneath his shirt. She introduced him to the glee of crystal methadrine, then clamored for a big score. Cranked to beat the band, he sweated so much at the table that his computer shorted out and ignited his chest hair. Two bouncers broke one arm outside the casino as Jean pleaded with them to spare the other one because she couldn't drive herself back to New York. Shaken up, she repaired, on her mother's tab, to the pricey clinic where she met Victor in group therapy; he was the runaway talker who lied so much and so sloppily everyone studied the ceiling when he spoke.

Except Jean. She reveled in the baldness of his jerrybuilt deceit, saw in it a forlorn, childish craving she could feed. Mink and Jean were neighbors across the hall and they had laughed together, soon after Victor started coming around, as she mimicked his blowhard storytelling in the nut house. They had laughed about a bunch of her guys but Mink just couldn't find the right time—she was either head over heels, strung out, or in rehab—to pitch his own increasingly hangdog woo. So when Victor started staying overnight at her place Mink could spark only weary rage as he pressed his ear to his door when the two of them came home—Victor's goofy braying and then her familiar laugh.

"Fe fi fo fum, I smell the fun of loaded gun." Victor came

356

thumping down the stairs stuffing the armory—a .38 pistol—in his back pocket. "I thirsted and the Romans gave me Muscatel," he announced as he scooped a cup of the river water.

"Careful, could be full of bad microbes," Mink said.

"Then we'll feed it to Zarg. Open up his sluices. Retentive bastard probably only shits when the prime rate drops." Victor wore an Australian safari hat, a withered ostrich feather flagging off one side. A tall boy even in socks, he loomed creature-feature size in his Arctic-proof mountaineer's boots. He gulped two cups and regarded the third warily.

"You know the septic tank from the gun club leeched last fall. Maybe we should've melted some snow instead."

"Brainstorm, sweetheart," Jean said. "But a bit on the tardy side for you."

Mink thawed unhappily by the Franklin and emitted a hollow chuckle. "We're pioneer stock," he declared, standing in shorts as he wrung out his pants over the stovetop. Victor and Jean, eyes aglare, smiled loonily. Once again, and how many times has it been since he slipped on a Popeye mask behind a dumpster last night, Mink wished himself gone, wished himself home sprawled on the bed, his head sandwiched between two pillows.

"How's the czar?" Jean asked as she sat cross-legged at the kitchen table. She had begun mincing magic mushrooms with a wrist-thick Swiss Army knife. Zarg was known as the "Parking Czar" of Manhattan. "Still bug-eyed. I've never seen eyes that *really* did look like saucers?"

"It's that touch of duct tape on the mouth," Victor said,

stroking his chin. "Accentuates the upper face. Actually, he's not so scared now. Pissed-off is more like it. Being hog-tied to a bunk bed overnight will do that." He grinned loudly, his many teeth appearing to jostle for prominence.

"He can breathe, can't he?" Compassionate Mink.

"Sure, sure."Victor stood behind Jean cupping her head in a pair of large, putty soft, almost babyish hands. "He'll be fine. Just needs to relax a bit and Suzy Homemaker's dose of fungi oughta turn that trick."

"Victor's a strict behaviorist, you know," chirped Jean. "He studied with Pavlov, Smirnoff and Stolichnaya." She measured out two chopped mushroom caps and dropped them in a simmering pot. "Am I on target here? Don't want to knock his brainpan loose or anything."

Mink nodded yes without looking, thinking instead about Zarg's bug-eyes. The *Citybest* article about him said he was fifty-six. Maybe he had a heart condition. But then the magazine also said he played squash like a demon. "Hey, I wanna check on the buzzard," he said.

"I said he's dandy," said Victor.

"Just look in on him." Mink made for the stairs.

"You no believe your compadre?" Habitual lying had spawned in Victor a need for regular testaments of trust.

"I know he's OK but I wanna visit. I'm a card-carrying kidnapper, too."

"All right, all right. Remember, no names. And don't

forget your mask. And don't take mine. He knows I'm Brutus. We've got a rapport."

Mink fumbled among the coats on the couch and retrieved Jean's Olive Oyl mask. Clomping up the wooden stairs, he saw her stirring at the stove, her other arm loose like an undone belt part way around Victor's waist. She found Mink's eyes and closed hers, as if she'd caught his look and then hid the evidence behind her shutters.

Air as dirty as it was cold made the upstairs root cellar dank; an ancient paste of wood smoke, moldering boots, camphor, and creosote slathered across Mink's face as soon as he reached the top of the stairs. The milky light that illuminated two plastic covered windows penetrated only a few feet into the gloom, enough to brighten the steel frames of four military bunk beds. In the lower bunk of the bed against the far wall lay Zarg. A propane lantern hung overhead. The yellowy tableau reminded Mink of church crypts in Italy where withered saints were laid out like blue-plate specials. He sweated into his mask and gulped his own trapped breath. Small detonations of claustrophobic panic scattered through his chest. He squinted hard through Olive Oyl's eyes and fidgeted with the elastic band that dug against his ears. Bearing down on Zarg, he wondered *Who*, singing to himself, *who wrote the book of love.* Eddie squinted too, the lantern light pouring over his face as his eyes skipped frantically behind the narrowed lids. Mink settled warily onto a chair at the foot of the bed, careful to be quiet, non-threatening, interpretable as perhaps even friendly. *Who, who, who*, he tapped out silently, *who wrote that book of love.*

He summoned up suave Ben Casey for proper bedside manner, "Are you okay?" Jesus, Mink thought, what a question. Of course he's going to nod yes sir, quite wonderbar, I'd smile for the camera if I could just move my lips underneath this remarkably adhesive tape. In fact, Zarg did nod yes, his eyes still dancing. Checking that the knots were all knotted, each arm and leg to a bedpost, Mink edged closer and dropped a line he'd only heard used by cartoon characters like Snidely Whiplash, "You can scream all you want but we're miles from anyone so it's best you keep quiet." Zarg's rubbery jowls pulled taut as Mink tugged the tape off his mouth. When the last bit came off with a snap, Mink jerked back anticipating a scream or a viper's spit. But Zarg lay quiet, flexing his jaw and sucking air. More little bombs now going off in his knees and belly, Mink forced himself to study a tiny mole on Zarg's chin, one neatly set within the parenthesis of two nasty shaving cuts. The words, *Lindbergh baby* flashed in newspaper print through his head. He remembered Patty Hearst and the Getty kid with his ear in the mail.

"Thanks," Eddie Zarg, the parking lot lord of New York, croaked huskily. "I thought I'd suffocate. Howabout the ropes? Be nice to sit up, stretch a bit." Pressurized calm, an imploring lilt in every word. Fear's lyric.

Mink stood, shoulders shot back with a military jolt. "The ropes have to stay for now. You can sit when we go down for breakfast." The air felt chewable as gum. Mink's voice vibrated against the mask which then tingled his cheeks. I'm Torquemada in Olive Oyl drag, he thought. I'm doing slapstick on a Bob Hope special. His eyes clenched shut with obliterative force; he shuffled backward.

"Breakfast. How nice." The sweet gone sour in Zarg's voice. "Do I get to see a menu?"

"Don't be an asshole, Zarg," Mink said shakily, "this is serious shit."

"Serious shit. You shaggy-assed punk," Zarg growled, his hands bunching into fists. "You're gonna see serious shit. You have no fucking idea who you've messed with here. No idea how bad you fucked up."

A sauna cooked beneath Mink's mask. *Who wrote that goddamn book of love?*

"Listen, you don't seem like a bad kid," Zarg started in with his dealmaker's pitch. "If you help me you're gonna walk away clean from something you know will turn out bad."

Charging in from the shadows, a magic show's outsized rabbit, Victor elbowed between them, pistol in hand.

"We'll see who's fucked here, Mr. Eddie. I know about the Mafia shit-birds you hang out with but I don't give a fart in France." Probably miles tall to a supine Zarg, Victor started rocking the bunk bed side to side. "As your doctor and a proud gun owner, I'd advise a copasetic demeanor." He let the bed settle gently, then bent to pull each rope tighter. Zarg's fists opened like flowers, and he became ever so still. The two of them, Mink could now see, really did have a rapport.

"You think ducks know?" Jean asked, Socratic depths in her airy pitch. She was scrambling eggs as she regarded a row of duck decoys lined up along the counter.

The boys brooded purposefully, chins secure between fists as if their heads would plummet through the floor without that heroic support. "Know what?" they harmonized.

"That they're being duped. Do they really go for a wooden duck?"

Victor bore down studiously, his overbite devouring his lower lip, sucking it in like he was trying to swallow his own mouth; he wanted very much to answer correctly. "Sure some know something's up, but they can't resist their biology."

"Yeah, born suckers." Mink piped this direct to Jean but she let it pass, her eyes now fixed on the sparks visible behind the stove's grate. Belly, she thought. What a sexy word for something filled with ashes and made of iron.

"Get Zarg," she said. "Breakfast is served."

A gun at the old man's back, Victor walked a blindfolded Zarg downstairs for a platter spiked with psilocybin fungi. All of them cozy within the radiant ambit of the Franklin stove— which had taken on the aspect of a host, a silent, stolid old-timer glad to have these city folks up for some real country weather—sat Bonnie, her Clydes, and Zarg. No masks now, since Victor decided Zarg's blindfold was enough. Outside the wind drove the snow crazily, the windows like television screens between stations. Mink pushed his fork through neatly built piles and watched egg erupt between the tines. Drift, he commanded himself, far enough away, out of this overstuffed chair, out of this cabin, out of this deep scatter and blown snow. There was silent chewing all around as the wind tinkered with every loose joint in the cabin. Zarg used his foot to explore the rope that connected his ankle to the cast iron stove. He regarded it like a new appendage, something whose mechanical possibilities had yet to reveal themselves. Hungry but sightless, he scooped haphazard forkfuls.

"What's with you people. Come on, what's the story here." Plaintive, much put out was Moneybags. Victor looked up to see him gesturing with his fork and lurched like a drunken waiter to grab it. He scared a girlish yelp from the fat man.

"Sorry, Mister Eddie," Victor said through a mouthful of egg. He offered a plastic spoon. "Wouldn't want you to accidentally stab anyone."

"You're here for some re-education. A new spool for your loom," Jean said, starting in like a tough new teacher in a baddass school. "You've got an unhealthy way with the world, thinking everybody is your personal withdraw window. Step up, show your porky mug, and the dollars fly. Well, a line's got to be drawn with you, your kind in general. And we're here to help you draw that line yourself. We're going give you a guided tour to Eddie Zarg."

"What the fuck are you talking about?" Zarg snapped.

"We're talking about, for instance, the building on 55th Street where Sal Mineo lived," Jean shot back. "The one you're going to tear down for another friggin' parking lot." Mink watched her incandesce then cool, and marveled at the ease with which she let herself feel things.

"What are you guys, communist types? You know my grandfather was socialist. He used to go to big meetings down in Union Square," Zarg said.

"Yeah, comrade," Victor laughed. He checked and tightened the ropes, then gave Zarg a slap on the back. "And we're Stalin's lost grandchildren in search of our roots."

Mink hadn't thought about this part, the afterpart. They spent so much time working out the abduction—grabbing Zarg as he left his girlfriend's place in the East '80s—he never believed that they would actually end up with a living, breathing Zarg of their own. No ransom, no demands, just some silly notion about screwing with a rich man's head.

Jesus, Mink flailed at himself and then he turned to Victor. "Don't hit him, man," he said.

"Don't hit him, maaan," Victor whined. "Don't worry about it."

"I'll worry about what I want to." Schoolyard. Mink might as well have said, It's a free country.

"You worry too much. You never really got behind this. I've been working my ass off. Jean too. But you've just been playing tag-along."

True enough, Mink never was behind it. Maybe he hated his city job answering complaint letters from subway riders, but who wouldn't? It was practically a job requirement. But it paid well enough. And there was great vacation time. So what if he never went anywhere, at least he could if he wanted to. Jail would not be a good thing. He'd lose his seniority, all his accumulated sick leave. His discount subway pass. In Victor's voice he heard his father's exasperated What-are-we-going-to-do-with-you tone, the same accusation that he wasn't really trying. Underachiever. Daydreamer. Waterboy. "Go fuck yourself," he said.

"Children, children." Jean was on her feet, palms up like a referee. "What is important here? Let's not trip on our own feet, OK."

"Children, you bet you are," Zarg said. "I wouldn't let any of you help my Puerto Ricans park cars."

Jean spun around at Zarg. "Look, shithead, nobody's interested in what you've got to say. But if you've got something so important to say, maybe you should try it with

364

your fat tongue cut out."

"Cut your freakin' tongue out," Victor echoed.

Mink stiffened. Tongue? This was not on the menu. He thought of Jean with the Swiss army knife and he wondered where the gun was. His stomach tightened around what felt like a dozen struggling fists inside.

"I'm going to be sick," Zarg announced, his voice suddenly wan and distant.

Jean nodded *yes, yes* and silently mouthed the words, "He's getting off." Another proud mom pleased her cooking has hit the spot.

"You'll be fine," Victor told Zarg. "Relax and let it happen."

"Let what happen?" Zarg's head rolled around, a balding antennae frantically trying to tune into the source of Victor's voice. "What the fuck is gonna happen?"

No one said a thing. The cabin quaked in a blast of wind and coals shifted in the stove. Thick and animal deep, Zarg's panicky breathing filled the room. Mink felt its stuttered rasp envelop him, clog his own throat. *Who wrote, who wrote the book of drugs*. Mink was underwater yet still could hear Jean and Victor, their angry whispers barely audible at his spongy depth. He wanted to ask if something was wrong, to ask Jean, but he could not make his mouth move. Eddie Zarg had begun moaning—a soft, exhausted sound that Mink felt had been stolen from his own mouth.

"Coffee?" Jean leaned down and set the cup against Mink's

open hand. Her hair poured across his face, lemony shampoo, the closed smells of winter. I am immune to this, he thought. "You still with us?" Jean spoke close to his ear, her sibilants like brushed cymbals. He took a couple of her fingers and tugged. Make the world right that way. Victor had pulled a chair opposite Zarg and talked quietly to him. Mink heard Zarg say the word *dizzy*, heard Victor soothe, *It's as harmless as dreaming.*

"You would think dreams are harmless," Mink said.

Now standing behind Zarg, whose blindfold he was removing, Victor flashed wide, wild eyes before pulling on his Brutus. "This is a conversation here," he said, punching each syllable with exaggerated precision. "Put your mask on or get out." Jean already wore her Olive Oyl and she offered Mink his Popeye. He took it but headed for the door.

Snow, snow, snowed away, Mink stepped down from the porch to end up knee-deep in the stuff. Like a blanket pulled over the head of a sleepless world, snow made a place where you crawl down beneath its weight, blind yourself in its forever white. The big, wet flakes startled him, a cold pin prick on his face every time one landed. Mink had taken a personal day for all this and he recalled that he only had two left. He so hoarded his time off that he had argued for the kidnapping to be done over a weekend. Now he was down to one personal day. Personal day. That's choice, Mink thought. What could be more personal than a Federal crime punishable by life imprisonment. That's something you just might want to keep close to the vest. But sick time also fits, he figured, since he was doing this to be close to a woman who may be crazy, was sometimes cruel, and was certainly fucking someone else.

As he shivered against the raw, wet air, he imagined he

was a lost trapper bereft of fire, then a beggar expelled from his sheltering doorway. But those dramas would not serve; the Popeye mask in his hand was the only place to cloak himself. With his thumb in the hollow of its puffy cheek, Mink's fingers grazed across the embossed corncob pipe. Popeye the Sailor Man. The cartoon was never a favorite but he'd watched it almost every day for years as a kid. Sally Starr, the cowgirl kiddie-show host, featured Popeye and Clutch Cargo everyday at five. He would eat on a foldout TV dinner stand while eyeing "Our Gal Sal," keenly aware of her sizable breasts, especially when the line of fringe that crossed her chest danced as she twirled her gun. *I'm strong to the finish*— Mink turned face up to blank sky and tumbling flakes—*cause I eat my spinach*—and opened his mouth. He was thirsty and the snow teased his dry tongue.

"Whatcha doing, trying to swallow the blizzard?" Jean asked from the porch. Her head rose out of a quilted bundle; she held herself tight at the waist and shoulder.

"No, just chewing air." Mink climbed back up the stairs, kicking snow free at each step. "What's going on?"

"Doctor and patient are doing fine. Victor's got Zarg talking about growing up. The fat man is definitely launched—he's all inner-child with a pinkie ring."

After loosening Jean's hair from the blankets, Mink tugged a collar into shape around her neck. Like sending her off for her first day of school. Their breath steamed together in knotty, evanescent whorls while Jean dabbed her nose with a tissue.

"It's going to be fine, babe," she said. "We'll walk away from this. It's just something Victor needed to get out of his system." Partial truth. "And then maybe you and me…"

Probable lie, even with the maybe. She sank down into her body wrap—mischievous eyes barely visible, "I really do want to make love to you, Minkovski."

Mink ran through a list of possible responses—the echo effect, *And I want to make love to you*, something gutsy, *Do you think saying that erases everything else?*, or maybe blunt and dirty, *One promised fuck—I'll pencil that in on my calendar*. Before he could choose, Victor's head peeped out, puppet-like, from the door.

"People, perhaps a little help in here."

Mink said nothing; Jean too was silent and as still. They both knew they looked guilty but neither could come up with the word or gesture to break the spell. The snow-spiked wind burned his ears; his feet ached with cold.

"Are you both deaf?" Victor said as he lifted his mask and smiled clownishly, but hard. Lots of effort. "Pretty please with piss on top. And don't forget your masks."

Balled up on the couch, his umbilical rope snaking across the floor to the stove, Zarg chewed absently on the fringe of the pillow he hugged to his chest. When Mink sat down across from him his eyes widened, their pupils as big and dark as old 45s. With that slack, unshaven face, the bruised blue circles, and the comb-over tuffs all shot to hell, Mink could see Zarg was having a rough ride. All the polish had been rubbed away; he was a sagging old man whose dye jobs, manicures, and squash games were, in truth, a slack defense against decay. A spoiled tomato, soft and wrinkled. And now his mind all mushy, too.

"So Eddie." Victor hovered behind him, massaging his

shoulders. His voice low, soothing, therapeutic. "What I really want to know is how you feel about getting rich on bits and pieces of empty asphalt. You don't make widgets, don't cure anyone, you don't build houses. You don't even sell dope. You just nickel-and-dime people to park their cars." Victor bent to whisper, soft, endearing through his Brutus mask, "I mean, even among parasites you rank pretty low."

Zarg mumbled into his pillow as if it were a microphone, "Just putting bread on the table. I work twelve hours a day to put something…to save for my family, but even they don't know what I'm trying to…I don't talk…they don't talk…"

"Talk to who?" Victor asked.

"To people. To people like…I don't even talk to my own daughter anymore." He shut his eyes for a long time and then opened them with a child's Christmas morning surprise. "Christ, that's one helluva movie. Do you folks do this stuff a lot?"

"What about your daughter?" Jean asked.

"She married an asshole. A deadbeat. I told her he'd run her around the block and leave. Now he's suing for alimony."

"And that's why you can't talk to her? Cause you're so pissed off?"

"Yeah. Because I'm pissed off. She's pissed off. Every time I try to say something…one time she said I sounded like poison." The batteries died on Zarg's voice. He found the damp corner of his pillow and started to nibble, a newborn at the breast.

"You mean like a snake?" Victor said. Olive Oyl glared at

him, then she turned to Mink for commiseration. *Don't look at me*, he wanted to say. *You brung him, you dance with him.*

"This stuff is getting to me," Zarg moaned. "It just won't stop. When is it going to stop?" He raised his arms over his head and spread them as far as the rope would allow. "I give up. Whatever you want." Mink saw the unclutched pillow slowly spring back into shape, revealing dark, distended palm prints. Afterimage of panic. We always leave our mark, he thought. Sweat, some piss, a carving in some rock. They were leaving their mark in Zarg's brain. A slash of neon, the mildew musk of a prehistoric couch, and a dose of jagged fright. Fear is what they had burned into Eddie Zarg's head. Maybe he knew it before, but now he would know its every color, high voltage.

Jean went to a window, breathed on the glass and drew an angel in the fog. She flicked the moisture from her finger against her sketch and watched the drops course down through the portrait, devouring its lines, gathering force as they severed the wings in two. Mink and Victor collected behind her. The storm had stopped and it felt like the house had landed after wild flight. Not in Oz, but somewhere empty, somewhere tired.

"Let's wrap this up," Jean said. "We drop him, we go home, we watch *Kojak* on TV."

"But we're not done yet," Victor pleaded.

"We're done."

"What about Sal Mineo's place? What about that?" A spoiled child keening for ice cream, Mink thought, as he squirmed with embarrassment. But anger quickly overtook him—how could he have taken up with these people. Same beat question. Still drawing a blank.

"Victor, we are done with this," Jean said, words popping through barely parted lips. "Get Zarg ready to go. Mink, you should start digging the van out. We're going to drop him just like we planned."

But as soon as Mink stepped out on the porch he heard angry voices. He held the door open a bit. Victor blindfolded Zarg, who launched a bovine cry that seemed to swallow itself as his darkness returned.

"We should do what we came to do," Victor shouted. He manhandled Zarg, tugging the ropes tight, and then tighter to make his point. The old man sucked hard at the newly applied tape, a small gray cleft deepening in his mouth.

"Let it go," said Jean. "It's just something we did. It ain't the crusades." Darting around, Jean gathered up the few things they brought in a backpack. As she passed between the stove and couch she laid her hand against the small of Victor's back as he bent over a wriggling Zarg. "Just don't hurt him." Her touch had a mechanical effect on Victor, making him stand up and lift both arms above his head. For a second, he seemed to pose like a victorious boxer, but then with a sledgehammer swing he brought his clasped fists down on Zarg's stomach. The blow bounced Zarg's body on the couch as it vibrated with an unformed, buried cry. Reflexively, he curled tight like a centipede.

"What the fuck are you doing!" Jean screamed. Grabbing Victor around from behind she staggered back with him, bumping the hot stove. She screamed again but held on. Mink bolted across the room and drew up short, stopping to figure just how to separate the two. Just as Victor pried Jean's locked

371

arms from his chest, Mink saw his chance and reached out to snatch the .38 in Victor's belt.

"Stop it. Stop it right fucking now," Mink shouted, his voice wire-thin and breakable. He pointed the pistol in a vague way at Victor's feet, unable to fix on a lethal target like his head or gut. Jean slipped loose and moved off to the side, her eyes tracing and retracing the line between the muzzle and Victor.

"Hey, guys," she said, a wooden laugh threading through her words. "Come on now, we should be cool. This shouldn't be going this way."

His open palms at shoulder-height, Victor could have been someone refusing an extra portion of dessert. "That's right, Mink," he crooned. "We should be cool here. A little family squabble but there's no need to get overly bent." He rocked easily from foot to foot, inching slightly forward. Zarg groaned but lay still. "I'm behaving, buddy. Sweetness and light."

A dozen gun-wielding movie guys fluttered through Mink's head, condensing into one generic shot—a dark-haired man wearing a jacket with big lapels holds his weapon a bit forward from his waist as he points with his free hand. So Mink pointed at the couch, "Just sit."

Shuffling closer, Victor's piano-mouthed grin overtook his lower face.

"Get back, man." Mink mustered some tenor, but Victor kept coming, rocking like a robot toy. One step back, Mink knew, was as good as giving up. Still, he couldn't point the gun at Victor's head. "You'd better sit down now." This time his voice crackled in the upper register.

"Come on, listen to him," Jean begged, her jaw working after the words stopped, as if she were badly dubbed.

Victor shot her an ugly look and took one giant step forward, lunging for the gun. Mink slammed back against the wall, the gun suddenly heavy, his every nerve packed into the palm of his hand. The trigger felt like someone's finger that he was unbending, maybe so he could take hold of their hand. The pop was surprise enough to press him back against the wall again. Zarg bellowed and Jean crouched down, her eyes shut, her teeth dug into the soft pad of her thumb. Alone in his lack of reaction to the shot, Victor calmly inspected the front of his body and saw the hole in the toe of his boot. Blood had begun to leak from underneath the sole.

"Jeez, you shot me. You ruined my brand new boot," he said blankly. The gunfire had shorn him of any menace.

"You're lucky he didn't ruin your shirt," Jean said. She lead him to a chair, knelt and untied the perforated shoe. "Mink, there's a first-aid kit under the sink." The bullet had passed between his big toe and its neighbor taking a healthy bite of skin from each. "Nothing serious," she said as she peeled back his wool sock. "You'll flamenco before the weekend."

Gun in one hand, the open first-aid box in the other, Mink stood slack-armed beside Jean. She took out a roll of gauze and scissors. "Why don't you check Zarg, then sit down and cool out. And take the bullets out of that gun."

Mink was gripping the pistol so tight, his hand had cramped. The pebbled butt was slick with sweat. Firing it, he thought, had made it a part of him. It was the biggest thing in the room, as hot as the stove, and it was taking root in his hand.

"I'm sorry, Victor. But you shouldn't have…I mean…"

"Watch with the names," Victor said distractedly, intent instead on Jean's handiwork. "I'm sorry," he said to her.

She daubed peroxide on some cotton. "It's OK." She didn't look up, wouldn't meet Victor's thirsty eyes.

The sharp pinch of antiseptic rose up to make Mink wince. He remembered skateboard brush-burns and bicycle cuts, the bathroom cabinet mirror folding his reflection as he opened the door. Ancient bust-ups, home cures. Small scars with small stories. Now he'd get top billing in someone else's war wound tale. *The fucker almost blew my foot off.* What could he say himself, *So I told 'em, one more step and I'll dust your Tom McAnns.* History, Mink decided, would not absolve him.

Once the van tumbled into the deeply tracked road that ran along the river, the going got better; plowing down from the cabin had been a gear grinding chore. Swaddled in blankets and bouncing on the cold steel floor, Zarg sat across from Victor in the back. Navigator Jean rode up front and pitched warnings at Mink as he attacked the drifts with engine at full gun and wheels spinning. He was a Panzer tank pilot driving toward Stalingrad, or the spearhead of an Arctic rescue mission. Mostly, though, he was nervous, stalled too long in the first reel of an unfinished movie, no gear to shift him free.

On the highway, a brooding quiet settled in as the winter sky bled down from a chamois-soft blue. They were headed back toward New York, specifically Van Cortlandt Park in the Bronx. Plan was to stop in a secluded spot, give a tied and blindfolded Zarg a shove, then speed off free and clear. The Parking King would have been gone less than 24 hours. Between his wife and girlfriend, each figuring he was with the other, there would be hardly enough time for the cops to get involved. And what could he tell them: That two guys and a woman wearing cartoon masks took him to a cabin somewhere. Mink could see the tabloid headlines—*Psychedelic Quicknap*, or *Parking Czar Pinched by Popeye*. A one-day joke around town and then consigned to forgottenville.

When the George Washington Bridge came into view, Jean turned to the passengers in the back, "Are we hunky-dory?" Victor squeezed a dozing Zarg, eliciting a cranky grunt. "We're good," he said. "I'll get him ready."

A river of rush-hour headlights poured northward from the city. A torchlight procession of penitents, Mink thought. His eyes relaxed and the white beams blurred. The traffic around him seemed to buoy up and carry the van forward; he was gliding down the grooves of a concrete funnel, moving inexorably toward the distant, luminous spires. The heat blowing from the dashboard was like stale booze. Suddenly, a driver in the next lane blasted their horn. Mink, who had drifted across lanes, swerved back sharply, sending Victor crashing onto Zarg. Sprawled in the rich man's lap, Victor snatched at the air for some non-existent handle while Zarg, sightless and just miles from freedom, slipped his arms over Victor's head and snapped the rope that joined his hands tight against Victor's neck.

"Hello fucker," Zarg hissed through a hole he had chewed open in the tape.

The rope dug down across Victor's windpipe. He sputtered and coughed. He kicked against the walls, but Zarg held on and pulled tighter.

"I've got a gun pointed right at your head, fat man," Jean

shouted. She didn't, but she was rifling through Mink's coat hoping to find one. She almost had a gun and that should count for something.

"So. what. So you've got a gun. I'm gonna break your boyfriend's neck if you don't stop this truck right now."

Mink looked to Jean as she shook her head violently No way.

"How 'bout you do that while I shoot you dead." Jean had found the .38 and rapped the muzzle against the roof as audible proof. Oncoming headlights cast enough light through the van so she could see Victor's swollen face, his lips wet, his nose running.

"Check the chamber, little girl," Zarg said. "The last I heard was bullets getting emptied on some table. Just like you asked for."

Mink sank deeply in his seat, several vertebrae lopped from his spine. He bent toward the steering wheel and locked his mind on the car in front of him. He was Richard Petty tail drafting in the Daytona 500. No way was he going to turn to catch Jean's simmering eyes.

"You're way too smart for me Eddie Zarg." She fired the pistol through the roof and an electric jolt caromed around the van. "That's what a little girl's got a purse for, asshole. To keep the bullets." She laughed. "Now, let him go."

Zarg uncoupled from Victor and cringed in expectation of a shot. Up on his knees and panting like an animal after a chase, Victor spat and wiped his mouth.

"Pull over," Jean told Mink.

"Here?"

"Pull over!" Her voice was metal, foreign. Mink pulled to the shoulder, rumbling over gravel and hubcaps, and stopped beneath an underpass. "Throw him out."

Victor staggered out the back door dragging Zarg with him. A truck barreled past, its wake rocking the van. Mink gripped the wheel like a ring-buoy.

"Just dump him." Jean strained to be heard above the traffic. At the sound of Zarg hitting the ground, Mink felt as if the ballast had been cast; he was free for ascent. Jean put her hand over his as Victor climbed back in. "Let's go home," she said. But Mink had already found the door handle, had already given it a tug. A glance back into the traffic to see if he could swing it open, and he slid from his seat to the ground.

"What are you doing?" Jean said.

"Fucking flake," Victor cursed, as he pushed up-front between the seats. "We've got to go." Mink measured the breaking wave of traffic, then sprinted across three lanes to the asphalt medial strip. Turning around, he saw Zarg struggling to his feet as the van lumbered out into the middle lane, cutting off cars, brakes squealing, tires skidding. A pickup just missed them. Zarg was tearing at his mouth and eyes and Mink could see motorists were slowing down at the sight.

Who wrote the book, he shouted into the storm of passing cars. He started to run, aimed at the sweet spot somewhere in the traffic that would allow him to dash between the speeding cars like an Olympic hurdler, or a doughboy dodging shells at

377

the Somme. Or Minkovski, maybe, running hard, terrified by a burst of reasonless joy. Running nowhere farther than just away, an unmoored world roaring in his open face.

SHITTY MICKEY

John Reed interviews Mickey Mouse

Recently, I was afforded the opportunity of interviewing Mickey Mouse at his Chelsea art complex. In a spartan loft of 6,000 square feet, the Marlon Brando of the mouse world sat in a warm buttermilk bath and sipped papaya smoothies (evidently excellent for the bowels) while we discussed his most recent body of work, which surrounded us. The colorful sculptures came in all shapes and sizes. From simple, abstract conical mounds, to large splattered globs, to flattering busts of famous Johns (John F. Kennedy to John Belushi).

John Reed: Mickey, what a wonderful chance this is for people to get to know the real mouse.

Mickey Mouse: Yes, I often think how exceedingly difficult it must be to get a sense of my importance through just my films—and I so rarely give interviews, as I can only sustain my enlightened state of awareness by way of a quiet, contemplative life, rich with meditation and debased stupors. But of course, even if the audience of the Earth can only glean the most transient sense of my holiness through my movies, it must do them a great deal of good, anyway.

Reed: Meditation and stupor? Is that the secret to your amazing longevity? You must be nearing eighty, which, as I understand it, is quite advanced for a mouse.

Mouse: Seventy. It's all about quality healthcare. As it stands now, mouse health care is extraordinarily evolved. The testing process for mice, in terms of therapies, medicines, etceteras, is far more developed than it is for humans. Indeed, if a mouse receives the very best in the way of proper medical attention, he might expect to live forever. And that's true, by the way, because mice are foremost supporters of the medical establishment—and the medical establishment can't afford to lose me, as the world's preeminent mouse.

Reed: You mean you sell a lot of candy?

Mouse: And soda, and so forth. But the medical industry owes a great deal to mice, not only because of my candy and soda, but because of Lyme disease and the Hanta virus and the Bubonic plague, and, moreover, because the general social theory of mice—that they can live anywhere, on any food supply, in any level of toxicity/adversity—has been a wellspring of surgical and medicinal necessities, and, henceforth, applications.

Reed: And, aside from your excellent health and prospects, as of the Sonny Bono 1998 copyright extension, you've been made a protected species, virtually in perpetuity.

Mouse: Yes, as of the Sonny Bono bill, I won't become public domain in 2004, but will remain protected under the new copyright law.

Reed: Which is currently being challenged in the Supreme Court.

Mouse: But that challenge will fail. And that means, pretty much, that I'll be around until the sun burns out. And with all the helpful Disney lawyers and all the helpful non-Disney lawyers who don't want to do anything that might spark a lawsuit, as that would be expensive, and require they rise from their leather couches, in the current, and probably permanent state of things, well, not only am I immortal, nobody can even make fun of me.

Reed: As a matter of fact, I was recently challenged to try

publishing a parody of Disney. How long do you think it will be before I hear from the lawyers?

Mouse: Eh?

Reed: How do you feel about being emblematic of the total impunity afforded large corporations? Let's take, as an example, your own adaptation of the *Hunchback of Notre Dame*.

Mouse: Hugo would have loved it.

Reed: Why?

Mouse: Because audiences loved it. We tested and tested, and our boards finally came up with exactly what the target market wanted to see. No individual could do that. Besides, our Quasimodo was cuddly.

Reed: I'm not so sure I agree with your assessment of what Hugo would have thought of a "cuddly" Quasimodo. It seems to me you had nothing to add to the story, and that, quite the opposite, you subtracted rather liberally, and that, in terms of justifying your version, there is no critical or satirical element whatsoever—merely a bottom-line of capital gain, and the exploitation, and subversion of an individual's—

Mouse: Individuals die. Corporations don't die.

Reed: Like Walt, you mean—corporations continue to exist, unchanging, in perpetual stasis. Come to think of it, that harkens to your own untouchable, immortal state. Would you draw a parallel—

Mouse: I'm not immortal like Walt. Nobody had to freeze me. And nobody's gonna have to thaw me out. I can lick the back of my own knee if I want to—you call that frozen? Besides, even when he was alive, Walt was just my hand puppet. I had my forepaw so far up his—

Reed: Ehem. We're already pushing this.

Mouse: No, we're not. This is nothing. You're the one who asked the stupid question. You think you're going to rattle me? You should have seen the time I sold the flammable pajamas to toddlers. I've got balls the size of my own head. Look.

Reed: Yes, uh, they are big, comparatively—but isn't that just because you're an animated figure, and you can have whatever you want? Much like the giant conglomerates can have or do whatever they want—and anyone who attempts to express something at odds with their agenda is—

Mouse: I'm not animated, I'm real, ask Wall Street. I live and change and there's no reason to make fun of me in the first place. I'm on top of it. You make fun of me, you're probably out of it anyway.

Reed: People worry about machines taking over life on Earth, but maybe the real threat is animated figures. You're like a higher form of life—you reproduce more easily, live forever, get loved and respected like a living being, and yet suffer no moral or physical consequences for anything. You can kick anyone—push anyone off a moving train. You can eat a whole cake if you want to, and only get fat if you're so inclined. In some ways, you, as a representation of Disney, truly are a kind of divine mouse. God and mouse—everywhere and nowhere, free and yet totally dependent on the laziness and waste of others. And, best of all, as supreme vermin—no glue traps.

Mouse: I told you I'm real. And if that's some kind of threat about the glue traps, let me tell you—nobody sets glue traps for me. You set a glue trap for me, that's punitive, and nobody wants a punitive judgment as far as The Mouse is concerned. Nobody messes with The Mouse.

Reed: Yes, I'd agree that's a fair assessment. And, in a genuine sense, you are real. Did you know that in the nineteenth century corporations were afforded the rights of individuals?

Mouse: Enough about the damn corporations, the damn copyright law, and your damn campaign of disinformation. I thought this was going to be about my art.

Reed: Uh huh. Well—

Mouse: And, by the way, I saw those articles, in the *New York Press* and *Publisher's Weekly*, about you ripping off George Orwell, and I hope they throw your ass in jail.

Reed: I don't think there's too much chance of that. Even with the Sonny Bono extension, which kept Orwell's work out of the Public Domain in 2000—the year that marked fifty years after his death and the end of the previous term of copyright on his works—my book is pretty clearly a parody. And I'm not the only one taking a second look at Orwell— George is facing some legitimate reassessment after the attacks last September. *Animal Farm* in particular represents a cold war mindset, a formulation that the enemy is out there, while, contrary to that formulation, we must now realize that, to a large degree, the enemy is within. By applying the Orwell model as it currently stands, via *Animal Farm*, there's little room for the realization that we're not living up to the ideals of our own society, and that, especially abroad—

Mouse: Shut up, Orwell was a great man. Great men can

pump heavy metals into frog ponds, if it's for the greater good.

Reed: Oh?

Mouse: If this isn't in *Artforum*, I'm gonna sue.

Reed: Uh, how about *The Brooklyn Rail*?

Mouse: What the hell is that?

Reed: *The Brooklyn Rail*? Oh, I don't know. I've published a couple of reviews in the *Rail* and I've been surprised by not only the number of people, but the number of really good people who read it.

Mouse: Yeah, well, I better get the cover.

Reed: That's really not up to me, but I'll mention it to Phong and Ted.

Mouse: What? Who are they? And get me their social security numbers. And just forget plugging your stupid knock off of *Animal Farm*.

Reed: *Snowball's Chance.*

Mouse: Jail, buddy.

Reed: I really don't think anything will happen. Everyone close to the publication is frothing at the mouth, but all that's happened so far is we got one kind of grumpy, not-too-bright e-mail. The representative for the Orwell estate wouldn't even talk to *The New York Times*.

Mouse: The *Times* should be ashamed of itself. They must be getting their writers out of the same cesspool that spawned you.

Reed: I'm not sure how much importance you'd attach to my opinion, but I found myself amazed by how—

Mouse: Anyone who wants to be a writer, anyone who wants to be an artist, they should have to get a license, which could get taken away at a moment's notice. You have to have a license to do everything else, and, generally, a creative person is more careless and destructive than a drunk driver. Frankly, I think it should be illegal to be an artist at all.

Reed: I see, but don't you consider yourself—

Mouse: Not me, you moron. Everyone else. And I want approval on the text in this "interview."

Reed: Okay.

Mouse: Run it by my lawyers.

Reed: Okay.

Mouse: Hey, wise guy, try asking this question—in what ways are you, Mickey Mouse, the most influential artist this century? In what ways does your latest, brilliant sculptural expression bring yet more enlightenment to a planet you have already brought enlightenment?

Reed: All right, what of it?

Mouse: Well, I developed film, obviously, and animation, and special effects—almost entirely on my own. Music as well. Consider what we did for Rock n' Roll on *The Mickey Mouse Show*. Certainly the music video—I had fully reconciled music

385

and image in the 1930s. And art—figurative, and abstract. Just look at *Fantasia*. That says it all. From that source alone, you could trace almost all of contemporary culture. From MTV to Jackson Pollock.

Reed: What about Walt, didn't he—

Mouse: Without me, Walt wouldn't even be a hunk of ice. By the way, Marc Quinn owes me big time on that.

Reed: Hm, you think so? Could you explain that in more—

Mouse: Stick to the subject. Ask about my new medium.

Reed: Oh—just consider yourself asked.

Mouse: I'm working with excrement and pigment, much in the same method that I have for all of my animated pieces. (Incidentally, I've always had that technique on the table, and I'm investigating whether artists such as Paul McCarthy, Mike Kelley, Franz West, Tony Labatt, Chris Ofili, John Miller, Wim Delvoye and Piero Manzoni don't owe me royalties.) It's an organic process of intake, digestion, and yield. The medium has always been crucial to me, and I've always spread it literally throughout my projects—as a kind of fertilizer in which the viewer might take root. But now, I'm looking for a more pure art. All excrement. Next, the theme park.

Reed: That's heavy.

Mouse: Now, ask me about my influences. And be sure to print it just the way I say it—I mean, that should be easy for a plagiarist like you, but you never know.

Reed: Whatever you say.

Mouse: You're darn tootin'.

Reed: Please, go on.

Mouse: Right, then. Influences. As for myself, I studied alongside Anthony Quinn, under Picasso. As for influences— Andy Warhol, Matthew Barney, Damien Hirst and Jeff Koons. All totally influenced by my work. And totally derivative, I might add. Looking back at this period, the only other artists of any merit will be David Bowie, David Byrne, Paul McCartney, Johnny Rotten, and maybe, Sylvester Stallone, who made some pretty important paintings when he was—

Reed: Righto. Moving on. Not to be a rumormonger, but what about the 1994 article in *Star* mag—

Mouse: No. Absolutely no basis to it. There was never anything between me, Liberace, and a forceps.

Reed: But it does seem to, pardon me, fit in with your artistic concerns.

Mouse: No, it doesn't.

Reed: What about the talk of homosexuality at the old Disney studio? If you look at the photo documentation, there are quite a few dapper-looking fellows in v-neck sweaters.

Mouse: What is this, a smear piece?

Reed: No, not at all, to tell the truth, I thought it made Disney more interesting.

Mouse: No comment.

Reed: What about CBGB Gallery's recent "Illegal Art" show—of parodic images that have been quashed?

Mouse: Huh?

Reed: Disney was featured prominently in the exhibition. Most notable, of course, would have to be Wally Wood's 1967 "Disneyland Memorial Orgy." I guess Disney really got into the bacchanal spirit of the sixties.

Mouse: I don't know what you're talking about.

Reed: Oh, well, what about the theory published last month in *Zoology* mag—

Mouse: No, not so. I am not a rat.

Reed: But straight-up, Mickey, you must be tipping the scales at 12 pounds.

Mouse: Listen, I'm too important to be a rat. You, you're a rat, and that's pretty good. Most of the global population is maggots, and those are only good for between-meal snacks. Me, I'm so damn important that I can be whatever I damn well please.

Reed: Aha. Lastly—and I must say your nose does seem a little smaller lately—what about the rumors that you had an eye enlargement as early as 1940, and that, as of 1985, you've been sharing a plastic surgeon with Michael Jackson?

Mouse: No, untrue, and as far as I know Michael hasn't had any surgery either—though he does give excellent sleepovers. And, just for the record, I gave him his first sleepover back in the late seventies when we briefly brought *The Mickey Mouse Show* back to prime time. Returning to the subject of cosmetic surgery—you know, I lived in Hollywood a long time, and for all the talk in the tabloids, the only celebrity that I know of who, notwithstanding the gossip, really has had some work is Pinocchio. And that was just a little shave of a nose job—back when he was still made of wood.

Reed: And on a more personal note, how's Minnie?

Mouse: Actually, that's a common misconception. We've been replacing Minnie with a new mouse about every four months since—

Reed: Is that so?

Mouse: Yes, to be perfectly honest, we've got a whole new litter to choose from in the back.

Reed: But what about the males?

Mouse: Don't you know anything about mouse fathers?

Reed: You mean?

Mouse: Yes, occasionally one hankers after more than a maggot.

Reed: Um, thanks. That's just about all I'll need for—

Mouse: Yeah, yeah, hotstuff, we'll see. You think you're real? I could have you erased. I could have this erased. I could have the whole *Brooklyn Rail* erased. All I have to say is the magic words—Abracadabra the mouse gets his way, with a wave of his tail this newspaper...

MRS. MUNCH

by Kurt Strahm

From: Mitch Kakuski
Helmsley/AMC Gitford Hotel
737 Seventh Avenue
New York, New York 10019

To: Cynthia Munch, Comptroller, Grants Division
Ronald McDonald Foundation
22278 Ronald Reagan Pacific Coast Highway
Newport Beach, California 92663

Dear Mrs. Munch,

This is in reply to your response to my EMERGENCY request for more money. Let me remind you, in case you missed the messages I left on your machine over the weekend, that I am down to my last few thousand dollars, which won't even cover the bill for last week here at the hotel. I know that by Third World (or even terrorized New York) standards, I'm not that bad off yet, but it makes me sick to think about having to go back to my old life. It would be like a genie giving you a magic carpet and flight lessons, then pulling the rug out when you got airborne. Anyway, you asked me to "give a thorough accounting" of the money already sent to me. Of course I've been too busy to keep track of every little thing, but here is what happened, from the beginning:

The Postal Service Delivers Hope

I received my Ronald McDonald Genius Grant by certified mail. Though I'd never applied for one, I wasn't too surprised when it came. I'd seen an infomercial on TV about thousands of grants, worth billions of dollars, that foundations are desperate to give away.

I did think it was strange my name was misspelled on the envelope, and that the grant was for "Distinguished Work in the Flavor Dynamics of Recycled Fast Food Grease," but people make mistakes, even when large sums of money are involved. And sure, someone could question my credentials as a genius and say I should've known the grant wasn't meant for me. But just because I was a substitute clerk at RadioShack doesn't make me an idiot.

It's true my mind can get lazy; I can't count the number of times it's spit out the command to "just *do* something!" when it got tired of thinking. And yes, I could barely put two words together on a page for the first few decades of my life. It took years of honing my craft, sending letters to the editors of local free weeklies, before I was able to write with my current coherency. But I did make it through nearly two years of community college, and have always been an *avid* collector of information, sometimes so much that I don't know where to put it, so it just sits where I dropped it on the floor of my brain. I've also noticed that a lot of people have a hard time following my elaborate logic once I get rolling on a topic, and isn't that an indicator of genius?

I really was surprised when I saw the amount on the check. You people are *very* generous. Of course I guess you can afford to be, with all the billions of hamburgers you've sold, even after all those cows went crazy from that "mad cow" brain disease a few years ago.

Moving On Up

After getting the cash (minus the 8% fee) at one of those bulletproof check cashing places and putting it in an old backpack, I found a "suite" at a nice hotel near Times Square (almost $300 a night). Spending money like that made me nervous at first, but it was just a drop in the bucket now that I was rich. I needed a quiet place where I could concentrate and make sure I didn't squander the chance to turn my life around.

My new suite was sunny and spacious, with big TVs in both rooms. I ordered meals from room service (about $120 a day including tips), and sent one of the bellhops out to The Gap for three of everything in my size when I ran out of clean clothes (another $120 a day).

I spent a few days watching really interesting stuff on satellite TV and realized I was a sucker for living without it all those years. There's a world full of knowledge out there, with channels dedicated to every subject you can think of, from debutantes to dictators, being broadcast on invisible waves right through our bodies 24 hours a day from broadcast towers, microwave dishes and satellites, but we can't pick up any of it without the proper equipment. So I signed up for the hotel's premium TV package ($50 a day), and bought a few DVD recorders ($1000 each) to record some of the stuff that was on when I was watching something else or asleep. You never know which nugget of information might turn out to be the missing piece of the puzzle. Did you know *Xena the Warrior Princess* is based on fact, according to the Amazon Network?

To top off the luxury, I didn't have to lift a finger to keep the place spotless. The maid would come through every day at 11:00 AM, when I was watching *History's Greatest Bloops and Blunders* on the What Happened Channel. I tipped her $20 a day, spreading the wealth.

After a week at the hotel, it occurred to me that I could afford a nice apartment. But I found it didn't bother me at all to live in a place where I was always treated as a guest, and didn't have to fill rooms with possessions like a pharaoh getting ready for the afterlife (thanks, Mysteries of History Channel). Instead I could become a more "evolved" human being, by realizing that "wisdom is the only luggage allowed on the soul train to enlightenment" (thanks, Don Cornelius Zen Channel).

The idea of becoming more evolved really appealed to me— I could almost feel the new "lobes" growing on my brain as I soaked up the satellite TV—so I decided to stay at the hotel.

Now That You Can Have Anything, What Do You Want?

Of course my first thought when I got the grant was to hire a beautiful young "escort" for a night out. We'd start in Chinatown, dining on the exotic deep-sea creatures I'd only dreamed about. I'd learned from the Green Channel that sadly, a lot of these species are nearly extinct because of demand from a wealthier China, and I wanted to try a few of them before the Pacific Ocean was vacuumed clean. But I found out escorts are really expensive. You could buy a decent *used car* for what they asked, and still have enough left over to buy gas and cruise suburban strip malls for bored and lonely housewives, happy with dinner and drinks at a freeway-exit steak house. Not that I would ever do anything so sleazy.

The last escort service I called gave me the number of an "adult entertainment" line. But I was so disgusted after talking to three of the girls there that I gave up. They each had low, husky voices and said the most perverted things I've ever heard. I was pretty turned off by the phone bill, too, when I found out the "girls" were really inmates at a prison upstate, and that the calls cost $19.99 a minute. You'd think being locked up with a bunch of sweaty thugs would dull the sexual imagination, but I guess not.

Peacock Feathers Are an Evolutionary Necessity (Thanks, Natural Broadcasting Corporation)

After that experience I realized there was a hole in my new life—I was kind of lonely. I was pretty sure I'd have a better shot at getting a girlfriend now that I could afford to maintain a decent appearance. I even considered getting plastic surgery to make myself look really good, but then thought about the *burdens* of beauty, and imagined how terrible it must feel for someone like Brad Pitt to be sitting around the house half drunk one day, then look into the mirror at those long eyelashes and suddenly realize it won't be long—before they fall out, his gut spills over his belt and pops his shirt buttons, and he's staring into the pink eyes of a fat leprechaun at the tail end of a bender.

Beauty is like fruit—the moment it reaches its peak is the moment it starts to rot.

Plus I wasn't sure what I wanted to look like. Studies show that women prefer "pretty" men like Brad, but then so do men, and I wouldn't be comfortable with a bunch of men's eyes crawling all over me—I don't know how you women stand it. Then I thought about going for a more "thuggish" look, but could guess the outcome: me and my new girl are the only passengers in a subway car late at night when some teenage lowlifes sit down across from us. They stare at us and smile, then ask if we want to go "party" with them. When I say "no thanks," they laugh and say "that's OK, *you* don't have to go..." then start praising the finer points of her anatomy. Pretty soon she turns to me and asks "Did you hear what they said? Are you gonna let these punk m...........s say this s..t to a lady?!"

There's no way this scene can have a happy ending. Looking like a thug just attracts trouble, and doesn't scare off a real one, who can smell the killer inside like a shark smells blood (yes, sharks do smell underwater somehow (thanks, Cousteau Channel), while we humans get underwater in the bathtub so we *do not* smell). I can get angry and boil for weeks, but don't have a violent bone in my body, and want to keep all my bones. I decided that being average-looking and sort of invisible, like I've always been, isn't so bad—you can pass through the world without anyone noticing and see it as it really is, like a reporter from another planet—so I skipped the surgery.

Prisoner of Love

No matter what you look like, it seems like most relationships either go bad, with a nasty divorce and decades of child support, or the marriage works out and the rest of your life is cast in stone, so there's hardly any point in waiting around to see what happens. Either way, the husband will have to spend his entire life:

1) working indoors, stuck in a dead end job at an airless office surrounded by incompetent bureaucrats, working for a petty fascist whose only enjoyment in life is spreading misery, until the poor guy has stewed in the pressure cooker for so long that one day he "goes off" and "takes out" everyone

around him with an assault rifle, but then has to confront the ultimate, predictable humiliation when he can't "take out the trash" that is himself, and winds up begging the SWAT squad to do it as he sits on the floor rattling hand grenades and whimpering in the smoke rising from the carnage, looking like a Big Baby Destroyer of Worlds, or,

2) working outdoors, where the monotony, scorching sun and freezing rain break him down day by day, like erosion eating away at a mountain, until his face is shriveled up like a walnut, his fingers and toes are all crooked, and it hurts every time he moves, so he winds up drinking and taking pills all day to numb the pain and silence the alien voices that rise every afternoon like scavenging pterodactyls on the whistling wind.

(Venus Trap)

(Yes, as I'm pretty sure you're thinking, I shouldn't look so far ahead and snuff out the embers of romance before they even catch fire. It's not that I don't feel the longing and desire that makes you want to drop everything and follow a beautiful stranger into the unknown. I get that feeling all the time here in New York, like an outline of her was tattooed under my eyelids at birth, so when my eyes lock onto her the world slows to a crawl and the DNA in every cell in my body starts screaming to leave this low-rent vessel and move into hers, to sprout a new branch of the family tree. The trouble is that after a while, instead of imagining the branch growing toward the sun in a sky blue future, I feel it wrapping itself around my ankles, then smothering me like vines on a dead tree trunk.

You're right, I need to stop thinking so much, it gets in the way of my happiness. But without funds, you can bet I won't have much else to do.)

So, after all that, I bought one of the Japanese key-chain pets ($29) I saw on the Spend 'n' Save Channel. It's a digital leech named Froyd, and I have to push a button to feed him blood a few times a day or he starts saying "Froyd vants blood—a virgin vould be good" like a vampire, louder and louder until you feed him. It's really embarrassing to have Froyd go off in my pocket in the middle of a crowd, so I'm pretty religious about feeding him.

The World Turns Out to Be a Super Titanic Death Match

NOTE: I have to warn you that things take off from here. Current events suddenly hijacked my new life and turned me away from luxuries like love and happiness, back to the irritated frame of mind I had when I wrote letters to the weeklies. Or even more irritated, because the topic in the weeklies was usually just an excuse for an argument, and now it's the fate of the world. After the terrorists murdered thousands of people for the greater glory of Allah and dimmed every beautiful day (like 9/11 was here) with a lurking sense of dread, I started wondering if my happiness was the only thing that mattered. I tried to think of what I could do to improve the world.

Of course my first thought was to go on a personal "jihad." I'd buy a plane ticket to Pakistan, grow a beard, and infiltrate the local scene. I'd act deaf and dumb, and carry a Koran with a picture of Osama bin Laden, then point to the picture and hold up a piece of paper that said "Please help me find my daddy!" I knew from watching the King Fahd Channel (KFC) that family is the most important thing in that part of the world, and some of these people have upwards of 50 children. (Maybe that's why the women wear those big black robes? Imagine what having so

397

many kids does to your figure.) Sure I didn't look much like bin Laden, but if I started smoking opium when I got there it would give me the same deadly serenity, and after I played my KFC Islamic Science video that shows how infidels are descended from twelve-breasted rats and how Allah invented the nuclear bomb to eradicate them, there would be no question about my sincerity. I was sure I'd find "daddy" in no time.

And when I found him and his bloodthirsty crew I'd martyrize them on the spot: I got a bomb recipe from the Militia Channel (fertilizer, sugar and Diet Coke), and some tips on how to be a suicide bomber from the Al Jazeera Network (remind yourself that your victims are ants; eat garlic to cover the smell of the bomb; chant (something that sounded like) "God is good, God is great! Let's go, let's go, Mississippi State!" until you're in the mood). It's true this act would go against my nonviolent, self-preserving instincts, but all I had to do to get past them was psych myself up and push a button, then let everyone else worry about cleaning up the mess afterwards.

The only thing I wasn't clear on was what I'd say just before I set off the bomb. People would want to understand my motivation—was I doing it for God, for my People, for spite, or just to get on TV? I needed something clever, something an action hero like Bruce Willis would say, but he had millions of dollars worth of Hollywood screenwriting talent to think up his lines, and all I had was myself. So I decided I'd have to put off the bombing, keep watching TV, and hope some of that talent rubbed off on me.

Is the World Such a Wreck That It Deserves to Be Blown Up, Along with All Us Inhabitants?

Meanwhile I'd continue to think about what was wrong

with the world. Some people said the terrorists had the right to kill as many random strangers as possible because their People were being disrespected and the world is not fair. These people are idiots, but it's true the world's not fair. It never has been and probably never will be. But the terrorists don't want a fair world anyway, they want a "perfect" one, under their thumb, just like the commies did. (Conclusions formed after weeks of grueling TV watching.)

After the terror attack, you could feel the hole blown in the side of reality, like America just found out it was mortal. All of a sudden nothing mattered but survival, and all the stuff we normally argue about was submerged under a river of grief and anxiety. But it wouldn't take long for the thieves to learn to breathe underwater and get back to work.

Thank You Ronald

I walked by a group of half a dozen street people every day near 51st and Broadway, up the street from Times Square. A few of them looked like pirates, with shifty eyes and missing teeth, trolling for spare change in the stream of potential suckers that flows by every day. It was pretty obvious they ran the lives of the more disturbed members of the crew, "managing" their disability checks and medication.

Once in a while I stopped to talk to the ringleader, a loud woman who went by the name "Squirrel Girl." In between her twitching and profanity, and while I tried not to stare at what looked like algae growing on her teeth, she told me her story. She said she and her friends used to live in the crevices around the World Trade Center, "till them terror morons blew it up for virgins," and they were forced to migrate north, driven out by the smoke from burning computers and by rescue workers who didn't appreciate her and her friends standing in line with them for free sandwiches and coffee.

"I can't believe they think they're killin' everybody for God! God don't give a damn what people do, or He'd take care 'a these morons," she said, pointing a thumb at her friends. These lost souls passed their days buzzing around garbage cans and muttering complaints at passing shadows, living in private worlds that barely intersect this one. I realize this doesn't mean they have no purpose here, though I doubt they know what it is. Their job, since the day the other Ronald (Reagan) started emptying the insane asylums, has been to keep the rest of us in line—by reminding us that this ledge we're walking on is narrow, and when we fall off, it's all over. (Thanks to FOX's *World's Craziest Homeless People* for this conclusion.)

God Helps Those Who Help Themselves, Thank God!

Reagan's followers, including the current president, Bush Jr., claim that personal responsibility is the cornerstone of a healthy society, and that's one of the world's greatest ideas. But then these ungrateful parasites don't want to pay taxes to support the system that helped them get rich, so the rest of us suckers get to pay their bill, a.k.a. "the deficit." This is because they believe either that:

1) it will cost them less to put up electric fences and hire a private police force than to help support a healthy society (this is known as the "Republican Model," according to the Popular Front Channel), or,

2) the meek *shall* inherit the earth, but only after assertive people have chewed it up and spit it out, and are relaxing in cryogenic tubes on luxury space ships speeding toward a fresh planet (thank you, Popular Mechanics Channel), or,

400

3) they are geniuses who could have made it anytime, anywhere—selling heaters in Hell—and are upset they haven't received recognition from a genius grant foundation like I have, or most likely,

4) they are *blessed*, and God has given them the *moral right* to live better than everyone else.

The Promised Land

Just before Bush and his "religious right" attorney general, John Ashcroft, began advertising their White House prayer meetings, the president said we are blessed, and it's our natural right as Americans, practically our duty, to burn energy like there's no tomorrow. Meanwhile the "religious right" Reverend Pat Robertson bought an old, broken down oil refinery and tried to start it up, hoping to raise more money for the cause.

Then Osama bin Laden, a product of the Saudi royal family's oil wealth and official fundamentalism, came along and made self-serving righteousness look bad—and momentarily distracted the Republicans from their endless attempts to move the U.S. closer to the Saudi "religious right" model.

What's this relationship between God and oil, anyway? Is His spirit locked inside the stuff, and we have to burn it to spread the spirit? To the lungs, which are next to the heart? Or have these people been tipped off that *there is no tomorrow*, and there's no point in conserving anything or worrying about the mile-high wall of flame about to engulf us because, in the words of Bush's favorite Supreme Court Justice, Antonin Scalia, "for the believing Christian, death is no big deal." (These facts kept pouring out of the Nonstop

News Network; I quit watching, it was too depressing.)

(Or maybe something even more sinister is going on. I watched a show on the Ripley's Science Channel about how oil comes from dead dinosaurs. After some animations showing gigantic brontosaurus graveyards turning to liquid under the hot sands of Arabia, the show went on to hypothesize that we've inhaled so much dinosaur DNA from burning oil and gas fumes that some of us will start mutating into dinosaur-like beings pretty soon. Of course my first thought after learning this was that the Texas and Saudi oil people are part of a secret cult planning to resurrect the dinosaurs and take over the world. But then I remembered that they *already* rule the world.)

The news always shows pictures of politicians going to church, but it's considered too personal to ask exactly what kind of weird religious beliefs they have. Maybe this is because half of Hollywood belongs to the Church of Scientology and the media doesn't want to advertise the fact? I won't even go into the contorted fantasies these people base their lives on, because I don't want to get sued or murdered. But they are just *actors*, the off-screen shells of the characters they play on screen, and their beliefs don't affect anyone. Until they run for office.

The Moral Quandary of Being Protected by Republicans

The ruthless, gun loving Republicans are naturals to defend us from the terrorists. But just like the fresh new kid in a maximum-security prison full of perverts, we're going to have to pay for the protection (thanks for the nightmares,

402

Scared Straight—After School Special, AOL Time Warner SuperStation). It makes me sick, but the facts are:

1) someone has to stop the fundamentalist mass murderers, because they see everyone as slaves to the *next* life,

2) the Republicans have their own fundamentalists, and have always been comfortable with the rest of us being slaves in *this* life,

(and like the fundamentalists, their success depends on keeping a large percentage of the smelly, sweltering "masses" desperate and ignorant enough to thank them for table scraps (thanks, Comrade Central)),

3) no one's going to save you from the Republicans, now that the Democrats are deflated from: (a) finally figuring out that the world will never be fair, (b) losing faith in their plans to make the world as safe and caring as a daycare center,

(run by robots, where everyone is so pampered that they turn into bloated parasites, fed liquefied Happy Meals by intravenous tube as they lay in their hammocks watching the Wrestling Channel all day, until no one has enough muscle left to dust off the robots, so they all break down and everyone starves to death (thanks, Twilight Zone Channel)),

and (c) getting slapped like sissies by the Republicans for so long. Now they just sit and watch, and let the money and corruption creep over them like clouds over the sun. Why should the Republicans be the only ones getting fat?

Meanwhile Bush, like Reagan, thinks reading the teleprompter with some TV emotion makes him a real leader, when it just makes him the "front man" selling the facade to the suckers. And instead of growing into greatness with his new popularity, he still spends most of his time selling the same old "pump gas, print money & pray" philosophy he was before the terror, just like the Saudi oil princes. Of course there's plenty of time for him to change, but I'm not holding my breath. Unless the terrorists spray me with nerve gas.

I Had a Dream

By the way, if hearing the stuff above would upset all those rabid right wing Republicans out there in California, and cause them to vote at their next convention to let the Bush clan, Nancy Reagan and the Christian Coalition stand me up against the wall of an abortion clinic and execute me without a last meal, fine. I just had another one of those dreams, where a jet with its tail blown off and people spilling out the back is flitting all over the sky looking for a place to crash, so I don't care. If we're all going to die, we should at least speak our minds and face Judgment Day without a slick lawyer at our side.

You aren't one of those rabid right wing California Republicans are you?

Go Forth and Multiply the Right to Bear Arms?

The humiliation of being protected by Republicans has given me a feel for the NRA, militia nuts, and people in Utah, Afghanistan, Pakistan, etc., who feel everyone needs their own assault weapons to protect themselves from everybody else threatening their paranoid way of life. Like those weasels at the U.N., who are always looking for a way to force Americans out of big, comfortable cars.

(When everyone knows the U.S. was *built* on gas-guzzling cars, that they are its blood and the freeways its veins. If that fact chains us to humiliated, corrupt oil countries whose proudly ignorant and spiteful citizens want to blow us up just because Britney Spears won't answer their creepy love letters (People Magazine Channel), well, what can I say? It's the best deal we could make with the devil.)

And after taking our cars and forcing us onto slow, crappy solar-powered buses, they'd raise our taxes to pay for (1) condoms in poor countries, so they can all go buck wild and have safe sex all day for free, and (2) abortions in poor countries, where all the peasants want boys who can pull a plow and inherit 1/50th of the farm some day, which means no more girls would be born there, which means pretty soon our shores would be choked with rusty boats full of horny foreigners trying to get at our women, including you (Repent! Channel).

So the pro-gun, anti-sex nuts do have a point. But how will assault weapons protect you from a jet plane without a tail? It's almost like defending against an asteroid from outer space, and for that everyone would need their own assault spaceship with a nuclear device. Maybe that's what this Star Wars program they've been working on is going to do? Spaceships are too expensive, but they would give everyone on earth their own miniature nuclear device, and the threat of getting blown up would make everyone respect the rights of others?

At first glance this might seem like a reasonable approach to security. But with six billion people on earth, there's bound to be a few kids, religious nuts or drunks who go ahead and push the button, causing a chain reaction of 5,999,999,999 more nuclear explosions, and burn us all off the face of the earth (no TV necessary for this one, just common sense). Of course that *would* end our suffering—unless the religious nuts are right, and we're all sentenced to their next life.

You aren't one of those religious nuts, are you?

Back to Reality and Squirrel Girl

Anyway, in spite of all my bellyaching about Republicans, I definitely do not agree with people who say "nobody deserves to go hungry or homeless," when everyone knows some people don't deserve to *breathe*. But I do believe everyone deserves a few chances, and it struck me that Squirrel Girl and her friends—who were working hard to eke out a living as bums in the wilderness of Midtown, and making a more honest attempt to cope with reality than the terrorists—deserved another chance.

So I bought them all plane tickets to L.A. ($3800 one-way), gave them $600 cash for drinks before, during and after the flight—they were worried about security—and enough for some new clothes, two weeks at a motel near the beach, three nutritious meals a day, and a chauffeured limo to take them to job interviews ($8800). I was sure the fresh air and new opportunities out west would help them turn things around, but gave them your address just in case. I guess that's what the message from your assistant Eldridge was about. I could tell he was agitated, but that was about it—it sounded like he was shouting and drowning at the same time. You'd think a Digital Surround Sound answering machine ($600) could take a message without garbling it.

I have to admit I thought about escaping to L.A., too—there's no center to it, so the terrorists would have a harder time figuring out what to blow up. But I've decided to stay

406

put, because New York needs all the help it can get. Which means I need you—to send more money.

So Thanks for Everything, But Please Send More

The grant transformed me, like an ugly "larva" turns into a majestic Monarch butterfly (Wings Channel), and I owe it all to you, Ms. Munch. But there *is* a problem. After all the accounting above, I guess it's obvious I need a higher level of income to maintain my lifestyle than I used to. Without being accusatory, I'd like to respectfully point out that *you* made me dependent on this lifestyle. And now that I'm out of money and facing life in the gutter, it's pretty obvious you should've given me a *fishing pole* instead of a *bucketful of fish*, as I'm sure Ronald Reagan would tell you if he could.

From what I've seen on TV, he wasn't right about much of anything, but he sure was right that welfare is poison, and that you shouldn't just send people a check in the mail. The grant freed me from worries about basic survival, but then I started worrying about all these other problems. And how can I solve them if I can't think straight because I don't know where the next dollar is coming from? How can I go back to RadioShack after living so well, thanks to you?

When you sent the grant, you saved my life. And it's a well known fact that you're responsible for someone after you save their life. It's just like saving a dog from the gas chamber at the pound—you can't decide a week later you don't like the slobbering Rottweiler after all, and ditch him in the suburbs with a bagful of burgers. You made yourself *responsible* for the poor creature, and it's your duty to love and feed it till it drops dead of old age or a brain disease.

You bet on my future, too, financing my genius in the hope it would improve the world. If you invested in a company, would you turn your back the first time it hit a bump in the road? If everyone did that, pretty soon the whole economy would collapse and we'd all be sitting in mud drinking rubbing alcohol and trading army surplus grommets for zippers like they were in Russia a few years ago, before they struck oil.

It All Depends on the Future of the World

And speaking of Russia, the only way out of this mess is to put *more* money on the table and *spend* our way out—the same strategy Reagan used to beat the commies. I just need time to regain my footing and learn how to "fish," maybe with some foreign language classes at a small, elite college, so I'm ready when the future arrives, and either:

1) Bush and the Saudi princes become the biggest heroes in history and establish a world government that gives everyone freedom, education, fresh air, health care and satellite TV. Then space aliens reprogram the satellites to suck our brains out and transport all our thoughts to their galaxy for a new reality show called *The Universe's Craziest Planets*, or, more likely,

2) earth becomes a boring European socialist utopia where everyone sits around sidewalk cafés all day, meditating and reading poetry, and complaining about tourists, Hollywood blockbusters, and the three-day work week that's running them into the ground, or, just as likely,

3) we're neck deep in strife, as the world keeps contracting and everyone gets more and more irritated, like the inside of an atomic bomb, or a family in a hot motel room with a broken TV.

If (1) comes true, it doesn't matter what I do. If (2) comes true, I'll have to learn French and etiquette just to get a job as a busboy. If (3) comes true, an executive-level CIA job in Paris or Rome might be nice—so long as I get to wear a disguise that makes me look un-American and I don't have to visit the embassy, which would be a prime target.

We have to worry about getting blown up nowadays because everyone in the world hates America. We were stupid enough to give them TV, they've seen all the stuff we have, and now they want it for themselves. They hate the way we run the world, too, as though they could do a better job. I just saw some Norwegian on the World Channel talking about what vicious idiots we are—this from an icicle of a country where nobody's worked a lick since *they* struck oil, and like the Beverly Hillbillies, decided to buy some class; this from a country whose main export for centuries was seafaring thugs called Vikings, who would chop your head off as soon as look at you (Nordic Pride Network).

Everyone else had, what?, thousands of years to make the world a decent place to live and they failed miserably. We've been at it for less than 100 years, and now even the most backwards village in the world can drink Coke and watch MTV. What are these ingrates complaining about?

But I guess it's natural for people from old places to be jealous after they've spent centuries cultivating the best cuisine, art and ideas, and then an upstart nation stumbles from one success to another without even trying, like a *blessed* idiot. It's got to be galling to feel the *haute* blood of royalty coursing through your veins under the stupid uniform, as you call out "Un Big Mac, sans le pickle!" from the counter day in and day out, even if the work does ultimately result in such high-minded and necessary programs as the Genius Grant.

Conclusion: There's Only One Right Thing to Do, I'm Pretty Sure

No matter how the world turns out, I'll need more money right away (on top of living expenses), so I can pay tuition, buy books and get some clothes in the school colors. Beyond school spirit, I'll need *faith*, *purpose* and *money*, like the right-wingers, religious nuts and terrorists have, but more positive and less deadly. Unless you think it's more important for the future of the world that I blow up the terrorists, in which case I'll sign up for a screenwriting class so I can come up with my final statement. Or if all the cows start going crazy again and threaten the fast food business, I could either take science classes and discover a cure, or take public relations classes and talk people into accepting the risk of going insane from cheeseburgers. It's the least I can do after all you've done for me.

With that kind of purpose and more money, all I need is faith. No matter what classes I take, I'll have to cultivate myself, so I have faith in myself. And I'll need to cultivate my faith in humanity, so I care about it enough to help save it. My faith in humanity, and maybe humanity itself, depends on you and your continued support—please don't disappoint me.

Thankfully yours,
Mitch

CONTRIBUTOR BIOGRAPHIES

Diane Williams, the author of six books of fiction, has a new book forthcoming from FC2 entitled *It Was Like My Trying To Have a Tender-Hearted Nature*. She is the founding editor of NOON.

Brian Evenson is the author of seven books of fiction, most recently *The Wavering Knife* (FC2, 2004). A new novel, *The Open Curtain*, will be published by Coffee House in October of 2006.

Caila Rossi has completed a novel and a collection of stories that have appeared in, among others, *Brooklyn Review*, *Shenandoah*, *Gettysburg Review*, *TriQuarterly*, *Witness*, and *Gulf Coast*, and have been anthologized in *The Year's Best Fantasy and Horror* (St. Martin's Press). The piece here is from her novella, *Seeing A Specialist*.

Prizewinning author **Lynda Schor's** latest short fiction collections are *The Body Parts Shop* (FC2) and *Adventures In Capitalism* (Unicorn Press). She is the fiction editor of the online literary magazine *Salt River Review*, and she teaches at The New School.

John Yau is the author of books of poetry and fiction, including *Hawaiian Cowboys* (1995), *My Symptoms* (1998), and *My Heart Is That Eternal Rose Tattoo* (2000). He is a Guggenheim Fellow in Poetry (2006-2007), and teaches at Mason Gross School of the Arts.

Barbara Henning is the author of several books of poetry, as well as two novels, *Black Lace* and *You, Me, and the Insects* (Spuyten Duyvil). After living in New York City for many years, she has recently relocated to Tucson, Arizona.

Michael Martone's new book is *Michael Martone* (FC2), a memoir composed of contributor notes that first appeared in the contributors' notes sections of various magazines.

Jacques Roubaud is one of the most accomplished members of the OULIPO, the workshop for experimental literature founded by Raymond Queneau and Francois Le Lionnais. He has published extensively in prose, theater, and poetry.

Susan Daitch is the author of two novels, *L.C.* and *The Colorist*, and a collection of short fiction, *Storytown*. Besides appearing in *The Rail*, her work has been published in *failbetter. com*, *The Pushcart Prize Anthology*, *Ploughshares*, and *The Norton Anthology of Postmodern Fiction*, and featured in *The Review of Contemporary Fiction*.

Jim Feast is a member of the Unbearables writers' group. His excerpt is inspired by the book *Fear of Milk* by the late John Penn.

Martha King's latest collection of short fiction, *North & South*, was published by Spuyten Duyvil in spring of 2006. She lives and writes in Brooklyn, New York.

Lynn Crawford is a fiction writer and art critic who lives outside of Detroit. Her books include: *Solow, Blow, Simply Separate People, Holiday, Detail*, and *Fortification Resort*.

Lewis Warsh's most recent books include *Ted's Favorite Skirt, The Origin of the World* and *Touch of the Whip*. He is co-editor of *The Angel Hair Anthology*, editor and publisher of United Artists Books, and is an Associate Professor at Long Island University in Brooklyn. A new novel, *A Place in the Sun*, is forthcoming in 2007.

Pat MacEnulty is the author of two novels and a short story collection. Her fourth book, *From May to December*, will be published in 2008.

Will Fleming is a native of Baltimore, Maryland who now resides in Brooklyn. He has an MA in Creative Writing from the City College of New York and has recently completed a novel called *Baltimore Son*.

Carmen Firan, born in Romania, is a poet, fiction and play writer, and a journalist living in New York. She has published fifteen books of poetry, novels, essays, and short stories.

Bart Cameron grew up in the Midwest, moved to Boston, then Brooklyn, then, with the help of a Fulbright, on to Reykjavík Iceland, where he stayed. He edits the English-language cultural and political magazine the *Reykjavík Grapevine*.

Constanza Jaramillo Cathcart wrote the novel *Subtitles for Life*. She lives in Brooklyn with her husband Blake and her son Lucas.

Aaron Zimmerman is the author of the novel *By The Time You Finish This Book You Might Be Dead* (Spuyten Duyvil, October 2003), and his fiction and poetry have appeared in numerous literary magazines. He is also Founder and Executive Director of NY Writers Coalition, a non-profit organization that supports the creative writing of people deprived of a voice in society.

Sharon Mesmer is the author of *Half Angel, Half Lunch* (poems, Hard Press), *The Empty Quarter* and *In Ordinary Time* (stories, Hanging Loose Press), and *Ma Vie B Yonago* (stories, Hachette Littératures, France, in French translation).

Jeremy Sigler is the author of two books of poetry, *To and To* (1998) and *Mallet Eyes* (2000). His next book, *Crackpot Poet*, is forthcoming from Black Square. Sigler is Associate New York Editor of *Parkett* and teaches at the Maryland Institute College of Art. He lives in Brooklyn.

Jill Magi is the author of *Threads*, a hybrid work of poetry, prose, and visual art, forthcoming in fall 2006 from Futurepoem Books, and *Cadastral Map*, a chapbook published by Portable Press at Yo-Yo Labs. She is a 2006–07 writer-in-residence with the Lower Manhattan Cultural Council and teaches literature and writing at the The City College Center for Worker Education and the Eugene Lang College of the New School. Jill runs Sona Books, a community-based chapbook press.

Blake Radcliffe is a novelist and an editor at Words Without Borders, wordswithoutborders.org. He lives in Brooklyn.

Meredith Brosnan is a novelist, songwriter, and musician. He plays bass in Peacock's Penny Arcade.

Evan Harris is the author of *The Art of Quitting* (Barrons). She lives on the east end of Long Island with her husband, sculptor Hiroyuki Hamada, and their son.

Canadian author **Douglas Glover** has won his country's highest literary prize, the Governor General's Award for Fiction. His novel *Elle* was a finalist for the International IMPAC Dublin Literary Award.

Johannah Rodgers' work has appeared in *Fence, ChainARTS, Fiction*, and *The Brooklyn Rail*. Her chapbook *Necessary Fictions* was published by Sona Books in 2003, and her collection of experimental short fiction, *sentences*, is forthcoming from Red Dust in 2006.

Brooklyn native **Jonathan Baumbach** is the author of three collections of short stories and eleven novels including *Reruns, B, Separate Hours, Babble, Chez Charlotte & Emily*, and *On The Way to My Father's Funeral*. His stories have been anthologized in *O. Henry Prize Stories, Great Pool Stories, Best American Stories, Full Court, All Our Secrets Are the Same*, and *Best of TriQuarterly*, among others.

Marie Carter has been published in *Hanging Loose*, *The Brooklyn Rail*, paintedladypress.com, and turntablebluelight. com, among others. She is working on a book of creative non-fiction called *The Trapeze Diaries*, and has received a residency at the McDowell Colony for September 2006.

Doug Nufer is the author of the novels *Negativeland*, *Never Again*, and *On the Roast*, all of which appeared in 2004, and of the novels *The Mudflat Man/The River Boys*, 2006, published in the double-fronted format that was made famous by Ace in the 1950s. He also writes poetry and pieces for dance performances, in which he moves around, bellowing.

Leslie Scalapino's entire *The Forest is in the Euphrates River* will be included in 2006 in a collection of the last eight years of her work, *Day Ocean State of Stars' Night*, published by Green Integer. Her most recent fiction is *Dahlia's Iris*, published by FC2.

Born in Geneva in 1919, **Robert Pinget** studied law before turning to painting and moving to Paris. He published his first novel while in his early thirties, then went on to write a dozen more before passing in 1997.

Elizabeth Reddin is a poet and performer living in Brooklyn. Her first book is forthcoming from Ugly Duckling Presse, and she is producer/director of Deerhead Records.

Kenneth Bernard's books include the long poem *The Baboon in the Nightclub*, *From the District File*, and the short story collection *The Man in the Stretcher*. He has been active as a playwright, fiction writer, and poet since the late 60s.

Jean Frémon has published numerous works in France, and only a handful have been translated into English. They include *Painting*, translated by Brian Evenson (Black Square Editions), *The Paradoxes of Robert Ryman*, translated by Brian Evenson

(Black Square Editions), and *Island of the Dead*, translated by Cole Swensen (Green Integer).

R. M. Berry is the author of the novels *Frank* (Chiasmus: 2005) and *Leonardo's Horse*, a *New York Times* "notable book" of 1998, as well as the story collections *Dictionary of Modern Anguish* and *Plane Geometry and Other Affairs of the Heart*. Since 1999, he has been publisher of *Fiction Collective 2*.

Thomas D'Adamo was born outside of Weehawken, NJ in a teepee made of lipstick tubes to a hobo mother and an intergalactic anthropologist with whom he rode the rails until the age of 16. Following a brief stint as Secretrary of State under Warren Harding, he settled down to a career as an obscure writer in Manhattan where he is currently working on *The Savage Heart*, an account of the exemplary life of Mr. Bob Friendly (a.k.a. Idi Amin), America's second-most beloved motivational author and speaker.

Albert Mobilio is the recipient of a Whiting Writers' Award. He teaches at the New School and is the fiction editor at *Bookforum*.

John Reed is author of the novels *A Still Small Voice, Snowball's Chance*, and *The Whole*.

Kurt Strahm is a slave to creativity living in NYC. Sometimes he thinks he's the greatest, then a few seconds later thinks he's the worst; his hobbies include waiting for the roller coaster to come off the tracks.

EDITOR BIOS

Donald Breckenridge is the Fiction Editor of *The Brooklyn Rail*, in addition, he is the author of more than a dozen plays as well as the novella *Rockaway Wherein* (Red Dust '98), and the novel *6/2/95* (Spuyten Duyvil '02). His second novel *Arabesques for Sauquoit* is currently making the rounds and he is working on his third novel.

Jen Zoble is the Assistant Fiction Editor of *The Brooklyn Rail* and the Director of Education of New York Theatre Workshop. She lives in Prospect Heights, Brooklyn.